NEVER TRUST A ROGUE IN WOLF'S CLOTHING

MICHELLE HELLIWELL

ISBN: 978-0-9940357-7-6 (ebook)

ISBN: 978-0-9940357-6-9 (print)

Cover Design: Selena Blake

Editor: Donna Alward

❀ Created with Vellum

For the caregivers

ACKNOWLEDGMENTS

Funnily enough, this is always the hardest part of the book to write. Not because I don't know who helped me along the way, but because I am so extremely grateful for their support, it's hard to express it in words.

I would like to thank my husband Rob, and my sons, for not only their patience with me but their support, sometimes through gentle nudges, sometimes by the delivery of tea when I'm flailing a bit and I need a pick me up, and also just being the supportive people they are. I also want to thank all my friends, acquaintances and readers who ask "how's the next book coming"? It tells me that people care, and that is always a nice thing.

Several people in particular were instrumental in helping me bring this book to you. I would like to thank Dr. Roger Hamilton, for polling his colleagues and answering my question, "what drew you to this profession?"(which, I suppose, is a nicer question than "how can you tell how long someone is dead" that he entertained for me when I wrote Not Your Average Beauty). Roger is a very dedicated physician and the profession is lucky to count them among their own. To Margaret Poitras, who checked my Canadian school French, and entertained my questions about appropriate French swear words, *merci beaucoup.* As always, I must thank Anne MacFarlane, Nikki Figueiredo and Annette Gallant for getting this story off on the right foot, and to my editor, Donna Alward, for making sure it stayed on track.

I would also like to that all the caregivers in my life—some in formal roles, many who are not, who strive to help someone else get through the day and give up a bit of themselves each day to do it. Love ya sis. Go take care of you.

CHAPTER 1

Yorkshire, January 1796

THEFT. Bribery. Intimidation.

Bastien DuMont had committed a litany of sins in his nearly thirty years. If someone didn't hurry up and answer the damned door, he would break it down himself and add vandalism to his list.

He pulled up the collar on his last good coat and cupped his hands, bringing them to his mouth to allow a wisp of warm breath to drive off the chill before rubbing them together. English winters were so damned cold. He hated being cold. Stomping his boots to push blood into his feet, he stood on the step of a modest but tidy Tudor home in a sleepy Yorkshire village. For the second time in as many minutes, his knocking had gone unanswered.

Bastien shoved his hand into his pocket, his fingers curling around the edge of a letter of introduction of a new surgeon, Bastien DuMont, to one Dr. Timothy Brayden, the local physician. The letter stated Bastien was here under the invitation of the Marquess of Barronsfield, to assist Dr. Brayden with his practice. The seal on the parchment, bearing the house of Barronsfield, was genuine and provided an identification of sorts to the man Bastien thought would be expecting him. If he ever came to the damned door.

The note was purely theater. Its purpose was to deflect any questions about Bastien's real reason for being here—to hunt down *Le Veneur Rouge* and, according to his orders, capture him.

But Bastien had other plans. Plans that involved exacting some very personal justice.

Le Veneur Rouge, whose dedication to furthering the republican cause in England bordered on lunacy, had been trying for six months to kill Bastien. It was the price Le Veneur Rouge demanded for having his plans to bring the revolution to England disrupted. Bastien had spent two years trying to infiltrate his inner circle, and had come close to succeeding. It had all gone up in smoke because, damn it, his friend Edmund Pembroke had got himself in trouble with a handful of English Revolutionaries. All because of a woman and Edmund's so-called honor. It was not a total failure. Bastien had discovered information—names, places, plans—that successfully upset much of Le Veneur Rouge's network, but the spider at the center of the web had scuttled away and remained safely in hiding. Waiting for a chance to tear Bastien apart, piece by piece.

All because he'd helped the damned English. He should have helped himself and sold the list of names to the French. To the Irish. Or even back to the British. Instead he gave it away. And the reward for his charity was a life on the run.

Good deeds always came with a price. He'd been a fool to forget that lesson.

Hunched against the cold pin pricks of icy rain that had begun to fall, he pulled a long iron file out of a special pocket sewn inside his coat. He was finished with patience. He'd been in hiding for nearly six months. That had given him more than enough time to think about what the hell he'd done. And while he was skulking away in the shadows, the mysterious ringleader of one of England's most successful revolutionary networks had discovered the familial link between Bastien DuMont—the Wolf de l'Ardoise—and the

Baroness D'Anville. Le Veneur Rouge had lashed out at her to get at him.

Ten days ago, Bastien had been hiding in London when Sir Richard Hamilton, one of the King's best spymasters, had tracked him down with news that Tante Marie had been gravely wounded. The baroness was the very public face of the *Émigrés*—the French nobility that had fled their lands for the safety of England. She was also the last bit of family Bastien had left. Their relationship had been a strained one, to say the least. But when the message arrived, it had driven a hole into Bastien's heart. Which was remarkable, given he didn't think he had much of a heart anymore.

She'd lost part of her arm, but she was alive. She'd managed to shoot the attacker herself. A man working for Le Veneur Rouge. But she'd also gotten a vital piece of information about where the dreaded Red Hunter was hiding.

Your prey is a lost Prince of Weymouth and bears the mark of the Wolf. He hides where the Beast rules over the land.

It had been cryptic, even for her, though the implication of one aspect of the message was clear. They had met once, Bastien and Le Veneur Rouge. The mark of the Wolf told him so. Would Bastien recognize him?

He slid the file into the locked door of the modest home, which stood only a few miles away from the estate of the Marquess of Barronsfield, once infamously known throughout England as the Beast. Jiggling the file in the lock, he turned the mechanism about until a satisfying click told him he'd accomplished his task. He quickly slid the file back into his pocket.

Bastien wrapped his hands around the iron door handle, the cold stinging his fingers. As he pulled down on the latch, the door opened from the other side.

"Good afternoon."

Bastien straightened at the greeting. Across the threshold stood an older gentleman with thick shoulders, a balding head wreathed by gray hair, and a countenance that suggested he would brook no nonsense. The man stood absolutely still, and Bastien felt the force of his keen appraisal.

"Don't tell me," the gentleman began, before Bastien had the chance to say a word. "You're the favor I am doing for Lord Barronsfield."

Bastien bowed, then presented the letter, complete with the Barronsfield seal. The marquess, upon learning of Le Veneur Rouge's whereabouts, had authorized this mission.

"I trust everything is in order?"

The doctor opened it, skimming the contents. Apparently satisfied, he folded it up and handed it back to Bastien.

"Trust." The doctor glanced down at the door lock, then back to Bastien. "Funny you should use that word. Come out of the weather. I've got enough work here this winter. I don't need you to be catching your death."

Bastien stepped out of the cold and into the well-appointed home. A servant took his overcoat. He followed the physician into his study, appraising the room. To one side stood a case filled with texts, some medical in nature. In one corner stood a cabinet filled with powders and the tools of the physicians' trade. On the wall was a drawing of what he assumed was the Barronsfield Infirmary, which he'd passed on his way.

"Brandy?" the physician asked.

Bastien nodded, and walked to the fire so he could soak up its warmth. His host put a glass in his hand, the liquid inside glistening in the firelight.

"Are you really a surgeon, or is that a fiction?"

Bastien smiled at the question. Dr. Brayden wasn't a man who wasted time with pleasantries. Neither was Bastien.

"Does it matter?"

"If someone shows up here with a broken bone or a gangrenous foot, it damn well does, yes."

"I assume you know I am here for specific reasons, and those

4

reasons aren't doctoring." Bastien took a healthy sip of the brandy, and savored the heat of it at the back of his throat.

The physician shook his head. "You are here because Lord Barronsfield asked me, and I have a tremendous respect for His Lordship. Whatever mission you are on must be important to him. But if you are under my roof, masquerading as one of my staff, you will goddamn well tell me if I can trust the skills you proclaim to have."

Bastien swallowed the rest of his brandy, unmoved by the doctor's dedication. Still, he needed an ally. He planted the glass on a nearby table. "Edinburgh. I studied at Edinburgh. Until 1792 I worked under Desault in Paris." And for Marat, in his presses. Until September. Until his world exploded.

The doctor must have been suitably impressed, because all he did was nod.

"His Lordship was thin on details about why you are here," he continued, "except that I am to introduce you as my assistant." He paused, clearing his throat, apparently waiting for Bastien to fill the silence with an answer. Bastien decided it was best to fill it with as much of the truth as he dared.

"I am searching for the man responsible for the kidnapping and attempted execution of His Lordship's cousin, Mr. Edmund Pembroke." He left out the fact that the bastard had nearly killed his great-aunt Marie. "There is credible information this man is in the area."

"I see. Do you know who you are looking for? This isn't a place with a lot of coming and goings, especially this time of year."

Bastien shook his head. "The gentleman—and I believe he is one— is probably able to converse well in French, and has access to considerable resources. And he is believed to bear a red mark—a scar—on his left shoulder." That scar would be unmistakable.

Dr. Brayden put a hand to his chin as he appeared to be considering Bastien's description. "The neighborhood has gentlemen enough in it, some who wear their wealth, and others who choose not to. I've seen several people with some nasty scars—including some I've given them, truth be told. My stitching isn't the best. But those are mostly folk who can barely manage the King's English, never mind a second tongue."

A tray of sandwiches was brought in, and the two men shared an uneasy silence. Brayden was insistent on hearing about Bastien's surgical and medical experiences—something Bastien was not keen to share. Tante Marie had sent him to school. Believed he was capable of greatness. Occasionally, since he left Paris, he had tended to the odd broken bone, or sewn up a gash. The last time he saw a patient was the summer before, when Tante Marie had dragged him to tend to a sick child.

Saving lives had been his calling, once. He'd lost many to poverty and the ravages of hunger that made them susceptible to disease. The Revolution had promised change, and Bastien helped rally the people to rise up against the corrupt nobility of which, ironically, he was a part. And when the ideals of *liberté, égalité, fraternité* had turned deadly, it had done so, in part, due to the puritanical zeal of men like Jean-Paul Marat, the famous revolutionary turned near deity in France. Before long, the new revolutionary government had become as corrupt as the old regime, and death was meted out in part by the national razor, developed by Joseph Guillotine.

Joseph Guillotine. Jean-Paul Marat. Bastien DuMont.

They'd all sworn an oath to first do no harm. An oath shattered and strewn over the blood-soaked streets of Paris.

After those horrible days in Paris, after the September massacres, Bastien decided it was time to stop trying to save the world, and turned his mind to another occupation. He left Paris for Normandy, spent his nights tracking down the men who'd preyed on the weak, or who'd hunted down noble families fleeing the country; men who had delivered them to the guillotine in the name of the revolution and lined their pockets with blood money. He became the Wolf de l'Ardoise, hunting the hunters, and delivering his own sort of rough justice.

Right now, there were no crowds to save. The only lives that hung in the balance were his own and that of Tante Marie.

"Come, I will show you the infirmary," Dr. Brayden said as they finished their meal. "I have to prepare for some visits tomorrow. You should at least come and get familiar with it. People will be expecting you to be there."

Bastien wiped his mouth on the serviette and stifled a yawn. He'd been up for nearly eighteen hours. But the man was right. He was here to play a role, and the better he played it, the more information he might find to aid his capture of Le Veneur Rouge.

He donned his coat once more, and followed the physician along a small lane to a larger stone building, which, compared to many other structures he'd seen upon his arrival, was of relatively new construction.

"It's empty now, but we've had it full many times." The doctor opened the door that led to his office and examination space. "His Lordship had it built nearly fifteen years ago."

On one wall stood a cabinet with a small collection of powders and tinctures. In another cabinet were several other implements: a bloodletting fleam, cupping jars, and a few obstetrical tools. Missing were the cruder instruments of the surgeon's trade. Those he'd brought himself, just in case. Not that Bastien expected to do much doctoring. That wasn't why he was here.

The physician led him to the ward which held four beds, all empty. It was well lit and clean—unlike many such institutions where Bastien had spent his time. He had no intentions of performing procedures if he could help it, but he could not help but admit the space was excellent.

The door flew open, the heavy creak drawing their attention. "Dr. Brayden, sir!"

Both men looked up to see a young boy, perhaps twelve, breathing heavily.

"Yes, Master Gordon, what can I do for you?" asked the doctor.

"My mum's ready, but da said the babe's coming out the wrong way."

"Right then." He turned to Bastien. "Do you wish to accompany me?"

Bastien shook his head. "I'm not here for this, remember," he said, his voice low, deliberately averting his gaze from the lad who, he knew, was no doubt hanging on every word and gesture. "I'll be of no use to you."

Brayden's eyebrows dipped into a deep frown, before he turned back to the young lad who'd come in. His voice was the measure of confidence. "Meet me out back. I'll grab my things and we'll go straight away."

The boy nodded, then bolted out the door.

"Now," Brayden put a finger up to Bastien's face. "The next someone who comes through that door may need you. I don't care who you're chasing. You will help them."

Bastien watched the doctor disappear out the door, then walked to the smaller examination room, which also served as the physician's office. Dr. Brayden's rebuke lingered for less than a moment. Bastien needed to get to work. And his work wasn't to deliver babies or tend to patients.

He sat down at the spartan desk, lit a candle, and began rooting through the drawers, unsure of what he was looking for. Among the collections of quills and ephemera, Bastien found a small brown journal. He flipped through the pages, which were full of notes about the doctor's patients. Bastien sank down into the chair and pored over them. Somewhere—between the notes about the births and deaths, the pox and pus and foul humors—there might be a hint as to a patient who bore a red scar on his shoulder.

After several hours, light began to bleed away the last of the short winter day. Bastien rubbed his eyes and stretched. Through a nearby window, the snow that had been falling steadily for the past hour had begun to accumulate. There was no sign of the doctor's return, and little more Bastien could do here. He rose, stretched his stiff back, and reached for his coat and hat, eager to return to a comfortable bed.

"Dr. Brayden!"

A female voice echoed across the stone walls, laced with panic. "Dr. Brayden, are you there?"

"*Oui?*" Bastien grimaced, flung his hat aside, and walked toward the main ward. A woman ran toward him, not much more than twenty, her cheeks ruddy from the cold and her breath heavy from exertion. She was draped in a heavy woolen cloak of the deepest crimson. She came to an abrupt halt, her boots skidding on the wooden floor. He ran toward her, catching her before she tumbled to the floor. Her hood fell back, revealing a delicate face framed with flaxen hair. Her eyes, a remarkable green, widened at the shock of her near fall. Her gloved hands gripped tightly on his collar. Even through the thick fabric, a shock of awareness bolted through him.

He cleared his throat, determined to shake away whatever unwelcome connection had just occurred. *"Attention,"* he muttered, almost under his breath, as the two struggled in an awkward dance until the girl was safely on her feet.

"Who are you?" she asked after a moment, her delicate brow furrowing in confusion. "I need Dr. Brayden at once."

"I am Bastien DuMont. Dr. Brayden has just left to see to a patient," he said, forcing himself to sound professional. "How may I help you?"

"I think I've killed a man."

CHAPTER 2

$\mathcal{E}$leanore swallowed hard as she fought to catch her breath, unable to break the hold of this stranger's intense silver stare, peeking out from behind a lock of black hair that had fallen into his eyes.

It took her a moment to realize she was still holding on to him—whoever he was. He'd interrupted her fall with reflexes so quick it took her half a moment to realize she was back on her feet. She looked him up and down, forcing herself not to be distracted by the strong line of his jaw or the squareness of his shoulders. The man in front of her was most definitely *not* Dr. Brayden. This man was much younger—and much rougher around the edges.

Steady, Eleanore. She was on a serious errand. Daniel, one of Barronsfield's most faithful servants, was injured—grievously so—and it was all her fault.

"Did he deserve it? This man you say you've killed?" The corner of the man's mouth curled up slightly, as if he was holding back a smile. Shaken out of her daze, Eleanore stepped back and brought her arms to her sides, her fingers curled into fists. Was he amused by her plight?

"Of course not!" Daniel didn't deserve to be anything other than safe in London, attending to her brother's horses. Instead, he'd taken her back to Barronsfield on a fool's errand in the dead of winter. Perhaps she should have gone to Cheshire, to visit her cousin Edmund as she'd originally planned. Not that visiting Silver Cross had been much of a plan. Her only real scheme had been to run. "Answer me. Are you a physician?"

The man seemed to hesitate a moment, then nodded.

"Then come." She started to turn on her heel when a hand landed on her arm, forcing her to remain in place. She reached up to push the stranger's arm away, but he clearly was not having it. Instead, he caught her other hand, and stepped in so that he was mere inches away.

"You said you killed him, *mademoiselle*. If so, he is beyond my help." His eyes narrowed and he put a gentle hand to her brow. "You on the other hand, are quite alive, and bleeding. I should attend to this."

No. The only person who needed attending to was Daniel. She backed away and put her fingers to her temple, shocked by sight of her own blood staining her gloves as she realized for the first time she'd been hurt as well. But she was on her feet. Daniel most certainly was not. "Perhaps, but another time. Come."

Without another thought, she grabbed the doctor's hand and led him out the door and down the road to where the coach had skidded off the road, throwing Daniel off his perch and onto the ground.

It took only a few minutes to reach the scene. A small crowd had already gathered.

"Make way please!" Eleanore called out, letting go of the doctor's hand and returning her attention to Daniel. His eyes were open and, thankfully, he was breathing. "I brought help."

"Let me see him," the doctor ordered. He examined Daniel head to toe. "Back away *s'il vous plaît!*" he yelled over his shoulder, forcing the crowd that had gathered to move away. He pulled back the coat someone had draped over Daniel to keep him warm, then laid his hands over him, his movements careful but efficient. Two or three times Daniel cried out, the sound slicing through Eleanore's heart.

"You've got a few broken bones, *monsieur*. Perhaps a cracked rib or two."

"You mean I haven't killed him?" Eleanore asked.

"Not yet. Are you disappointed?" He flashed her a smile, then looked to the crowd, his expression serious once more. "We need to get him out of this weather."

It took a few more minutes for a cart to arrive. Several men lifted Daniel into the rough conveyance and took him back to the infirmary, where he was soon lying in one of the beds. His sharp cries filled the room, letting all know he was very much alive, to Eleanore's relief. And yet, guilt coursed through her with every sound. If only she'd stayed in London. If only she'd managed to swallow her Pembroke pride and not toss aside her engagement to Lord Ramsay. Surely there were many of his ilk who'd dallied with the servants and created an offspring who'd carry the taint of a single moment. Eleanore knew about that more than most.

Her mother had baked tarts in the kitchens at Barronsfield and her father had been Barronsfield's master. And though her half-brother was a powerful man, in the eyes of much of society she was still the daughter of a baker. Now history had repeated itself. But rather than join herself to a man who'd created an unwanted child and an unthinkable burden for some poor servant, Eleanore had unceremoniously broken the engagement. Adding to what would no doubt be a horrid scandal, she fled London, unable to bear the hypocrisy where she was considered tainted merely by being born in the same circumstances under which Lord Ramsay would remain blameless.

To selfishly distract her from the sounds of Daniel's pain and her own maudlin thoughts, Eleanore ran to the supply room and gathered up extra pillows and linens. With that task completed, she and Mr. Darling, the vicar, who'd helped bring Daniel to the infirmary, kindled the fire. The hearth was soon raging, chasing away the icy chill of mid-January.

"What happened, Eleanore?" Mr. Darling asked, his voice low as they stood near the bright flame. "I am surprised to see you back from London so soon."

Eleanore pasted a smile on her face. The vicar had been a surrogate uncle to her, and with his wife had raised Eleanore since she was a small child. It was an arrangement, she'd learn much later, that had allowed her father, the marquess, to watch over her at a close, but careful distance.

Her parents had loved one another, but their love had not been enough to allow them to be together. Unlike many children in similar circumstances, Eleanore, at least, had been wanted. She'd been loved and cared for. Sheltered from the harshness of society, she'd been given a chance for a life that was unattainable by so many others in her circumstances.

It was that gift, she'd decided, that she could give to others. The gift of a loving home and a chance at a vibrant future. If she had Lord Ramsay to thank for anything, it was for strengthening her resolve to see it done. She'd spent much of the journey home working on the details of how, and where. The "when" was the next question to be answered.

"I found London not to my liking," she replied, as she gave Mr. Darling a guarded smile. There was so much she had to tell, but no one, not even the Darlings, to tell it to. "Daniel had to return and offered to bring me home. The roads were adequate, the weather clear, until we'd come nearly to Barronsfield. We must have hit a rut."

Blessedly, Mr. Darling ended his inquiries, perhaps sensing her reticence. She returned to Daniel's bedside, watching this new physician work. He was utterly focused on his patient, who lay as stoically as possible.

"How can I help?" she asked.

"Stay with him." He took her by the arm and guided her toward Daniel's upper body. "Your pretty face should help distract him while I set his leg."

He spoke so directly that Eleanore was unable to decide if the doctor was being condescending, or if he'd attempted humor that had somehow failed in translation.

"That's not funny," she replied.

"It was not my intent to be," he said, not bothering to spare her a glance. He was fixed on his task, arranging a section of splints for Daniel's lower leg. Apparently satisfied with their position, he stood, pulled off his coat, and began rolling up his sleeves. "Laudanum might make him ill, and he cannot strain his ribs further if he vomits. The distraction will help."

Eleanore wanted to protest, but this was not the moment for it. She sat beside Daniel and took his hand, holding tight as they set the bones in his lower leg. He let out a sharp cry, and Eleanore bit down on her lip, keeping her gaze on his face. When that was done, the doctor sat Daniel up and bound his chest with a plaster that was just tight enough that breathing wasn't much of a chore. At last, Daniel was comfortable. Or, at least, as comfortable as he could be.

"I'm so sorry, Daniel." Eleanore breathed in deeply, forcing her voice to steady as tears stung the backs of her eyes. "I promise Barronsfield will take care of you. You shan't have to worry about a thing."

"Can you send word to Allie that I'm here?" Daniel closed his eyes, a troubled look on his face.

Another wave of guilt washed over her, sagging her shoulders. Allie worked in the kitchen at the manor. She and Daniel were sweethearts. More than that, they were engaged. "Of course. I will tell her myself."

"You." A male voice laced with a French accent caught her attention. "Mademoiselle with the red hood. You're next."

"Excuse me?" She frowned and glanced over her shoulder. The doctor—his shirt sleeves rolled up to his elbows, his black hair pushed out of his face—was cleaning his hands on a fresh piece of linen. With a curt nod, he gestured to a second bed on the opposite side of the room from where Daniel lay.

"Here, please."

Eleanore stayed fixed to her seat. "But Daniel needs my help."

He grimaced, spectacularly unimpressed. "Monsieur Daniel needs rest. You have been hovering over him for the past hour."

"But—"

"I'm fine, Lady Eleanore," Daniel replied, his voice groggy. "I feel like shuttin' my eyes anyhow."

Daniel's eyes fluttered closed, wincing slightly as he took a breath. He looked so battered.

"You can't keep me waiting all day," the doctor called out. "A man has to eat, and I understand the innkeeper makes a palatable roast chicken."

Eleanore tensed and glared at the Frenchman. Roast chicken? She rose, let go a low sigh, marched across the hall, and plunked herself down on the bed. Where on earth had Dr. Brayden found this man? His skills seemed up to the test, but his manner with patients was hardly nurturing.

"Remove the cape, s'il vous plaît," he began.

Eleanore was confident she blinked at his order. "Excuse me?"

"I need to examine you. You do not need to disrobe any further at the moment, but it would be helpful if you remove the cape."

"I don't even know who you are."

"I believe I already gave you my name. Bastien DuMont." He paused, and regarded her carefully. "You do have memory of this, oui?"

"Of course I do." She bit her lower lip, his gaze throwing her off kilter. "You must own that this has been a rather trying day." She was barely able to withhold her annoyance. Really, this was becoming quite tiresome, even if he was terribly handsome. She unfastened the three clasps that kept the cape in place, letting it fall off her shoulders onto the cot. Though she was wearing a very modest frock, she nevertheless felt a little exposed. It didn't help that he was standing over her, his shoulders square, arms crossed.

"You have yet to give me the privilege of your name," he replied, a hint of judgment in his voice that pricked at what little remained of Eleanore's civility.

"I am Lady Eleanore," she said. "Of Barronsfield."

A glimmer of recognition widened his astonishing silver eyes. "Well then, you may thank His Lordship for my presence here. I am a surgeon who is assisting with Dr. Brayden. I arrived only today."

Eleanore blinked, confusion clouding her thoughts. Her brother confirmed this? Without her knowledge?

"When did the marquess make these arrangements?"

Thinly veiled annoyance came over him, as if she'd asked a question too many. "A week ago, perhaps less."

Curious that her brother Stephen had not mentioned it. Dr. Brayden had once discussed the idea of bringing on an apprentice, but that was a very long time ago. Bastien DuMont was hardly the age of a physician's apprentice. Indeed, if his treatment of Daniel's injuries were any indication, Mr. DuMont was an experienced surgeon. Eleanore glanced down at her hands, then to the door that led to Dr. Brayden's private office. Though Stephen had founded the Barronsfield Infirmary, in the past few years he'd allowed her to assist with the day-to-day running of it. That neither of them would have mentioned something as important as the hiring of new staff was a bit of a mystery.

She sat quietly, studying him, which she could not help but admit was a pleasant enough task for her eyes. His movements were fluid and quick, yet methodical. His dimpled chin was shadowed by a day's growth, the roughness a contrast to the lushness of his lips. His voice was clearly accented, but his English was excellent. His eyes were gray and hard—like a frozen January afternoon.

"May I ask about your qualifications?" Eleanore asked, turning her mind to where it should have been.

He shrugged. "I spent two years working as the only medical man in one of the more destitute areas of Paris. I trained as a surgeon, but I have also acted as a physician, and very occasionally as apothecary when required. The birthing I leave to the midwives. But mostly I did what needed to be done, and killed no more or no less than then next doctor. Does this satisfy you?"

Eleanore shifted in her seat. If Stephen had authorized his appointment, and Dr. Brayden accepted it, Mr. DuMont must be qualified. But his direct manner would take some getting used to. It was clear to Eleanore, at least, he was not accustomed to being questioned in such a way. "My apologies if my question offended you."

Mr. DuMont's face broke out into a most disarming smile, and with a flourish no Englishman could muster, bowed deeply, then straightened, winking at her as he did so. "I am, my lady, both humbled and honored by your trust in me."

"I—" Eleanore was uncertain if it was her injury, or the fact she hadn't slept well in two days, but she was quite suddenly at a loss for words. Was he playing with her?

"Now, if you please, I should examine your wound."

"There is nothing wrong with me," she insisted. Nothing wrong except being born a bastard. Nothing wrong except she'd just thrown away what was probably her best chance of a good marriage, and had done it in such a scandalous fashion that not even her brother's power and position in society could fix it.

"I am not certain that is the truth." He took a clean cloth, dabbed it in some sort of liquid, and held it to her temple. A brief flash of pain caught her off guard, but quickly subsided.

"I feel perfectly well," she grumbled, though she sat quietly as the surgeon finished his ministrations. Indeed, as direct as he was in his manner, there was something about his touch that was remarkably soothing.

"You have a nasty bump. Be thankful it will not require stitching. Hopefully we won't have to lance it." He looked over at Daniel, then back to her. "This is hazardous weather for both man and beast."

The question was in his tone, if not his words. *What were you thinking?*

What had she been thinking? She'd been thinking of escape. Escape from the whispers, well out of earshot of her brother.

Why should she care if Ramsay dawdles about? She's only a bastard after all. She'd be lucky if anyone would have her.

She stiffened as the whispers from that horrible night when she discovered Lord Ramsay's tryst flooded her memory. "We were trying to beat the weather. It was getting worse, but we knew we were close, so we decided to press on."

He tidied his little tray and carefully corked the bottle he'd been using. "You are lucky, then. Your driver might even be lucky, if he heals well enough."

A fresh surge of guilt settled in her chest. "He will heal, won't he? He'll be able to walk?"

"I'm a surgeon, mademoiselle, not a fortune teller. If he gets adequate rest, nutrition, and is able to stave off fever, then, after many weeks, he might. Some of that is in his hands. Some of it is not."

"He will want for nothing."

He raised his eyebrows. "Those are strong words, my lady. He is your lover, this gentleman?"

Eleanore blanched at the question. "What?"

Were the French always so *laissez-faire* about these things?

He shrugged. "You seem to care about him."

"He's worked for our family for over a decade. And he's lying in that bed because of me."

The surgeon shook his head softly. "I see."

"He has to be well. He plans to marry." Eleanore looked over at the bed where Daniel lay, sleeping, though fitfully. "I will stay with him tonight."

"You will not."

He said it lightly enough, but it was clearly an order. An order she was in no mood to bear.

"Excuse me? Dr. Brayden has allowed me to assist in tending to the infirm. I've been doing it since I was fourteen."

He smiled, but the warmth in it did not quite reach his eyes. "He must have overlooked that when he spoke about his practice. I recall nothing about allowing impetuous young ladies to martyr themselves and ignore their own injuries."

Eleanore's mouth fell open. The gall of this man!

The creak of the heavy front door drew her attention. Over her shoulder she recognized the sturdy frame of Mr. Schofield, Barronsfield's trusted steward. She pushed back a mix of grief, sadness, relief, and shame as he approached, a worrisome expression on his face.

"My lady! Tell me you are well."

"I am fine, Mr. Schofield." Eleanore replied. "And sorry to be the cause of so much apprehension and discomfort."

"Come now, my lady," he replied, his mouth turned up in a gentle smile. "I'm just glad to know you are unhurt." He turned to Mr. DuMont. "She is well, I assume?"

"She has a few bumps and bruises, though it is the one at the side of her head that concerns me the most," the surgeon replied, his tone all business, the concept of "concern" hardly making an appearance.

"I do not believe I have had the pleasure, sir," Mr. Schofield said, his stance guarded. Clearly, Mr. DuMont's presence was a surprise to the steward as well. Interesting.

"Bastien DuMont. I arrived only today." He went to his coat, pulled out a carefully folded piece of paper, and handed it to Mr. Schofield. "I am here at the request of the marquess, to provide the people of the area with my services."

Eleanore rose and stood next to Mr. Schofield, reading over his shoulder. The hand was clearly her brother's, and the bottom of the page was emblazoned with the seal of Barronsfield. She pursed her lips. It seemed Mr. DuMont's story was entirely true. Still, there was something about it that did not settle well. Mr. Schofield folded up the parchment and handed it back to the Frenchman, apparently satisfied.

"And my best driver?" Mr. Schofield looked to where Daniel slept, an anxious expression on his face.

"His situation is more complicated. He has several broken bones, which I have set. I shall keep him here for a few days, to observe his condition, and then he can be moved. But he will be unable to work for several months."

Mr. Schofield glanced at Eleanore, concern in his brow. He would not ask the questions she dreaded to be asked, thank goodness. It was not his place to inquire about broken engagements. The answers to those questions would wait. At least until Stephen and Rosalind returned.

"Where is our physician?" Mr. Schofield asked.

"Assisting with a birth," Mr. DuMont replied. "I will have him take a second look at your driver."

"Tell him we will be 'round in the morning to check in on the lad," Mr. Schofield replied, glancing over at Daniel.

Mr. DuMont only nodded at the steward's orders before Mr. Schofield turned to Eleanore, his expression softening. "Let's get you home, my lady."

"A word, monsieur, if you please." Mr. DuMont took Mr. Schofield aside, just out of earshot. Mr. DuMont's hands moved in the air, using them to underscore whatever direction he was providing the steward. Occasionally Mr. Schofield's gaze would stray to Daniel, and he'd nod, obviously in agreement with the doctor's words. But most of the time Eleanore found her attention unwittingly drawn to Mr. DuMont, who must have sensed it, for more than once did his gaze slide to her. Each time she looked away, as if she'd been caught doing something she oughtn't. Which was ridiculous.

After a moment or two, their voices rose again, signaling that whatever business between them had concluded. Mr. Schofield's shook Mr. DuMont's hand, then went to Eleanore. As they walked past Daniel, remorse tumbled in her chest.

"Mr. DuMont will want to see to your wound again soon, my lady. I will answer to His Lordship if anything happens to you," Mr. Schofield replied, then pointed a finger to Mr. DuMont, who was back at Daniel's bedside. "And so will he."

"I have to answer to my brother regardless," Eleanore replied, her heart sinking as Mr. Schofield helped her into the comfortable seat of the carriage he'd brought to bring her home. "Did Mr. DuMont have any further orders?" He was certainly good at giving them in his unconventional way. She wasn't sure if it was because he was French, or just a self-centered boor.

"None at present. Let's get you home, shall we?"

Eleanore gazed out the carriage window, the warm lights of the infirmary getting smaller as they drove away. Soon she'd be home. But this was not the homecoming she'd imagined, nor wanted.

Surely, Daniel's injuries were the horrible reward for her thoughtlessness.

Perhaps it was the price of her freedom. She only wished she was the one to pay it.

CHAPTER 3

*B*astien lay on one of the infirmary beds in the little ward. His patient slept nearby. Bastien had every intention of going to the inn and getting a hot meal once Dr. Brayden returned, but it appeared the physician was having an equally late night. So Bastien stayed put. He spent restless hours fading in and out of wakefulness.

The low creak of a door put Bastien on alert. He remained motionless as footsteps approached, stopping a few feet away. A frantic idea gripped him.

Had Le Veneur Rouge found him? The man had never failed to be one step ahead. And though Bastien never used his own name when he was on missions, the man had obviously discovered the link between the Wolf de l'Ardoise and the Baroness D'Anville. And if he'd done that, then perhaps the next step, linking Bastien DuMont to the Wolf, had also been accomplished.

It would have been easy for Bastien to run instead of fight, if it was just his own life in the balance. He was going to hell, no doubt, though he was in no particular hurry to get there. But Le Veneur Rouge had made the critical error of harming the one person in the world

Bastien still cared about, and for that, the Red Hunter would pay dearly.

He opened his eyes to little more than slits and kept his breathing steady. The figure had his back turned to him. There was barely enough light to see.

In a fluid movement he'd practiced many times, Bastien sprang out of bed, snatching a small blade he kept in his boot. He wrapped his arm around the person's neck, his blade in his other hand at the ready. A dull whooshing sound cut the air as something fell from his attacker's arms. A pair of hands gripped his arm, as his prey struggled in his grip. The scent of lavender and vanilla wakened his senses.

"What are you doing?" The voice, high pitched from fright, was female. And familiar.

Panic and confusion shot through him. Bastien relaxed his grip and spun the girl around. *Merde.* Lady Eleanore stood in front of him, her eyes wide. She stepped back, pushing Bastien away with such force he had to catch himself before he fell on his backside.

"I said, what on earth are you doing?" Her question came out as in a harsh whisper. The fear in her voice had melted away, replaced with anger and indignation.

"*Pardon.*" Bastien nodded and slid his small dagger back into its place. "You shouldn't sneak up on a man like that."

"I wasn't sneaking. It's cold in here. I thought you might have need of a blanket." She bent down, scooping up a heavy wool blanket in her arms and pushed it at him. "Do you make it a habit of trying to choke people when they approach you?"

He caught the blanket in his hands, his fingers brushing over hers. Her skin was soft and warm, and he found himself wishing the touch had lasted a few seconds longer. Pushing the unexpected sensation aside, he pulled the blanket from her hands.

"When it's the middle of the night, it's sneaking," he grumbled. Goddamn it, he could have killed her. Too many years of hunting. Of being hunted.

"It's not the middle of the night." She pointed to the window, where a soft gray sky hinted at the dawn as the last minutes of the

22

long winter night faded away. She scowled, her arms crossed, clearly unimpressed with his assessment of the situation. "And that is not an excuse to scare people so. Heavens, this is an infirmary. Surely you are used to being interrupted at all hours?"

He was, in fact. By demons of all kinds. Some living, and some merely shadows of his past. But never by a woman who thought he might deserve a small kindness. There were few left who thought he deserved any.

"I am sorry." He did not make a habit of trusting. Softening his stance, he stepped closer, telling himself it was so he would not have to raise his voice and wake his patient. "I told you I worked in a destitute part of Paris. It was a violent place, and it bred a certain response I have yet to get past." It was a rather selective version of the truth, of course, but as she uncrossed her arms, he suspected she accepted his explanation. For now.

She looked over her shoulder at her wounded driver, then back to Bastien. "I will leave you to rest. I have work to do."

She left him, and Bastien found himself strangely compelled to watch her until she disappeared through a nearby door. She was so trusting, that one. Too trusting.

His patient rested nearby. A patient that was going to need some supervision. When Brayden returned, Bastien would apprise him of the man's status and leave the physician to do what he was paid to do. Bastien was going to spend the day narrowing down his potential targets, not watching the driver with broken bones.

Both had had a restless night. The driver, with his bandaged ribcage and aching leg, had good reason. Bastien, on the other hand, had been robbed of rest by a sensation he thought he'd lost—good old-fashioned nervousness. It had been three years since he'd set a bone. He'd lost the patient anyway, from wounds inside he'd been unable to heal. There were too many ways to break a body, and far too few methods at hand to mend them.

He looked over to see his patient smiling weakly at him. "Good mornin' doctor," the man said, his voice thick with lingering fatigue.

"How are you feeling?" Bastien forced himself to be civil. Though he knew he'd have to tend to a patient now and then, having someone so badly injured was going to slow him down and distract him from why he was really here.

"Like I lost a fight with the devil, to be honest," the man replied.

He was young, this fellow. With a lifetime worth of work ahead of him.

"Then it was a good fight," Bastien replied, setting the blanket aside and lighting several more lanterns to get the best light possible. "Let me take a look." He bent over the man, checked the braces where he'd secured the driver's leg, and made him wiggle his toes. His patient was stoically agreeable, the lone indication of his discomfort being the sporadic sharp intake of breath. And though he did not expect to find it, Bastien found himself examining the man for the red scar borne by the Red Hunter. The Wolf's bite. It was nowhere to be found.

"Where's Dr. Brayden?" the man asked at last.

Bastien stood upright, satisfied with his handiwork. "He attended to a birth last night. I have not yet seen him."

He put a hand on his chin, his gaze fixed on his patient, plans churning in his head. Of course the patient would need to stay. Bastien could insist on moving the driver to his home, but this was why the infirmary was here. If he'd hurried the man out the door—while he was still at risk for fever and his chest was still vulnerable—he'd cast suspicion on himself. Bastien needed to be trusted. To be considered part of the scenery. It would be easier to discover where Le Veneur Rouge was hiding.

"Am I dying?"

Bastien gave himself a mental shake, then refocused his attention on the driver. "Excuse me?"

The man nodded toward Bastien, concern crinkling his brow. "You had a sour look on your face there. If I'm not going to make it, just tell me."

Damn it. This was not the time for distraction.

"Pardon. I was considering how we might keep you occupied while you heal, as it will be some time," Bastien replied, deliberately lightening his tone. It was, of course, perfectly plausible the man could die.

But not if he could help it. "In a few weeks, depending on how you are doing with your chest, we can try a crutch, but it will be spring before you can walk on that leg."

The man's face fell at the news.

"I understand you have a fiancé. Spending hours in the company of a lovely lady cannot be the worst punishment." Not that Bastien could remember such a pleasure. His thoughts strayed but a moment to wherever Lady Eleanore had gone.

"We were supposed to be married soon," the driver replied. "Will I be able to work?"

"If you take care of yourself, rest, and eat well, I do not see why not. Of course, I am merely a surgeon, monsieur. I don't make God's plans for him." Indeed, Bastien wasn't entirely certain that he and God were on tremendously good terms. And to think that for a time, Tante Marie thought he might become a priest. Of course, for all of the times he'd spent in the arms of a woman since the Terror began, he might as well have become one.

"Just Daniel, if you please, sir."

Bastien paused. "Excuse me?"

"I'm just Daniel, sir. Daniel Morehouse. No need to give me any fancy titles."

When Bastien left France, everyone had gone by a single title —*citoyen,* or *citoyenne.* It had become a test of people's devotion to the cause. And like much of the revolution, the ideals of it had been marred over time. The use of the term became almost a badge of one-upmanship—he'd seen men hurled in jails as traitors when an official, pumped up on his own newfound importance, was somehow slighted by the misuse of the term.

"Monsieur is a basic sign of respect, from one man to another. Do you not feel you deserve it?"

The man paused a moment, perhaps mulling over Bastien's words. "Right then. Thank you, Doctor."

"Monsieur. Mister."

"I thought you was a doctor?"

"I'm a surgeon, Monsieur. We don't have fancy titles either."

Bastien paused, the memory of the woman who'd brought Daniel Morehouse to his attention. She had a fancy title. And she probably knew much about the comings and goings of the area.

"I thought I heard Lady Eleanore's voice," Daniel asked, as if reading Bastien's thoughts.

"She is here, indeed. She's very concerned about you."

Daniel nodded, which only served to fuel Bastien's speculation. Though he saw no particular signs of attachment, he could not help but wonder if there was something between them. She was obviously of the Barronsfield family and not the household, but her devotion to a servant's welfare was remarkable for a woman of her station. The smallest prick of envy twisted his lip. Why it bothered him at all that the two might be a pair eluded him. Indeed, he should have been thrilled at the possibility—people with secrets to hide were always valuable to someone like him. Secrets were a currency all their own and he had no trouble using others to get what he needed.

"She cares about everyone, Lady Eleanore does," Daniel said, then sensing Bastien's unasked question, continued. "She is the marquess's sister."

"I see." When they'd met ever so briefly in London, the Marquess of Barronsfield had made no mention of his family. And though Bastien had arrived here with the reluctant blessing of the marquess, Bastien had little doubt that the man would not approve of Bastien being in close quarters with his sister. Lady Eleanore's arrival home must have been unplanned. If the marquess thought there was a threat in Barronsfield, Bastien could not imagine he would allow her to be so close to it.

A door creaked open, and before Bastien could ask his next question, the titter of female voices intruded on his thoughts. *Goddamn it.* He would get nowhere if he couldn't find the information he needed.

Emerging from the threshold were two women. One of them he recognized instantly as Lady Eleanore, a tray of food and drink in her hands. The other was of the servant class. Her eyes widened and she ran toward Mr. Morehouse.

"Daniel!"

"Allie," Mr. Morehouse answered, the female's presence putting a smile on his face. He reached out with effort and clasped her hand. "I'm fine."

The young woman kissed his hand. "Oh, Daniel."

The two regarded each other with such obvious affection that it was clear that Lady Eleanore's concerns about her driver were fueled by nothing but a genuine sense of responsibility. A fleeting sense of relief at the notion buoyed him.

"We brought some of Emily's famous healing broth," Lady Eleanore called out, her voice bright despite the early hour and the dim light of a pre-dawn winter morn. She turned to Bastien, and he caught a subtle falter in her smile. "If that is amenable to you, Mr. DuMont."

She set the tray on a nearby table and stepped to one side, hands clasped in front of her, as if waiting for Bastien to inspect it. Her gaze lingered where Mr. Morehouse lay, guilt robbing her of what was no doubt an ordinarily beautiful smile. She was without her red cape and was simply dressed, her flaxen hair pulled back in a simple knot. Her features were very fine, with slender wrists and a neckline that, even in this setting, Bastien found very inviting. The thought that he'd nearly attacked her only a few moments ago, without provocation, weighed in his gut.

He cleared his throat, forcing his scattered thoughts from his mind, and concentrated on the sustenance she'd laid before him: a savory broth, eggs, coffee, some cheese, and a bit of stewed apples and cinnamon that was still warm.

"He cannot stomach this. You'll make him ill," Bastien grumbled. The last thing the man needed was to be heaving and putting strain on his already damaged ribs.

"It's not for him. At least, most of it isn't," Lady Eleanore replied, the smile now frozen in place. "I thought you might like a bit of breakfast."

Bastien paused. *Merde.* He didn't realize until this moment how unaccustomed he'd become to kindness. In France, food had become so scarce and paranoia so rife, it had turned some of the most gentle

27

and hospitable people in Europe into animals. Since he'd crossed the Channel, he'd spent so much time with those focused on political havoc that he'd forgotten that there were a good deal of people out there without ulterior motives.

But he wasn't one of them.

"*Désolé.*" He bowed his head. It would be easier to pry information out of her if he was civil. And easier still if he was charming. "Thank you, my lady, for your kindness."

He examined the victuals intended for his patient. Clear tea, the English cure-all which may have no other purpose than the notable quality of comfort. The broth, also clear, had scents of onion, chicken, and thyme. On a separate plate were two hard boiled eggs, some cheese, and apple tart, as well as a small pot of coffee. His stomach grumbled, demanding the feast in front of him.

"Is this acceptable, Mr. DuMont? May I take Daniel some broth and tea?"

He glanced up at Lady Eleanore, her hands still clasped at her front, strained politeness masked by a thin smile. Bastien was struck by a need to see what was beneath her veneer of goodness, but it was not the time or place. Besides, he was famished.

He put on his best smile, and with a sweep of his arm, gestured toward where Mr. Morehouse lay. "Of course."

While her back was turned, he took a bit of the strong, hard cheese and savored the sharpness. It had been too long since he'd had a decent meal. He watched as she took Mr. Morehouse his breakfast, as if bewitched. Then, with far more resolve than should have been necessary, he tore his gaze away, gulped down some coffee, and reminded himself why the hell he was here. And it was not to gawk at the sister of the local lord.

Her face lit up, highlighting her beauty. Evidently the act of giving made her happy. Good for her. Lady Eleanore was clearly active and engaged in her community. Given her position and her charitable nature, she would, no doubt, be apprised of all the comings and goings in the neighborhood. She looked guileless enough, and no doubt privy to information that might aid him. And she was most desperate to help.

He would use that desperation to help himself.

ELEANORE WATCHED Daniel and Allison from a respectful distance, taking in the smiles and tears of a couple clearly in love. Truth be told, Daniel still looked in miserable shape, but his wounds were well tended. Allie helped Daniel grip the sturdy cup that held the broth as he gingerly sipped. A pang in Eleanore's chest betrayed a hint of envy.

The two were supposed to marry in the spring. Indeed, Eleanore was supposed to have been married shortly thereafter. Her bouquet was to feature blooms from Barronsfield's famous roses. The design for the dress had been approved. And though Eleanore could not summon up the excitement or deep passion that her brother had for his bride, she had accepted Lord Ramsay's hand with a resigned contentment. Lord Ramsay, she'd thought, was an honorable man, and one willing to overlook Eleanore's tainted parentage. The marriage had been arranged down to the smallest detail.

Until Eleanore had insisted she leave London at once, and had asked— ordered—Daniel to take her away. Perhaps if they had stopped at Cheshire to see Edmund and Gwyneth, as she'd originally planned, this mess with Daniel would never have happened. But she'd changed her mind. Like a frightened, petulant child, she'd wanted to go home. The cost of her selfishness was in Daniel's broken bones and a delayed marriage.

She would pay it back one hundredfold. Daniel and Allie would have a wonderful wedding in the spring, when Daniel was better. Even if Eleanore was not destined for the fairy tale happiness of her brother's union with Rosalind, or her cousin Edmund with his new wife, she could bestow it elsewhere.

Now that Eleanore had returned home, there was so much to do. Foremost in her mind was her plans for a foundling home. Merely an idea when she'd arrived in London in late autumn, it had consumed her thoughts entirely on the way home. A place for the unwanted to be wanted. A safe place where children could be reared. It was the gift her parents had given her—their one shared legacy. If they could not have been together, they had at least seen to Eleanore's care together. And she'd flourished in a loving home, raised by Mr. and Mrs. Darling. There were so many who were destined to a crueler fate, like the poor woman who'd been put upon by Eleanore's former fiancé.

Eleanore would offer those children another chance. In a warm home, with wet nurses and a school room and a garden.

There was the small matter of getting support from the neighborhood, but she'd already decided to enlist the assistance of the Darlings and Dr. Brayden. Indeed, she would speak with them today. And of course, she would have to consult Mr. Schofield about what to do about the unexpected, secret guest at Barronsfield, which meant she needed a chaperone to be in her own house. Eleanore's shoulders sagged at the very idea. Maybe she could ask Mrs. Darling about that as well, and save Mr. Schofield the trouble. And at some point she absolutely had to write Stephen and Rosalind a note that she'd gone to Barronsfield directly, instead of visiting Edmund. Maybe that could wait until tomorrow. Or maybe she should do that first—

A sharp pain to her temple interrupted her list-making. She put her fingers to the bump on her head. The swelling had increased since yesterday, and even as she'd put up her hair in the dim light of her mirror this morning, she could see the lump had turned a spectacular shade of purple.

"Lady Eleanore."

Though it was neither loud nor edged with anything resembling anger, Eleanore jumped at the sound of Mr. DuMont's voice. She turned and found him watching her with a scrutiny that was not a little disconcerting. His expression was mostly unreadable, but there was a distinct undercurrent of deliberation in his countenance.

"Can I help you, Mr. DuMont?"

He shook his head, his tongue making a gentle tsking sound as he did so. "I told you to rest. But since you are obviously more interested in indulging your conscience than good sense, I will take the opportunity to examine you more thoroughly." He turned and walked toward his office, held up two fingers, and gestured for her to follow.

Eleanore was certain her mouth fell open. Not in all her twenty-one years had she seen manners so mind-bogglingly horrid, and she'd been treated to some of the largest egos in the kingdom. She was tempted not to move even half an inch. But her head ached.

She walked to the office, but made no effort to rush. Mr. DuMont leaned against the desk, arms crossed. As she approached, he pulled out a chair and waited for her to sit.

"How bad is it?"

"T'is nothing. Just a little ache," she replied, trying not to be distracted as he moved in close, staring into her eyes. There was nothing more than clinical curiosity in his gaze, but she became conscious of her every breath. He held a lamp up to her eyes, then moved it away, watching them intently. Apparently satisfied, he began to examine the wound much more thoroughly.

"You are not fine, by the looks of you. Did you rest?"

"Of course," she protested. He cocked his head in the most beguiling way, then raised his eyebrows as his countenance softened. Uncertain if it was because of the soft expression around his eyes, or her own emotional fatigue, Eleanore sank into the back of the hard wooden seat, unable to keep up her brave front. "But not well."

"And not, I suspect, due to your injury."

She shook her head. Gently. He bent down, cradling her chin in his hand, gazing into her eyes, then touched his fingers from her forehead down to her neck, examining her for other indications of injury. She took in a quick breath, then closed her eyes, embarrassed by the involuntary way she'd reacted to his touch.

The examination took but a moment, and the sensation was immediately calming, even as the ache persisted.

"Have you had dizziness of any kind?" he asked, his tone completely clinical in nature.

"None."

"*Bon.* Still, you must not overexert yourself. Mr. Morehouse's bones will not knit any faster because you are fawning over him." He raised his lips into a condescending sort of a smile, which made his appearance inexplicably fetching and irritating all at once. He was without his coat or cravat, and though he hadn't shed his waistcoat, his collar was open at the neck, and his shirt sleeves rolled up to his elbows. His features were not sharp, but neither were they soft. He was perhaps approaching thirty, but had a weariness about him that occasionally made him seem older. His chin was dark with stubble, the whiskers interrupted on one side by a scar that ran along part of his jawline. He was tall, but perhaps not quite as tall as her brother. His black hair was somewhat tousled from the rude awakening, which he must have tried in vain to comb with his fingers, to little avail.

Eleanore squared her shoulders. It didn't matter if he was fetching or not. The subtle jab at her efforts to comfort Daniel Morehouse rankled. Who was he to tell her who she should or shouldn't be caring about?

"Emily's broth is well known in Elmsdale for its restorative properties," she insisted.

Mr. DuMont shrugged, his mouth crinkling in that Gallic way that suggested he could not care less about Emily's broth. "I'm sure it is. And does part of the recipe involve it being delivered by a beautiful girl in a red cape?"

Eleanore started at his words. "No."

"Then I would suggest it could have been delivered by anyone else. Like his fiancé, perhaps, leaving you to take care of yourself." He paused, then lowered his voice, which had the effect of drawing her closer to him. "You must have those English lords lined up just to survey your beauty. But I am prepared to be denied that pleasure in the higher service of your well-being."

Eleanore would have rolled her eyes if her head didn't ache so much. "Mr. DuMont, this is hardly appropriate conversation."

"I only wish to point out that if you had stayed in bed and let yourself rest, you would not have to suffer now." He pulled his lips into a tight smile, and it struck Eleanore that the gentleman was genuinely grieved by her refusal to tend to her own needs.

"I take a great deal of interest in the well-being of the people in this village." Eleanore replied. And she did. Unlike in London, people here accepted her for who she was. They didn't care if she was the bastard child of a nobleman and a kitchen servant. She belonged here. "Daniel is my responsibility—I wished to ensure he had managed through the night."

"At the moment, he is my responsibility, mademoiselle." He paused, then gave just the slightest shake of his head, as if his own words took him by surprise, before composing himself. He dug into Dr. Brayden's cabinet, picking over bottles and powders until he'd found the combination that satisfied him, then began mixing a poultice of sorts. "Mr. Morehouse is doing as well as could be expected, considering his injuries."

"Do you know when Dr. Brayden will return?" she asked.

His left eyebrow arched ever so slightly. "Bone setting is the province of surgeons, not physicians. You do not trust my remedies?"

"Of course I do," she protested. His manner was another matter, but she kept that to herself. "When I was in London I went to see Coram's Foundling Hospital." Seeing so many unwanted children nearly broke her heart. "While there are some problems with the institution, I think the idea is a good one. It is my intent to create a home for the area, right here. Dr. Brayden was quite interested when I mentioned it to him last fall."

Mr. DuMont barely paused, giving no indication that he had heard any such idea at all, and he certainly betrayed no interest. "He may have gone directly home. I need to confer with him about Mr. Morehouse." He turned his back to her, and finished the task of mixing his salve. "I will advise him that you wish to speak with him. I have not the insights of a nursemaid, nor how to care for a houseful of baseborn children."

Eleanore's eyes widened and she swallowed, blindsided by his callous, if casual, insult. An awkward silence filled the room, and Eleanore, eager to press on, decided to turn her attention to exactly why Stephen would ever think such an unpleasant person would be an appropriate assistant to Dr. Brayden.

"How did you come to discover this post?" she asked. "I'm surprised my brother did not mention your addition to the staff here."

"I was recommended to His Lordship by an acquaintance." He turned to her, his manner confident as he applied a bit of the salve he'd mixed to her temple. Though he was careful, she flinched as his fingers touched the tender parts of her wound. "It is something of a trial, which is perhaps why the marquess may not have wanted to mention it."

Eleanore pursed her lips, considering his answer. It was possible, she supposed, that Stephen didn't want to disappoint her. Just not probable. She opened her mouth, about to ask another question, when he continued.

"Of course, perhaps he took pity on me, given the circumstances in my homeland that led me away."

A small pang of guilt settled in her chest. Eleanore had read about the horrors across the Channel. Who knew what Mr. DuMont had been running from? "Is it as bad as people say, in France? One never knows what to believe."

"I have been away for two years, but when I left, I no longer recognized the place I loved. There are few winners in the fight for power. And the people at the bottom always lose. " He paused, and there was a softening in his looks, a echo of painful recollection perhaps, that caught Eleanore off guard. But just as quickly he threw off whatever memory had trapped him. He walked away, put down the bowl on his desk, and wiped his fingers on some nearby linen. "Now, it is time for you to return to your home and rest that pretty head of yours."

"But what about—"

"If you care as much about the people as you say you do, then you will take my advice. It will do your little kingdom here no good if their angel of mercy falls down dead, will it?"

He was smirking. It was positively infuriating.

"I have no intention of falling down anywhere, Mr. DuMont." Eleanore sprang up from her chair, eager to put the surgeon's sarcasm behind her, when the room began to spin. She reached out to steady herself, only to find Mr. DuMont catching her arm and gently lowering her back down to the chair. She'd become acquainted with the man only yesterday, and thus far he'd caught her every time she was about to fall.

"You did not need to prove my point so quickly, mademoiselle." He knelt down at her level, and surprised her with the concern in his silver stare and gentle smile. "You will not appease any gods I know by ignoring your own well-being. Mr. Morehouse needs rest and so do you. Time and rest is all the medicine I can offer you. Please take them."

Eleanore grimaced, her cheeks hot from the embarrassment, the low timbre of his voice lingering on her as surely as if he'd touched her. She closed her eyes a moment, trying to throw off both sensations. She'd come home to avoid trouble, but it only seemed to give her a different kind. Mr. DuMont was right—she needed to look after herself. She couldn't help Daniel or begin work on her foundling home if she was sick. And she could hardly bear to think of what Stephen would say to her if he and Rosalind arrived home to find her ill.

Her brother had kept away from her for years, the fear of his now infamous curse depriving both of them of the family they so desperately needed. Her brother Stephen was once known as the infamous Beast of Barronsfield throughout much of England. Devastated by the deaths of so many women he'd loved, Stephen had isolated himself from almost everyone. His retreat from society had provided opportunity for others who'd wished to hurt him and those he'd cared about. With the love of Rosalind Schofield, the remarkable woman who would become his wife, he'd overcome the fears that had kept he and Eleanore apart.

Still, Eleanore could not help but feel his pain at her illness. So she would do what Mr. DuMont asked.

He stood there, patiently waiting for her, his expression soft. "Is there someone to accompany you home?"

Eleanore bit her lip. She'd sent the driver home with instructions to come back in a few hours. She'd expected the morning to go differently. She'd expected to be needed, rather than being the one in need.

"I believe it can be arranged," she replied. "I will walk to the vicar's home. It is close by. I know they will help me return."

"You will stay right here, and I will go," he said, with an edge in his voice that told her he would brook no argument.

"Very well. But are you certain it is no trouble?" She gave him directions.

He bent over in a deep bow, the solemnity of the action lightened by the flourish of his hand. He raised his head, wearing a sly smile. "Of course not. You wouldn't want my employer to find out that I had mistreated his sister, would you? I would be put on the next coach out of this fair town before you English could say 'roast beef.'"

Eleanore attempted a smile. She was certain Mr. DuMont couldn't understand the edge in his jab. Being the sister of the Marquess of Barronsfield had changed her life completely. Most of it was wonderful. But there were moments when she wondered if life would have been simpler if she had remained Eleanore Martin, parlor border of the Darlings and daughter of no one in particular. She could have married a farmer or a baker and had an ordinary, respectable life. Her fairy tale dreams would have remained just that—dreams.

But now they were gone.

CHAPTER 4

*B*astien stood outside the door of one of his patients, the broken snoring of the man so loud that it would have woken the dead. Snoring was a good sign; the man was still alive.

Four days had passed since Bastien had arrived in Elmsdale, looking for Le Veneur Rouge, without much he could account for as progress. While he had no qualms about using his status as a new tradesperson in Elmsdale to insert himself into the fabric of life there, the intent had been to use his position as surgeon as a means to uncover information about his prey. Instead, he'd found himself genuinely busy, spending practically every damn moment since he'd arrived tending to farmers, millers, and local gentlemen. He'd discovered little thus far, except that he'd become the object of singular curiosity in the village. Either that, or Daniel Morehouse was an exceptionally popular man. There had been a string of callers to the infirmary. He'd learned a few faces and several names, but no more. No one attached to the house of Weymouth. Scattered amongst the curious were people with genuine complaints for him to attend to. It did provide him with the excuse to question the locals about scars, though it was not a subject one could easily bring up in random conversation. He'd seen the normal assortment of faded marks that came as a result of everyday mishaps, but nothing of the remarkable sort that would identify Le Veneur Rouge, who bore the Wolf's bite. After days with no substantial leads as to the identity of his prey, he was beginning to wonder if the information he'd been given was false...and that Tante Marie had nearly lost her life for a dead end.

His skills beyond bone setting, however, had been required once since his arrival. A grisly accident at a local estate had required Bastien to put his knives and surgical skills to the test. A mishap with a musket had taken most of the hand of the poor bastard who'd been on the wrong end of it—the man who was now snoring on the other side of the door. The scene had reminded Bastien of some of the wounds he'd seen in the early days of the revolution when gunfire and cannon had been the tools of terror. Indeed, the scope of the man's injuries—singed hair, black powder, and considerable bruising on his back, left Bastien questioning the true nature of how his patient had been hurt. Mr. Wakefield, the man's employer, had been insistent it was from the misfire of a weapon, but even Bastien's limited time in the King's Army made him doubt that story. The patient himself was far from forthcoming, and Bastien had a feeling his patient was not keen to share the truth with his employer present. He'd probably been in his cups when a weapon discharged with his hand on the wrong end of the barrel.

The remedy was as terrible as the injury itself. Fueled by a generous quantity of black rum, held down by a couple of terrified footmen and biting down on a hard piece of leather, the man endured a quick, if not painless, amputation of what little remained of his left hand. It had not been the man's first such procedure, as Bastien noted a missing lower right leg. When it was over, the patient—a grizzled, weathered man named Grimm—lay back down quietly, and offered Bastien a swig of his bottle. He'd accepted.

It had been two days since the incident. After the knocking proved unsuccessful, Bastien opened the door, letting himself into the man's room, which was located in the servant's quarters.

The space was small but comfortable, and spartanly furnished. Only the smallest bit of ephemera from the man's life marked the room; a small slab of wood with the word "Trimbel" scratched into it hung on the wall. Bastien put his bag down on a nearby trunk, then pulled the bottle of rum out of Grimm's hand. The action roused the man.

"Give me that, you bastard," Grimm yelled, flailing in response to being awoken. "I don't need ye sniffing 'round here."

Sniffing was an interesting choice of words. Day-old sweat, urine, and alcohol assaulted Bastien's nose. Still, it was far more sanitary than the slums of either London or Paris, which no doubt helped with the man's recovery.

"You're still alive, monsieur," Bastien said. It was the closest he would dare come to sympathy or surprise at the man's condition. He set the bottle down on a rickety table, out of the man's reach. "Let me take a look at my handiwork, and I'll return your medicine."

The man glared at Bastien, his face red and bloated from drink, and, no doubt, the lingering pain in his limb. Nonetheless, he held his arm out to Bastien. "I've seen better stitchin' by topmen."

"You were in the navy, then," Bastien said, by way of making conversation to distract Grimm from the task of redressing the wound. "Is that where you lost your leg?"

The man nodded and took a quick intake of breath. Bastien worked as quickly as he could to minimize the discomfort. As with surgery, speed was a virtue.

"Merchant ships," Grimm corrected. He gestured to the weathered splint of wood Bastien had spied earlier. "I've been damn near killed more times than I have fingers." He grunted, obviously taken with the macabre observation that that number had very recently been halved. "They plucked that piece of wood out of my leg. Surgeon didn't think I'd live the night, but here I am. I ain't goin' nowhere."

Bastien examined the wound. It was red and swollen, but clear of putrefaction. He rewrapped it in fresh linen, then left another clean one on a nearby trunk. "I'm going to leave some fresh bandages here. This should be rewrapped every few days. The old ones should be cleaned in hot water. I will leave instructions," he said.

"I can do it myself." Grimm furrowed his thick wiry brows and nodded to the rum bottle. "Just give me my medicine."

Bastien held the bottle to him, Grimm exerting every bit of energy to lunge forward and snatch it from Bastien's hand.

Bastien rose and closed his bag. "Far from me to point out the obvious, but you have one less hand to work with. Wrapping that stump might need two."

The man grunted and settled back in his bed, clearly content with his situation. "I'll be fine. You don't need to come round again. Me master's got work for me do to, and I'm going to be gettin' to it. You go find someone else's rum to steal."

Bastien shook his head, grateful for Grimm's rough manner. He was giving Bastien permission not to waste a single moment of concern for him. Whether the ex-sailor realized it or not, it was a welcome gift.

Without another word, Bastien took his leave. He had another patient to visit today—Lady Eleanore. Though she had not demanded his concern, he found himself uncommonly distracted this morning. Was it anticipation at seeing her? Perhaps. Her delicate hands, her astonishing green eyes, her expressive little mouth. The mere thought of her, he'd discovered, was tempting. Of course, Bastien was quite certain that if Lord Barronsfield knew Bastien had entertained even a hint of such thoughts about his sister, the Beast would probably feed Bastien to Le Veneur Rouge himself.

He trudged on toward the village, the cool air taming his thoughts and his body. Perhaps, he thought as he strode down the frozen paths, his anticipation was attributable merely to the notion that Lady Eleanore could be a welcome source of information. An unknowing pawn to aid him on his quest.

He let go a long breath, which hung in the cool air. The idea of her being an unwitting accessory to serve his plans did not sit well, but he pushed it aside. Now was not the time for emotion, for sentimentality, or the scruples that would interfere with his hunt. He was still the Wolf de l'Ardoise. The women in the red hood was a means to an end.

And no more.

***

Eleanore sat in her favorite chair in her bedchamber and rolled the thin charcoal pencil in her fingers. As ordered, she'd been at home for the past four days, straying no farther than the door of her bedchamber. Mr. Schofield had been by to see to her condition, and dispatched the note she'd written to Stephen informing him of her whereabouts and about Daniel. What had she been thinking, leaving in the middle of the night with only a note telling her brother she was breaking the engagement? Leaving him to deal with the scandal?

She leaned forward, rested her chin in her hand, and gazed out the window. London, Lord Ramsay, and those horrid tittering voices were miles away. She could only hope Stephen and Rosalind would forgive her. They were the only ones who mattered.

But now that she was here, her thoughts turned in another direction. Mr. DuMont's placement at the infirmary was a puzzle. That Stephen would not have mentioned it, even in passing, pricked at her.

Mrs. Darling had been overseeing her care since the morning Mr. DuMont had sent Eleanore home. She was a most diligent caregiver, and paid strict attention to the surgeon's orders. Part of those orders included quiet, with minimal visitors. To the gentleman's credit, he'd done her the favor of staving off the wave of visitors that would have brought a bevy of unwelcome questions about Eleanore's unexpected return.

However, it gave her far too much time to think.

She gazed out the window. A brilliant blue sky filled the view, the sun beaming brightly off the thin cover of snow on the hilled landscape below. She opened the sketchbook on her lap, idly flipping through the pages. Her sister-in-law, Rosalind, had given it to her last year as a birthday present, along with a new set of charcoal pencils. It was beautifully bound, with exceptionally fine paper. At first, she'd been afraid to mark in it, convinced her scribbles would somehow mar the volume. But Stephen and Rosalind loved her work, and it provided a private place for her to sketch out random sights and thoughts. It was nearly full now, not only with drawings, but sketches and lists and plans for her foundling home.

The ability to create with her hands went beyond Eleanore's love of drawing. Baking was tactile, useful, and created joy for those around her. When she had been a parlor border, she often baked with Mrs. Darling, making loaves of bread or pies for the patients at the infirmary. Even though Mrs. Darling had a kitchen servant, both Eleanore and Mrs. Darling found it a worthwhile occupation. It gave Eleanore a link to her mother, too, who'd once baked in the kitchens at Barronsfield.

She still baked from time to time. It wasn't particularly lady-like, making biscuits and tarts. Drawing was sanctioned by polite society. Baking bread was not. While Stephen indulged Eleanore completely, she learned upon her first trip to London it was not a pursuit society smiled upon. It, along with a hundred other things ladies did *not* do, was a constant reminder to Eleanore that despite her brother's name and protection, she did not quite fit in London's posh parlors.

Eleanore settled on a fresh page, and after a few cautious strokes with her pencil, started to sketch the perfect little place where she'd establish her foundling home. It would have a small orchard and garden, and maybe a separate building where they could make a school. It would have a foundling wheel, where babies could be left safely. Where they would all have their chance for a happy ending.

She had not yet had the opportunity to discuss her plans with Dr. Brayden. Both he and Mr. DuMont had come by to see her, as promised, but Eleanore had been sleeping when they'd arrived and Mrs. Darling had been instructed not to wake her. Apparently Mr. DuMont had been satisfied with her condition, because he had not returned since, the idea of which left Eleanore oddly out of sorts. Not that she missed him. Indeed, she'd much rather he spent his time attending Daniel and anyone else who truly needed his attention. Still, she found herself awaiting his return, if for no other reason than to be released from her confinement.

A knock at the door broke the silence, and she laid down her pencil. "Hello?"

"Good morning, Eleanore." The door creaked open, and Mrs.

Darling appeared with a tray. "I thought you might like a bit of tea and some gingerbread."

Eleanore closed her sketchbook and smiled, buoyed by the sight of the vicar's wife. "Most definitely. And company too, if you are offering."

Mrs. Darling nodded and set the tray on a table by the hearth. Eleanore rose from her chair and reached for her robe.

Besides her family, the only other people to call Eleanore by her first name were the Darlings. Since her mother's death, Mrs. Darling was the closest thing Eleanore had had to a mother. And, since Eleanore had learned they had a houseguest—the very eligible Colin Middleton, the Marquess of Ellsworth—Mrs. Darling's presence was even more vital. Stephen had mentioned Lord Ellsworth's plans to stay at Barronsfield as a respite from the marriage-minded ladies in London, but Eleanore, involved in her own schedule of parties and social occasions involving her Lord Ramsay, had quite forgotten it until she'd returned home. Lord Ellsworth's visit, Mr. Schofield had shared, was not commonly known, and under her brother's orders, was to remain that way. That Mrs. Darling could attend to her as a nurse, instead of as a chaperone, only assisted with the subterfuge.

"I thought you might like some time to yourself."

Eleanore frowned, and continued pulling on her robe. "I've had quite enough of that. Indeed, I'm becoming quite bored with myself."

"I suppose it wouldn't be the end of the world if we chatted for a short while," Mrs. Darling replied, pouring the tea and adding a touch of honey to Eleanore's. "Perhaps we could start with something simple, such as why you're not in London."

Eleanore paused a moment before accepting the gold-rimmed porcelain cup, wondering if she'd spoken too soon about her lack of companionship. She leaned into her chair, her mouth crinkling in a light grimace. "That is not so simple."

Mrs. Darling's eyes were kind, but the thin line stretched across her brow betrayed her worry. She leaned forward and put a hand on Eleanore's arm. "I simply need to know that you are well." There was no judgment in her countenance. Only concern.

Eleanore set her cup down on a nearby table. "I learned some unfortunate truths about Lord Ramsay that made a union to him impossible. I thought it best to leave after that. I was not up to facing the crowds." Eleanore let go a sigh, squeezed Mrs. Darling's hand, then sat back in her chair. "Perhaps I am a coward."

"You are hardly that, my dear," Mrs. Darling said. "The London rumor mills are vicious at the best of times."

Eleanore knew that all too well. Years ago, those mills helped to give rise to the myth of the Beast of Barronsfield—horrible stories that had claimed her brother, under the curse of a local witch, turned into a beast at night and wreaked havoc on Elmsdale. The fire of gossip had been stoked by stories planted by her wretched uncle and cousin, but London society had happily devoured them and created more all on its own.

She could only imagine what they were saying about the bastard daughter of a marquess who'd run from a desirable match only because her intended had sired a bastard of his own. And that sin, of course, would not be borne by that so-called gentleman, but rather by Eleanore for rejecting him, and the poor soul now growing his unwanted child. Thanks to Mr. DuMont's instructions, she had nothing but time to think about it while awake, and dream about it when she was not.

Enough of that.

Eleanore sipped her tea, letting the lightly sweetened warmth soothe her worries.

"How is Daniel getting on?" Eleanore asked, then helped herself to a piece of gingerbread. She needed to turn her mind to other topics more pleasant and productive.

"From what Mr. Darling has told me, very well," Mrs. Darling replied. "Daniel is eager to return to Barronsfield, but Mr. DuMont does not wish the lad moved until he is satisfied with his cracked ribs. It might be another week before he's home."

And months before he could walk again. Eleanore's heart sank at the very idea. She had to make it up to him, and to Allison. "We shall have to make arrangements for his own room while he is healing. I shall discuss the matter with Mr. Schofield. And then I will speak with Allison about the wedding. I was thinking about it just this morning. We shall have to make it a merry celebration—I'm sure Stephen wouldn't mind giving her some of his roses, and we can use some bunting for the church, and—"

"Eleanore," Mrs. Darling began, interrupting Eleanore's planning. "You are good to attend to these things, but you cannot put the troubles of the world on your shoulders. Perhaps it would be best to leave it to Allison and Daniel."

The subtle reproach in Mrs. Darling's voice caught Eleanore off guard, dampening her enthusiasm. She only wanted to help.

"Of course," she said, perhaps too brightly. "I suppose this is what happens when I am confined to my chamber for too long. I need to keep my mind busy. I have something else I wish to discuss with you. I believe you know about the Foundling Hospital in London?"

The Foundling Hospital was full of children whose only sin was being born to a family who could not afford to care for them, or a mother who'd perhaps succumbed to the charms of a man who would never marry her. Like the poor woman, Eleanore thought, who'd found herself bearing Lord Ramsay's babe.

"Of course."

"While I was in town, I took the opportunity to visit with Rosalind. She left a rather generous donation at the hospital, but I cannot put the place out of my mind." Eleanore fiddled with the ends of the sash around her robe. "And I was thinking that perhaps I could start such a thing here, in Elmsdale. On a much smaller scale, of course. What do you think?" If she could not be the lady society demanded of her, she could do this. And she knew, more than most, what was at stake. But she had not yet decided to speak to Rosalind or Stephen about her plans for a program here, in Yorkshire.

Mrs. Darling paused, pursing her lips slightly. Clearly she was surprised by the idea, but after a moment, her face broke into a smile. "My dear, I think that is a splendid venture. A challenging one to be certain, but that does not mean it is not worth pursuing."

Eleanore popped out of her seat and kissed Mrs. Darling on the cheek, then sat back down. "Thank you. Perhaps we can think about how we might raise both awareness and some funds."

"There is much to consider." Mrs. Darling put a finger to her chin in thought, then brightened. "I think I have just the thing that might assist you."

Eleanore leaned forward, a flutter of excitement lifting her spirits. "Tell me."

"I had already been speaking with Mr. Darling about hosting a small gathering to welcome Mr. DuMont to Elmsdale. I thought it might be beneficial for him to get to know his neighbors," Mrs. Darling said. "We can take the opportunity to speak to your cause and the issue of foundlings, and perhaps build support in the neighborhood for the idea. What do you think?"

"It's brilliant, of course." Eleanore clasped her hands together, buoyed by the idea, though not quite certain how enthused Mr. DuMont would be with the notion. With his dark, inscrutable expression and pragmatic sensibilities about life and death, she was not sure where he might feel at home outside of the infirmary. He looked to be a man living his life on the edges of society. Part of her envied him for it.

"It's a first step," Mrs. Darling continued, "but with the support of the Marquess and Marchioness, it will be a simple task to convince the village of the merits of such a program here."

Eleanore paused, quite deliberately pouring herself a second cup of tea. While Stephen and Rosalind would no doubt happily support her cause, Eleanore wanted to do this on her own. A gift, of sorts, to her mother—a gift she wanted to give. She kept her gaze focused on the stream of tea pouring into her cup, and her tone light.

"I have not yet spoken with them about my plans. I will, once they return home." She finished pouring the tea, and braced herself for the reply she knew was coming.

"Eleanore." Mrs. Darling's brows raised slightly. "Do you not think it wise to discuss this with them first? This is a rather large undertaking for you alone."

Eleanore studied her friend's guarded countenance and nodded, eager to reassure her. "I would not be alone. Rather, consider this a head start. Using a social occasion to welcome Mr. DuMont to the neighborhood would be just the thing to gauge that support."

Her friend paused, and Eleanore held her breath. While Eleanore easily outranked Mrs. Darling, the woman's support meant everything to her.

"Perhaps you are right," Mrs. Darling said at last. She set down her teacup and clasped her hands together. "Of course Mr. Darling and I will support you, my dear. And perhaps Dr. Brayden and Mr. DuMont would be willing to speak to the idea, which would give it a boost."

Eleanore wrinkled her nose. She didn't share Mrs. Darling's optimism that Mr. DuMont would be so eager. His earlier, dismissive tone about baseborn infants still rankled. And somewhat odd, perhaps, given the care she'd witnessed. Perhaps he simply did not care for children. Mr. DuMont was a surgeon—practiced with knives, needles and saws. He said himself that he left the birthing to the midwives. She was entirely uncertain what the people of Elmsdale would make of him, with his French sensibilities and brusque manners.

But Dr. Brayden most certainly would support her. He was a practical man, and his guidance would be helpful in planning the details of how such a scheme might work. As for Mrs. Darling, it was something of a tradition for her to welcome new people to the village. Indeed, Eleanore had met her future sister-in-law Rosalind at just such an event years ago.

"That's a splendid idea," Eleanore said at last. "We could have the tea here, in the library."

"Are you certain? It would be a lovely setting," Mrs. Darling said. "But do you think it wise, with Lord Ellsworth here? He wishes to keep his visit private."

Lord Ellsworth was a private man, but an amiable one, and she considered him a friend.

"I will speak to him. I am certain he would be happy to remain in his rooms for a couple of hours while we entertain. And it would add to the ruse, you see. If he remains invisible, then no one will suspect a thing." Lord Ellsworth was good friends with her cousin Edmund, and, after a fashion, with her brother as well. He'd visited Barronsfield several times in the past. Though perfectly proper in his manners, the marquess was man of singular passions—all of them of a distinctly scientific nature. His absence in London over the holidays had been noted by every family with a marriageable daughter. Lord Ellsworth was *the* catch. But Colin had no interest in being caught, to no greater disappointment than that of his aging father, the Duke of Weymouth.

"Excellent. Indeed, you are correct," Mrs. Darling replied. "So, where do we begin?"

Eleanore's mind turned immediately to the menu. Savories, cakes, biscuits. "I'm not sure of Mr. DuMont's tastes. But it might be nice to serve him something that reminded him of his home. Do you think it would be imprudent to ask him?"

"Of course not. And he's spent a few days with Dr. Brayden. Perhaps he could advise you."

As if on cue, there was a knock at the door. Mrs. Darling rose, and welcomed Dr. Brayden.

"I came to check on the patient."

"Dr. Brayden," Eleanore beamed. "So good to see you."

He came in the room, Mrs. Darling closing the door behind him. "May I have a look at your wound?"

"Of course," she replied. She found herself looking past the physician, her lips crinkling as she realized the man was alone. A peculiar sensation of disappointment settled in her belly, but she brushed it aside.

She set down her cup and sat while Dr. Brayden inspected the cut along her hairline. "I'm certain Mr. DuMont will want to have a look, but to my eyes, this is healing nicely. No more headaches?"

"Certainly fewer than before, thank you." Her interest was immediately piqued at hearing Mr. DuMont's name, though she owed it to his unexpected arrival in Elmsdale. She used the mention as an invitation to satisfy her curiosity. "Mr. DuMont is an unexpected asset to the infirmary. I had no idea of his appointment."

"Having a surgeon's skills is fortunate, and I am not getting any younger. I can use the help." Dr. Brayden smiled, lines creased around his eyes as if to emphasize his point. "Many physicians and surgeons have been displaced in France. The marquess must have heard of him through a contact in London and thought to send him to me."

Eleanore tried, with some difficulty, to keep her expression neutral. It still seemed out of character for Stephen not to mention it. But then, she had been unaware of Dr. Brayden's wish for help, or that he was feeling overburdened. He had been the physician for as long as anyone could remember. Maybe she was being oversensitive—a residual effect of uncovering Lord Ramsay's infidelity. It was time to stop it from clouding her judgment.

"And how is he settling in? Is he the asset to you that you had hoped?" she asked.

The gentleman paused a moment, thoughtful as always. "It is an adjustment for both of us. Each of us are used to our own way of doing things. But he is skilled, and thus far people are giving him a chance." He picked up his black bag. "Indeed, he is at the steward's cottage, conferring with the housekeeper about arrangements for Mr. Morehouse."

He was here? The thought, quite independent of Eleanore's good sense, brought a smile to her lips.

"Dr. Brayden, would you and Mr. DuMont have time to take some refreshment with Mrs. Darling and me? If you are not busy?" She watched him carefully, his expression guarded. "There is some fresh gingerbread in the kitchen and it would be a shame to see it go to waste. That is, if you feel I am well enough."

"I have no concerns." Dr. Brayden paused, turning his gaze to Mrs. Darling and back again. "Are you certain we are not imposing? I would appreciate the refreshment, and I think my colleague would appreciate a look at your wound."

She was hardly certain Mr. DuMont would appreciate it, but that was of little consequence. "I am quite certain. I would like to hear Mr. DuMont's report on the arrangements for Daniel. And, I confess, I have an ulterior motive," she replied. "I have a little project I am considering, and I would appreciate your perspective." Eleanore forced a smile on her face. She was determined to have a foundling program in Elmsdale.

She had little hope, if any, of convincing Mr. DuMont of the virtues of a foundling home. He'd already made his thoughts on the subject quite plain. But there was also a small part of her that anticipated the gentle touch of his fingers, the timbre of his voice and the subtle rolling of his r's as he spoke. There was a mysterious alluring quality to the man that felt dangerous and welcoming at the same time. A quality that made her wonder what it would be like to touch him. To have him brush his lips up against hers.

Had her mother felt this way about her father? Was this how she had been tempted by a man who was otherwise out of reach? Those feelings led to a brief forbidden time of happiness that ended with Eleanore's birth.

Heavens, Eleanore. She gave herself a mental shake. Mr. DuMont was a visiting surgeon. She was, for the moment, his patient, and nothing more. That she would entertain any thoughts about him was silly at best. The aftereffect of a tumultuous week.

Maybe she needed to go back to bed after all.

CHAPTER 5

*B*arronsfield Manor stood tall against the cloudless blue sky a contrast to the biting cold in the air. Bastien braced himself against the stiff breeze as he gazed up at the imposing structure, which seemed impervious to the wind that whipped the thin layer of snow into small eddies over the courtyard. The only color to be found in the otherwise barren landscape came from the rosehips clinging to frost-laden rose bushes that skirted the manor. Their brilliant red hue could not help but remind him of the crimson cape Lady Eleanore wore the day they'd met.

While Dr. Brayden was attending to Lady Eleanore, Bastien had met with Barronsfield's steward, Mr. Schofield, to discuss Daniel Morehouse's return. After a brief discussion, it was concluded that Daniel would be billeted in a makeshift room at Mr. Schofield's home. It was an unusual arrangement, but then Bastien was discovering that Barronsfield, and the people who lived there, were an unusual group who seemed unduly concerned with the well-being of everyone on their estate.

A stiff breeze cut into the flesh on Bastien's cheeks, interrupting his reverie. He resumed his journey toward the manor's massive front entrance, when a hint of movement from a window above caught his attention. He paused and cast his gaze upward to the second story, anticipating he might catch a glimpse of Lady Eleanore, or perhaps one of the servants. It was neither.

In the window stood a gentleman looking off into the distance, as if lost in thought. Though it was difficult to make out a tremendous amount of detail, Bastien was positive the man was not one of the servants, the marquess, or Brayden.

His pulse quickened. Ignoring the chilled wind, he put a hand to his brow in an attempt to shield his eyes from the brilliance of the clear sky, squinting to get a better look. But the man in the window stepped away, disappearing from view. *Merde.*

Bastien moved toward the door, quickening his pace, while attempting to keep his gait steady in case he was being watched from above. He dashed up the steps and knocked on the great door, glancing up at the window where he'd seen the figure. The building probably had eighty rooms—too many to search. Plenty of places to hide.

He let out a deep breath. *Slow down.* The figure could be one of Lady Eleanore's relations. *Or her lover.* The idea curdled in his gut like a stomach full of bad wine. Shaking off the idea, he threw his energy into pounding on the door. Why the hell should he be concerned with Lady Eleanore's romantic connections? He pushed the idea aside. He had other, more pressing things to concern himself with. Like the notion she could be inadvertently harboring a traitor. A lost prince.

The door opened and on the other side stood an older man, thin, with hair whiter than the snow beneath Bastien's boots. He gestured for Bastien to enter.

"Mr. DuMont sir, Lady Eleanore is waiting for you in the library."

Bastien stepped inside and forced himself not to gape at the grandeur of the entryway. A huge fire blazed from a nearby hearth, bringing welcome heat on the cold day. A chandelier hung high over the entrance hall, and a grand staircase lay ahead. Barronsfield Manor was at once a testament to the power and hospitality of its owner.

He followed the butler, all the while taking in every possible detail

—staircases, corridors. Where they might lead. Every possible place to hide.

"Is only Lady Eleanore home at present?" he asked. "With her injuries, I want to ensure that she is resting."

"Lady Eleanore and Mrs. Darling, who is here to assist with any care due to her wound," the butler replied. "She has had no visitors."

"Are you certain?" Bastien pressed, his impatience getting the better of him.

The man paused and turned so slowly, Bastien was worried for a moment he was going to fall. The man stood two steps above him, and though he was a butler, he looked down at Bastien with a look so thunderous, he might have been the lord of the manor.

"I have been opening the front door of this house since before you were in swaddling clothes," he said. "Lady Eleanore has had no visitors."

Bastien bowed his head, embarrassed by his conduct. "I had not intended to offend, sir." He straightened. The butler nodded his head ever so slightly by way of acknowledgement, and then turned back around, leaving Bastien to wonder if what he'd seen had been a trick of the light, or a figment of his imagination.

At last they arrived at the most astonishing room Bastien had ever encountered. A red carpet spilled out across the floor. Three walls were lined with shelves of books that went from nearly floor to ceiling. In one corner, a small winding staircase led to a smaller, half level alcove with even more volumes. A great hearth blazed, and light streamed in from grand windows that faced south. The famed library of the Marquess of Barronsfield lived up to every description his friend Edmund had used to describe it, and more.

A bolt of awareness cut through the splendor, diverting his attention away from endless rows of books to a figure sitting near the fire. Lady Eleanore sat in a chair so large it seemed to engulf her delicate frame. She was wrapped in a shawl, her cheeks flushed ever so slightly, deep in conversation with Dr. Brayden and Mrs. Darling.

"Mr. DuMont," the butler announced in a clear voice, nearly

causing Bastien to start. He'd been so preoccupied with Lady Eleanore, he'd nearly forgotten he wasn't alone.

She turned her head toward them and smiled. "Thank you, Hanley."

At the mention of the name, Bastien turned to get another glance at the man before he left the room. Hanley. His friend, Edmund Pembroke, had taken the name Edmund Hanley as an alias for many years. He said he'd adopted the name in honor of a man he knew who had always done his duty and shown remarkable loyalty to his family.

The ancient butler must have been the man. Interesting. Bastien could not help but wonder about the man's truthfulness regarding his answer about visitors. His loyalty would, perhaps to his last breath, be to the family.

Bastien acknowledged Dr. Brayden with a nod before turning his attention to the ladies. "Good day, Lady Eleanore, Madame Darling. I am pleased to see you are looking well."

"Thanks to your excellent care, Mr. DuMont," Mrs. Darling said. "Please, sit with us and have a bit of refreshment to warm yourself on this brisk day."

"I will warn you now, DuMont," Dr. Brayden said, "the ladies have been scheming, and I am afraid you are part of it."

Bastien turned his gaze to Lady Eleanore, cocking his brow. The idea of her conniving seemed farfetched, and yet intriguing. "I had no idea Lady Eleanore was capable of anything that sounds so dastardly."

A delightful flush of pink stained her cheeks, which had a remarkable effect on him. A gentle warmth grew in his chest, driving away the chill as surely as a glass of the finest cognac.

She smiled, her eyes lively despite the lingering marks of her injury. "It is not a scheme, Mr. DuMont. An idea, perhaps, and I hope you agree, a very pleasant one." She put her hand out, gesturing to a seat near Dr. Brayden. "Please sit, and have something warm."

If he didn't know better, he'd think she was going out of her way to flatter him. And damn it if there wasn't something about her smile that drew him near and encouraged him to sit.

"Please," he said, taking a seat opposite her. "Tell me about your very pleasant idea."

"Mrs. Darling has a tradition of hosting a tea for newcomers to the area," she began, her hands clasped in front of her. "If you are agreeable, we would like to host such a welcome for you. Tea, here in the library, with our neighbors."

An intimate gathering with most of the neighbors sounded like a perfectly horrid way to spend an afternoon. But Bastien recognized an opportunity to search for Le Veneur Rouge when he heard one.

"Excellent," he replied, smiling at the chance he was being offered. "I would be honored, my lady."

"Really?" Lady Eleanore's eyes widened and she looked to Mrs. Darling a moment, as if she wasn't quite certain she'd heard him.

"You look surprised, my lady." He lifted a hand, gesturing in the air with a somewhat overly dramatic flair, but he was eager to be seen as amiable. The more she trusted him, the better. "I am French, you see. Some good food, some pleasant company—I cannot think of a better way to spend an afternoon. On one condition, of course."

"Of course," she replied. "Which would be..."

"I would like to examine your wound, and confirm, for myself, that you are improving."

"Well, Lady Eleanore, it seems Mr. DuMont is not so disagreeable after all," Dr. Brayden replied. "I told you he can be quite pleasant."

Bastien shot a glance at Lady Eleanore, whose cheeks deepened from pink to a red as rich as the cape she'd worn the day they met.

"I—didn't say you were disagreeable," she protested. "Just that you might not be agreeable to the idea of a tea party."

"You might find that I am agreeable to a great many things, Lady Eleanore."

She bit her lip. It was an artless gesture on her part, but Bastien's body reacted. She seemed completely unaware of her beauty. He swallowed, forcing his body into check. She was, at the moment, a patient. An innocent. And if Bastien DuMont's moral code had degraded over the years, he knew somewhere inside that he was still, at the very least, a gentleman.

"How is Mr. Morehouse?" Mrs. Darling asked, clearly trying to fill the awkward silence that had descended on the room.

"He is doing as well as can be expected, madam," Bastien replied. "I have just seen to the arrangements for his return, which should be satisfactory for his recovery."

Lady Eleanore's brow crinkled, and sadness dulled her eyes. Lady Eleanore's guilt of the man's condition had not abated, and Bastien found himself struck by a desire to alleviate it.

"Which is to say, he is improving." He smiled, determined to show confidence.

Her eyes brightened, which Bastien found gave him immense satisfaction.

"Now, so you can get on with your party planning, let me take a better look at your injury." He rose and gestured to a spot near the windows, far enough away from the others he could speak to her privately, and yet close enough as to not be suspicious. "If we could take advantage of the light, I will examine your wound. This way."

He walked ahead, inviting her to follow. He led her to a small writing table in the far corner of the library, pulled out the chair, and motioned for her to sit.

She frowned, her delicate mouth crinkling at the edges. "Tell me, Mr. DuMont, is your professional manner always so charming?" She settled in her chair and leaned her head in such a way that he was able to easily examine the wound.

He did not miss her sarcasm. "I am not here to be charming, my lady." *I am here to hunt down a man and kill him if I have to.* "I am here to ensure you are well. And I hope you are."

"I am doing much better, thank you."

"*Bon,*" he said, more to himself than to her. He put his fingers gently to her head, near her wound, though careful not to touch it. The swelling had decreased considerably, and the color of the bruising suggested she was starting to heal.

"Well?" she asked. "Please tell me it does not need to be bled, or worse, leeched." She shook slightly in disgust, which made Bastien smile. He hadn't smiled very much—genuinely—in a long time. "I know they are small and helpful creatures," she continued, "but I cannot say I enjoy the idea of having them attached to my head."

"I think we can leave the leeches for now." He cast a quick glance toward the hearth, where Dr. Brayden and Mrs. Darling appeared to be in conversation. Seizing the opportunity, he put two fingers to her throat, feeling her pulse. It wasn't necessary, but he needed time to prod her about the figure he'd seen in the window. "You have been following my instructions?"

"Of course. Please do not tell me I have to be confined to my room any longer. I feel much better now."

He pulled his hand away, almost reluctantly. "You are here alone, oui?"

She nodded. "Except for Mrs. Darling, no visitors. Indeed, you've probably done me a favor, keeping some of my...more inquisitive acquaintances away, at least for a little while."

Interesting. Lady Eleanore was interested in throwing parties and caring for injured servants. She hardly seemed the sort that would avoid company. Unless she had a reason she was hiding.

He kept his voice deliberately playful. "And there is no one else here? No visiting relations, keeping you up at night with boorish stories or trouncing you at cards?"

"How silly," she said. "Of course not. All my relations are in London and Cheshire at the moment."

"Very well. It's odd then," he pushed. "It must have been a trick of the light, unless the manor has apparitions."

Her lips fell into a thoughtful frown. "I don't understand."

He shrugged. "I thought I saw a gentleman earlier, as I was coming in. But it must have been merely my imagination."

She hesitated a moment, and pink crept up into her cheeks. "I don't know what you saw. But it is just Mrs. Darling and me, and the servants of course." She smiled, but the expression stopped at her mouth.

She was lying, the little minx.

"Well, it must have been my imagination," he repeated.

"Or a ghost," she replied. "Are we done, then?"

Bastien smiled. He was far from done. In fact, he may have been just beginning.

❧

PARANOIA DID NOT AGREE with Le Veneur Rouge.

Neither did the fact that the Wolf de l'Ardoise still eluded him.

The Red Hunter sat in his study, staring off into the flames of the stone hearth. He hated this house. It was far too small for a man of his power and potential. Hated this brutally small market town with its petty comings and goings. But they'd been convenient places to hide. Until now, perhaps.

If he had a guinea for every Frenchman who'd passed through town since last summer, he could have bought the crown himself. England was awash with Frenchmen—aristocrats fleeing justice polluted London's ballrooms and cafés. That bitch D'Anville—who'd he discovered recently was, despite his best efforts, still alive—had been smuggling them out of France since Robespierre had arrested Louis.

He'd been in Paris the day they'd executed the King. It was a transcendental moment. A moment when he'd known anything was possible. The day he realized that no matter how powerful a man believed himself, he could be defeated by a righteous cause. A cause like his own—where he would gain vengeance against those who'd stolen his rightful future. It had happened in France. It could have happened in England. He would have been their avenging angel, their Michael, leading the English down the same glorious path, freeing himself and everyone else from the shackles of the aristocracy.

Until that bastard the Wolf had, almost singlehandedly, torn it to pieces.

He'd built his network using the wayward few who'd heard his message and wanted to bring the glory of revolution to England. He'd built it from almost nothing, using nothing but his wits, the power of a promise, and quiet ruthlessness. He'd been one of the most effective of the hunters, gathering those noble families who'd run like rats toward England. Turning them over to the revolutionary authorities was, as it happened, a profitable business. A business that, in part, gave him the means to bring his crusade back to his homeland. His network was going to be his path to glory.

And now it was all but gone.

It was rumored the Wolf had once been a tremendous asset to the cause in France. He'd been in Marat's inner circle once, a disciple of the Revolution's ideals. But he'd betrayed them. The Wolf had then turned his eye toward the hunters themselves—dispatching them in the night, in the wood, when they had strayed across his path.

It hadn't taken long for news of the new surgeon to reach his ears. Winter in Yorkshire was dreadful and dull—a new presence would be met with all the curiosity Elmsdale could muster. A visit to the local pub or bakery provided much of the information he needed. The man's name was DuMont. He was a French surgeon. He served in the King's Army at the start of the Revolution, then left not long after.

He could be the Wolf. And he could be no one.

For now, he would watch. And he would wait. And if this seemingly respectable surgeon was the man whose treachery had destroyed his dreams, then the Wolf would die.

CHAPTER 6

*B*astien sat on a hard, ancient stool in the Elm & Thistle, the local public house, pondering his encounter with Lady Eleanore. He stared down at his food, idly pushing the contents of his bowl around with his spoon. There were times when he found himself content in England. The theater was entertaining, and the rather polite way the English had of insulting each other amused him. Springs were horrible but the summers were delightful, and while much of London was a sewer, the countryside was still lush, green, and inviting. But as he swallowed a mouthful of beer to wash down a mouthful of questionable stew, he found himself longing for his homeland.

"Good day to you, Mr. DuMont. Can I refill your ale?"

The voice came from Mr. Roderick, the establishment's keeper. Bastien lowered his tankard and gave it to the innkeeper, who filled it to the brim.

"Word has it that Daniel Morehouse is on the mend," Mr. Roderick began, resting his meaty forearms on the bar opposite Bastien. He leaned in, almost conspiratorially, and lowered his voice. "And Lady Eleanore? She's doing well too, I hope?"

Bastien suppressed a smile. He knew a gossip when he saw one. "She is improving."

"Well, that's good to hear," the man replied, his face lighting up in genuine happiness at the news. "She's everyone's angel, Lady Eleanore. Glad to know she's home safe from London and all. We weren't expectin' to see her back again until at least spring. Maybe not until after the wedding."

Wedding? Bastien shifted in his seat, the very notion of Lady Eleanore being joined to another man discomforting. *Ridicule.* He lifted his pewter tankard, and took another sip of the warm draught. The last thing he wanted was to appear eager to know about Lady Eleanore's marital status, but information was a weapon, and the more he knew of her, the better. He set down his ale. "I did not realize Lady Eleanore was affianced."

Mr. Roderick shook his head and made a tsk-tsk sound. "Not any more."

"*Excusez?*" He leaned forward, inwardly chiding himself for his eager reaction. He found himself uncommonly relieved at that news, for no particularly good reason.

The action seemed to encourage the innkeeper, who crossed his arms across his broad chest and nodded. "She was to marry Lord Ramsay, a Viscount from Essex. Sad for her, but we'd have missed her if she'd have left, that's for sure."

Bastien nodded, inwardly searching his memory for anything he knew about a Lord Ramsay, but nothing was evident. "What happened?"

Mr. Roderick cleared his throat, leaned over the table and lowered his voice. "I heard from Lucy, over at Oliver's bakery, who heard it from Bess Hargrove who works at Barronsfield, that Lady Eleanore broke off the engagement."

Bastien stilled, careful to keep his apparent interest in check. It explained much—including her sudden need to vacate London, her guilt over her driver's injuries, and given that her brother was still in London, her desire to keep any male visitors to Barronsfield an absolute secret.

While Mrs. Darling could play nurse, her role as chaperone would have been more important if there was, in fact, a gentleman in the house that was not a relative. Bastien looked up at the innkeeper with a new interest.

"You seem to be in possession of a great deal of knowledge about the comings and goings of the area," Bastien said, deliberately nonchalant in his manner. He wanted to encourage the innkeeper to continue.

"There's not too much goin' on I don't know of," he beamed, then grew serious. He straightened his apron. "Mind you, I'm not a babble merchant. I run a quality establishment."

"Of course," Bastien said, digging into his bowl and, with great effort, swallowing a lump of something that might have optimistically been called beef. "I am new to the area, as you are no doubt aware, and I want to ensure that all of Dr. Brayden's patients are well looked after. And in my position it's always good to be extra careful with the people who can command the highest fee, if you get my meaning."

The innkeeper winked, learned forward on the bar, and scratched the back of his head. "Mr. Battersby is a well-respected local gentleman, as is Mr. Waterstone. His wife gets gout from time to time. Then I suppose there is Mr. Wakefield. He's in trade, does fairly well for himself I'd wager."

"*Merci.*" Bastien couldn't pry much further without raising suspicion, and he'd soon be meeting many of these men anyway. "And of course, the marquess."

Mr. Roderick looked around the common room, which was nearly deserted, then leaned in close. "How'd you know about him?" His voice was little more than a whisper.

Bastien stilled. Why wouldn't he know about the Marquess of Barronsfield? But it was clear from the innkeeper's manner something was amiss. He shrugged, feigning nonchalance, and took a risk. "I saw him yesterday, during my visit to check on Lady Eleanore's injuries," he lied.

The answer seemed to satisfy the man, for he nodded, though he still kept his voice low.

"The marquess is as fit as a fiddle even if 'e can't see too well without his spectacles," Mr. Roderick said. "Word 'as it he don't get on too well with the old duke. They say he's got some strange habits, Lord Ellsworth does."

The name Ellsworth shot through Bastien's chest as surely as a musket ball. "The Duke—do you mean the Duke of Weymouth?"

The innkeeper paused then look over his shoulder, his attention drawn by the heavy wooden door groaning on its hinges as several local gentleman entered and took a seat at a table near the hearth.

"Yes sir," he said, keeping his voice low. "The Duke of Weymouth."

The spoon slipped from Bastien's fingers, clattering in his bowl. Was that the man he'd seen? It certainly wasn't Lord Barronsfield, whom Bastien had seen in London a few days before he'd arrived. And if it was Ellsworth, what was he doing here?

"Want some more stew?"

Bastien looked up at the innkeeper, who seemed oblivious to the implications of the news he'd shared. Bastien shook his head, shoved another spoonful of the lukewarm gravy in his mouth, and forced himself to still. Lord Ellsworth was a friend of the Pembroke family, most especially Edmund. Indeed, they'd renewed their acquaintance only last summer.

And not long after, Edmund Pembroke had been kidnapped under the orders of Le Veneur Rouge.

Maybe it was coincidence. Or maybe not. More than a few men lived double lives. Edmund Pembroke had been one of them. And so had Bastien.

He turned the idea over in his mind a moment. If Ellsworth was a guest at Barronsfield, it was highly likely even the Beast himself was unaware of the marquess's identity. If, in fact, he was the lost prince. The lost prince who bore the Wolf's bite.

There was only one way to find out.

&

THE BELL that announced customers to Oliver's Pastries rang clearly as Eleanore walked in the door. The establishment was an institution in the village, selling some of the best cakes in the county. Cinnamon, cardamom, sugar, and lemon wafted in the air, and as she closed the door behind her, Eleanore took a long, deep breath.

"Good afternoon, my lady," Mr. Oliver said from the other side of the counter. "It is an unexpected pleasure to see you about."

She pulled down her hood. When Eleanore was a girl, she would come here with the Darlings for the occasional treat. Then, she was known simply as Miss Martin. After six years, there were times when the change in her address still struck her as odd.

"Mr. DuMont said I was well enough to go out of doors, and just in time." Her gaze went to the shelves, which were artfully arranged with tarts and pastries. Daniel was coming home today, and she wanted to purchase something a little special for him. "I will take three of your currant cakes, and a lemon tart for me, please."

"Excellent," Mr. Oliver replied. "If it pleases Your Ladyship, I will bring you a small service of tea to warm yourself while you wait."

She nodded enthusiastically. "That would be splendid, thank you." She took a seat at one of the little tables.

"Mr. DuMont was here just yesterday," Mr. Oliver said as he brought over a small tray. "He's an interesting fellow, that's for sure. Asked me if I knew how to make canelé."

"I've never heard of it," Eleanore replied. "Is it a dessert?"

"It's a little cake, just for one, with a sticky glaze. I don't have the exact tin, but I reckon I can make one of my other molds suffice. I've found a recipe I'm going to try."

"That is excellent information, Mr. Oliver!" she replied as she plopped a bit of milk in her cup, inexplicably excited by the insight. "Perhaps we could order some for our tea that we are having for Mr. DuMont? I hope you are able to attend."

The door swung open again, cool air rushing in as the bell announced another customer. A gentleman stepped inside.

"Good afternoon, Mr. Wakefield, sir," Mr. Oliver called out in his ever-cheerful greeting.

"Good afternoon! The usual, if you please," Mr. Wakefield returned in kind. At forty, with blond hair, a reddish beard, and a sizeable fortune, he was still a very eligible bachelor. He had a pleasant countenance, and was generally well regarded. He'd garnered a respectable fortune in trade, and though he was sometimes away with his business ventures, when he was home he was always at the center of village activity. And a potential contributor for her foundling home.

"Mr. Wakefield." Eleanore waved to him. "How are you? I thought you might be taking advantage of some exotic venture to escape the cold and damp of Yorkshire."

He took off his hat and gloves and walked her way, nodding respectfully. "Business keeps me here, for the moment at least." He gestured with a look to her injury, which was still quite visible. "I heard of your mishap. Can I safely assume your injuries are not of a serious nature?"

"I am making a quick recovery, thank you," Eleanore replied, touched by his concern.

"And your driver?"

"Fortunately Mr. DuMont's particular skills were expertly suited to Daniel's injuries. Though it will be sometime before his bones are mended, we expect he will recover," she replied. "Indeed, he is being settled in at Barronsfield this very day."

"Excellent news." Mr. Wakefield gripped the edge of his top hat. "Indeed, we too have been witness to the surgeon's skills at Hawley Park."

"Oh dear—I hope nothing too serious," Eleanore replied.

"Alas, the man lost his hand. Mr. DuMont is most efficient with the saw and the needle. It was most fortuitous of the marquess to bring him here."

"Indeed it was." Eleanore swallowed, trying not to grimace while the grisly image intruded on her otherwise cheerful thoughts. She could not help but wonder if it was the harsher elements of Mr. DuMont's practice that inspired his occasionally distant manner. "That is sad news."

"Indeed. Of all my servants and associates, Mr. Grimm is one of my longest serving—we have been through much together. He is the hardiest of souls, and has already survived more trials then most men do in a lifetime."

Mr. Oliver returned with a package each for Eleanore and Mr. Wakefield. The gentleman pulled several coins out of his purse and put them in Mr. Oliver's hand before donning his gloves and hat. He then turned to Eleanore, bowing his head slightly as he doffed the brim of his hat.

"I must be on my way. A pleasure as always, Lady Eleanore."

"A moment if you please, Mr. Wakefield," she called out before he had the chance to take a couple of steps.

He paused, then turned.

"If you are not otherwise engaged, I am hosting a small gathering at Barronsfield Manor this Friday to officially welcome Mr. DuMont to the neighborhood," Eleanore said. "I hope you are able to join us."

He looked away for but a moment, his lips turned up in a polite smile. "Sounds like a pleasant afternoon. I would be eager to speak with him under less professional circumstances. Good day, Lady Eleanore."

Eleanore finished her tea, picked up her package, and walked out to the carriage that Mrs. Darling and Mr. Schofield insisted she take into Elmsdale. She would have much preferred to walk the distance, but thought it best, under the circumstances, not to risk becoming ill when she had so much to do to prepare for Friday's activities.

The driver opened the carriage door and took the parcel so she could climb inside. She grabbed her skirt, put her foot on the step, and reached out for his hand to steady her when a shiver of awareness ran from her fingers straight to her chest. She paused and looked up to see Mr. DuMont, his hand outstretched, supporting her. His eyes narrowed slightly into an appraising stare, and it took a moment for her to find her voice.

"Good afternoon, Mr. DuMont," she said at last.

He nodded, putting his other hand to the brim of his hat. "*Bonjour*, Lady Eleanore."

She looked down at her hand, still wrapped around his, and with a shocking amount of reluctance, released her hold on him.

"I wonder, at times, Mr. DuMont, how you are able to move so quietly," she said, her heart inexplicably fluttering in her chest. "You have taken me quite off guard."

"When I said it was fine for you to stir out of doors, this is not what I intended." He motioned to the package in the driver's hands. "Surely this fine fellow could have gone about this errand for you?"

She pursed her lips. "Of course he could. But I enjoy doing things myself." She leaned in a tad, in a conspiratorial fashion, catching a hint of his scent. "Mr. Oliver makes the best lemon tarts in the county. Possibly England. I am not as selfless as you think."

His mouth twitched, and then, as if almost against his will, he smiled, which changed his countenance entirely. Despite the chill in the air, it made her feel…warm. Tingly.

"You should do that more often, Mr. DuMont."

His brows dipped slightly in confusion. "Give you grief for not following orders? Trust me, I am far from stingy in that regard."

"No, silly. Smile. You have a lovely smile. I would wager it puts your patients at ease."

He paused, melancholy casting a shadow over him that made Eleanore's heart lurch.

"You are kind, my lady. But most people do not smile when I approach. Indeed, they are usually doing quite the opposite. I am a source of pain, or even terror, when I am doing my work." His smile remained, but his eyes betrayed his nonchalance. There was something else there. Sadness, perhaps. Regret.

Eleanore's thoughts went to her discussion with Mr. Wakefield and the image of the saw and the needle. There was no remedy for the pain those inflicted—for the patient, or the person wielding them.

"Perhaps," she replied, growing serious, eager to soothe him. "But I know when I first came to you, to help Daniel, I only felt relief. Relief that you might be able to take something horrible and painful and make it better. So I would say you also offer hope. A second chance. Would you not agree?"

FOR THE FIRST time in a very long time, Bastien did not know how to reply. His thoughts scattered like autumn leaves on the ground. They'd been pushed aside by the sparkle in Lady Eleanore's exquisite green eyes and loose strands of flaxen hair that flitted in the breeze.

But more than that, he was distracted by her words, and how, for just a moment, they'd allowed him to see himself as someone different. The man he'd once thought he could have been.

What was she speaking of? Relief? Hope? People didn't regard him that way—not anymore, if indeed they ever had. Jacob Grimm certainly did not. And that reaction had become far more familiar. Even comfortable.

"Ask the man whose hand I removed," Bastien grumbled. "Trust me when I tell you that he called me a thousand names, but none I could repeat in front of a lady."

"I heard, just a few moments ago, from Mr. Wakefield," she replied, clearly not in the mood to indulge his testiness. "Will he survive, do you think?"

"If he can stave off fever, then perhaps he will."

"Well, then." Her mouth teased at a smile that threatened to beguile him. "I think you have proven my point entirely."

Lady Eleanore looked up at him from under the rim of her hooded red cloak, her cheeks ruddied by the air. If he was not in the middle of a public square, he would have been tempted—so tempted—to quiet her with a kiss.

"Sometimes," she pressed, completely unaware of the spell she was casting on him, "healing requires us to walk a rocky path. But the path would not be possible without another to offer it. Someone like you."

For just a moment, he wanted to believe her. Believe that there was more to his work than pain and suffering. But he'd walked that path. Heartache and failure were his rewards. He hardened.

"You are a romantic, Lady Eleanore," he said. "Perhaps what I offer is false hope—and any healing that happens is mere chance."

She laughed, but he could not help but notice a note of bitterness in it. "As much as I would dearly love to be a romantic, Mr. DuMont, life has given me another path. Still, I know what I felt when I first saw you the night I'd returned."

"Confusion?"

"I suppose, yes. Confusion. Surprise. And perhaps a little frustration. But when you took my hand, I had hope."

Hope?

As if sensing his disbelief, she squared her shoulders. "And that is not just my opinion. Mr. Wakefield agrees."

"That is good to hear," he replied at last, eager to move on from the subject, but not willing to be impolite. "Please express my gratitude for his good opinion."

"Indeed, you will be able to express it yourself, on Friday. Mr. Wakefield promised me he would attend the tea."

"Of course." He smiled, almost as an afterthought. Lady Eleanore's tea party—to welcome him to the neighborhood and provide a break in the monotony of the cushioned lives of the landed gentry— provided the perfect opportunity to search the house for Lady Eleanore's secret houseguest, Lord Ellsworth. She'd asked him and Dr. Brayden if they might speak to the guests about her well-intentioned, if misguided ideas about starting a foundling home. "I'm certain Dr. Brayden has something to say that will be to your liking. I am not blessed, as you might have guessed, with the ability to charm people with my words."

"The initiative is mine, and it is up to me to convince my neighbors it is an idea worth their support," she said. "I merely thought you might be inclined to consider my arguments, and if they seem reasonable to you, you could support them."

Did Lady Eleanore have any idea of the hell that could exist in a foundling hospital? Because he did. That he was here, now, was nothing short of a miracle. He'd been fortunate in a way that most of the poor souls he'd shared his first years with were not. Little though he knew of Lady Eleanore, he couldn't believe she'd be so inclined to replicate it here if she understood the folly of her idea. Of course, she'd lived a sheltered existence. If Bastien could put her in his shoes for even a night at *l'Hôpital des Enfants-Trouvés*, she undoubtedly would reconsider.

"It would be just a very small part of the afternoon," she pressed.

"I will consider it," he said at last, carefully noncommittal.

"Wonderful!" Lady Eleanore continued, her face lit up which almost had the remarkable effect of chasing away his ill humor. "Well, I shall be on my way. I look forward to it."

He nodded, struck by the urgency to keep her here longer. Though it was but two days away, Friday was now too long to wait.

The sun had begun to be crowded out by heavy clouds that promised the choice of snow, or worse, a cold icy rain. He helped her climb into the cab of her carriage, and was about to close the door when the clanging of bells piqued his attention.

"What is that?" Lady Eleanore asked loudly, leaning back out the carriage.

"Church bells, my lady," called the driver.

"At this hour?" She looked to Bastien, worry in her face. "Something is wrong."

"How far is the church?"

"Close," she replied. She called out to the driver. "Please take me to the church. Mr. DuMont, if you would be so kind as to accompany me."

She did not need to ask twice. He hopped in, and the door was barely shut before the carriage was in motion.

"Where is Dr. Brayden?" she asked.

"Last time we spoke was this morning. He was attending to some patients on the other side of the village. I do not know if he has returned."

The bells kept clanging ever louder as the carriage approached. Though it took them only minutes to arrive, tension had kept Lady Eleanore deathly still.

The equipage barely came to a stop before Lady Eleanore threw open the door. She jumped out, running toward the church, Bastien at her heels. The parson came out to greet them.

"Eleanore—have you seen—" The man stopped short, looking past her. Looking, Bastien realized, for him.

"Mr. DuMont, I thank God you are here," he replied. "It might already be too late. Please, come."

Bastien exchanged a confused look with Lady Eleanore, then followed Mr. Darling to the vicarage. Blood pounded in Bastien's ears, a familiar rush of excitement mixed with dread.

"We found him, my dear," Mr. Darling called out to his wife as he threw open the door to his home. "We found him."

Bastien followed the parson into his front parlor, Lady Eleanore at his heels. Ahead was Mrs. Darling, pacing in front of the fire. Her face was drawn. In her arms was a bundled infant.

Bastien swallowed, then shook off his trepidation. "Show me."

He rushed to her, and she held out her arms.

"We found him by the church, just a short while ago," she said, her voice edged with fear. "There had been a few little gasps of breath from him at first. We were trying to keep him warm."

He pulled away the bundling, and his heart dropped. The infant, perhaps a day old, was cool to the touch. He put an ear to its tiny chest, but there was no sign of breath, nor the faintest evidence of a heartbeat. A hint of blue stained the child's lips.

He said a silent prayer for the child's soul, then pulled the bundling over the child. "He is in God's hands now."

A stifled sob cut the air, and Bastien looked up to see Lady Eleanore, her hand over her mouth, her eyes bright with unshed tears.

Mrs. Darling took the babe, her countenance one of grim resignation. She swallowed.

"Thank you, Mr. DuMont."

"I have done nothing but perform the grim task of pronouncing death," he replied. "In this weather, an infant would have little chance of survival. It is unfortunate the mother did not at least present the child to the infirmary. It is never locked."

"Unfortunate," Lady Eleanore repeated to herself, her gaze fixated on the bundle in Mrs. Darling's arms. She wiped away a stray tear with the back of her hands. "Who knows what circumstances led to this?"

A hushed silence filled the room. At last, Mr. Darling spoke.

"I baptized the child when we found it," he said. "I shall see to a proper burial for him. Mr. DuMont, Lady Eleanore, if you would excuse me."

He left the room, and Mrs. Darling followed, leaving Bastien alone with Eleanore.

"I'm sorry."

She sank down into a chair, and stared into the fire. "That poor thing was probably doomed from the moment he first took breath. There was nothing you could do."

There was nothing he could do. Too often there was nothing he could do. And he hated himself for it.

"But there is something I can do."

The steel in her words caught Bastien off guard. He gazed at her, enthralled by the determination that had set her emerald eyes ablaze. She stood, adjusted her cloak on her shoulders, and walked past him to the door, pausing only to look back at him one last time.

"And you, Mr. DuMont, are going to help me do it."

CHAPTER 7

*N*ight had fallen, and a bitter wind howled at the windows in Dr. Brayden's home where he and Bastien were sitting in front of a blazing fire. Though Bastien had planned on staying at the local inn, Dr. Brayden insisted that he had plenty of room, and despite his own occasionally brusque manner, seemed to appreciate Bastien's company. And on a night like tonight, Bastien was more than happy not to have to venture out of doors.

"Always a dreary business, burying a babe," Dr. Brayden said, staring off into the fire, a glass of brandy in his hand. He looked over at Bastien, a single eyebrow raised. "I'm surprised, frankly, that you bothered."

"So am I," he replied. Bastien tipped back his own glass, savoring the burn of the liquor on his throat. "Why wouldn't the mother have brought the child to the infirmary?"

"Who can say? Perhaps the mother died in childbirth. Or perhaps she was afraid of being seen. It is not for me to judge the poor soul's motives," he replied. "Though plenty would, I am afraid."

The burial had been a brief, solemn affair. Bastien helped to dig a little grave, breaking up the partially frozen soil with a pickax. The vicar read from his prayer book, and Lady Eleanore stood in the cold, her red cape whipping in the wind.

"What do you think of Lady Eleanore's plan?" Bastien asked Dr. Brayden. "To have a foundling home?"

"It is a bold one. And not without merit." He shuffled in his seat, and took another sip from his glass. "I have known Lady Eleanore since she was little more than a child. She has a good heart. Perhaps too good. And she can be most determined when she puts her mind to something. Though it's not terribly surprising, I suppose."

"In what way?"

His companion hesitated a moment. "It is perhaps not speaking out of turn, for it is common knowledge. Lady Eleanore is the marquess' half-sister. Her mother was a servant, and only when the girl was fifteen, did Lord Barronsfield reveal the truth of her parentage to her."

Eleanore Pembroke was a bastard? *Mon dieu.* Bastien's memory wandered back to his offhanded remarks about baseborn infants. *Idiot.* He put his hand to his temple as a heaviness settled in his gut. "Why did he wait so long, the marquess?"

"He had his reasons. Much of it had to do with his concern that if he owned their relationship, he would put her in jeopardy. He'd believed himself cursed. When it became clear to him, and everyone else, that his curse was nothing but a ruse, the first thing he did was to speak with Lady Eleanore," he said. "She moved to Barronsfield not long after, and has remained there. The Darlings were her guardians before that."

Which would explain the familiarity between them. Indeed, it would explain much about her need to rescue foundlings. Because she could have very easily been one of them. As he had been.

"I have seen many a foundling hospital in France." *From the inside*, Bastien silently added to himself. "The end result for most of the inhabitants is not unlike the poor soul we found today. Though they meet their end more slowly." With more anguish.

"I have not seen the institutions you speak of, though I know their reputations." Brayden shook his head. "Coram's has had its challenges, but also its successes. If Lady Eleanore can learn from what the others did wrong, as well as what has been done right, I do not think I have the right to naysay her."

Bastien shrugged. Of course Dr. Brayden was correct. And when he recalled the look of utter commitment while she stood at the graveside, he knew he would be a fool to try to dissuade her.

Lady Eleanore's cause, however, was not why Bastien was going to tea. The Wolf de l'Ardoise had one last prey to hunt. Still, there was something about her quiet resolve he found fascinating. She was starting to become a distraction to him at all possible levels, and he could not afford the complication.

Bastien settled into his chair further, his head back, looking around the comfortable salon. Dr. Brayden was a man who clearly was passionate about his work, and about learning. There were texts scattered about the room.

"You have a medical library here that would rival many schools," Bastien said, rising out of his seat and examining the spines of the books. Some were written in languages he could not identify.

"His Lordship is a great supporter of knowledge and the written word, as you have no doubt deduced for yourself," the physician replied. "I have been most fortunate, as a part of my practice, to be supplied with whatever new knowledge that can be put into print. Indeed, there are medicines from the Holy Land and the Far East that I find fascinating."

Bastien smiled, impressed by the man's enthusiasm for learning.

"Of course, one can also learn from careful observation," Dr. Brayden continued. "What do you make of this?"

The doctor's outstretched arm directed Bastien to a nearby shelf laden with almost a full row of smaller notebooks of various sizes. He picked one off the shelf. Inside was page after page of the doctor's handwriting.

"Is this what I think it is?" Bastien rose, drawn by the discovery, and marveled at what he was seeing.

"I have been in practice for nearly thirty years," the doctor said. "The newer volumes are in the infirmary. Every birth. Every fever.

Every cough. Every death I attended. There is always something to learn."

"Impressive." Bastien raised his eyebrows, closed the book, and put it back on the shelf. In all his time, he had hardly bothered to keep a single note on his patients. Any field reports he had to write during his short time in the King's Army felt like an exercise in tedium.

"Are you enjoying your practice?" Brayden asked him, his eyes narrowing slightly. "Or perhaps it interferes with your real business."

"It is serving my mission nicely." Indeed, the invitation to tea provided the perfect opportunity to track down Lord Ellsworth, without having to pick a single lock. He'd leave the charity speeches to Dr. Brayden.

"And you would not consider taking up your practice full time?"

Bastien nearly laughed aloud at the physician's question. "I think that's better for everyone if I remain safely out of the surgery business."

"And why is that?" the doctor pressed, clearly incredulous. "Your work to date has been excellent. And heaven knows I could use the help. I am eager to learn about Desault's approach to debridement, if you are willing to teach me. What are your plans after you've caught your man? Return to France?"

Bastien pursed his lips and stared into the orange flame. What were his plans? He had no idea. He had been fixated on this singular target for nearly two years. It had consumed his waking hours and not a few of his dreaming ones.

He shrugged. "By the time I left, the revolutionary government felt that keeping trained physicians and surgeons smacked of elitism, and in their wisdom, replaced them with anyone who thought they could do the job."

"That is a shame. Even many English physicians will grudgingly admit that some of the best surgeons have come out of Paris." The doctor smiled at the idea, then took another sip of his brandy.

There was a part in Bastien's heart that yearned to return to France, but there were too many trials there he wanted to forget. Eager to change the subject away from those painful subjects back to the issue at hand, he returned to the matter of Lady Eleanore's plans. "Speaking of which, you never answered my question. What are you going to say about Lady Eleanore's foundling program? She is counting on you to convince the neighborhood of its merits."

"Lady Eleanore will have to count on you, my boy," he replied. He reached into his pocket and held up a small letter. "And so will the rest of the village, at least for a fortnight."

Bastien blinked, unease tightening the back of his throat. "Excuse me?"

"I have a letter from my sister. It arrived this morning. She has long suffered with consumption and I fear she might be coming to her end." Brayden shook his head. "I will be with her, until she passes."

"I am sorry," Bastien replied, chiding himself for his selfishness. But this was damn poor timing.

"We both knew this day would come, sooner or later. Indeed, she has survived longer than many," he replied. "I must leave first thing in the morning."

Bastien stilled, realizing the implications of being the only medical man in the area.

"I have no idea when this mission of yours will be over, but I will ask a favor of you, which is, to the best of your ability, take over my practice until I have returned."

What the hell could he say? There was only one answer.

"I will take care of business here. Go to your sister."

❦

ELEANORE TAPPED the edge of her pencil against her cheek as she sat in the kitchen, contemplating her list.

That special blend of tea favored by Mrs. Waterstone. Mr. Battersby's cherished currant cakes. And of course, canelé for Mr. Bastien DuMont.

She looked back down at the scrap of paper lying in front of her, studying as surely as a general reviewed a plan of attack. And it was, after a fashion.

It had to be perfect. The food, the company. Not just because she wanted to impress Bastien DuMont. Indeed, despite his enthusiasm, she'd seen the disdain he'd shown for the very notion of a foundling home. More than disdain, in fact. But as long as Dr. Brayden was there, she knew she would be able to count on him to lend his support and convince the local populace of the merits of her idea. And the Darlings, of course, but then she knew she could count on them for anything.

Mr. Darling had conducted a lovely little service for the baby they'd found yesterday. Only the Darlings, Mr. DuMont, and she were there to see the poor thing put to rest. To Eleanore's great shock, Mr. DuMont took it upon himself to hollow out a grave. There was no marker for the child. When Eleanore returned home, she'd asked Mr. Schofield if a little wooden one could be fashioned.

She shook off her morose mood, determined to use it as fuel for her cause. There had, over the course of the years, only been a few abandoned children in the area. At least that anyone knew about. Infanticide and abandonment were, by their very nature, hidden from all but their mothers.

The smells of the breakfast meal still lingered. She folded over her paper, tucked it into her sketchbook, and set it aside. Later, she would discuss her plans with Mrs. Darling, Mr. Schofield, and the cook. But for now, she had another more immediate task ahead of her—visiting Daniel. He'd been staying in a room in Mr. Schofield's cottage on the estate. They'd turned his front parlor into a makeshift bedchamber for Daniel, where he could be attended to. Mr. Schofield had his own housekeeper, and Emily would fuss over him as much as Allie.

Eleanore rose and walked to a rack near the oven where a few oatmeal biscuits and tea cakes were cooling. She grabbed a basket and tucked in a linen, filling it with treats and a little pot of preserves. If she walked quickly, they should still be warm by the time she reached him. Satisfied with the basket's contents, she pulled on her cloak and gloves, gathered the basket, and walked out into the bright, cool morning. She took in a breath, savoring the crisp air. Glancing over her shoulder, she looked toward Lord

Ellsworth's room. There was little doubt that even at this hour he was still fast asleep. He kept curious hours, given his interests. It had been a miserable evening, with blowing wind and icy snow that now covered the ground, so she could not imagine what manner of heavenly observations could have been done in such conditions. Still, she could not wonder if his serious nature would brighten if he spent less time peering at the stars, and a little more walking in the sun.

A thin crust of snow sparkled in the sunlight, forcing Eleanore to pull her hood up to shield her eyes as she emerged out of Barronsfield's shadow. Keeping her head down, she noticed footprints in the snow. Perhaps Colin had decided to walk in the daylight for a change. Since she'd returned, he'd been very careful not to make any appearances, especially since Mrs. Darling had come to the manor. Now that Eleanore's health was improving, there was no need for her to have a nurse, so for Mrs. Darling to stay on as a chaperone would only invite further comment.

"Good morning, Lady Eleanore."

Eleanore started at the sound of Mr. DuMont's voice. He'd turned the corner just as she'd approached, and she'd nearly walked straight into him.

"Good heaven, Mr. DuMont," she said, taken off her guard. She put a hand to her chest, her heart beating a little faster. "This is an unexpected pleasure."

Mr. DuMont bowed his head. "I apologize for startling you." He carried a leather bag in his left hand.

"Nonsense," she replied. "I was merely lost in my own thoughts. I am on my way to visit Daniel Morehouse. I trust you were doing the same?"

"Oui. Your steward has gone out of his way to see to his care," he replied.

"Mr. Schofield is a remarkable man. We are very lucky to have him," Eleanore agreed. He was one of Barronsfield's longest serving and loyal servants. And, in part, the reason why her brother Stephen had met his wife Rosalind, who was Mr. Schofield's niece. "I am bringing Daniel some of my famous oatmeal biscuits." She held out her basket.

"Yours?" he regarded her with ever increasing interest. "I did not realize that sisters of marquesses baked oatmeal biscuits."

"This one does," she replied, perhaps more tersely than intended. After spending months in London, it was difficult not to be defensive about such things. She smiled in an attempt to take the sharp edge off her reaction. "And they are the best you will ever taste."

His eyes widened slightly, and his lips parted as if he was going to say something, then thought the better of it. "I am certain they are magnificent. But I have tasted many delightful pastries, back in France."

"These are more than delightful." The recipe had been her mother's and a very special one. "Indeed, they are positively sinful. Especially when they are warm."

"Sinful?" The edge of his mouth teased at a smile, and his voice lowered to such a timbre it created a flutter in her belly. "Now that is quite the claim. And an enticement."

Eleanore swallowed, her breath catching just a little. "Do you wish to try one?" She took a step closer, as if drawn to him.

He reached out, his fingers gently brushing away a loose lock of her hair, tucking it behind her ear. A winding heat traveled from her ear through her body. She gripped the handle of the basket a little tighter as Mr. DuMont tilted his head slightly, his heavy-lidded gaze riveting her where she stood.

"These are meant for Mr. Morehouse," he replied, her heart skipping at his accent, which seemed even more pronounced. "I am tempted by something far sweeter."

Eleanore's breath caught as she found herself drawn up onto her toes.

"I—cannot imagine what it is." It was a lie, of course. Even she wasn't so innocent.

He lips drew back, his smile inviting and yet, almost predatory. "You, mademoiselle, are a horrible liar."

He reached down, his lips grazing hers, and Eleanore knew he was right. She was a horrible liar.

A heavy sigh escaped her as the warm sensation of his lips against hers countered the cold air around them. It was the first time she'd ever been kissed like this, and it was glorious and frightening all at once. His lips, gentle, explored only her mouth, but every other part of her body was coming alive.

She parted her lips, inviting him to explore further, but instead, he abruptly broke the kiss.

Eleanore opened her eyes to see Mr. DuMont looking quite at odds with himself.

"My apologies, Lady Eleanore," he said, his voice a little gruff. He stepped back and cast a hard glance aside, as if he was angry with himself. "I have taken advantage."

She swallowed, trying to calm the rush of blood coursing through her body. Squaring her shoulders, she shook her head. "I do not feel that way. Perhaps the stress of recent events has clouded our judgment."

"Regardless, you have been in my care, and this encounter was inappropriate."

Eleanore bit her lip, and looked to the ground, desperate to gain control of her breath. Her head was still spinning, and it took her a moment to fully comprehend him. And he was right, of course. What was she even thinking?

"Well, let us both agree to forget about it, shall we?" Eleanore smiled widely, as if she was speaking about something as facile as tying her boots.

He bowed deeply and mimicked her smile, which had the singular effect of making her feel better and worse all at the same time. Would he be relieved to forget the encounter?

Mr. DuMont pointed at the basket of biscuits that had led to that glorious, if ill-conceived kiss. "I will test your claim about your baking at the tea."

At the tea. Eleanore gave herself a mental shake. What was she doing, lingering here in the chill with Mr. DuMont—*kissing* him—

when there was work to be done? "Excellent. Dr. Brayden will vouch for it, of that I am certain."

"I am afraid your physician will be unable to attend." Mr. DuMont reached into his coat and produced a letter. "He asked that I deliver this to you with his sincerest apologies."

Frowning, she took the missive and scanned it, her heart sinking a little more with every word. She knew very little about Dr. Brayden's family circumstances, but by the physician's own admission, they were dire indeed.

"Thank you," she replied, folding up the note and handing it back to him. She let go of a long breath, more than a little crestfallen, then chided herself for her selfishness. Dr. Brayden was well respected. People generally heeded him in a way, she was aware, that they might not with her. "I hope that will not stop you from attending?"

"Of course not. I look forward to the afternoon."

Hope rose in her chest at his admission. There was something in his looks that made her want to believe him. But whether he did or not, she needed someone to speak about her foundling program. And if Dr. Brayden couldn't be there…

"And, perhaps, you might consider saying a few words about the foundling home in his place?"

Mr. DuMont straightened, any hint of softness evaporating. "I will do you the honor of being truthful. If I shared my feelings on the subject with your guests, I do not think they are the words you would like to hear, Lady Eleanore."

"Why ever not?" she pressed. "What possible objection could you have?"

His lips formed a tight line. "Plenty. Shall I list them for you?"

Eleanore knew she should have kept her response measured, but with the memory of that poor child fresh in her memory, she could not quite manage it. "No need. I have heard them all, Mr. DuMont." She held up her fingers and began to count. "Number one. Encouraging lose morals in women. Number two. Allowing the poor—"

He waved her off. "I care not for that."

She threw up her hands, the basket jostling on her arm. "Then what? I do not understand."

He stepped closer, his eyes ablaze. "How many do you plan to rescue, my lady? One? A dozen? A hundred?"

"As many as need rescuing!"

"And what will you do with them all? How will you care for them? When the beds are full?"

Every year had been different. Elmsdale would go a year, even two, with none, and others might produce three children in need of homes. The children were often left at the church.

"We will hire local women to care for them. It will provide employment as well."

"And what about nourishment? Heat? How will you tend to their welfare when there are more of them than you have beds?"

Eleanore paused, struck by Mr. DuMont's haunted, angry countenance. "It appears you have given this a lot of thought, Mr. DuMont. You might be the perfect person to help me."

"I am merely pointing out the challenges in this little project of yours."

"Little project?" Eleanore pointed off into the distance. "You were there, yesterday, at the Darlings'. That child's death might have been averted if there had only been a safe place to take it."

He let out an exasperated breath, as if he tired of the discussion. "I do not discount your feelings on the matter."

How dare he patronize her? "You have done nothing but discount my feelings since the moment I met you!"

His eyes fluttered, and he paused. If Eleanore didn't know better, she would have guessed he was hurt by the accusation. After an agonizing moment of silence, he spoke.

"That child lived a short life, I grant you," he said, his manner softening. "But it did not suffer a crueler fate—being warehoused in a crowded, filth-ridden building, forced to sleep in flea-ridden beds, huddled for warmth, wracked with starvation, only to die a slow, lonely death. Because that is what it means to be in a foundling home. And I cannot pretend to support it, not even for you."

He brushed past her, leaving her standing alone, quite bewildered, horrified by the image he'd just presented to her. She turned around and called after him.

"What sort of hell do you think I am capable of creating, Mr. DuMont? Because that is hardly my intention."

He paused, and turned on his heel, an expression of utter bitterness on his face.

"I have seen what havoc good intentions can do."

Mr. DuMont's vehemence on the subject went much deeper than moral objections. They felt more...personal. Eleanore regarded him closely, and caught a glimpse of another emotion, beyond his bluster, to the pain that fueled it. Realization slowly dawned on her. He must have seen similar establishments in Paris. Taking a tentative step toward him, she softened her voice. "Perhaps I cannot save them all. But I can try. And perhaps, with your knowledge of such horrors, you can challenge me to plan carefully, so I would avoid them. So I ask you again, Mr. DuMont, will you help me?"

He looked away for a moment, then back to her, tilting his head back ever so slightly. And in that moment, Eleanore suspected he was fighting to keep his emotions under control. At last, he spoke.

"I am not your hero, Lady Eleanore. When Dr. Brayden returns, he can do your bidding. Or your brother. He is a powerful man. I assume he supports this notion of yours?"

He would if he knew. But she wasn't ready to tell him, not yet. She wasn't ready to give up this dream that was hers, and for her mother. She just did not know how to do it without appearing ungrateful to the family that had given her so much.

"I cannot wait for the marquess' return. There is much work to be done, and the earlier it is started, the better," she said, her shoulders sagging. "If you do not wish to attend on Friday, I will make an excuse for you. It is not fair of me to ask you to something that you do not condone. It would be dishonorable, and despite your protests, I believe you are an honorable man."

He hesitated, then, turning on his heel, slowly approached her.

Eleanore frowned. In that moment, something had changed. His gray eyes had hardened. His countenance was more shrewd.

"Perhaps we could come to an arrangement," he replied at last. "You will introduce me to your houseguest, and I will have your neighbors so enraptured as to the merits of saving foundlings they will be queuing up to help you."

Eleanore started, at once confused and alerted. Did he know about Lord Ellsworth?

"I-I… There is no one else living here." She scolded herself for her stammer. "Except the servants, of course."

He smiled but there was almost a predatory quality to it, putting her on her guard.

"Don't lie to me again, Lady Eleanore. It does not become you."

She remained silent, but her heart pounded.

"All I want is to meet him," he continued. "Is that such a difficult thing?"

She cleared her throat. "I told you, there is no one to meet."

"Well then, I will bid you good day. Enjoy your tea." He turned away and began walking toward the courtyard.

"Wait!" Eleanore bit her lip. Surely to heaven it would not be the end of the world if he met Lord Ellsworth?

He turned on his heel.

"I would like to know your interest in my supposed houseguest."

"It's quite innocent, actually. Lord Ellsworth extended a great honor to a member of my family. I have long wished to thank him, but as you can appreciate, we do not travel in the same circles," he said. "And of course, I suspect that if you announced to him that I wished to meet him on this matter, he might decline. So there is some delicacy required."

Eleanore turned over his explanation. It seemed genuine enough, and heaven knew that Lord Ellsworth was not only a private man, but a humble one who shunned any kind of attention. It seemed like a reasonable enough request.

"If I can arrange an introduction, do you promise to speak as I've asked?"

He nodded deeply. "I am a man of my word."

"You understand his presence here could be compromising not only to himself, but to me as well," she said. "I am not ready for marriage to anyone, even Lord Ellsworth."

Mr. DuMont smiled at that. "Of course."

Eleanore squared her shoulders. His request seemed reasonable. Surely there was a way she could grant Mr. DuMont's request without Lord Ellsworth feeling put upon. "Very well then—I will do it. I will send you a note when there is an opportunity."

"Excellent," he replied. "Thank you."

"How did you know?" she asked. "I hope word has not gotten into the village."

To her immense relief, he shook his head. "I had received word from the relation in question that he might be in the area. I caught a glimpse of him when I came to see you at Barronsfield. I decided I would be daring, and broach the subject with you. You really are a terrible liar."

He bid her adieu, and went on his way. She continued on toward the steward's cottage, fiddling with one of the clasps on her cape, annoyed by the accusation. She had only been trying to protect Lord Ellsworth's privacy—and her own reputation. And then she remembered Mr. DuMont's passionate, personal objections to the foundling home. He claimed not to care, but such vehemence did not come from a lack of compassion.

He was a terrible liar, too.

CHAPTER 8

*B*astien uncapped a bottle from among Dr. Brayden's stock of supplies and sniffed. Rosemary oil. Satisfied, he poured a careful measure into a smaller bottle and pushed the stopper on tight. He'd been tending a young man, no more than eighteen, who'd been brought to the infirmary by his father. The boy had suffered a broken bone in his arm, which Bastien set without too much fuss. What was far more worrying to him was the rather persistent cough that wracked the young man's chest. Just as he was giving the boy's father the instructions on how to mix the oil with a quantity of goose fat to apply to his son's chest, a runner came to the door, a note in hand.

Since Dr. Brayden had gone, nearly all of Bastien's precious time had been siphoned away by complaints of croup, lancing boils, and tending to colds. He'd even suffered through the odd call of vague ills and headaches, which had been little more than ploys to have him sit for tea and to learn all about him, which served his own purposes just as well. He used whatever opportunity presented to him to check his assumptions about the identity of the lost prince of Weymouth. Thus far, no one seemed a more likely candidate than Lord Ellsworth.

He'd learned three things over the past few days: the villagers of

Elmsdale were just as curious about him as he was to learn about Le Veneur Rouge, Mrs. Waterstone was the source of the best gossip in the village, and everyone was truly sorry to hear about Lady Eleanore's broken engagement, no doubt learned from Mrs. Waterstone. Considering Lady Eleanore had not made a public announcement about her marital status, Bastien came to truly appreciate that keeping her mysterious visitor a secret may have been nothing short of a miracle.

The runner's note was from Barronsfield, begging Mr. DuMont to come see a patient as soon as convenience allowed. Bastien shook his head at the subterfuge. He couldn't help but smile. Lady Eleanore was wasting no time arranging a meeting.

Bastien had done everything in his power to put Lady Eleanore out of his thoughts, but the task proved to be impossible. Aside from being the most popular topic of conversation among the gentry in the area, the memory of their kiss echoed through his body. She kept trying to call him honorable and worthy, and if that kiss had showed her anything, it was that he was neither.

He was the Wolf de l'Ardoise. And he did not deserve to feel the way he did when Lady Eleanore looked at him with her kind green eyes—warm like the most lush summer day.

An hour later, Bastien was led through the grand hall of Barronsfield Manor, anticipation testing his patience. The aged butler, Hanley, was several steps ahead of him. As Bastien followed, he could not help but notice the man walked with a subtle limp that had not been present when he'd seen him last.

"Is your leg giving you much trouble?" he asked.

The man paused for just the slightest moment, then resumed. "Not at all, sir."

Bastien paid close attention to the man's gait. No doubt because Bastien had inquired about it, Hanley's limp lessened somewhat, but it was still clear to Bastien's practiced eye that the man still favored his right leg.

"This way please, sir."

As he came to a stop outside a door to one of Barronsfield Manor's many rooms, Bastien put a hand on the butler's shoulder. He faced the man, keeping his voice low, and his tone light, but firm. "Monsieur Hanley, when my business is concluded here, I will take a look that that leg." He could see the smallest flush of red come into the man's cheeks, even though he said nothing. "You may trust in my discretion. I merely wish to see your service to this household continue for as long as possible."

Hanley pursed his lips slightly, gave the most subtle of nods, then opened the door. A gentleman, and not Lady Eleanore, was on the other side.

He was Bastien's height, or a little taller, and the cut of his cloth was very fine, though he was not the dandy type. He looked to be Bastien's age, or a little younger. His hair, Bastien could not help but note, was reddish in color, cropped short in the newer style. He wore a pair of gold-rimmed spectacles and a rather worried expression.

"At last. Please come in." He stepped aside, urging Bastien to enter.

"I came as quickly as I could," he replied, stepping into the room. Bastien's gaze fell on Lady Eleanore, who was sitting upright on a chaise, her legs outstretched. Nearby was a lady's maid.

"Good afternoon," she called out to Bastien, as readily as if she was inviting him to tea. "I'm sorry to be taxing on your schedule. I know you are busy attending to other patients."

Bastien looked carefully at Lady Eleanore. "Not at all, my lady. What can I do for you?" Her color was fine, and he saw no clear evidence of distress.

"Silly me," she began, with a sheepish smile. "I am afraid I may have turned my ankle. Luckily, Lord Ellsworth was nearby to catch me, or it might have been far worse than it is now."

He looked over at Lord Ellsworth, who appeared distinctly uncomfortable. Bastien grabbed a nearby chair, placed it near Lady Eleanore's feet, and sat down to examine her ankle.

"Which is it?" he asked.

Lord Ellsworth and Lady Eleanore spoke at once.

"Her left—"

"My right—"

Bastien cast a glance at Lady Eleanore, who blushed slightly, then looked away to Lord Ellsworth. "You are correct, of course. It is my left."

Bastien cocked an eyebrow as he began to examine her ankles. Neither of them appeared swollen, and without removing her stocking, he could not tell which was bruised, though, he was becoming increasingly confident that neither had suffered any injury. Carefully, he ran his fingers over her left ankle. Her eyes were wide, and her mouth parted slightly as her gaze bounced between Bastien's face and his hands. Did she feel the same alluring sensation as he? Could she tell how utterly conflicted he was at this moment? Tearing his thoughts away, he cleared his throat.

"Does this hurt?" He squeezed her ankle—barely—and watched her. After a moment, she winced, but it was half-hearted at best.

Lady Eleanore was a mediocre actress, but her performance seemed to impress Lord Ellsworth, who, it seemed, would have been happier on the other side of the door. The man seemed genuinely uncomfortable. Perhaps he was a much better actor than Lady Eleanore. Or a better liar.

"Is there anything I can do to be of service?" Lord Ellsworth asked. "Shall we have hot water brought up?"

"Only if you want tea, monsieur," Bastien muttered, watching him. "Hot water does not cure turned ankles."

"Oh, how rude of me not to introduce you," Lady Eleanore interjected. "Mr. DuMont, this is Colin Middleton, Marquess of Ellsworth. Lord Ellsworth is a guest and a longtime friend of Barronsfield. Lord Ellsworth, this is Mr. Bastien DuMont. He has come to the area on recommendation of my brother, to assist Dr. Brayden in his practice. He is a surgeon." She gazed at Bastien, a coy smile on her face, before turning back to Lord Ellsworth. "Which may, or may not, explain his occasional lack of congeniality."

Upon mention of his name, Lord Ellsworth looked sharply at Bastien, then, to Bastien's shock, reached out to shake Bastien's hand. Bastien rose to greet it. Lord Ellsworth's grip was firm.

"Your name is not unfamiliar to me, Mr. DuMont."

"I am afraid you have me at a disadvantage, my lord," Bastien replied, trying not to appear as though he'd been taken off guard.

"We have a mutual acquaintance, I believe, in Mr. Edmund Pembroke. He told me you were instrumental in assisting in his rescue near Westemere this past summer," Lord Ellsworth said. "So I suppose I have to thank you for saving my friend's life."

A smile froze on Bastien's face. Fool. He'd committed a colossal error. It had never occurred to him that Edmund would mention Bastien to Lord Ellsworth. But until Tante Marie's note, Ellsworth had not been an object of Bastien's concern.

"That is perhaps overstated, my lord," Bastien said as he released the man's hand, deliberately keeping his response vague. "I was not aware that the two of you were well acquainted."

"We had not been in each other's circles for some time," Ellsworth replied. "Indeed, I only learned he was in Cumbria when we met, by chance, last summer."

By chance? Edmund Pembroke had disappeared from society for years. That Ellsworth should miraculously appear days before Edmund's kidnapping hardly seemed to be chance.

"A terrific coincidence then, you were present when his unfortunate kidnapping occurred. Perhaps fate." Bastien knew he was venturing into dangerous territory. Lord Ellsworth pursed his lips, then looked past Bastien, as if caught up in a tangle of his own thoughts. His distraction, however, disappeared almost as quickly as it had appeared.

"Perhaps. I do not subscribe to the notion of fate."

I bet not. Bastien was about to push further, when Lady Eleanore cleared her throat.

"You saved Edmund?" Lady Eleanore was staring at Bastien, confusion and amazement in her smile. "I had no idea. Edmund never said a word about you, nor Stephen."

For a perfectly good reason. Saving Edmund had turned Bastien into a marked man. At the moment, the way Lady Eleanore was looking at him, perhaps it was worth it. She looked at him with the same adulation that he'd read about in medieval *chansons*, where ladies would lavish their admiration onto knights who spent their days doing good deeds. But Bastien wasn't one of those. He knew the bitter truth.

Doing good deeds always came with a price.

"I merely happened to be at the right place at the right time." He shrugged, aiming for nonchalance while his mind raced. He had no idea that anyone beyond those directly involved, knew of Bastien's presence at Westemere, the estate of Sir Richard Hamilton, where Edmund had taken up the role of gamekeeper. Sir Richard had hosted a traditional hunting party for the Glorious Twelfth that had also brought Tante Marie to the area.

"Perhaps that's why my brother asked you to come here," Lady Eleanore continued, relief in her countenance. "A living, in payment for assisting Edmund."

Bastien did not bother to correct her. It was safer for everyone, especially her, if the real reason for his presence remained hidden. He bowed. "You have found me out, Lady Eleanore."

"Now, about her ankle," Lord Ellsworth interjected, keen to return to the matter than brought Bastien to the house in the first place. "I should leave while you examine her."

Bastien knew perfectly well there was nothing wrong with Lady Eleanore's ankle. And the last thing he wanted to do was send Lord Ellsworth away.

"I can deduce everything I need to know simply by palpating the area," he said, then sat and resumed his 'examination.' It was difficult not to be distracted by the warmth of her skin in his hands, even if it was covered by a woolen stocking. On cue, Lady Eleanore winced again, but kept her reaction appropriately modest. "It is not broken, nor is it swollen. I suspect that she will be well enough to be back on her feet by the end of the day, as long as you mind the furniture."

Lady Eleanore smiled, then looked over at her houseguest. "I apologize for completely overreacting."

"Not at all," Lord Ellsworth said. "In such cases, it is prudent to have these matters attended to as soon as possible."

"Thank you," she replied. "And I trust that Mr. DuMont will be sensitive to your need for privacy, won't you?"

At that, the man betrayed a hint of contrition. "My apologies, Mr. DuMont. I have imposed myself upon Lady Eleanore's hospitality. I am here for my own selfish reasons, which partially involve me hiding from the outside world, if only for a little while. Inspired, perhaps, by our mutual friend, Mr. Pembroke." He grew even more serious, if it was possible, as he turned to Lady Eleanore, "But I do feel, Lady Eleanore, that perhaps for your sake it is time to end the subterfuge. I will make arrangements to depart."

"I am certain Mrs. Darling would be able stay for a short time." Lady Eleanore protested. "I would not wish to have you go on my account."

"There is no need. My project will come to a resolution, one way or another, very soon." He was speaking to Lady Eleanore, but his gaze wandered past her, toward the window. "Very soon."

"Your project? I am intrigued." Another invitation to speak, which Lord Ellsworth accepted. Indeed, he practically sprinted to the window where he pointed to a wooden contraption he announced was a reflecting telescope.

"He is making star maps." Lady Eleanore proclaimed from where she remained seated. "This telescope is Lord Ellsworth's design."

"Not entirely," Ellsworth gently corrected, before he began reciting the publications he'd consulted and the tinkering he'd done. Bastien feigned interest as the marquess launched into a painfully detailed explanation of the wonder of refracting light, leaving Bastien confused about more than the difference between Newtonian and Keplerian telescopes.

Refraction. Not revolution.

Was this part of his ruse? Ellsworth was quite suddenly so completely animated it was difficult for Bastien to think.

The appearance of a servant at the door, package in hand, interrupted them.

"Excuse me, my lord," the servant said, speaking directly to Lord Ellsworth. "This arrived for you by special post."

Lord Ellsworth, paused, his gaze tearing away from his beloved contraption to the package in the servant's hands, his relaxed countenance gone. He practically ran to the door, took a small package from the butler's aging hands, and gazed down at it, appearing to study it intensely. He became deathly still, his knuckles whitening. At last, he swallowed deeply, his face flushed nearly as red as Lady Eleanore's cape.

"Lord Ellsworth, is something wrong?" Lady Eleanore asked.

The man fought visibly for control. "Not at all." He smiled, but it was utterly forced. "If there is nothing more you need from me, I will leave you to your privacy. Good day to you, Mr. DuMont."

He bowed, and departed quickly.

Lady Eleanore stared at the place where Lord Ellsworth had stood before he'd bolted from the room. She turned to her maid and sent her on an errand, leaving she and Bastien quite alone. "I wonder what happened. I'm sorry you did not get the chance to speak with him on the matter that brought you here. Though, if I might be selfish for but a moment, it was wonderful that someone else was the subject of his enthusiasm. I cannot pretend to be interested in his astronomical interests, try as I might."

"You can barely pretend to have a turned ankle," Bastien replied, trying to focus on his encounter with Lord Ellsworth. Not an easy task with Lady Eleanore smiling at him the way she was at present.

"Mr. DuMont," she admonished, a playful edge in her voice. She pulled her legs up and in a swift moment, had both feet firmly on the floor. "I'm not that horrible an actress, am I?"

Lady Eleanore might be everyone's angel, but she was more than that. There was something else about her, a vitality that threatened to distract him.

"I'm afraid your career on the boards would be short. But your scheme, as the English say, was 'brilliant.'"

She laughed at that, the sound musical to Bastien's ears. He leaned forward, as if utterly bewitched, took her hand, and put it to his mouth, kissing her fingers tenderly. They locked gazes, her eyes dazzling him. It was all he could do not to crush his mouth on hers. He'd tasted her once. What would he give to taste her again?

She was a patient. Or was she? At the moment, she was tempting his body and soul. Regardless, she was an innocent. He forced himself to break the spell of the moment.

"I should go." He stood, forcing himself away from her.

She nodded, but there was a reluctance in her look that was unmistakable. They were silent for a moment, the only sound the crackling of the fire in the hearth.

"I hope I did not pull you away from a more serious patient," she said. "It was the only way I could think of to introduce you to Lord Ellsworth without him being suspicious. I told you, he's a very private person."

"I would not have come if I could not be spared," he replied, his thoughts going back to the young man with the troubling cough. "I would not put my own needs ahead of my patients."

Bastien paused, as if taken aback by his own words. Indeed, he was very much invested in hunting down Le Veneur Rouge. But he found himself unwilling to throw away the trust that Dr. Brayden had put in him by completely disregarding his role as a healer.

"And yet you did not get the opportunity to thank Lord Ellsworth as you had hoped," Eleanore said.

Bastien smiled tightly. When Ellsworth recognized him, it had taken him off guard. And it did not help that Lady Eleanore was so attentive. "Alas, no. It was unfortunate he was called away."

Her face darkened, and she looked toward the door where the gentleman had left in such a mysterious manner. "I hope nothing serious has happened."

Bastien could not help but wonder. What business did he have that would resolve itself shortly? Had he received news that Tante Marie was still alive? That someone was on the hunt, looking for him, and that man was standing in the room with him? Or was it nothing? Still, the coincidence of his presence when Edmund was kidnapped was difficult to overlook.

"Why is he here? Why the subterfuge? It is your home," Bastien pressed. "He has not imposed himself?" An edge of protectiveness took him off guard.

"I don't know if Lord Ellsworth could impose himself on anyone if he tried." Lady Eleanore brushed a lock of hair away from her face. Bastien's fingers itched to do it for her. "Indeed, he should probably be a great deal more imposing, given he's going to be the Duke of Weymouth one day."

"The Prince of Weymouth," Bastien interjected, thinking aloud.

Lady Eleanore's brow crinkled, apparently confused by his statement. "Yes, though not a prince of course."

"No, of course," Bastien said, still trying to put the pieces of this puzzle together. "But he was here, in Barronsfield, before your arrival."

"Immediately after the Yuletide. Half the kingdom is after him, which I suspect is the reason he is here. Hiding. But the particulars to that reason, I cannot say. I assume that my brother knows." She crossed her arms, and tilted her head, regarding him in a way that made Bastien distinctly uncomfortable. "I didn't take you for a gossip, Mr. DuMont. You and Mrs. Waterstone will fit in famously, I should think."

Her observation gave him pause. He was asking too many questions. Getting far too comfortable.

But Tante Marie had been injured not long after the holiday. And perhaps, just perhaps, Lord Ellsworth was escaping London because people were after him. But not society matrons or foreign nobility, eager to match their daughter. Maybe he was hiding for other reasons. Reasons that might be tied to that package he held in his hands. He needed to find out what it was.

"Mr. DuMont, you are scheming."

"I am merely thinking," he protested. "That is all."

"Well, I hope you are thinking about what wonderful things you are going to say at the tea tomorrow. I have held up my part of the bargain," Lady Eleanore said. "Can I assume you are a man of honor?"

It was a dangerous assumption. But she had held up her side of the agreement. It was time for him to return the favor. A house full of people would mean busy servants and occupied guests that would give him the chance to investigate the mysterious package and the elusive Lord Ellsworth.

"Of course," he nodded, attempting to give her his most confident, earnest smile.

"I know the idea distresses you greatly."

Discomforted by the keenness in her observation, he shrugged and shook his head. "Not at all."

"Mr. DuMont," she admonished gently. "I know you aren't thrilled about helping me."

Bastien stilled. She was correct—he had made his thoughts clear on the matter. If she mistook his current distraction about Lord Ellsworth for any misgivings he'd had about tomorrow, it served his purpose well.

"I don't understand," she pressed, though perhaps more gently. "Why would you not want to give these children a chance?"

"Chance?" He voice broke slightly. Unwanted memories flooded him, and he stemmed them the way he always had—with anger. "What chance do you want to give them? The chance to live in a filthy, over-crowded room, reeking in summer, freezing in winter, with an empty belly? Going to bed every night fearing both death and surviving another day? Listening to the failing wail of a babe that would no doubt be dead by sundown from whatever illness they'd acquired? To let them die alone, quickly, is a kindness. At least the fear does not last more than a few hours."

Silence fell heavily in the room. He turned away, swallowing hard.

"My God," Lady Eleanore said, her voice barely above a whisper. He felt her hand on his shoulder as she firmly turned him toward her. Her brow furrowed, her cheeks flushed. "You didn't work in one, did you? You were raised in one."

She said it softly enough, but her words ripped like a ball through his chest. He did not answer. He would not. A lump formed in his throat.

Her eyes widened and she took his hands in hers. "I am so sorry."

Her touch was miraculously calming, and in that moment, he

wanted nothing more than to hold her into his arms and drink in whatever magic she wove that made him feel a little less alone.

"No wonder you abhor the idea so." The tenor of her voice was soft, but not condescending or dripping in false sympathy. It was, simply, understanding. "But even you must see that not all institutions are the same, just the way not all surgical men are as well trained as you must be," she said. "Surely you do not think me capable of creating such misery? My intentions—"

He pulled away, the security of his own feelings on the subject outweighing any comfort her touch offered.

"Do not speak to me about intentions, Lady Eleanore. I am sure yours are noble. But I have seen lives made miserable, peace sundered, by 'good intentions.'"

"Just because an idea was poorly executed doesn't mean the notion itself is flawed. I can learn from past mistakes, and do better." Her voice was calm, and she did not bother to plead with him. She took him by the arm and led him to a small desk. She pulled out a notebook, which was stuffed full of drawings, notes and plans, and shoved it at him. "Read this. Examine every detail, and critique it all. You seem to enjoy pointing out my failings—I am giving you permission to do so here. You know what is not to be done. Help me avoid the mistakes that others have made."

Bastien let go a bitter chuckle. "I have patients to care for. Real ones. I do not have time to dawdle over some fairy tale establishment run by a princess in a red cape."

He pushed the book at her, but instead of taking it, she dropped her hands to her sides. Taking a step back, she squared her shoulders and lifted her chin, making her slight frame seem somehow taller. And it was then he saw the same impervious stare he'd witnessed when he'd first met her brother, the Marquess of Barronsfield.

"You, Mr. DuMont, are in the employ of this estate. When you are not tending to Daniel or your other patients, you will make time."

Bastien's stomach clenched. He was not in the damn employ of this estate. He was working for himself. His purpose. His task. But he could not reveal it. All he could give her was a curt nod.

She softened then, her face lighting up in that way of hers that threatened to steal his anger.

"You have every right to despise the very notion of a foundling hospital," she continued, her voice quiet but losing none of its authority. "But I know this is what I am supposed to do. Most women born to my circumstances do not have the benefit of my position. I have the privilege to be able to help others avoid the situation in which I could have easily found myself. Did it ever occur to you that you might be the same?"

No.

Whether it was the magic in her touch, the challenge in her voice, or the way she looked at him with such expectation of goodness, Bastien was unsure, but he tucked her notebook into his bag.

Before leaving he made a fleeting visit to Hanley, who, much as Bastien suspected, was suffering from arthritic pain. He provided some suggestions, primarily in the form of rest, though he was doubtful the proud servant would abide by it.

Once outside, Bastien quickened his pace, walking along the frozen road back to the village. He'd been offered a carriage, but he savored the exercise.

He needed to clear his head, swimming with all that had occurred today. He could not rid himself of the notion that he'd come face to face with Le Veneur Rouge. The coincidences were too many to ignore. Still, he needed more. He needed proof. A search of Lord Ellsworth's rooms was in order.

Snow began to fall as the lights of the village came into view. Soon he'd be warm again. When he was little he'd always been cold. He'd hated it ever since. He threw his bag over his left shoulder and shoved his hands into his pockets, his mind turning away from Ellsworth to a softer, far more difficult moment when Lady Eleanore reached out to him. He hadn't for a moment intended to reveal that part of his past to her. It had taken all his strength to swallow the emotion that had threatened to spill over. What goodness she saw in him eluded Bastien. His purpose had always been to serve as the instrument of others. The Jacobins. The Home Office. Even Tante Marie. They'd demanded his devotion, or at least his loyalty, and with few exceptions offered nothing in return but promises. Lady Eleanore was asking him for his guidance. His opinion. The chance to shape an idea.

Mr. Roderick had called her an angel. Maybe she was everyone's angel, but in that moment, he wanted to believe that she could be his.

⁂

ELEANORE STOOD AT THE WINDOW, her fingers drumming on the sill, her thoughts scattered as she watched the snow fall. She hadn't intended for Mr. DuMont's visit to be so utterly provocative, but nothing about him seemed easy. Or rather, nothing about the way she was beginning to feel about him was simple.

She'd been waiting for Lord Ellsworth to return after that rather curious package had so clearly upset him. Had there been unfortunate news from his family home at Stormount? While his parents were of a more advanced age, the best she knew was that they were both in excellent health. Still, he had not returned.

She should have been feeling quite proud of herself, discovering a most convenient way for Mr. DuMont to meet Lord Ellsworth, and at the same time, preserve the illusion that the surgeon's appearance at Barronsfield was by absolute chance.

Yet nothing about the afternoon felt resolved. The delivery of the mysterious package that led Lord Ellsworth away had robbed Mr. DuMont of the chance to speak to the marquess on whatever matter had been so important to him. He'd taken her notebook, at least. That, she supposed, was something of a minor victory, though part of her doubted he would even look at it. Still, she could not rid herself of the topsy-turvy sensation in her belly. There was something about the entire meeting between Mr. DuMont and Lord Ellsworth that felt... off kilter. At the time, she'd been focused on ensuring the meeting occurred, and convincing Mr. DuMont of the virtues of her plans. It was not until both men had left that she could replay the scene in her head. And that scene prompted far more questions than answers.

Why was Lord Ellsworth here, in Barronsfield? As heir to the Dukedom of Weymouth, Lord Ellsworth had access to several estates across England and Wales if he required isolation. One of them, in fact, was not far from where Edmund and Gwyneth were happily situated, in Cheshire. And while she knew the Duke and Duchess of Weymouth were heavily invested in their son's marriage prospects, they were in London.

Eleanore could not help but shake her head and smile at the contrast between the two gentlemen. Mr. DuMont seemed the very opposite of Lord Ellsworth—as dark as the marquess was light. Lord Ellsworth was preoccupied with the heavens, and Mr. DuMont, with his silver stare and lined mouth, seemed so terribly worldly.

She exhaled, her breath leaving its mark on the cold glass, her finger idly moving to that spot on her cheek where Mr. DuMont's lips had been. His touch had unsettled her completely in a manner so alluring and yet dangerous. Whenever she thought of his fingers running along the bones in her ankle, a curious heat curled through her body, awakening it. And he felt it too—she was certain of it. She wondered about his hands, so masculine. And how it would feel to have them touch her again.

And his mouth. His lips were soft. All the better to kiss her with.

She thought about sending a servant to see to Lord Ellsworth's well-being, perhaps ask him if he would like to join her for dinner. Whatever the contents of the package he had received, its arrival had clearly thrown him. His expression, such as she could make out from her position, had gone from anticipation to abject disappointment. She recognized it, because she'd experienced it only a short time ago in London.

Her gaze strayed to the orangerie, where, amongst the lemon and orange trees, her brother's prized roses stood, encased in glass, defying the gray gloom around them with their shock of rich pink blooms. Those roses had, thanks to his wife Rosalind, gone from being a symbol of his doom and loneliness, to a testament to their fearless, joyous bond. Barronsfield roses had been present at every wedding that had taken place since in Elmsdale, whether that of a lady or kitchen servant.

They'd even managed to get some to Gwyneth, Edmund's wife, for their joining. Their love was no less remarkable in their own way, beginning in deceit, and ending with them risking their lives for each other and the love that had grown between them. Each of them had managed, against all odds, to find happiness. It was almost like a fairy tale.

Her parents had loved each other, too. A baker and a great lord, who found comfort, companionship—even love. But love had not been enough to give her parents a happy ending. Eleanore's birth had ensured their parting.

Still, Eleanore's place in the world defied the odds. Expecting a fairy tale love like Stephen or Edmund was perhaps more than she could hope for. And if a comfortable home and a loving family was the price Eleanore would pay in lieu of a loving husband and children of her own, she would be satisfied. Instead, she would focus on her foundlings. She would find a way to give them happiness. To have them loved the way she had been. Not left alone like Mr. DuMont.

Eleanore gave herself a mental shake, turned away from the window, and headed for the kitchen. She had a party to prepare for. Tomorrow, the library would be filled with her neighbors and friends. And, thanks to her bargain with Mr. DuMont, he would be there too, ensuring that everyone would understand the virtues of a foundling hospital.

He had been alone. A child, a babe, left for unknown reasons in what could only be described as a horror. Little wonder, then, he'd been against the idea. He'd spent the first years of his life cold, hungry, and afraid. The very notion brought tears to Eleanore's eyes. That he survived was incredible. That he'd thrived was nothing short of miraculous.

But he was still alone.

CHAPTER 9

"*B*reathe in for me."

Bastien put his ear to Daniel Morehouse's chest, listening for the telltale rattle of pneumonia. He had the man repeat the action twice more, just to be certain. The first breath was sharp, no doubt as a reaction to the lingering soreness, but to Bastien's satisfaction, Daniel's lungs sounded clear.

"How am I?" Daniel asked. He was sitting up in what had become a makeshift bedchamber in the front parlor of the steward's cottage. It was warm, clean, and comfortable, and with the added quality of having the steward's housekeeper able to watch over him.

"How do you feel?"

"A little sore by times, in my chest. Restless mostly. I'm not accustomed to spending so much time on my backside." Daniel carefully shuffled his weight. "Am I getting better?"

"Your chest appears to be healing. Your leg is straight, but then I am the best bonesetter this side of Bordeaux." He was amazed at how easily that rolled off his tongue, but it was, in fact, true. He'd earned that moniker a lifetime ago. "Before long we'll have you up and on a crutch."

Daniel nodded. "Thank you sir. Nothin' against Dr. Brayden, but I'm glad you're here."

The compliment struck Bastien silent, and he nodded in reply.

His patient reached for the bowl of steaming broth set on the table next to his bed. The telltale aroma of whatever local healing concoction was cooked up in Barronsfield's kitchens was a reminder that his engagement with Lady Eleanore's neighbors was fast approaching. But first, he was intent on discovering the contents of the mysterious package Lord Ellsworth had received. He needed proof, one way or another, that this man was the person he'd been seeking.

"You get some rest. And think of me, as I go into the lion's den," Bastien said, pulling himself to his feet. "I have to go and be respectable."

Daniel took a small sip from his bowl, then chuckled softly. "There's naught to be fearful of in that lot. They'll all be more interested in Lady Eleanore, no doubt."

Interested in her broken engagement, to be specific, if Mr. Roderick's information was correct. Bastien could not deny that there was part of him that looked forward to seeing Lady Eleanore. At the same time, part of him was truly terrified. He'd unwittingly exposed more of his soul to her in ten minutes than to anyone else in a lifetime. That Lady Eleanore was about to endure an afternoon where every word and look would be under scrutiny did not settle well with him.

Bastien rose, collecting his bag and his hat. "Perhaps Lord Ellsworth's presence might distract from other talk."

Daniel shook his head. "Allie told me that His Lordship had left by carriage before sunrise."

"Did he?" Heaviness fell in Bastien's gut at the news. If Ellsworth had gone, it was likely that Le Veneur Rouge was on the move. "I had the opportunity to meet him yesterday. He did speak of leaving, though not immediately."

Daniel shook his head. "Allie said His Lordship did not give any direction to send his belongings after him."

Thank God. Relief rushed through his body, allowing Bastien a genuine smile at the news that Ellsworth would be returning. With him temporarily gone, Bastien could search the rooms before the dreaded tea party.

"Speaking of business dealings, I must ensure I am punctual at today's event," Bastien said. "I shall check in on you again. Until then."

Bastien fought the urge to run to Barronsfield Manor. He slipped in through aservant's entrance and gained the attention of a young servant. Giving her his best smile, he soon discovered the location of Lord Ellsworth's rooms. Bastien could not help but wonder what Hanley would do if he'd discovered how easily it had been for Bastien to extricate the information from the young girl. No matter. He stowed his hat and bag, and raced up one of the servant staircases to the second floor.

The corridor was empty as all available hands were probably tending to the preparations below. Bastien slid down the hallway until he came to Lord Ellsworth's rooms. He paused and put his ear to the door, just in case the marquess had returned. All seemed quiet. A gentle tap at the door. Nothing.

Perfect.

One last check over either shoulder, and Bastien slid inside.

Bastien's gaze swept over the room. Like every other space in Barronsfield it was impeccably tidy, but not empty. Nor was there any evidence of belongings being packed up, which gave Bastien hope that Ellsworth would return.

To face justice.

A desk, near the windows, was the only thing in disarray. Broken quills, drops of ink, and wax littered the blotter. Bastien, taking care not to disturb the papers, carefully flipped through the scattered envelopes. He looked for the seal that was characteristic of all Le Veneur Rouge's correspondence, but there was none to be found. Not that he expected to. Something that identifiable would be kept on his person at all times.

Letters were scattered across the desk. Most appeared to be from Stormount, estate of the Duke of Weymouth, Lord Ellsworth's father.

To one side of the desk was a small book. He moved it carefully so he could review the papers underneath. As he did so, Bastien couldn't help but notice that the volume was lighter than it should have been. Much lighter. He picked it up and carefully opened the lid. Most of the insides of the book had been hollowed out, and where there had been pages, was instead a smooth round milky stone, quartz perhaps, not quite the size of his palm. He picked it up and held it to the light, where a remarkable star shape revealed itself, as if floating inside.

Odd. He set the stone back inside its hiding place, placed the book down, then continued his search. The hour of Lady Eleanore's afternoon tea approached, and he didn't want to be missed, especially if Lady Eleanore had even an inkling he was on the prowl. But there was nothing. Not even a scrap of a clue. Only a few letters, most of them of a scientific nature.

There. Tucked at the back of the desk, as if deliberately pushed out of sight, was an open package revealing a small stack of letters, carefully tied together with string. Another letter lay on top, half open. Bastien picked it up.

Lord Ellsworth,
  Our plans have gone awry. We miscalculated—

The sound of footsteps approaching put Bastien on alert. He grabbed the note and stack of letters just as the door creaked open. He dove under the bed and held his breath.

The swish of skirts and the click on sturdy shoes on the floor signaled a servant—perhaps tidying while Lord Ellsworth was away. He followed the footsteps intently with his eyes, but otherwise remained as still as possible. He needed to get out of here before his absence at the festivities below were noted.

Blood pounded in Bastien's ears. Lord Ellsworth was Le Veneur Rouge. He had to be. The news would probably be crushing to his friend, Edmund, who claimed to be friends with the man. But they'd not spoken for nearly five years, and, as Edmund himself knew, a man could change in that time.

The footsteps stopped near the bed. Pillows were being plumped, and blankets smoothed. *Hurry up. Vite. Vite.* Barronsfield must have the most attentive damn servants in the land.

But she didn't go. To Bastien's horror, he saw a hand reaching under the bed, clearly feeling for something else that needed attending to. Peering down at his side he saw a porcelain pot, the lid firmly atop. If she knelt down, she'd see him. As carefully as he might, he inched the chamber pot closer to the edge of the bed. A moment later, it disappeared, and a new one was put in its place. Finally, the servant left and Bastien let out a long, low breath.

Close. Too close.

He rolled out from his hiding place and sprang to his feet. Running the heel of his hand over his temple, he smoothed his disheveled hair back into place. He needed to present himself to Lady Eleanore, and later he would confront Lord Ellsworth. And if he was Le Veneur Rouge, he'd kill him.

❧

PERHAPS THIS WAS NOT as good an idea after all.

The Barronsfield library buzzed with the small talk of ladies and gentlemen from the area: the Battersbys, Mr. and Mrs. Oliver, who ran the tea shop in the square, and the Waterstones, an elderly couple with a small but delightful property a few miles away. At least two dozen families from the area had arrived, sipping tea and nibbling on sweets. They were smiling and convivial. It was, to any outsider, a merry gathering. People were engaged, the food was lovely, and the weather forgiving.

The only person missing was the guest of honor.

Eleanore's gaze strayed to the clock on the nearby mantle. Where on earth was he? Mr. DuMont had promised he'd arrive promptly at two, and it was nearly twenty minutes past the hour. She had no idea what the French considered fashionably late, but Mr. DuMont seemed determined to work on his own schedule.

"Lady Eleanore! So wonderful to see you!" A tall woman of seventy, elegantly dressed, approached. Eleanore took a sharp intake of breath. Mrs. Waterstone was a lovely, well-meaning soul, but her tongue was as loose as a set of hand-me-down gowns. "I hope you will allow me the honor of thanking you personally for the invitation."

"You are most welcome, Mrs. Waterstone," Eleanore replied. "I hope—"

"Especially since we had not anticipated your return for many months, given your impending marriage."

Eleanore pasted a smile on her face, then glanced past the well-meaning woman toward the door. Still no sign of him. Which was perfectly fine—she would do this herself if she had to. Though she wished it otherwise, Eleanore had known that the swirl of people in the room had come not only see Mr. DuMont, but also to gain knowledge of her broken engagement. Though no one dared to raise it directly, everyone must know by now. It was the price she was prepared to pay to raise awareness about the plight of foundlings and garner the interest of others willing to help. So each time they started to bring it up, she gently redirected them back to the reason why she'd asked them to come.

"Are you familiar with the concept of foundling hospitals, Mrs. Waterstone?"

Eleanore launched into her little speech, which she'd repeated three times thus far. A little speech she'd hoped Mr. DuMont would help her deliver. Perhaps he was with a patient. As discomfited as he was with the idea, she could not imagine him reneging on his promise.

"Mrs. Waterstone, how are you?" It was Mr. Darling, a cup and saucer in hand. "If I could impose on you for just a moment, Mrs. Battersby was inquiring after your new fan. If you would be so kind as to satisfy her curiosity on this matter, I think she would be much obliged to you."

"Of course!" the woman replied, popping it open as if on cue. "Lady Eleanore, it was a pleasure to speak to you. Your care for the unfortunates of the area is remarkable."

As the woman left, Eleanore breathed a small sigh of relief. "Thank you for coming to my rescue."

"Anything for you, my dear," Mr. Darling replied, and Eleanore knew it was true. The Darlings had been so good to her over the years. "Any sign of the guest of honor?"

"Not yet." He would be here. She turned to the door, tempted to ask Hanley if there had been any sign of Mr. DuMont when, out of the corner of her eye, she caught a glimpse of Mr. Wakefield. He nodded in acknowledgement and walked toward them.

"Mr. Wakefield! So good to see you again," Eleanore said. "I hope you are well."

Mr. Wakefield nodded. "I am in excellent health my lady, thank you. Though if not, I will avail myself of our new surgeon. Indeed, I wanted to personally deliver news about Grimm's condition."

"He is improving, I hope?" Eleanore asked. Given the reported state of the man's injuries, his recovery would be tenuous.

"Slowly, yes." He paused, and looked about the room. "Mr. DuMont *is* attending, is he not?"

It was difficult for Eleanore not to grimace. "He has not yet arrived. I would not be surprised if he is busy, tending to patients. He seems particularly dedicated in that regard."

Mr. Darling paused to take a sip of his tea. "He called upon me yesterday, with particular concerns about a young man in the village. Indeed, he does keep a full schedule."

Eleanore frowned, then chided herself for her impatience.

Mr. Wakefield smiled and leaned in, almost conspiratorial. "I was speaking to Roderick only yesterday. Apparently Mr. DuMont has been the subject of conversation for some of the young ladies in the village."

"Really? Well, that is—" Eleanore took a sip of his tea to fight away the curious tension that straightened her spine. Maybe Mr. DuMont was late for quite a different reason. Taken aback by her reaction to the very idea, she gave herself a mental shake. *Good heavens Eleanore, what are you thinking?* "I'm sure they are curious. They are so few new faces in town this time of year. If you would excuse me, I will see to one of my guests. Good day to you."

Mr. Wakefield and Mr. Darling bowed politely, and she took her leave, weaving her way across the room, trying to ignore the few hushed whispers and the stares directed at her.

A murmur rippled through the crowd, drawing Eleanore's attention. She turned around to see Hanley announcing Lord Ellsworth to the room. She was positively shocked to see him, seeing as he'd gone to so much trouble to stay hidden. He smiled, but his eyes were rimmed, as if he'd not had enough sleep. After going around the room, Eleanore was finally able to pull him aside.

"I thought you were in hiding. And in York," she said, her voice low.

"My business is concluded for the moment," he replied, a forced smile on his face. "I am your brother's guest. Mr. DuMont was correct. This subterfuge is unnecessary. And I cannot avoid society completely. At least here, people are not quite as mercenary as they are in London. I can understand why Edmund chose to avoid it at all costs."

Her cousin had never been a fan of London society. Indeed, after Edmund discovered his father and brother had tricked him into aiding their plans to take control of Stephen's title and fortune, Edmund had renounced his name and connections for years. It was only in the last year that Edmund had reclaimed his birthright, in order to save the woman he loved from harm. But he still preferred the quieter life in the countryside.

"Edmund cannot avoid it forever," she replied. "Far be it from me to tell a Duke in waiting what to do, but I give you my heartfelt permission to hide away for the duration of the afternoon if it pleases you."

"I am not sure if anything can please me at the moment," he replied, his smile so bitter and sad Eleanore thought her heart would break. She wanted dearly to ask him the source of his unease, but this was neither the time nor place. "But thank you for the escape. I shall endeavor not to use it. If there is a singular advantage to my position at present, it is that I can avoid speaking to anyone with merely a look. But I think you should go, Lady Eleanore. Your guest of honor has arrived." He nodded toward the door.

Eleanore turned, then weaved her way past the onlookers who turned to cast a curious eye at the new surgeon.

His dress was impeccable. He wore breeches, and cut a very fine figure. His coat was black, and he'd pulled his hair back off his face, which only accentuated his Gallic features and silver eyes. The moment he caught sight of her, he smiled, weakening her at the knees. She put a hand to her chest, then dropped it again as she made her way through the crowd to meet him.

Mr. and Mrs. Darling met him at once, helping to ease him into the room.

"Lady Eleanore," Mrs. Darling smiled as Eleanore approached. "Mr. DuMont has joined us at last."

"Mademoiselle." He bowed deeply, almost reverently toward her, then took her hand to his mouth, kissing her gently on her gloved hand. He looked up at her with a knowing look—and in that moment, Eleanore knew that Mr. DuMont was not here to be charming, nor to meet the neighbors. He was here to fulfill his part of their bargain. Which was all, in the end, she had asked him to do.

"I was worried you were not able to attend, Mr. DuMont," she said.

"I took a few moments to check in on Mr. Morehouse, and the time, I am afraid, quite slipped by me," he replied.

Tension leached from her shoulders. "I was afraid you might not come."

"I am French, Lady Eleanore. Provide good food and decent wine, and I cannot help but be enticed," he said, looking around. "Did you invite the entire village? I cannot believe they have all come just to see me."

Eleanore could not help but notice the way some of the younger ladies were regarding Mr. DuMont. With his remarkable eyes and the squareness of his shoulders, it was easy to believe most of them had come for this very reason. That it irked her, even in the smallest degree, surprised her.

"You are new to the area, and that makes you an attraction enough. Some are here to see the library. And some, no doubt, are here to ask me why I am here at all." Eleanore spied a couple of older ladies whispering behind teacups, occasionally glancing up at her.

He cocked an eyebrow, and the most remarkable tingling sensation rippled right down to her toes. She pushed it aside. She had her own reasons for wanting his presence. And whether he liked it or not, he would give her what she needed.

"Very well, then," she said, clasping her hands together in front of her. "I will introduce you to everyone in the room. I do not suppose you had even a moment to look through the notes I gave you?"

Though he did not go through the motion of rolling his eyes, it was clear to Eleanore that he had not, nor did he appreciate being asked. "Alas, Lady Eleanore, I am burdened by my trade. Some of us must work for our bread."

She stiffened at the jab, but would not allow his stubborn mood to interfere with her plans. He might not believe she was capable of creating a safe, loving foundling home, but she knew it could be done. And in the end, he didn't have to believe her. He just had to make sure everyone else did.

"No matter," she said brightly, then pasted a smile on her face as she spoke lowly through gritted teeth. "Even though you are not a nursemaid and know not the slightest thing about caring for base-borns, you are going to convince everyone in the room that we need a foundling home. Understood?"

He paused, the edges of his mouth tight, before relaxing into a pleasant, if rehearsed smile.

"Excellent," he replied, rubbing his hands together and taking stock of the task ahead. "Let's begin."

CHAPTER 10

*B*astien wanted nothing more than to get this damned business over with. He had a man to catch, and possibly to kill. And the quickest way to do that was to give Lady Eleanore what she wanted. Besides, he was good at playing roles and skirting the truth, all in the service of getting what he wanted. Today would be no different.

Still, the reminder of his ill-chosen words sat uncomfortably in his gut.

As promised, she took him about the library, introducing him to faces both new and familiar. Most were gentry from the surrounding area, as well as some of the more successful merchants. A few he'd already met informally; the Olivers had a little bakery that made an excellent bread, and the Battersby's housekeeper sent over a dozen of the freshest eggs he'd ever eaten after he'd seen to a kitchen maid who'd sprained her wrist.

With each new introduction he proceeded to answer the same three questions: his opinion on the revolution, how many arms and legs he had removed in his time, and his professional opinion on the malady of a relative. He remained neutral on the first point, exaggerated for sport on the second, and offered to make an appointment on the third. After their curiosity was sated, Lady Eleanore would launch into her crusade for her foundlings. She spoke about it so convincingly that he almost believed he could care about her plans for infants who were otherwise doomed to a short life of misery. Once she was complete she'd turn to him, smile, and ask for his thoughts on the subject.

"What is your opinion on the matter, Mr. DuMont? Do you think the institution would have value? Or do you believe the argument sometimes offered that it will encourage a certain wantonness of behavior that can only be rewarded by having the burden of raising children removed?"

"I doubt there is a woman who wishes the censure of being with child out of wedlock," Bastien said. "But—speaking strictly as a medical man—I do not see the value in punishing the child for the mistake of being born, particularly when the babe has no say in the matter."

She smiled at his response, which brightened her countenance in such a way that he'd continue, as if driven by a need to ensure it would not fade.

"Lady Eleanore's program would allow such children a second chance. These babes might otherwise freeze or starve in the first days of life. If raised in a warm, nurturing environment and given good sustenance, instead they could thrive. I have heard stories of children being settled quite happily with families with no children or who have lost their own. The older ones can be taught skills and become the next generation of farmers, clerks, or even surgeons."

They would smile at that last part, as if he'd been trying to cheerfully wrap up the plight of these castoffs like a fairy tale. Nice to believe, but out of reach for almost everyone.

He'd left out the horror of being underfed, cold and scared, of being whipped for crying for food, for warmth, for love. Or, even when that magical day came, and a kind stranger claimed you, took you away, and freely gave you the things that once were beyond reach, how guilt consumed you for taking them. For surviving, and God forbid, for thriving. Was this the task he was meant for, as Lady

Eleanore inferred? Lying to a willing audience in order to gain their trust so Lady Eleanore could gain their support?

Not so different from the spying business after all.

Tante Marie. Bastien scanned the room. He was here precisely because of the spying business, and his true purpose was to find the bastard who had tried to end her life. His hand went to his jacket pocket, where he'd stuffed the package he'd taken from Lord Ellsworth's room.

It took the better part of an hour to fulfill his part of their bargain. His plan, now that their agreement was concluded, was to make a public departure, sneak off to Ellsworth's rooms to lie in wait for his return, then confront him at last.

"I think you've spoken to almost everyone," Lady Eleanore said. "That wasn't so terrible, was it?"

The only thing remarkably pleasant about it was standing next to her, catching the flush in her cheeks when she laughed, or the way she played with the pendant around her neck.

Not that he was going to tell her that.

"Not too terrible." Bastien's gaze slid to the door. He needed to leave, no matter how damn tempting it had been just to stand beside her. "Now, are you satisfied I have held up my part of our agreement? If so, I should return to the infirmary."

"Of course," she replied. "Thank you for keeping your word. Especially when I know how difficult it was for you to do that. I hope you can trust me."

She smiled at him, so earnest in her countenance, and damn it if it didn't make him feel a little less than honorable. He pushed aside the unwanted pang of conscience, bowed, and started to walk away when an elderly, somewhat shrill voice slowed his pace.

"Lady Eleanore, at last."

He paused, and turned to see three elderly ladies, huddled around Lady Eleanore like clucking hens. Lady Eleanore took a seat next to them. A hint of worry flitted across her brow, and the smallest measure of discomfort tightened her smile.

Bastien forced himself to turn away again, though he did not seem to have the will to keep himself from eavesdropping.

"We were so pleased to hear about your charity, and we have all agreed to help," one of them said, her shrill voice intruding on his concentration. "We think this is a remarkable way to repay your esteemed father's memory. So thoughtful of you."

"Why—thank you, but—" Lady Eleanore's voice, much lower, began to answer.

"We were pleasantly surprised to see you at home, my lady. We hope—that is—we do not wish to intrude—but we hope all is well?"

He wasn't here to worry about how the village gossip wore on Lady Eleanore. Still, as he scanned the room, he quickly realized that much of the attention was focused on her, and not him. For Bastien, it was perfect. Being ignored meant he could watch and learn. And what he was learning was that Lady Eleanore was sacrificing more than a quiet afternoon for her cause.

"I thank you for your inquiries," she replied. Bastien could not help but detect a note of restrained sarcasm in her voice. "I am quite well, thank you. I found London to be taxing and decided it best to return home."

"Of course, my lady. I hope your fiancé was not distressed about your leaving."

"Lord Ramsay is no longer my fiancé." Her voice was absolutely steady, dropping what was surely the stuff of gossip in their lap without so much as a pause as her audience exchanged nervous glances. "So whether he was or not is no longer my concern."

A painful pause followed. Bastien, finding himself quite unable to bear another second of insipid, inappropriate gossip about Lady Eleanore, turned on his heel, away from the door, and back into the crowd.

"My dear ladies, I must ask you to indulge me," he began, using his most charming and yet professional tone. "While Lady Eleanore is committed to her cause and I am most grateful for the pleasure of meeting you all, I am concerned that after her accident, we must not tax her overmuch, lest her humors become unbalanced at a time when they are still recovering."

An awkward silence fell upon them. One of them pulled out a fan, fluttering it in front of her face to hide her embarrassment.

"Of course, Mr. DuMont," said one of them, with what Bastien could see was genuine remorse and concern. "How thoughtless of us. Please forgive our intrusion, Lady Eleanore."

"Of course, Mrs. Waterstone. Do not trouble yourself."

"If you could do me the great favor," Bastien continued, "of keeping the conversation subjects of a more general, less taxing nature, it would do her a tremendous amount of good."

A hint of a smile teased the side of Lady Eleanore's mouth, and she looked up at him, her eyes bright, with an expression that, for just a moment, made Bastien feel he was capable of goodness. That he was more than the Wolf de l'Ardoise.

He bowed deeply to them, and most especially to Lady Eleanore, then turned to survey the rest of the crowd. To his amazement, he saw Lord Ellsworth, engulfed by a small circle of gentlemen, no doubt eager to make their favors—and perhaps even their daughters— known to him. The man smiled politely, though his countenance was somewhat strained. Ellsworth looked up then and gave Bastien a nod in acknowledgement.

Every fiber in his being twitched, eager to confront Ellsworth with that damning package of letters. But this was neither the time nor place.

He stood, locked in his own thoughts, when a gentleman stepped in front of him, obscuring his view of Ellsworth. He was older than Bastien perhaps a dozen years.

"Hugh Wakefield." The gentleman held out his hand in greeting, which Bastien took. "It is good to meet you at last, Mr. DuMont. Grimm spoke well of your handiwork."

Grimm? He could barely imagine Grimm speaking well of anything. "I hope he is improved."

"He'll be back to his old self soon enough. He's a tough old bird. Spent many years at sea."

Bastien thought back to the hardened soul, lying on his bed, cursing at Bastien like he was the very devil while he was sewing him up. "Somehow that does not surprise me. Are you a sailor yourself?"

Mr. Wakefield was well-kept, confident, and pleasant, but not overly verbose, nor was there anything in his manner that suggested he was anything but comfortable in his own skin.

"I am but a humble merchant, though I have spent a great deal of time at sea plying my trade. Hard work and a little luck. Things you must be most familiar with, Mr. DuMont."

Bastien nodded. "Indeed. Some days, I am most happy for all the luck I receive."

"There's a man who requires neither," Wakefield said, gesturing with a single nod toward Lord Ellsworth. "Though perhaps he's already received all the luck he requires."

Bastien regarded Mr. Wakefield keenly, surprised at the baldness of the remark. Even though it was said low enough only the two of them could hear, it was odd that Mr. Wakefield would dare to comment publicly on Ellsworth's 'luck' in being born to privilege.

"Now if you will excuse me, I must take my leave," Mr. Wakefield said. "I am sure we will meet again, though. I hope you do not mind me saying that I pray it continues to be for purely social, and not professional, reasons."

Bastien nodded and smiled. "That is my wish as well. Though it is less profitable for me."

Wakefield left, allowing Bastien to return his attention to Lord Ellsworth. Except the man had damn well disappeared.

Bastien turned on his heel, his eyes searching every inch of the room. He found him being ushered by a servant through a small, nearly invisible door in the bookshelf that must lead to another room.

Merde.

Bastien wove through the crowd, making his way to where he'd seen Lord Ellsworth disappear, when Lady Eleanore approached.

"I thought you'd left, Mr. DuMont."

"I had just seen Lord Ellsworth—but he seems to have disappeared," he said, his words rushed despite his attempts to appear calm. "He seemed to prefer skulking in the shadows."

"Of course not," Lady Eleanore replied, a subtle rebuke in her voice. "He's not a criminal, for heaven's sakes. He was feeling unwell, and is resting in my brother's study."

Bastien's eyes narrowed as he stared at several women sharing hushed whispers in Lady Eleanore's direction. After being noticed, their expressions froze a moment, before dispersing like swatted flies.

"Why are you so vexed?" Lady Eleanore challenged, clearly impatient with him. "If you wish to speak with him, he is nearby. Let me attend to my guests, and I will show you after everyone is gone."

He was not interested in waiting. Ellsworth could slip through his fingers and he was not about to lose his chance. Bastien looked over his shoulder. People were starting to disperse, but not quickly enough. An idea formed in his head—one that would free Lady Eleanore from the strain of unwanted attention and get Bastien in front of his prey.

He leaned in closer and whispered into her ear. "Swoon."

She looked at him, utter confusion on her face. "Excuse me?"

"Do you wish to be put upon this afternoon by more well-meaning neighbors? Let me help you. Swoon."

Her eyes widened, and in a hint of recognition, she very publicly, and a little more loudly than required, fell into a swoon, and straight into Bastien's arms.

As if on cue, half a dozen people rushed toward them.

"Excusez!" he barked, as he scooped her up into his arms. He looked to a nearby footman. "Is there a private parlor nearby?"

The liveried servant rushed to them, nodded, and took them through the hidden door. Mrs. Darling ran to them.

"What has happened?" she asked, clearly worried about her friend.

"Nothing that a little clear air and a glass of wine will not cure." He spoke with authority, which did the trick of seeing the vicar's wife take command of the other room, leaving him only to be concerned with escape for the two of them. "If you could see to the guests, I will attend to the patient."

The door shut behind them and he looked down at the woman still in his arms. She lifted her head slightly.

"Can I open my eyes now?" she whispered.

She felt good in his arms. Very good. But it was not where she was meant to be.

"Yes," he replied, helping her to her feet. He did not miss the sigh that escaped her as he did so.

"He's gone," she frowned, looking about the room.

Bastien surveyed the space, which was obviously the personal study of the Marquess of Barronsfield. A mighty oak desk stood at one end of the room. The dark paneled walls held paintings of ancestors, though there was a single sketch of a small cottage. He recognized the style immediately as that of Lady Eleanore's.

Dammit. Ellsworth was nowhere to be found.

"You were speaking with him," he asked, impatience sharpening his tone. "Do you know his plans?"

"Of course not. Not beyond tomorrow, at least. He plans to leave for London in the morning," she said, her brow furrowed. "Not that it is your concern, Mr. DuMont. I think you forget yourself."

Bastien blinked, stung by her blunt reminder of the difference in station between the marquess and himself. But her reply gave him some relief. He still had time to confront Ellsworth.

A knock on the door intruded on his thoughts. Lady Eleanore quickly sat down in a nearby chair, and leaned back as Bastien answered the door. It was the vicar.

"I have come to see as to Lady Eleanore's condition. Is there anything we can do for her?"

Bastien softened somewhat. Mr. Darling was a good man, seeing to the health of the girl he'd spent a good deal of his life raising.

"She is well, sir. Just needing a little rest at the moment," he replied. "Perhaps a lingering tiredness from her accident last week."

"Of course." The man smiled, and Bastien cursed himself for the worry he saw edging the man's mouth. "I will not disturb her further. Mrs. Darling and I will see to the guests." He left, Bastien closing the door behind him.

Lady Eleanore rose. "I should return to my guests. Heaven knows what Mrs. Waterstone will say about this. Perhaps she will wonder if I am dying from a broken heart or some such nonsense." She sighed, then shook her head. "No matter. Let them think what they will."

Bastien grimaced.

"It matters." Mon Dieu, what was he saying? What was he thinking? He was angry for reasons he could not identify. "You have brought these people into your home, fed them, made them welcome, and you are repaid with being the object of gossip."

She blinked, clearly taken aback by his words. "Oh for heaven's sake, Mr. DuMont. Their daughters are married. They are idle, and I provide a pleasant distraction to them. It is not vicious. I have experienced that, Mr. DuMont. The cut direct of my so-called peers, the sneers of some of the finest bred women and men in the land. I would take a thousand of Mrs. Waterstone's well-meant, if ill-conceived questions about my marriage state if it meant I could never have to attend a single moment of ball in Grosvenor Square ever again."

Her eyes were bright, and in the moment, Bastien knew he'd unintentionally hit upon something raw. And like many of his most stoic patients, she was swallowing her pain with a smile. Pain he'd unwittingly caused. He needed to soothe it.

"*Désolé*, my lady. I have come from a place where harsh whispers and rumor could lead an innocent to their death."

"I am humbled by your care in these matters. But I have not asked for your protection or your concern," she said. "I do not need it. My brother is a powerful man. He provides me excellent protection."

Care? The last thing he was capable of offering was caring. He needed to check himself. For the past three years, he'd been doing his very damnedest to not care at all. Caring came with a cost that had become too high to pay.

"Why?" he pushed. "Why put yourself through this fuss when your brother, with all his wealth and power, could make your foundling dream come true? Does he not agree with the idea?"

"He does not yet know," she protested. "Though I'm certain he would, if I asked."

"But you won't."

"I don't want to, Mr. DuMont. I want to do this for myself. For my mother. I'd planned to tell him, when I was in London, but I went and did something horrible." Her eyes clouded over, clearly troubled. "And I didn't get the chance."

"HORRIBLE?"

Mr. DuMont's brow crinkled, and he sat down on the chair opposite her. "I cannot imagine it. But let me guess. And please do not disappoint me, as you had already promised me that you had killed a man, and yet, he is mending as we speak."

Eleanore could not help but smile at his devilish manner.

"Mr. DuMont, please—"

He held up a finger, and smiled, deliberately playful, which chased away the raging doubt in her mind and awakened a fire in her belly.

"Did you spill a very fine brandy on the muslin skirt of the Countess of Wheaton?"

Eleanore stifled a laugh. "No!"

"Well then..." He put his finger to his mouth, tapping his lips as he pretended to ruminate on her crimes. Whether or not he intended the motion to be hopelessly distracting, she found herself transfixed by the movement. "You stepped on the toes of a newly-minted Colonel, ruining the polish on his boots."

"No. I am, if you must know, an excellent dancer." And quite suddenly the idea of dancing with Mr. DuMont became a very attractive prospect indeed.

"Well then," he continued, his voice lowered, his silver eyes intoxicating her. He settled back in his chair, a devilish nonchalance that made her body tingle. "I cannot begin to guess."

The memory of that horrible moment rushed back, dampening her mood. "I broke an engagement."

His brow dipped, and he shrugged. "And this was the horrible deed?"

She rose, and began pacing the floor between them.

"Mr. DuMont, I do not pretend to know how things were in France when dealing with matrimonial matters, and no doubt, it seems like a silly thing compared with the calamity happening now," she said, by way of an apology. "But yes, in the eyes of society, breaking an engagement is not taken at all lightly."

He shifted in his seat, his countenance growing more serious. "Was he vicious, your intended?"

Eleanore shook her head.

"A drunkard? Or a...how do you say...a man who plays too often at cards?"

"Neither." She swallowed, closed her eyes, shame welling inside. "His vices ran in a different direction."

He nodded. "I see."

"It probably shouldn't matter, you see. Many married men take mistresses." She walked to the window, basking in the cold light of the day, melancholy squeezing her chest. "But I have seen what love looks like. I see it every time my brother and Rosalind look at each other. I saw it when my cousin Edmund married his fiancé only a few short months ago."

Mr. DuMont rose and walked to her, standing so close she could smell his cologne.

"I would not trust devotion. It has a way of making a fool of you, if you are not careful."

She turned to face him. "Love can only make you a fool if you let it, Mr. DuMont. And even I know love alone is not enough to create happiness." Her mother and father had loved each other. It simply hadn't been enough to overcome the differences in their stations.

She looked back out the window, unable, perhaps, to face him as her memory of that awful indignation came rushing back. She'd learned about it first not from him, but from hushed whispers in a ballroom. She folded her arms tightly in front of her, recalling the horrible delight on the faces of her so-called betters when they knew she'd overheard. "When I learned of Lord Ramsay's indiscretion, I could not bear it. So I left, that very night. Daniel was willing to take me. I told Lord Ramsay that he was free of his obligations to me, and left a note with my brother, informing him I was leaving London."

Mr. DuMont tsked, and cocked an eyebrow. The simple gesture was enough to weaken her at the knees. Lord Ramsay had never looked at her this way.

"You disappoint me, Lady Eleanore. I thought perhaps you'd stolen the heart of a married man who's now obliged to look upon the face of the black-hearted heiress he was forced to wed."

"Of course not!" Eleanore shook her head, smiling sadly. "I don't steal hearts."

He reached out and tucked a loose lock behind her ear. The merest touch of his fingers sent a shiver down her back. "Now that I cannot believe."

She stilled, her breath catching a moment, then touched her ear where his fingers had just been. He was watching her again, as he always did, but this time, there was a different kind of intensity in his gaze, one that threatened to take her breath away.

They stood in silence, a delicious tension that pulled Eleanore closer to him. His masculine scent, which hinted at cloves and bayberry, threatened to enrapture her. His gaze raked over her, and she tilted her head back slightly. He lowered his chin and parted his lips ever so slightly. She found herself reaching up on her toes, and she closed her eyes, expectation rushing through her.

And then nothing. There was nothing.

Eleanore blinked, her heels coming back down to the floor, and saw the door to the study softly closing on its hinges.

Her mouth fell open as confusion, frustration, and embarrassment swirled inside her. What had just happened? It seemed, for a sparkling moment, so terribly magical. Did she imagine his intention? And what did it say about her that she was eager to invite it? Was he being a rogue and tempting her, then, seeing how easily she might have been swayed, leaving her? Or was he a gentleman? Was he so desperate to escape the crowds he used her to do so? She let go a long breath, struggling to keep her composure.

So much for magic.

Eleanore sank down onto the settee and buried her face in her hands, replaying the afternoon in her mind. She hadn't spent every moment with Mr. DuMont, but for the most part it seemed like a perfectly sociable afternoon. Certainly, there were some questions about the war, the beheading of King Louis, and the guillotine that may have been a little insipid, but there was nothing about Mr. DuMont's manner that had suggested they had affected him so. Generally, people had seemed interested in him, and if she was honest with herself, far more interested in why she had returned and about her broken engagement. But their concerns were mostly that— concern. Not judgment. At least, not for the most part.

Mr. DuMont had seemed just as annoyed about the gossip about Eleanore than anything else. That, and the fact that he'd once again seemed fixated on meeting with Lord Ellsworth. Far more than his story would allow.

A knock on the door was a welcome interruption to her thoughts. She called out, only to see Mrs. Darling at the door. Thanks to Mr. DuMont's deception, she'd left the Darlings to wish her guests goodbye.

"Eleanore my dear, are you well?" Mrs. Darling stood at the door, concern in her eyes. "I thought Mr. DuMont might be here. He seems to have disappeared."

"Escaped. I think the word you are looking for is escaped."

CHAPTER 11

*B*astien stalked down the hall, his body on fire. He'd been hopelessly distracted by Lady Eleanore and it was damn time he put his energy where it belonged—finding Lord Ellsworth before he escaped. She was far too eager to protect the marquess, though he could easily imagine that Ellsworth would use her good nature for his own purposes. He pushed aside the idea that he was doing the very same thing.

He'd come within inches of smothering her with his kiss. Her scent lingered in his memory, tantalizing him still.

Both Lady Eleanore and Hanley would be preoccupied with seeing to their guests' departures. Which left the rest of the house, and Ellsworth, to him. The door was still ajar as he arrived at Ellsworth's chambers, a voice made sharp by anger immediately catching Bastien's ear.

"Are you quite certain?"

Bastien paused just outside, his ears perking up. It was Ellsworth, talking to a footman. Or, rather, barking at one.

"Absolutely certain, my lord," came the footman's reply.

"You know my instruction is to leave everything but my clothing completely undisturbed."

"Yes, sir."

Bastien peered through the crack in the open door. There was Ellsworth, pacing back and forth in quick, sharp steps in front of a hapless footman who stood as straight as a board. Even from this distance, the flush of color in the marquess' face was evident.

"You know I will speak to His Lordship myself and have you all tossed out if I discover—"

Heat pricked on the back of Bastien's neck, and his thoughts immediately went to the dagger in his boot. He let out a quick breath, squared his shoulders, and walked into the room, careful to keep his expression neutral.

"Good afternoon, Lord Ellsworth," he said, keeping his voice light. "Bored with tea? I know I am." He walked past Ellsworth to the sideboard, casting a deliberate look at the footman, who did not dare even acknowledge him. He poured two glasses of brandy, took a sip out of one, and handed the other to Ellsworth, who refused.

"No, thank you," he replied, his manner more polite, but strained so tight Bastien thought his throat might snap. Ellsworth glared at Bastien, who stepped toward the footman and held out the glass to him.

"And you, monsieur. You appear to need this."

The servant betrayed only the slightest hint of surprise, but otherwise remained rooted to the spot.

"Is that a medical opinion, Mr. DuMont? Or the opinion of a prig?" Ellsworth replied, the anger dampened and replaced with a more subtle tone of sarcasm.

"Perhaps both. Are you done with him? Or were you going to continue to threaten this hapless boy?"

Ellsworth blanched, his lips pressing into a tight line. The man was raging inside, and Bastien savored it. He turned to the footman and waved a hand, releasing him from his spot. Visibly relieved, the boy shot Bastien a quick look of thanks, then bolted.

"Is there something besides brandy I can get you for your relief?" Bastien asked.

"No, thank you." Ellsworth stood at the window, hands clutched behind him.

Bastien knew he had to be careful. Le Veneur Rouge was dangerous. And now, only a few feet away, he was clearly furious. Fury was a powerful propellant for a thousand horrible, deadly deeds.

Ellsworth turned on his heel.

There was no doubt in Bastien's mind that he stood in front of Le Veneur Rouge. He must have discovered the missing letters. Letters proving his true identity.

Before Ellsworth could pass, Bastien held out his arm, blocking him from leaving.

"What is the meaning of this?" Ellsworth asked, red creeping up from under his collar.

"I think we both know, monsieur."

Ellsworth took a step back, realization breaking across his brow with a mix of fear and fury. He reached out and grabbed Bastien by the collar.

"You." The man's heart was pounding so hard in his chest, Bastien could see his pulse thumping in his neck. "You have them."

"I have no idea what you are talking about," Bastien replied. "But if you let me go, we can discuss whatever has you so clearly upset."

The grip on Bastien's collar tightened a moment before the marquess released him. He pulled a handkerchief from his pocket and wiped his brow.

"I see. I should have bloody well known." He shook his head, and chuckled bitterly. "All your questions. Your interest in my work. No one is interested in my work."

"On the contrary. I take an extreme interest in your work, my lord."

Ellsworth's brows dipped, a flicker of confusion darkening his looks. His lips twisted a bit, and he shook his head.

"What is your price?"

"My price?" Bastien was thunderstruck by the man's nerve. "I don't know that even you have that much money."

"Is this what you do in your spare time? Pretend at doctoring and engage in bribery? No doubt that is where the real money is." Ellsworth adjusted his spectacles, then pointed a finger at Bastien. "Edmund told me there was a time he didn't trust you. That he never knew what side you were on. Well, I suppose I know now, don't I? Your own bloody side. I don't know how the hell you discovered I was here, but I hope you give them a cut of your earnings."

Bastien's fingers curled into fists, barely able to contain his anger.

"I knew you were here, you bastard, because before you had the last of your henchmen try to murder Baroness D'Anville, she got a message to me. A message that Le Veneur Rouge was here."

Ellsworth stepped back, clearly stunned. "The Red Hunter? Do you mean that lunatic who tried to have Edmund killed is here?" He stilled, put his hands on his waist and peered at Bastien as if he was a specimen to be studied. "Where?"

Bastien stood on his guard, the sound of blood rushing in his ears, waiting for Ellsworth to make his move.

"Bloody hell." Ellsworth's eyes widened as he dropped his hands to his sides, his lips twisting into a bitter smile. "You think I'm the Red Hunter. I don't know whether to be insulted or flattered."

"You are the Prince of the House of Weymouth." Bastien lunged at him, grabbing him by the throat. "Show me."

"Show you what?" Ellsworth said, his voice rough for lack of breath.

Bastien pushed him back. "Your left shoulder."

"I am not—"

On impulse, Bastien pulled the dagger out of his boot and held it to Ellsworth's throat. "Your. Left. Shoulder."

Ellsworth stepped back, holding up is hands as if in surrender, but not for a moment did Bastien lower the blade. Methodically, Ellsworth loosened his cravat, then struggled to remove his green wool coat and waistcoat. Pulling his shirt up, exposing his back to Bastien, there was a brilliant red birthmark.

That was all. Bastien pressed his fingers into Ellsworth's flesh, as if in disbelief. No scarring. And no evidence there had ever been any.

Unwilling to give up, Bastien lowered the knife and reached into his jacket, pulling out the pad of neatly folded letters, including the one he'd found on the desk.

"What is the plan? Your failed plan?"

Ellsworth turned to face him, lowering his shirt, then snatched the missive out of Bastien's fingers. He scanned the page, then shook his head. "My latest mirror. For my telescope." He sunk down into a nearby chair. "For months I have been working to source the best mirror. Even better than Herschel's. But my assistant found a flaw in the design. We have to start over."

Telescope? Mirrors? Bastien could barely comprehend what he was hearing.

"What about these?" he held out the stack of letters that had been carefully hidden away at the back of his desk.

Ellsworth practically lunged at them but Bastien stepped back, satisfied with Ellsworth's rash response. "Tell me about these."

"I already proved to you that I am not your madman. So unless you are interested in blackmail, you will give those back to me, and I will not have you tossed in prison for theft."

"You are a prince of the house of Weymouth." Bastien recited the words from Tante Marie's scrambled note. Unable—unwilling—to concede, he turned his back on the marquess, tore off the ribbon, and ripped open the letter.

Bastien pored over the missive, written in a woman's hand. A woman telling Ellsworth in the clearest terms that she was never in love with him, that he was a fool for thinking otherwise, and she was returning the rest of his letters to her, unopened. He shuffled through the rest, and all were addressed to the same woman—a Lady Amelia.

"Don't you want to read the rest?" Ellsworth's words, laced with vinegar, cut through Bastien. "Trust me, you'll want to up your price."

Trust me. Bastien closed his eyes, forcing himself to swallow back the bile in his throat. He folded up the letter, placed it with the others. Then, as methodically as if he were preparing for a procedure, he stacked them neatly, tied them up, and held them out to Ellsworth.

"Your price," the marquess repeated, his eyes red, clearly mustering what little pride Bastien had not yet stolen from him.

"Your forgiveness, my lord. And if that is too high, then your understanding."

Ellsworth grabbed the letters and shoved them into his jacket. He sank down into a chair, lifted up his glasses and rubbed his eyes. And then he started to laugh.

"I don't know if I should be horrified or flattered. My father thinks I'm shirking my responsibilities. My mother thinks I'm mad. And Lady Amelia thinks I am...nothing." He slouched backward and stared up at the ceiling. "I'll take that brandy now."

Bastien refilled the glasses and handed him one. "You should be locking those letters somewhere more secure. Or burning them."

"I locked my room," Ellsworth countered.

"Locks only keep out the innocent." Bastien drained his glass in a single shot. "It might cheer you to know I nearly ruined my trousers by almost knocking a pot of your piss all over them."

Ellsworth held up his glass in salute. "It does, in fact." He smiled, followed Bastien's lead and emptied his glass.

Bastien gestured to the marquess' coat, lying on a nearby chair, the letters buried inside. "Burn them. They are too much of a liability to you. And if the lady does not care for you, she is not worth your devotion. Find someone who is."

The marquess went back to the sideboard, and refilled his glass. "I am resolved, at present, to leave the subject of women and marriage to those much more invested in it than I am. My parents, for example."

Bastien shook his head. Far be it for him to lecture anyone on happiness, or worse, matrimony. The last time he'd made such observations, Edmund Pembroke went ahead and found himself a wife. The last person on earth he was even remotely devoted to—Tante Marie— had nearly been taken from him. If Bastien needed another reason to remain safely alone, Le Veneur Rouge had given him that.

His thoughts strayed, unwillingly, to Lady Eleanore. The woman he'd left, quite unceremoniously, on the edge of a kiss, his body raging. She would think him a cad, and she would be right. And all the better for it. She deserved a good man. Someone like Ellsworth, perhaps.

"What about Lady Eleanore?" The question slipped out.

"What about her?" Ellsworth's brows dipped, clearly uncertain what Bastien was asking.

What was he asking? More to the point, why? Because he was suddenly afraid of Ellsworth's answer.

"She would make you a good wife. You and her brother are on good terms, oui?"

"Until a week ago, she was nearly someone else's wife," Ellsworth said, sitting down.

"That was a week ago."

"Lady Eleanore is a lovely woman, yes," Ellsworth replied, looking up at Bastien. "But we are not well suited, her and I."

Relief flooded through Bastien at Ellsworth's declaration, for no damn good reason. "In what way?"

"She is looking for a love match, Mr. DuMont. And she probably deserves it. And I don't love her. I can't love her." He gestured to the letters in his jacket. "I am in love with a shadow. And Lady Eleanore deserves better than that."

He was right, of course. She did.

"Does Barronsfield know why you are here?" Ellsworth's voice cut through the awkward silence, and Bastien was happy for the change of subject.

"He does."

"He will be horrified to know Lady Eleanore has returned, if indeed the Red Hunter is here. How will you know you have your man?" Ellsworth asked. "I assume he has a mark on his shoulder."

"A scar." Bastien shook his head. "But there is more. This man is connected to the house of Weymouth. Do you have any idea who? You have no siblings, by chance?"

"Alas, no. At least none that survived infancy." Ellsworth looked over the rim of his spectacles, and grimaced. "Trust me, my parents are heavily invested in my requirements to produce offspring."

The two men sat together as Bastien continued asking Middleton about his parents, his cousins—any link to the mysterious message.

"What about scandals? Surely you can't have such a lofty history with any dark skeletons tucked away in a dungeon."

Colin shrugged. "Like many old families, there are no doubt cousins of mine born on the wrong side of the sheets." He stilled, frowning as though he was deep in thought. He tilted his head to one side, nodding to himself, then he spoke. "The only scandal—and it's not even in recent memory—was that of how my grandfather became Duke. He wasn't supposed to be, you see."

"Tell me more."

"His cousin was to inherit the title. But it came to light that his parent's marriage was illegitimate. His mother had been married before—married in some little parish to a horrible man, when she was very young. He abandoned her, and she returned home, pretending she'd been widowed. I suppose she never expected to see him again, nor for the truth to come out. She married my grandfather's uncle—the Duke of Weymouth, and had children. But the truth of the matter was discovered, and the title passed away from that line, to my grandfather."

Bastien listened, fascinated by the story. "And do you have any contact with this part of your family? Do you know anything about them?"

"No. They are not spoken of," Colin replied. "I will write to my father, and see what I can discover. It may be nothing at all."

Bastien rose. "Perhaps not. But I would like to be sure. Though you owe me no favors."

"No, I do not," Ellsworth replied, Bastien heart sinking at the answer.

He rose, knowing full well that this disaster was of his own making, prepared to make his leave.

"But I owe you for saving Edmund," the marquess called out.

Bastien paused, taking a moment to process what Lord Ellsworth was saying.

"So, then, you will help me?"

Ellsworth rose. "I will write to my father directly, and explain the urgency. One good turn deserves another."

❧

HE DID WHAT?

Eleanore raced to find Hanley. She'd returned from bidding the Darlings goodbye when she'd overheard two footmen speaking in confidence about an altercation between Mr. DuMont and Lord Ellsworth. Perfect. The day had gone from ridiculous to impossible in little more than an hour.

She should have been elated at what turned out to be an excellent and potentially profitable afternoon. The guests seemed delighted with Mr. DuMont, and were eager to accept his opinions on the virtues of a local foundling home. Lord Ellsworth's unexpected arrival only added another element of credibility to her idea. It was by all accounts a success—but she could not shake the sensation of failure. A failure capped by the memory of standing at the window in her brother's study—of all places—waiting for a kiss that did not come. The humiliation had sunk into her belly like a stone.

But perhaps that was not the worst of it, was it?

The aged butler reappeared from a nearby door. At least she could depend on him.

"Hanley," she called out. "Do you have any notion of Mr. DuMont being on the premises?"

"Yes, my lady," he nodded. "I handed him his cloak and bag but two minutes ago. Shall I have one of the footmen catch him for you?"

"No, thank you, Hanley."

Eleanore ran to the windows that overlooked the front courtyard. There in the dimming afternoon light was Mr. DuMont, his bag in his hand, his collar turned up against the cold air. Escaping.

Not this time.

She tore out the door, ignoring the winter air, the heat of her anger driving her on. Mr. DuMont had some mighty big explaining to do. She caught up to him and blocked him where he stood.

"What on earth are you doing?" he demanded. "You will catch your death being outside with nothing around your neck."

Eleanore swallowed a moment and caught her breath. "You will tell me what in the blazes is going on. And do not try for a moment to distract me with one of your kisses, because that will not work." No matter how wonderful they were. "You were interrogating poor Colin. Sneaking around his rooms. Invading his privacy and betraying my good will."

"I have no idea what you are talking about," he replied with a gentle shrug of his shoulders. "We merely had a chat, one gentleman to another."

"Do not try that condescending French business with me, Mr. DuMont." She poked her finger into his chest, which seemed somehow to amuse him, and vex her even more. "You drew a knife on him."

"That is an interesting account, but not complete. I believe you will find your Lord Ellsworth very much intact, and perhaps in better spirits than when I found him." He cocked his head to one side, frowned slightly, then shrugged and continued walking. "Now get inside, where it is warm."

She caught up to him, putting her hand out to his chest, stopping him in his tracks. "What did you want from him?"

"That is none of your business."

"When you are using my good will and sneaking around my guests for your own ends, it is every bit my business."

"Only because you make it your business to save everyone." He swore a little in French, and looked away. "Even if they don't deserve it."

"Like you, perhaps?"

"I don't want saving."

"Very well. Be a martyr, if that suits you."

He blanched then, taken aback by her words. "Martyr? I would take a good look in a mirror first."

Eleanore crossed her arms and cocked her eyebrow—a Pembroke trait she carried and used to its full effect. "I have no intention of sacrificing myself, Mr. DuMont. I know what I am doing—living to make sure others have the same chances I have had. To give a little comfort. I have no grand cause I am sacrificing myself to. That is your inclination. Not mine."

"You would not understand." He opened his mouth, as if to speak, then closed it, shaking his head as he did so.

The dismissive gesture increased her ire. "Despite what men think of the fair sex, we have brains in our heads. You will explain yourself to me."

He paused, and rubbed his hand across his chin. "I will explain nothing to you." He looked away for a moment, snowflakes falling softly on his shoulders, belying the storm between them, before he turned back to her. "I will not put you in harm's way."

She stepped toward him, an unexpected fury lighting her steps, and pointed her finger at his face. "Don't you dare make that decision for me. It is not yours to make."

He took her hand, pulling her toward him. "I have been on the run from a man who will kill anyone associated with me. The less you know of it, the better."

A cold realization dawned on her, and she pulled her hand away. "And you thought Colin Middleton was this man? He and Edmund are friends!"

"I have had many friends whose ideals left them on opposite sides of the Revolution. Friends I would no longer recognize. That cheered madly as old women and beardless men were marched to the guillotine. That reveled in the madness of chaos. Edmund had been in hiding for years, and the moment he reappeared, who should be there but his friend—a man who clearly has no interest in assuming his title, a man of sharp intellect. A man who knew Edmund's true identity and might decide to take advantage of it."

"You took advantage of me and my good nature to learn everything you could about him."

"Yes. That is what I do. I am not a good man. I am not one of your angels." He shook his head. "I have not had the liberty to think well of people as you do."

"You know nothing of me, or my life." Eleanore threw up her

hands, dumbfounded. "Your arrogance, Bastien DuMont, is astounding."

He flinched then, as if she'd struck him, and part of her could not help but own a little satisfaction at his expense.

"I have had every opportunity to be suspicious of the world," she said. "For years, people accused my brother of the most horrible crimes, to the point that he believed them. Believed them so intently, that he kept me away, depriving me of the only family I have, because he deemed it safer for me." Anger poured out of her. An anger that until that moment, she did not realize she carried. "And when at last I came here, and found a family who loved me, and protected me, I still had the whispers and stares of the so-called "gentle women" who would hurl insults behind my back, and sometimes to my face, because of my parentage. Men who would not look at me twice because my blood was not pure. So excuse me when I say that I could also be privileged to the liberty you claim for yourself to look upon everyone with suspicion or derision. And sometimes, heaven help me, I want to."

Tears, hot and unwanted, tumbled down her cheeks, cooling in the air. There was nothing between them at this moment except the dull quiet of the snow falling around them, the only light spilling from the lit windows of the house nearby.

He stepped forward and wiped the tears away from her cheeks.

"Your assessment of Lord Ellsworth is correct—he is an honorable man."

Eleanore nodded, but did not speak, for fear she would lose her composure entirely.

"I did not mean to desert you, this afternoon," he continued, followed by more gentle swearing. "No—that is a lie. I did intend it. I wanted you to think ill of me. To stay away from me. Because, God help me, I want you."

"I cannot think ill of you, Bastien DuMont," she said. And heaven help her, she wanted him, too.

He dropped his bag at his side and stroked her cheeks with his thumbs, wiping her tears. Then, slowly, tenderly, his lips caressed her cheeks, drying her tears with each tender kiss.

His hands were cupped around her neck, his breath hot on her skin. She felt herself melting into him as he put his lips to hers, savoring the taste of him. Savoring the luscious heat winding its way through her body, surprised by the hunger that desired even more.

The sound of hooves, thundering in the frozen ground, broke through their kiss. Daylight had already begun to fade, the courtyard lit by the windows from inside the manor.

Dear heavens, what was she doing? Thank goodness Stephen was not here.

"Is the doctor here?"

A strangled cry of frantic grief carried on the wind. Mr. DuMont lowered his arms, and Eleanore turned toward the voice, squinting in the dim light.

"*Ici, c'est moi!*" Mr. DuMont yelled, his voice sharp and alert. They both ran toward the rider, who Eleanore recognized as one of the local farmers.

"You've got to come," the man yelled. "I've been lookin' in town for ye. My boy—he can't breathe."

Grim resignation gripped Mr. DuMont's face. He grabbed his bag and ran toward the man, who pulled him on the back of his horse. He nodded to Eleanore, a pained look on his face.

"Get inside," he yelled over his shoulder. "You don't want to catch your death."

Suddenly, that had meaning.

CHAPTER 12

*H*e was too late.

Bastien trudged out of the small farmer's cottage that stood on a road leading out of Elmsdale. The horrible hacking cough of the young man inside was now forever silenced, the sound replaced with the low cries of grief from his parents. In Bastien's pocket was a single farthing they had pressed into his hands, insistent that he receive payment.

For doing *nothing*.

The rattle of cart wheels ahead caught his attention. The vehicle came to an abrupt stop, and a familiar voice rang out in the night.

"Ho there, Mr. DuMont." The figure climbed down and approached. It was Mr. Darling, a grim expression on his face. "One of the neighbors fetched me." He cast a glance toward the cottage, and shook his head. "A sad business, this is."

Bastien nodded. Sad, infuriating, horrible business. "Maybe if I had gotten here sooner." Or if the boy had been born in a dry, warm climate that was easier on lungs not made for England's damp. Or if, perhaps, they had a cleaner fire. There were too many or's, all out of Bastien's control.

"We both know that isn't true," Mr. Darling replied, as if reading

Bastien's thoughts. "You are a surgeon, sir. You maybe privy to some of God's miracles, and indeed, some of them work through you. But not all."

Bastien swallowed a curse. "Perhaps your God could have granted the boy's mother one more," he said through gritted teeth.

"If we relied on Him for everything, we would do nothing for ourselves," he replied, his tone measured and thoughtful. "Why don't you join Mrs. Darling and myself for dinner tomorrow? We are neighbors, of a fashion."

Bastien shook his head. "You are a good man. I see what you are doing. Perhaps another time. For the moment it is probably best if I keep my own company."

Mr. Darling smiled and patted Bastien's upper arm in tacit agreement. The two stood in silence for a moment before the vicar's gaze turned toward the cottage, his shoulders sagging as he surveyed the grim task ahead. "Very well. But if you change your mind, the invitation is open."

He turned, leaving Bastien alone to return to Dr. Brayden's home. He'd only gone a few steps before the same neighbor who'd brought the vicar offered Bastien a ride back into the village. The air had turned bitterly cold, and though part of him wanted to savor the trial as payment for his failure, he decided to accept, particularly as the man did not appear to want to take no as an answer. But instead of returning to his bed, he'd asked the man to drop him at the front step of the Elm and Thistle.

He pulled on the heavy door of Mr. Roderick's establishment and was hit by a rush of warm air thick with the tang of wood and pipe smoke. The place was pleasantly busy, and pleasantly working class.

Of course, he wasn't really of the working class. And he wasn't a gentleman either, at least not by English standards. He occupied some sort of no man's land, much of it of his own choosing. After he'd left France and came to England, he'd sometimes worked for the Home Office, sometimes fed information back to the more moderate factions in France. No man's land had become comfortable. It had become easier than picking sides—sides that still provided no relief to the people who needed it most. When Tante Marie had reached out to him, introducing him to Sir Richard Hamilton at the Home Office, he'd balked in the beginning. But she kept at him. In the beginning they were on opposite sides of the war, but she did not let him forget they were still family. And that he was capable of doing the right thing.

He'd fought against it. And then, he'd been tired of fighting.

His friend, Edmund Pembroke, had managed, somehow, to find love, devotion, and even a family out of nothing. A love so fierce and strong, it had given him the strength to rise above his own demons, claim his name, and have happiness. The happiness his cousin Eleanore desperately craved.

And though Bastien had been on the run since almost the moment they were reunited, he'd seen the determination on the part of Edmund's wife, Gwyneth, to brave the danger to save him from the clutches of revolutionaries egged on by Le Veneur Rouge.

Edmund's life had begun a new chapter, and by all accounts, it was filled with a new sort of contentment. And that night, Bastien realized he was finished trying to decide whose secrets were worth keeping, and for whom. What plans for mayhem he would try and foil and which ones he would not.

He'd become tired of the game. Or maybe he was just tired.

The inn was barely half full—a mix of travelers and local faces Bastien was coming to recognize. He found a seat in a dark corner, not far from the hearth. A moment later, his view was filled with the wide expanse of the innkeeper's impressive belly.

"Can I get ye some supper, Mr. DuMont?" he asked. "I'll be honest, it's not me best, but it's hot and will fill—"

"Just bring me whatever in your cupboard passes for brandy," Bastien grumbled.

"Tough day?"

Bastien didn't bother to look up. "Bring the bottle."

Mr. Roderick disappeared behind the bar and returned with a tray. He placed a bottle, a horn cup, and a small plate with bread and what looked to be some sort of cheese in front of Bastien.

"I'm not pretending to be yer mother," he started, crossing his arms, "but I know you Frogs—sorry—Frenchies—like cheese. So I brought you some. And you don' want to be drinking too much with nothin' in your gut. Got to mind my floors, doctor."

Bastien glared up at the innkeeper.

"I'm not a doctor," Bastien said. "As any doctor would no doubt tell you."

"Word has it you fixed up Daniel Morehouse something good, and helped out with Daisy Moore's wrist. That's doctoring as far as I know. And Dr. Brayden aside, I don't know too many of your kind who's helpful, if you don't mind my saying."

Bastien opened the bottle, poured his cup to the rim, then drank it down, relishing the warmth in his chest.

"I don't mind. I've probably killed more people than anyone sitting at Newgate."

"Well, now, I don't know about that. You can't fix 'em all. But you can save a few that would never have had the chance, and that's something."

Bastien wasn't so sure. But he was sure about getting off this bloody topic.

"Lady Eleanore is in the business of saving people, I see."

"We love Lady Eleanore, Mr. DuMont," Mr. Roderick said. "She's become a proper lady and everything, but she remembers where she came from."

Bastien watched the innkeeper as he returned to his post, turning over the man's words in his head. They were soon replaced with an image of Lady Eleanore, standing in Barronsfield's shadow, her words fierce, her sadness threatening to tear at Bastien's heart.

She had no place in society. Of course, she had her brother's protection, to be sure. But even in the library at Barronsfield, he'd overheard the gossip directed her way, even amongst her neighbors.

The papers in London were probably tearing her to pieces. And goddammit, he shouldn't care, but he did. He didn't want to rescue her. Even if she was a bastard, she had a good home, a powerful name, and a fortune that would keep her with a roof over her head and servants to care for her. And if she felt she needed to repay her good fortune by filling her days by feeding the poor and rescuing the sick, so be it. Bastien had tried that once. The poor were still hungry, and the sick never went away. And it had been too much for him to bear.

He grabbed the bottle of brandy as if his life depended on it, and poured himself a generous glass.

"Please do not tell me that spending a few hours in the company of your neighbors has inspired a man to drown himself in Roderick's cheap spirits."

Bastien gazed up at the man standing over him, recognition cutting its way through his cloudy brain.

"Not at all, Mr. Wakefield." He held out his hand, clumsily gesturing to the chair opposite, inviting him to sit. He then called for the innkeeper to bring another cup. And another bottle to accompany it.

Wakefield removed his hat and sat down, accepting the glass Bastien poured him.

"How are you coping with our damp English winters?" he asked. "Or perhaps you have become accustomed to them."

"Well enough. It's not Paris." Bastien laughed bitterly. "But then, Paris is not what it was. So I will get used to it." Of course, the heat from Lady Eleanore's kiss could turn any thoughts of cold weather into a memory. The very thought of it enlivened his body, even as the liquor dulled his senses.

"If you ever need a more palatable reminder, I can help you."

Bastien raised his eyebrows. He wouldn't take Wakefield as a smuggler, but no doubt every merchant doing well for himself these days were dabbling in the trade of goods that were 'extra-legal.'

"I will keep that in mind," he replied. "Do you do a lot of business that brings you to France?"

"The past year has been particularly difficult," he replied, leaning back in his seat. "But I am not a man to gnash his teeth when opportunities disappear. I merely look for another one, and I am rarely disappointed."

"I did not realize you were the charity-minded sort," Bastien said, changing the subject.

"When the sister of the most powerful man in three counties invites you to tea, you go," Wakefield said. "One learns not to cross the Marquess of Barronsfield."

Bastien sat up, his interest piqued by Wakefield's choice of words, but also his reasons. Is this why he chose to come to Lady Eleanore's aid? He could not help but think back to her protests about wanting to accomplish this feat—to have her foundling home—without her brother's help. And yet, Wakefield's words suggested that Lady Eleanore's wishes had already been thwarted.

He thought back to his own impressions of Lord Barronsfield. They had met only briefly, but Bastien had the distinct feeling that the man was gravely concerned not only about aiding the Baroness D'Anville— Tante Marie—but also for the danger this would have presented for his neighbors. But he was, as Wakefield suggested, a powerful man—and all such men, as he'd learned himself in Paris, were subject to the whims of their own ego. Regardless of whether they were born paupers or peers.

"I have not met the man," Bastien lied.

"The last man who crossed him ended up packing his family and moving them half way across the kingdom." Wakefield took another sip from his cup. "I picked up the house for a bargain. Opportunities, Mr. DuMont. They are everywhere. Is that what brought you here?"

"You might say that," Bastien said. "The powers that now rule France had decided, in the interests of *égalité*, that requiring surgical or medical training to practice smacked of elitism. So, as you might say, I took the opportunity to find other work." That other work included printing leaflets for the revolutionary cause. Later, it involved smuggling families out of France, and secrets back in. Or hunting down the men who'd tracked down those same families Bastien had tried to save, and turn them over to the authorities in exchange for more *livres* than a regular man could make in a year.

"How are you finding Elmsdale? Are there enough bumps and bruises to keep you fed?"

"There is always enough," Bastien replied. "People have been more curious. The youngest ones like to be horrified by the knives and implements. The oldest ones are skeptical of any cure, and no doubt, rightly so."

Wakefield placed his glass on the table, picked up his hat, and nodded. "Well, Mr. DuMont, I must leave you. Enjoy the rest of your evening."

Bastien nodded, watching him leave, then drained his cup. Then the bottle. Then ordered another.

An image of Lord Ellsworth popped into his head, his expression one of utter indignity as Bastien had torn into the letter from his ex-lover. Bastien shook his head and drank deeply. The liquor was godawful stuff, but it was good enough to do the job he'd demanded of it. After downing his second glass, he leaned forward, putting his head into his hands.

He was a goddamned failure.

Days wasted, fixated on the wrong man. Precious energy misspent. Another face intruded upon him, this one of a young man, his skin pale with a growing blue pallor. Bastien knew it was energy that could have been directed better by attending to patients.

He poured himself another glass and drank, desperate to drive the image from his mind.

He drank until there was no more to drink. Or, at least, no more Mr. Roderick was prepared to give him.

He rose, taking a moment to steady himself, then nodded to the innkeeper before heading out into the cold. The air was damp, soaking through his clothes, but helped to clear his head. He pulled his collar around his throat and went into the night, weaving past a few scraggly characters near the door. He ignored them, focusing instead on keeping his steps clear.

"Hey there, froggie!" one of them called out.

Bastien paused a hair of a second, then kept going. He'd heard the insult, along with a multitude of others, over the years.

"Where's your striped short pants, froggie?"

"E's not a frog. Word 'as it, he's a Wolf. Can't you tell by how shaggy he is?"

The word stopped him cold. The Wolf was his family crest. The code name he used to send messages. Only the Home Office and Tante Marie knew him as the Wolf.

He turned on his heel, damn near falling over in the process. "Excuse me, gentlemen, can I help you?"

"You already did," one of them answered. "Now boys, let's go."

Bastien's stomach lurched. He reached out and grabbed one of them by the lapels. "Where are you going?"

"None of your business, that's where, frog." The man sneered, and Bastien was soon surrounded by three others. "Now, I think you should be letting me go, or you're going to need someone to be setting your bones."

Bastien pushed him away so forcefully the man fell to the ground. Bastien put a boot to his throat. "Don't call me frog, you English pig."

His advantage was shattered with a blow to his jaw, which forced him back. He barely had time right himself when a second blow came to his gut, and doubled him over. He never had the opportunity to stand up. A furious volley of blows to his face, followed by a blinding flash of pain in his shoulder, brought him to his knees.

And then he felt nothing at all.

CHAPTER 13

*E*leanore rushed to the door as Lord Ellsworth came in with Mr. Schofield, who was calling out for assistance. Between them, they carried Bastien DuMont. Thick black hair hung about his face, slightly matted from where the cut over his left eye had bled into his hairline. His knuckles were bloody from a fight, and his entire body shook from cold. A veritable cloud of alcohol hung in the air around him.

"What happened?"

"Found him near the square," Mr. Schofield replied. "And not a moment too soon."

Eleanore picked up her skirts and ran ahead. "Bring him this way."

They took him upstairs to one of the manor's eighty rooms and deposited him on the bed. A footman removed his boots. By the time they'd done that Hanley and a handful of servants had arrived.

"You're freezing." She'd already covered him up in a heavy blanket, but they'd found him lying on the icy stone square. She ran her hands up and down his right arm to invigorate his blood. "Hanley, we need a fresh pan of coals for the warmer."

"Are you trying to put me out of my misery?" Mr. DuMont growled.

"Hush," she replied, taken aback by his roughness. "I'm trying to warm you up."

He patted himself on his chest, as if looking for something. His eyes were little more than slits. "Cognac."

Eleanore's lip curled and she scrunched her nose. "I think you've had enough to drink already."

"Au contraire, mademoiselle," Mr. DuMont replied. He groped for his coat, which was hanging over the back of a nearby chair. He looked up at her, his eyes wider now, his smile magically playful despite his condition. "Please, *chère*, would you not aid a dying man?"

"You are not dying, monsieur."

"Is that your medical opinion?" he mumbled.

She rolled her eyes but otherwise ignored his sarcasm, and against her better judgment, searched his coat pockets. She soon found a small silver flask, and placed it in his hands. His fingers lingered on hers for just a moment, before she pulled them away. He twisted off the cap and took a generous swig before handing it back to her. "Perhaps you are right. A taste of good cognac, and the touch of a beautiful woman is all a man needs to be convinced to live." He smiled, but Eleanore could tell it was forced through a wall of discomfort.

"So the man can speak after all. What the devil happened, DuMont?"

Eleanore's attention snapped to the doorway, where Lord Ellsworth stood, with Mr. Schofield nearby.

"I had a disagreement with an idiot in the square." Mr. DuMont let out a long breath, followed by a drunken laugh, then closed his eyes. "He didn't like my accent. I might have made some unwelcome references about his parentage. You English are devoid of humor."

"I cannot say I disagree," the marquess replied.

Eleanore shook her head. There was more to this than what he was telling her. "And what did your opponent look like at the end of this disagreement?"

"Unfortunately for me, he had the aid of several companions," Mr. DuMont replied, as he shifted his weight in an effort to be more comfortable. "But in the end, I am here with a beautiful woman, so it didn't turn out so bad for me, oui?"

Eleanore pressed her lips together. He'd been lying in the cold for heaven knows how long.

"Watch yourself, Mr. DuMont," Lord Ellsworth replied. "What the English lack in humor we make up for with propriety."

"Of course, monsieur. Which is why Lady Eleanore is raising money for all the throwaway infants conceived outside the bonds of very proper English marriages," he spat. He closed his eyes a moment, a pulled expression flashing across his face.

"Enough of this," Eleanore said, unable to hold back her exasperation. "Lord Ellsworth, is there something I can do for you at this moment?"

The marquess, apparently chastened by her gentle reproach, shook his head. "My concern was for you. Unfortunately for everyone, Mr. DuMont will probably be fine in the morning, and no doubt in only slightly better humor than he is at present."

Mr. DuMont let go a low, guttural laugh, then cast a look of grudging gratitude in Lord Ellsworth's direction. "Merci."

"Mr. Schofield, could you ask someone to bring up some coffee? Lots of it."

The steward looked to her, then to Mr. DuMont.

"I will be fine. He's not going anywhere. Bess is here," she replied, referring to one of Barronsfield's servants who was busy tending the fire. "There was a time I helped Dr. Brayden with his patients. I miss it."

Mr. Schofield nodded and left, Lord Ellsworth in tow. Soon a servant appeared with a fresh linen shirt and a pot of coffee. The two of them helped get Mr. DuMont into a clean dry shirt and under the warm blankets.

"Do you have any idea who perpetrated this vicious act?" she asked as he settled. "Can you describe—"

"It was dark," he grumbled. "They were buffoons. It does not concern you."

"Of course it does," she protested, though not too much. "You are an employee of this estate. For that, if for no other reason, it does concern me." It concerned her for many reasons, but she suspected he would push back against them.

"Of course." His lips twisted into a bitter smile. "An employee. Well, chère, I am asking my lovely employer not to pursue it. You need not add me to your list of concerns."

He shifted in the bed, letting out a thin hiss of discomfort.

"Damn that Ellsworth," Mr. DuMont said, his words a low mumble, his tongue dulled by alcohol. "Now I owe him. Serves me right for accusing him of being someone he isn't."

Eleanore paused, her fingers wrapped around the edge of a heavy quilt she was pulling up around him.

"Who?" she asked quietly. "Accuse him of what?"

"Wrong prince."

He faded out of consciousness for a moment, and she wasn't certain if it was the bottle of whatever spirits that were claiming him, or the cold. He was mumbling under his breath in French. A woman named Marie. Someone called Le Veneur Rouge.

The only sound in the room was the crackling of the fire. He looked to be in much less pain now, but he was lucky. If he'd been there an hour longer, he might not have been able to recover from the elements.

"Are my injuries so dire, my lady?" he asked, his eyes open only half way. "You look pale. Do not worry. I have no intention of dying yet. I have work to do first."

Eleanore's attention snapped away from her own thoughts. She looked at him carefully. He was watching her far more closely than she thought.

She returned to the matter at hand. "Did you think Lord Ellsworth was this prince? Why are you looking for him?" She took a warm cloth and began to clean away the drying blood from the gash on his scalp. The flow had lessened somewhat, but it had not stopped. Carefully, she reapplied the pressure.

He closed his eyes, and he spoke softly, almost under his breath.

"I have to kill him."

Eleanore started, uncertain she'd heard him correctly.

He closed his eyes, still smiling, though there was absolutely no joy in it. Indeed, he wore the look of a man holding back tears.

"I couldn't save the boy. I couldn't," he said, his words still clumsy, his voice thick with emotion.

She tilted her head, and instinctively put a hand to his cheek. "Do you mean the man who came for you earlier? His boy?"

He nodded. "His father was begging me to save him. But I couldn't."

"Oh, Bastien." She wrapped her hands around his, her heart breaking for him. "I'm so sorry."

He lay there, quiet, holding on to her, his body still shaking, though, she suspected, it was not just cold that caused the heaving in his chest. It was complete and utter grief. Eleanore just sat with him, understanding for perhaps the first time, why he was harsh with his words, so gruff in his manner. He wasn't unfeeling. Quite the contrary. He cared deeply.

She sat with him until wakefulness finally succumbed to fatigue and alcohol. The fire blazed in the hearth, and the crackle of the fire mixed with the tinkling of icy rain pelting the windows. She put a hand to his cheek, and wished she knew how to help him. Though, no doubt, he would not desire it.

In the morning, she would go to Elmsdale, and make some inquiries about what had happened. Perhaps Mr. DuMont would protest, angry he'd been placed on her list of concerns, but it was too late.

He was on it.

CHAPTER 14

"*E*leanore."

The sound of her name wafted through her dreams. The voice sounded familiar. And not a little perturbed.

Perhaps a lot perturbed.

The insistence in the voice shook her out of her sleep, which had been intermittent. She opened her eyes—it was not yet dawn.

Her gaze went immediately to where Bastien DuMont lay, snoring to wake the dead. It was amazing she'd slept at all. It wasn't he who'd called her name.

"Eleanore."

It was then she was aware of a light from a taper coming from behind her. She rubbed her eyes and stood, turning to meet the speaker.

Stephen.

"Stephen!" Her heart hammered in her chest as she jumped to her feet, smiling to mask her nerves. "What are you doing here?"

"Funny you should ask me that," he replied. "I am tempted to ask you the same thing."

He looked tired, as if he'd been riding most of the night, and he probably had. Still, it was good to see him.

"It is good to see you."

"And you have no idea how happy I am to see you," he replied, taking her hand. "Who is that?"

"The surgeon you sent," she replied. "Don't you remember?"

"Right. I sent him to Dr. Brayden" he said, his voice strangely flat. "What is he doing in my house? And more importantly, what in the blazes are you doing in this room, with him?"

"It is a long tale. He'd been beaten in the street and left for dead."

"It smells like a public house in here."

"Yes, well, he was also quite inebriated, which didn't help matters," she replied, looking back over her shoulder at him. "I was nursing him. Just like I do from time to time at the infirmary."

"Right. Well, it is late. Or early. I can no longer tell," he replied. "Time for both of us to get some rest."

The sound of Mr. DuMont's loud snores cut through the silence.

"It's a good thing my chamber is on the other side of the house," he said. "I will walk you to your room, so we don't need to wake any of the servants."

Eleanore looked over her shoulder one last time, but Mr. DuMont appeared to be sleeping soundly, and she needed rest too. She followed Stephen down Barronsfield Manor's hallways in silence. Agonizing silence.

"Stephen—I—"

"We can discuss it in the morning, Eleanore." Fatigue was heavy in his words. "At this point I am just glad to find you in one piece."

They came to the door of her bedchamber. She turned to her brother and opened her mouth, unsure of what even to say.

"Good night," was all she could manage.

He nodded, his lips a tight line. Maybe he was just tired. But there was an edge of disappointment that dug into her heart. There was so much she wanted to tell him. To explain.

"Good night, Eleanore."

He turned and walked away.

❧

If someone had bothered to put an axe through his skull, Bastien would have been grateful for the favor.

He put his fingers to his temples in a vain effort to soothe the pounding in his head. He hadn't drunk that much in a long time, and thank God for that. He ached from head to toe, but if there had been one blessing last evening, it was that the drink had taken the edge off the pain that would have wracked his body when Lord Ellsworth and Mr. Schofield had delivered him to Barronsfield. Why on earth they hadn't dumped him on Dr. Brayden's doorstep, he had no idea. They owed him nothing. Ellsworth especially.

When he'd heard Lady Eleanore's voice and saw her enchanting face, even through the blur of the drink, he knew instantly that he would recover. And yet, that she had seen him in such a disgraceful state gnawed at him.

He sat up gingerly in his bed, situated in a sumptuous cake of a room that would even impress Tante Marie. Marie had done well, marrying an English baron. That they'd had no surviving children was one of the disappointments in her life. She'd turned her attention to Bastien then, a poor but still gently-born nephew, plucking him out of l'Hôpital des Enfants-Trouvés where he'd been abandoned. She'd arranged for him to live with some distant relation in l'Ardoise and then when he was old enough, sent him to Edinburgh to study. That he'd decided to return to France, and throw himself into the revolutionary cause hurt her greatly, no doubt. A disappointment. And it had not been easy to disappoint her. She had not loved him like a son. She had loved him in the way of the great mentors—helping him seize the opportunities where he could excel. She expected greatness, or at least goodness. He had given her neither.

Using the bedpost for support, he pulled himself to his feet and waited a moment to steady. He still wore only the shirt they'd given him last night, his own clothes gone. He needed strong coffee and lots of it. The pain he could deal with—he was prepared to pay a little penance for his utter stupidity. Why he'd let these Englishmen get under his skin, he had no idea. They were often so goddamn smug. They'd had their civil war. Their king had lost his head, and then, tiring after a decade of puritanical zeal, they brought another back. A Scottish king, hiding in France. It was all a dim history to them. Whether all the bloodshed in France would end in a similar way, he had no idea. And he didn't care anymore who won or lost. All he cared about was exacting his revenge on Le Veneur Rouge.

If there was one possible highlight to the evening, it was that the Red Hunter may have played his hand too soon, confirming his presence in the town. Bastien had managed to garner his attention—a test of sorts. He would have to be exceedingly careful. Hopefully Ellsworth would find some news.

But before he could do either of those things, he needed his trousers.

He reached for the pull, hoping some poor soul could track down his clothes, when there was a knock at the door followed by the click of the latch.

The door swung open. In the doorframe was Lady Eleanore's ancient butler, carrying a silver tray and what smelled like a full pot of coffee.

"Good morning, sir." He walked in and placed the tray on a table near the hearth and poured a cup. Bless the man.

"Bonjour," Bastien replied, ignoring the ache in his head. He studied the man's gait. "Did you get the treatments I recommended?"

Hanley nodded, a little too stiffly for Bastien's liking. It took a liar to know one.

"I hope so," Bastien prodded. "They will take a few weeks to work to good effect. Perhaps I should check in with you in a few days."

"That is not required, sir," the butler replied. "I am quite capable of seeing to it."

"I would never doubt your capability in any manner," Bastien replied. "I have heard tales of your service. You are, I believe, quite the legend."

The older man's lips turned up ever so slightly along the edges, but he said nothing.

"You would not have seen the rest of my clothes by chance?" Bastien continued. "I have imposed long enough."

"I think your duties can wait just a little while longer, Mr. DuMont. But perhaps a robe might be in order."

The commanding voice coming from behind the butler took Bastien off guard. He straightened, his attention snapping to the doorway, where a well-dressed gentleman, older than Bastien, stepped into the room. He found himself being wrapped in a thick velvet dressing gown Hanley had pulled out of the dresser. Bastien recognized the man instantly.

Lord Barronsfield had returned. And he was most definitely not happy.

"Thank you Hanley," Lord Barronsfield acknowledged. "Please give my regards to the kitchen for the excellent biscuits."

Hanley nodded, gave Bastien an ever-so-slight grin, then left.

"I keep insisting he retire, but he refuses, despite my offer of a pension and a cottage. I don't know what we would do without him."

"He has an arthritic ankle, your Hanley," Bastien said, gesturing to the butler who'd disappeared on the other side of the door. "He dismisses it, of course. I have prescribed him a therapy but I suspect he is not taking it."

Lord Barronsfield cocked an eyebrow, and pursed his lips as if in thought.

"He is a proud man. I will find a respectful way to broach the subject." He grabbed a biscuit, sat down, and motioned for Bastien to do the same. "Please, Mr. DuMont. These are a wonderful antidote to some of the more inconvenient side effects of overindulgence."

Bastien paused, wary of Lord Barronsfield's manner, before accepting the man's invitation. He sat, took a cup of coffee, and drank it down without milk or sugar. It was dark and bitter, and he savored it. Bastien suspected that Lord Barronsfield's return must have had something to do with Lady Eleanore's flight from London. That he'd arrived to discover he was entertaining a bruised, hungover, uninvited houseguest under the same roof as his sister was no doubt contributing to his somewhat sour disposition.

"I had no idea that when I agreed to this plan of Hamilton's I'd be entertaining a spy who'd found himself on the losing side of a public house row," Lord Barronsfield said, his manner brisk. "I did not suspect this was a normal part of your methods, though Edmund did warn me you could be somewhat unorthodox in how you handled your affairs. Tell me—how goes your progress on this matter of finding his kidnappers?"

Bastien knew that for Lord Barronsfield, Bastien's sole value had been in saving his cousin's life.

"Not as well as I had hoped. But I might have some new information coming to me. Lord Ellsworth has offered me his assistance."

"Ellsworth?" Bastien wasn't certain if Lord Barronsfield was impressed or suspicious of Bastien's claim. "He told me you accused him of being your Red Hunter."

"At the time, he seemed a very likely suspect. He is, of course, the heir to the Dukedom of Weymouth. And that he was here, hiding from society—he seemed to be the obvious target."

The marquess shook his head. "I've known the man since he was in swaddling clothes, DuMont. He's incapable of that level of deception. Or interest in earthly matters, to be honest. He's too busy dabbling with his lenses and telescopes. Even his poor father has had the devil of a time getting him ready for his role."

Bastien thought back to the moment he'd confronted Ellsworth. The stack of letters from he held on to, from a woman he could not free himself of. And it occurred to him that despite Ellsworth's status in society, there was little respect for the man himself.

"Of course I was wrong. But after our discussion—"

"You drew a blade on him."

Bastien shrugged. "You question my methods?"

"Only when they involve my friends."

"He has offered to investigate certain aspects of his family tree," Bastien said. "It may be helpful."

"Ellsworth has a birthmark." The marquess pointed to a spot on his own neck, near his collar. "They run through his entire family line."

Bastien let out a derisive laugh, and put a hand to his throbbing head. "I can only imagine the irony. I wouldn't be surprised if Le

Veneur Rouge had been tempted to rid himself of the taint of nobility."

"Taint?"

Bastien dropped his hand in his lap, the fatigue of the conversation catching up with him. "Only a year ago, a peasant found with such a well-known mark could have easily found himself condemned to death. That a man who spent his days hunting down others for this sin only seems like madness because you are living on this side of the Channel."

Lord Barronsfield remained silent, quiet appraisal in his looks. Unlike his sister, it was clear to Bastien that the marquess did not view everyone as a potential saint.

A knock at the door interrupted them, and Hanley reappeared.

"Excuse me, Your Lordship. Lady Eleanore is looking for you. Shall I have her wait in your study?"

Lord Barronsfield's mouth pulled into a tight line, as if the idea of meeting with her was about to give him a headache. "I will see her in the morning room. Tell her I will be down in a few moments."

Bastien shifted in his seat, watching the marquess's troubled expression.

"Lady Eleanore is quite a favorite in the community," he said, overcome with the need to speak to her character. "A remarkable woman." A passionate, beautiful woman.

Lord Barronsfield's gaze shot to Bastien, his eyes narrowing.

"That she is. She is an extraordinary young woman. I understand you treated her and kept her from over exerting herself after the injury she received from her ill-conceived voyage home." He paused, looking squarely at Bastien, who did not miss the protective edge in his voice. "I have to ask you how you managed to have her heed your advice."

Bastien shrugged. "I did nothing but remind her that she could not look after everyone else if she succumbed to her injury."

The marquess started, genuine concern in his furrowed brow. "Was it that serious?"

Bastien held up his hand, waving away Lord Barronsfield's worry.

"No. It certainly could have been. But she did need to rest. A small lie to accomplish a greater need."

"I shall have to remember that trick. Though heaven help you if she finds out," the marquess said. "And Daniel Morehouse? Schofield told me that you'd set the bones of one of my best drivers, as well as tended to several of the cottagers to everyone's satisfaction."

"Mr. Morehouse is improving. He does not like to be idle—perhaps there is another, more sedentary task he could do, that would use his wits while his bones heal." Bastien shifted in his seat, his mind turning to more personal worries. "Do you have any further news from London?"

Lord Barronsfield shook his head. "I have had no news of the baroness's condition. They must be keeping it deadly quiet, which is quite the trick in London."

"I have heard nothing save what news Hamilton sent in his last coded message to me. She was very lucky." The woman carried a dagger with her everywhere. "I would trust Hamilton to advise me if her condition had changed. I have not seen her since last summer, near Westemere. It was not safe for either of us."

"And now you are here, in my house, my sister nearby," he said.

"Which is why I intend to leave immediately," Bastien replied. "I know exactly what I am dealing with. I first discovered what had happened to the baroness when someone left me a note. It was attached to a knife thrust into the eye of some poor whoreson's body." Bastien's stomach turned at the memory.

"Why would it be so important for them to tell you about the baron—" Lord Barronsfield rose and paused, realization dawning on him. "Who is she to you? She can't be family?"

"Of a kind, yes. She is my great-aunt. And the only family I have left." Bastien paused, letting the shock of the declaration settle. "So, you see, I understand the need to protect family from this monster."

"Of course. I will make sure Hanley finds your clothes." Lord Barronsfield rose, nodded, and headed for the door. "This scuffle that nearly had you killed, do you think this was his handiwork? Do not even think of deceiving me in this matter. I have more lives than your skin to protect."

"I believe so, yes." Bastien bit off a curse. "It is possible he knows who I am. Which has him at a distinct advantage."

"You are certain of this?"

"No. But I am certain he is here. I have forced his hand." There had to be a way to use that. Tante Marie would know how. She was loud, boisterous, and entertaining. When the cock is always crowing, no one expects any meaning in the pauses. She taught him that. "I must find a way to turn disadvantage into advantage."

"I will aid your quest, on two conditions," Lord Barronsfield said.

"I am not in the habit of accepting help from others."

"I have heard. But I am indebted to you for saving Edmund's life, and I am owed the opportunity to repay it. Unless I can convince Eleanore to return to London, the sooner you find this lunatic, the better. And since I am the lord of this manor, I will get my way." He smiled then, and Bastien could not help but admire this man's authority and dedication to his family. "So I suppose that is three conditions. One. You will accept my help."

Bastien nodded. "Help" was not something he was used to, but if he wanted to end this—to stop running, to keep Tante Marie safe— then perhaps he needed to make an exception.

"Two. You continue to act as surgeon to the community." His eyes narrowed, and Bastien saw the protector.

"My skills did not leave me." His capacity for caring was another matter perhaps. But people didn't pay him for that anyway.

"Excellent. I am off to see Daniel Morehouse this morning, though Schofield told me he's doing well."

The butler appeared with Bastien's clothes, cleaned and pressed. "Mr. DuMont sir, your attire is ready. Please ring when you need assistance to be dressed."

"Merci." Bastien nodded, and smiled tightly as a fresh wave of pain rolled through his head. "I will manage on my own, thank you."

"Mr. DuMont does not wish for help Hanley—his revolutionary

morals forbid it," Lord Barronsfield replied. "Do not take it personally."

Bastien opened his mouth to protest, but thought the better of it.

"Of course, my lord," the butler replied. "And if you please, my lord, Lady Eleanore is downstairs in the morning room. She insisted on making the apple tart herself."

The mention of her name caught Bastien's attention. When he heard her voice last night, it was as if heaven itself had smiled on him. Her dogged determination to bring him aid, the concern in her brow as she watched over him, and the authority in her voice as she ensured his needs were attended to, warmed Bastien even now. Perhaps he could have been anyone, and she would have done the same. Lady Eleanore cared about people. That she saw to his care was nothing more or less than her approach to the world. But he felt cared for in a way he had not in such a long time—perhaps ever. That she was downstairs, eating breakfast—so close—and had not yet come to see him, created a curious yearning in his chest.

Lord Barronsfield's answer broke Bastien's reverie. "Excellent. Tell her I shall see her directly."

Bastien watched the door close, and turned his gaze back to the marquess, who was eyeing him closely.

"I must leave you now. Do not hurry yourself out the door. Take time to rest, settle your stomach. Wounded prey is easier to hunt— you should know that, Mr. DuMont. In some circles in London, stories of the Wolf are legendary. But I think there is one more story left for you to finish."

It was now Bastien's turn to be surprised.

"I must leave now, and see my sister. We have much to discuss."

"Of course. Before you leave, you spoke of three conditions, but we have discussed only two."

"Right. The third. My sister. Stay away from her."

CHAPTER 15

*E*leanore tried to bask in the sun streaming through the windows in the morning room, but the approaching click of her brother's footsteps robbed her of the ability to truly enjoy it. Normally she loved this room, where the family took their more informal meals together. Eleanore wished Mrs. Darling was here, as a buffer, perhaps. No. It was time for her to grow up and own her decisions. Even if they had caused such an unintentional uproar.

As the sound grew louder, however, her new found bravado began to waver. She'd hardly slept a wink last night. The look on Stephen's face when he'd found her, curled up half asleep in the room where Mr. DuMont was recovering, played on her mind. It had been part relief, part dismay, and all disappointment. A good night's sleep was impossible.

Eleanore reached out for her coffee, grasping the delicate handle of the cup, and took a long breath. She had to face him. But she also knew Stephen had never, ever, been angry with her. Indeed, he was all that one could want in a sibling.

An unwanted image of him, his face tight with worry, clouded her thoughts. There was always a first time.

The footsteps got louder, until Eleanore could no longer stand it.

She set down her cup, the porcelain rattling on the saucer, nearly spilling the contents. Pushing away from the table, she rose and hurried to meet him. She had to get this over with.

"Good morning, brother," she said, smiling far more cheerfully than was warranted.

"Eleanore." He took her by the hands and pulled her into his arms, wrapping her in a hug that threatened to make her cry with relief. They stood a moment when at last he released the embrace and looked her over. "I am not certain whether I should hug you or throttle you, but I am happy to see you."

"I am—"

"What on earth were you thinking? I've been across half the bloody country looking for you."

Eleanore's heart sank. "You went to Cheshire." Eleanore closed her eyes, heat flooding her cheeks as a stone sank in her belly. She'd initially thought to see her cousin Edmund, and then changed her mind and continued home. "I'm so sorry. Oh—this is worse than I thought."

"When I got to Silver Cross, and you hadn't arrived, I only prayed you were safe here. If Schofield's note hadn't arrived when it did, you would have had both Edmund and me standing here."

"I did not intend to cause anyone such distress."

"I have already dispatched a letter to Rosalind. She tried to convince me you must have had a good reason for running off as you did." He stood over her, pulling at the edge of his waistcoat in that way he did when he was distressed. "Now, tell me, in a way I can explain to my lovely wife who was up half the night with worry about her dear sister-in-law, why you tore away in the middle of a winter's night leaving only a note?"

"I—"

"It was foolish, Eleanore. Dangerous. You know these roads are not safe to travel, especially for a woman alone."

"Daniel—"

"Yes, I know. Daniel's lucky that he will keep his job, because I am a reasonable master who knows he was put in a precarious position by a woman of rank."

"Stephen, it was not his—"

"You could have been robbed, or worse on these roads. There could have been a terrible accident—more terrible than the one here. Again, you were lucky and so was Daniel. If Mr. DuMont wasn't here—"

"Stephen—"

"—to set Daniel's limbs and tend to your head wound. You were very—"

"Lucky. Yes. I know," she blurted out. She blinked, trying to push back her tears. He hadn't raised his voice, but it was laced with exasperation and a hint of anger. "Believe me when I say I have not felt particularly lucky of late."

It took all of Eleanore's gumption to stay where she was planted. Did he doubt her?

"And then I return to find you alone, unchaperoned, in the middle of the night with that Frenchman?"

Eleanore did not miss the edge in his voice. *That Frenchman.*

"He was hurt, Stephen. Mr. Schofield and Lord Ellsworth brought him here. I only saw to his care, just as I would have if I had been volunteering at the infirmary. Just as I would have if it had been *anyone.*"

He was unmoved. "I don't think I need to remind you, but this isn't the infirmary. And that man isn't just anyone."

"The door was open, as you no doubt saw for yourself, and the man was clearly incapacitated." She didn't dare tell him about Mr. DuMont's intent to kill Le Veneur Rouge. Or the kisses they'd shared.

"Because he'd gotten his hind quarters kicked in a public house row."

"Regardless of how he came to his condition, he needed care. He has been caring for everyone else—he deserves the same attention," she replied. "Indeed, Rosalind told me of a time when she'd done the same for you, after that time when someone poisoned you at the assembly." Her brother had nearly died that night—an ill-fated attempt to put his so-called "curse" on public display.

"That was different," Stephen said. "You are my sister. Rosalind is my wife."

"She wasn't then."

"And Bastien DuMont is definitely not like me."

Eleanore's eyebrows dipped as she puzzled through his implication. "Are you saying he's not an honorable man? Why would you agree to have someone who isn't honorable come to work with Dr. Brayden? He saved Edmund's life. Lord Ellsworth told me this himself."

"Yes, and I owe him a tremendous debt." Stephen walked away, raking a hand through his hair. "But that debt is not so heavy that you are part of the bargain. There is no debt so high that I would trade your honor or your life."

Eleanore blinked back tears at the implication, her voice barely above a whisper. "Stephen..."

His countenance softened, and opened his arms. "Come here, you silly girl."

Eleanore went to him, letting him fold her into his embrace, and at last, she let relief flow through her tears. After but a moment, she collected herself and released him.

"Perhaps we can sit, and discuss this over breakfast," she said, wiping away her tears, gesturing to the table. "And in private." There were a hundred wonderful things about being the sister of a marquess —lovely clothes, invitations to country dances, and all the paper and charcoal needed to sketch as much as she liked. But it also came with a bevy of servants who were, it seemed, everywhere. And while the awkwardness of the distinction between them had faded over time— which as the daughter of a servant herself she was keenly aware of— the feeling of being watched and listened to at every moment did not.

Stephen gestured to the footmen, and they were alone at last. He sat, and took a generous sip of coffee.

"Eleanore, my dear, we were worried, and truth be told, disappointed. The servants came to us very early the next morning, fearful you had been stolen away in the night. It wasn't until hours later we had discovered the note. We had people scouring the neighborhoods looking for you. And then to find you had left because of Lord Ramsay."

Eleanore was unable to hold back her tears, but she bucked up the courage to look her brother in the eye and meet his disappointment head on. "I couldn't marry him. I just couldn't. It was all so horrifying, and I could not think of what else to do but leave. I know I've brought scandal to the family. Lord Ramsay—"

"Eleanore." His voice lowered, calm, and he reached across the table, taking her hand in his. "Hang Lord Ramsay. If he did something to drive you away, he doesn't deserve a single moment of my attention. And you know there is nothing the London rags could say about me that hasn't already been said."

"He fathered a child with a servant," she blurted out.

Realization flickered across Stephen's brow. "I see."

"I cannot be with a man who would be unfaithful—and who would burden a poor woman so," she replied. "I shouldn't have run. I shouldn't have. But I was so—hurt. And I didn't find out from him. Not at first. He only confirmed it later." Eleanore closed her eyes, the memory of that awful moment rushing back. She could still see the sneer of condescension and undisguised glee from the harpies in the glittering ballroom—so-called gentlewomen all—as they sipped lemonade and shared with Eleanore the gossip they'd heard from below stairs. Pretending they didn't know she was Lord Ramsay's fiancé, even when it had been publicly announced. "It was made known to me in a most inappropriate manner. I confronted him about it privately, and he confirmed it. And he couldn't even understand what he'd done wrong."

"London can be a harsh, harsh place, and the marriage mart can be absolutely mercenary. Why do you think Ellsworth is hiding here in Yorkshire instead of filling up dance cards in Almack's?" He let go of her hand and began tucking into his food. "I wish Rosalind was here. She would be so much better at this than I."

"Better at what?"

"Decoding female behavior. And you may get a second opinion on the subject from her, because I expect you to write her today and explain the entire mess to her, if only to let her know you are not dead on the side of the road somewhere."

Eleanore's heart squeezed at the thought of causing her sister-in-law—and dearest friend—worry. "Of course."

"But I think she would say that the reason you have been treated so poorly by your so-called equals is because they are jealous."

"Jealous? Of me? I am a former parlor border who was miraculously transported into the shoes of a lady, but to them I do not belong. I am a servant wearing a lady's dress."

"You are every bit a lady, and then some. You have a brain in your head, and a heart larger than any person I have ever known. Your drawing is exquisite, you speak two languages, and your apple tarts are the best I have ever tasted. You are also quite pretty, if that matters to you. Although I fear you may have the Pembroke flair for self-persecution."

"You said you were disappointed in me."

"I was disappointed that you felt you could not trust to speak to me or Rosalind about this when it happened. I am disappointed you felt alone, when you have us." Stephen swallowed deeply, and grew serious. "If anyone should be disappointed, Eleanore, it's you. For over a decade I kept you at arm's length because of my fears that, as the Beast of Barronsfield, I would bring you harm. That was my own weakness not to see past the lies and inconsistencies of our uncle's scheme. I kept you from me, for no other reason than I was afraid. And perhaps that is why you chose to run home, rather than come to me. Perhaps I am disappointed in myself."

Eleanore stood and threw her arms around Stephen. "You are the most wonderful brother."

"I shall endeavor to remember that," he replied, kissing her on top of her head. "Now, enough of this. I am starving, and I understand from Hanley you were bribing me with your apple tarts. After we've had breakfast, I was going to visit Daniel Morehouse. Do you wish to come? I am eager to see the new surgeon's handiwork."

Eleanore swallowed. "He is quite capable. I had a welcome for him but a day ago. People are generally pleased with him."

"And Mr. Roderick is no doubt happy that DuMont can pay for his brandy," Stephen replied. "It was cold last night. He's lucky Ellsworth found him. Colin told me he wasn't even sure he was alive when he picked him up."

"You were speaking with Lord Ellsworth?"

"He keeps unusual hours, as you well know. I arrived home very late last night, and Colin was still up, studying his notes." Stephen took a bite of apple tart and cheese, wiping the crumbs from the corner of his mouth with his thumb. "Mr. DuMont told me the rest this morning."

Eleanore blinked. She could imagine that conversation. "You spoke to him? Please tell me you are not going to send him away."

Stephen wiped the corner of his mouth with a napkin and cocked an eyebrow. Eleanore stifled a groan. She knew that look.

"You take an uncommon interest in his well-being."

"Not uncommon." Completely, utterly uncommon actually, though she did not wish to own it. Besides, she needed him—for her foundling home. "I have asked his opinion about a little project I am working on. He has some particular expertise that I think will be very valuable."

"What little project is this, pray?"

Eleanore swallowed a bit of her breakfast, and forced a smile. She was not ready to discuss it.

"We can discuss it another time perhaps—it is nothing of consequence."

"Eleanore, my dear," Stephen replied, earnestness in his tone, "when it comes to you, everything is of consequence."

"I was just thinking it could wait until dinner." *When I find my nerve,* she added to herself. "After you've had a chance to rest, visit Daniel, and see to whatever other affairs you need."

He nodded, apparently satisfied with her response. "Very well. But I warn you Eleanore, I want you to stay away from Bastien DuMont."

The warning in his voice took her off guard.

"Do you have a particular concern about him?" Besides the fact he was dashing, occasionally infuriating and with the power to make her feel wonderful and vexed all at once?

"Just take care."

❦

HE WAS BEING DEFEATED by his damned trousers.

The Wolf, who once struck fear into the noble hunters on the highways between l'Ardoise and Calais, who'd been under the gun of both the Home Office and Paris for his secrets and once disarmed an assassin after a long night of drinking, was now laid low by a fickle set of laces on a pair of trousers. They weren't even his. He'd stolen them from a gentleman last spring, when Bastien had been in London for a time. The man had been too busy being pleasured by his mistress to notice their disappearance.

The bastards had done a superior job with him last night, he had to admit, if lacing up his own trousers was far more work than it should have been. Of course, that his head was still foggy and his stomach weak was his own damned fault. Both conditions, however, had been notably lessened by Lord Barronsfield's offerings of strong coffee and ginger biscuits, though another day's rest was what his body required.

Clearly his capacity to deal with punishment—self-inflicted or otherwise—was not what it was. If he kept this up, he would be dead before he was thirty—an age he would see if he survived the year. There were far too many days when he felt twice that old.

He sat down, damn trousers still loose at his waist, and poured himself another cup of coffee. It had cooled but he drank it down anyway and savored the bitterness. Coffee used to be his favorite drink—it reminded him of the heady days when he was little more than eighteen and sat in coffee houses in Edinburgh, between lectures, full of ideals and passion about the world. Now, more than ten years later, he barely recognized that version of himself. There was little he cared about now. His struggles were more modest. Like getting his

169

trousers laced. There was only one thing that drove him—finding Le Veneur Rouge. And killing him if he had to.

Lady Eleanore still had passion. Perhaps she didn't want to change the world, but she certainly wanted to improve her corner of it. But there was an element of restraint—of fear. Of what, it was difficult to say. But it was fear that had driven her from London. Was she so afraid of judgment from her so-called peers? He could scarce imagine anyone her equal.

A knock roused him from his thoughts. They probably sent someone up to dress him. Damn it all, he probably needed the help.

"Un moment, s'il vous plaît." He swallowed, stood, steadied himself, and managed to get his fingers to work well enough to get his trousers fastened. "Come in."

The door opened and Lady Eleanore stood before him, a servant beside her. He recognized her as Allison, Daniel's sweetheart. She placed a tray down where the coffee and biscuits had been, scooped up the coffee pot, then disappeared as quietly as she'd come in.

Lady Eleanore smiled at him, and he forced himself a little straighter, buoyed by her appearance.

"Good morning, Mr. DuMont," she said, her eyes bright. "How are you feeling this morning?"

"A little sore, but I will manage, thanks to Lord Ellsworth." His gaze darted toward the door. "What are you doing here, my lady? I suspect your brother would be eager to finish off the job those ruffians had started if he found you with me."

"He's gone to see Daniel. And I'm not staying long. I simply wanted to make certain you were feeling better," she replied. "I would think you should still be abed, Mr. DuMont."

Bastien couldn't help himself. He raised an eyebrow—which hurt like hell—and smiled. "I am sure you do."

Her face colored a delicious shade of pink, but she recovered quickly. "When I injured myself, far less than you are now, you sent me to bed for three days. I fail to see the difference in that prescription between you and me."

"You are, perhaps, correct. But I cannot spare myself the time. You, my lady, are valuable to many people in this community. I am not."

"Mr. DuMont, surely to heaven there is someone out there who cares for you?"

Was there? Tante Marie, yes. But as he looked at Lady Eleanore's flaxen hair, like a halo around her face, for just a moment, he hoped it might have been her. "I am not as valuable as you make me out to be."

"But what about Daniel, and the others? The people of this neighborhood who have come to rely on you?" Lady Eleanore replied. "Why, when I spoke to Mrs. Waterstone she shared her high regard of you. And I...would not want to see any harm come to you."

His heart jumped then. He wanted to believe her words. But it was easier not to.

"Because you do not wish to see harm come to anyone," he grumbled.

"That's not true," she protested. "My uncle was a wicked man, and I felt no remorse when he died, wretched soul that he was. Despite what you may think, I am not a saint, Mr. DuMont." She looked away, a smile creeping on her face. "In fact, there are a few ladies I met in London who could stand a bit of comeuppance. Though, perhaps, more damaging to their pride than their bodies."

The idea of Lady Eleanore doing anything that was even the smallest bit untoward amused him. "I could help with that."

She tilted her head ever so slightly, her eyes raking over him as she crossed her arms. "I am certain you can. My brother said he didn't trust you completely. I wonder why that is."

"And yet, here you are," he challenged.

A curious pause filled the room. Both of them knew she should not be here. And despite her claims she was checking on the state of his injuries, Bastien could not help but wonder if something else had drawn her to him.

She cleared her throat, the noise cutting through some of the tension between them.

"I am sorry to hear of your patient. You mentioned it, last night. I don't know if you remember."

Bastien swallowed, a wave of nausea rising once again. Truthfully he could not recall much of the evening after he'd landed on the cold ground not far from Roderick's inn. He shook his head, not daring to speak.

She tilted her head, her brow furrowing slightly. "Is this why you were foxed last night?"

"Of course not," Bastien grimaced and turned away, unwilling to face her. "A man is entitled to get into his cups now and then." It was a miserable lie.

She took a few steps forward and reached out, putting a hand on his cheek. "It hurts you."

He stepped away, unwilling to bear the comfort of her touch. He didn't deserve it. "I'm a surgeon, mademoiselle," he said, bitterness flowing through him. "Do you know how many people I have had die in my care? More than you care to imagine."

"And it kills you a little bit every time."

Oui.

"No," he lied. "There are limitations to the science. To our methods. It is the way of it. The physicians are no better. Maybe worse."

"You are a horrible liar, Mr. DuMont."

Enough. He couldn't abide this. He grabbed his waistcoat from a nearby chair, a coin falling out of the pocket, rolling onto the floor. He picked it up. The farthing that had been pressed into his hands by a grieving father.

"What is that?" Eleanore asked.

"A donation," he said, his voice thick with emotion. He placed it in the palm of her hand, wrapping her fingers over the coin, savoring the soft touch of her skin. "For your foundling home."

She looked at the coin, then to him, in a way that made him most uncomfortable. It wasn't pity. That would have been intolerable. It was just…empathy.

"Thank you," she said. She rose to leave, which made him want to call her back, as if spending another moment without her was somehow unbearable. But she had no reason to stay, and he had no reason to beg her company. At least, none he cared to own.

She took a few steps, then paused and turned around. "You said a curious thing last night."

"Did I?" Bastien buttoned up his waistcoat, his body still stiff. That he'd probably made an utter fool of himself was something he wanted to forget. "Any drunken confessions of your beauty were not exaggerated."

His attempt at comedy had no effect. Her expression remained one of utter seriousness.

"You said you were here to kill a man."

Of course he said that. He'd been on a streak of rabid incompetency...why should he stop? "I was probably rambling about my patient last night."

She shook her head. "Perhaps. Did you treat a man known as Le Veneur Rouge?"

Merde.

"No idea."

"I see," she said, and for once, Bastien feared that she did, in fact, see right through him. He never realized he was so transparent. Or perhaps, except for Tante Marie, he'd never spent time with someone who seemed to read him so well.

"My brother has told me to stay away from you, which is an odd command given he was the one who brought you here. And because of everything you did for Edmund."

"It is probably because you are the sibling of a marquess, and I," he gestured to himself with a flourish, "most certainly am not."

"Half-sister, as you well know, and Stephen doesn't give a wit about those things."

"He should. You have a considerable fortune, no doubt. You need a man who doesn't require yours to get by." Bastien's mind went to the situation of Lady Gwyneth, who had become Edmund's wife. Her life was almost ended because of her wealth—and a devious plot to get it. "He is protecting you from those who would want you for your wealth alone."

"I am not like Gwyneth," she replied, as if reading his mind. "Of course that's a concern. But I think if an honorable man asked for my hand, and had not my fortune, it wouldn't matter." Her shoulders slumped a bit, and she saddened.

"What is the matter?"

"Nothing," she said, brightening, but Bastien could tell at once that she was masking another, darker emotion. "I was just thinking that Stephen's concerns were not about my fortune. You saved Edmund."

She looked at him anew, as if a connection was made. One that was making him uncomfortable.

"Your cousin had a history of getting in over his head. Lady Gwyneth was testament to that."

She crossed her arms. "Really? How do you know?"

"How did I know what?" Bastien said, his head growing cloudy. He put his fingers to his temples. "Perhaps we can finish this intriguing conversation about your hapless cousin another time. He is content now, and making his wife fat with child."

"How did you know that Edmund had a long history of getting himself into trouble?"

Merde.

"You were a spy, weren't you?"

"Lady Eleanore, I—"

"No." Her eyes widened, and she broke into a smile, like a person who'd just solved the last piece of a puzzle. "You *are* a spy."

Merde. Merde. Merde.

"You have an incredibly excitable imagination, Lady Eleanore," he said, trying to deflect her conclusions. "Perhaps you should stop drawing pictures and write fairy stories instead. About spies and foundlings. I am sure it would be charming."

"Maybe I will," she said, suddenly pleased with the notion. "The babies will all grow up happy, and the spy will capture the villain and find his one true love."

"I am too dashing to be a spy. Good spies are bland. Like Edmund."

"You don't look terribly dashing at the moment," she said playfully. "This all makes sense now. Stephen didn't bring you here to help with the infirmary because you saved Edmund."

"You keep saying that," he protested. "Lady Gwyneth saved your cousin. Probably in more ways than one. I merely provided the opportunity. I am no hero. My head hurts. You need to go."

She tilted her head in a way that he was coming to find both exasperating and yet intoxicating. "You can't send me away just because you know I'm right."

"I'm sending you away because I feel like I've been trounced by a quarter horse and I would enjoy a shred of dignity to suffer alone, as I finish getting dressed and take my leave."

"You can't go back there, not today. Not in this condition."

"I have patients to see."

"I was hurt far less than you are now, and you made me stay in for three days."

"That's because you're a woman."

She crossed her arms. "Nonsense. Women have babies one day and are back on their feet the next. Do not tell me about the delicate constitution of women, monsieur. You cannot adequately serve your patients when you are in this state. And even though you tell me you are not a spy, the truth of the matter is, whoever you made cross last night might decide they aren't finished with you. I will address this with my brother."

She had a point. Not that he was going to publicly agree with her.

"Besides," she continued, walking toward the door, "perhaps once you've recovered a bit more, you can tell me your thoughts on the plans I have given you. We could discuss it at dinner, if you are feeling up to it."

Lady Eleanore had her grip solidly on the door handle. She was leaving? Bastien willed himself to stand still, searching his mind for any reason he could give her to stay.

"I do not have anything appropriate to wear," he said. If he could have kicked himself for his idiocy, he would have. He couldn't remember the last time he had worried about his attire, and certainly never because he was dining with "quality." So what if they were peers of the realm? This wasn't his realm. But it had the desired effect. Her hand dropped back to her side.

"But that is of no matter," she answered, as if reading his mind. "I know my brother is not bothered by such things. I am certain we can find something here for you to wear. I will speak to Hanley about it."

"Of course," he replied. *Just let her go.* He had plans to make. "Thank you."

The ache in his shoulder, coupled with the pounding in his head, bested him. "If you will excuse me, Lady Eleanore, perhaps I will take the opportunity to rest before dinner." He held out his arm and reached for the chair beside him. A shot of pain ripped through his arm, and it buckled. He bit back a curse. He began to tumble forward when he felt someone catch him.

"Here you go." She guided him back toward the chair. "Quickly now. I'm not that strong." She helped him settle in the chair, her arm still wrapped around one side of him. She slowly started to disentangle herself, and left one arm resting on him while she examined him. Their gazes locked, and he reached out, transfixed, and ran his finger along her cheek, tracing her jaw. "Better?" she continued, her voice growing softer.

He nodded, and looked up to see her hovering only a few inches away. Through the rush of discomfort, a second sensation—pure, heady desire—followed. He was still holding on to her, still sensing the heat of her skin beneath her muslin gown, catching the scent of lavender in her hair.

What beautiful skin. Soft, inviting. Her breath caught as his fingers traced their way down her neck, to her shoulder, heightening his own desire. Her lips—soft, full and pink—were there for the tasting.

"I can think of a better treatment," he said, his voice low.

And he tasted them. Gently, with soft, teasing strokes, until a small sigh escaped her. Her hand, still wrapped around his arm, tightened its grip, and he thrilled as he felt her pulling him closer to her. Her lips parted. Accepting her invitation, he kissed more deeply, hungrily. He was aware of her fingers lacing through his hair—a most heady sensation—and he wanted to do the same. Wanted to pull down her hair, free it from the pins and baubles that adorned it and see it lay, like gold lace, over her bare shoulders, skimming over what he was certain were perfect breasts.

Breasts that he would never see. He didn't deserve them. Didn't deserve her kiss. Her soft skin. Or the way she shook her head at him when he said something she clearly didn't agree with. She was an angel. He was the Wolf. He didn't want just a kiss from her. He wanted far more. And before his lust could devour her, he broke the kiss.

"Your brother told me to stay away from you," he said, his voice still thick with desire. "And he was right."

She hovered there a moment, her lips deliciously plump, frustration clearly warring with her senses. Then she stood, ramrod straight, and backed away. She put her hands to her cheeks, then crossed her arms in front of her and walked toward the door, barely able to look at him.

"I will send one of the footmen in to help you. And then you should rest. You don't want to be worn out. You still have patients to see."

She looked over her shoulder but once, then fled.

CHAPTER 16

*E*leanore ran to her bedchamber and paced the floor before sinking down on her bed. What on earth was she thinking? Rushing off to see Mr. DuMont the moment Stephen left the house? And not only was he half dressed, but she let him kiss her. Until she decided to kiss him back, of course.

She buried her face in her hands and shook her head. Nervous energy swirled through her body.

She'd kissed a man—and not just any man. She'd kissed that French ne'er do well who was hell-bent on getting himself killed tracking down the Red Hunter. Of course he was handsome, but he was also trouble. Beautiful, dark, handsome trouble.

And the worst part of it all is that she enjoyed every tantalizing, teasing minute of it.

She fell back on the bed, gazing up at the patterned ceiling, and sighed. She replayed the kiss in her head, and each time, warm tingles twirled through her body. She could have so easily fallen prey to her own carnal desires; desires she had not fully known until Bastien DuMont walked into her life.

She sat up, a horrid, horrid thought side swiping her, driving every last drop of pleasure from her body.

Was this how it had been for her mother? Had she been swept away by a handsome man, a man she couldn't have?

Eleanore wasn't destined for a fairy tale. She wasn't like Stephen, or even Edmund. Her mother wasn't a lady. Her parents may have had deeper feelings for each other, but it hadn't made it possible for them to be together. It hadn't saved her mother from going to an early grave.

Eleanore had received several proposals of marriage and none of them, until Lord Ramsay, had felt like more than a business transaction, which so many marriages were. With Lord Ramsay, she had talked herself into the notion she could fall in love with him. He was handsome, his manners had been perfect, and he could, when the moment was right, almost make Eleanore laugh. In the end, he'd been far more accomplished at making her cry.

No. She hadn't really cried when she discovered the truth. She'd just felt...empty. And humiliated. Humiliation for herself, for her family. Fairy tales didn't end like that. But her story certainly had. And with her very public broken engagement, it was unlikely that another suitor would come calling. It hadn't bothered her. Not until Bastien DuMont had come into her life.

She hopped off the bed and rushed to the tall armoire in her room. The doors creaked as she opened them and, pushing aside skirts of linen and silk, she pulled a simple wooden box from a shelf inside. On it were carved two initials: S.M.

Sally Martin.

Eleanore carried it back to her bed, carefully opening the box. Inside were a few of her mother's ribbons, a rattle, and a small locket with a piece of her hair set under a sliver of glass. This, aside from a few letters from her father, was all that Eleanore knew about the woman who had given birth to her, and cared for her for the first few years of her life. There was no portrait hanging in the halls. Not even a miniature.

The clock on the mantle struck the hour. Eleanore frowned, then tucked away the contents and placed it back in its safe place in the cupboard. The heat from Mr. DuMont's kiss had faded, but Eleanore knew all she had to do was close her eyes and she could feel the sensation of his mouth on hers. It felt good. And bad. But mostly good. And it shouldn't.

Mr. DuMont had to be a spy. He had to be. Eleanore frowned, vexed at the idea that Stephen knew all about Mr. DuMont. Bastien DuMont had tried to throw her off, but it made everything—his interest in Lord Ellsworth, his appearance in Elmsdale, and Stephen's reaction to him—make sense. He was here to kill someone. Why? Why would a man who'd clearly filled with sorrow at the loss of a patient feel the need to take a life?

Did Stephen know? He clearly knew why Bastien was here, but there was so much the Frenchman kept carefully hidden away from everyone.

Le Veneur Rouge. The Red Hunter.

She wanted to ask Stephen about it, but he was still out, no doubt speaking with Mr. Schofield about business and the estate. It was unlikely he'd welcome the question, and given everything that had happened of late, she was loathe to raise it. Not today.

Eleanore idly picked up one of her older sketch books from its place on a small shelf in her room, sat down on her bed, and flipped through the pages. In it were scenes of Elmsdale—the infirmary, the vicarage, Oliver's. The world she loved—full of its comings and goings, its gossip and people. Even Mrs. Waterstone. She'd captured a decent likeness of her as she sat in Oliver's one rainy afternoon. Indeed, as she looked through the pages, she realized she'd captured much of Elmsdale. Since coming to Barronsfield, she'd become ever more involved in the community comings and goings. She knew people.

Did she know the Red Hunter?

Maybe she did.

LATER THAT MORNING, Eleanore hopped out of the carriage, the Yorkshire sky a beautiful blue. Her red cape fell heavy on her shoulders, sheltering her from winter's bite. Clear skies meant cold days, but the clear air also invigorated her weary body and cleared her mind. She gave instructions to the driver to return home, as the weather was good and despite the chill, the walk back to Barronsfield would no doubt help chase away any lingering feelings that had been plaguing her since Mr. DuMont's kiss.

A small basket in her hand, her secondary motive was to visit Oliver's and pick up some of his famous chocolate drops, which were Stephen's favorites. A little bribery, she thought, was never a bad thing, especially when she would tell him about her ideas for a foundling home.

She walked through Elmsdale's square, greeting people as she went by. Though nothing had changed, she found herself watching everything—and everyone—with a more critical eye. There was someone here who'd badly hurt Mr. DuMont. Someone who might be very dangerous. Or, at least, dangerous to Bastien DuMont.

Was he a dangerous man?

Perhaps. But not in the way Stephen had suggested. Even Mr. DuMont himself had insisted that he was not one of "her angels." Not a hero.

And yet, she found herself quite at odds with that notion. Indeed, there were elements of Mr. DuMont that were soft and compassionate. He was haunted. Haunted by a sadness that he buried under a brusque manner, and, occasionally, a little too much brandy. Was the kiss meant to scare her away too? Because it was having quite the opposite effect.

The inn was nearby, a steady plume of smoke rising from the chimney. While she had no reason for being there, Eleanore found herself drawn to it. This was where Mr. DuMont was discovered. She stood outside, lingering for a moment. While Mr. Roderick ran a quality establishment, walking in alone would bring her undue attention. Slowing her gait, she put her head down, watching the ground for any sign of the scuffle, when the innkeeper came out onto the steps with a black leather satchel.

"Good afternoon, Mr. Roderick!" she said, deliberately trying to be cheerful. "How are you this fine day?"

"Well enough I suppose," he replied. "I was just heading down to the infirmary."

"Are you hurt?"

He shook his head, then held out the bag. "Mr. DuMont was 'ere yesterday, and when he left, he was a little worse for wear. Forgot his doctoring supplies."

Eleanore was fascinated and held out her hand. "The infirmary is on my way. I would be happy to take it to him." Mr. Roderick handed her the bag, which was heavier than she had anticipated. She looked down at the worn case, feeling uncommonly protective of it.

She wasn't about to share with the innkeeper, or anyone, Mr. DuMont's true location. Not at the moment. But Mr. Roderick might have seen something that would give her insight into who was the source of his injuries.

"I do have a matter to speak with you about," she asked, keeping her voice low. "One that requires your discretion."

Mr. Roderick's thick eyebrows dipped, and he leaned in, the model of confidentiality. Which was not his natural state, Eleanore reminded herself. Mr. Roderick was good-hearted, a fine innkeeper, and rivaled the finest society salons when it came to gossip. Still, he was the only source she had at the moment.

"When Mr. DuMont was here, can you tell me, was he speaking to anyone in particular?"

The innkeeper's mouth turned up on one side into a conspiratorial grin. "Well now, if I might be so bold, my lady, you have quite the interest in our fair doctor."

Eleanore blinked. She was interested in Mr. DuMont. But purely for altruistic reasons—the same way she might be interested in Daniel Morehouse, or anyone else. At least, that was what she told herself.

"You are being too bold, sir." The square was full of its normal comings and goings, and she needed to be quick. "Mr. DuMont was attacked by a bunch of hooligans—at least as far as I can tell. He suffered a grievous beating just outside your establishment. I need to know if you recall anyone who might have had words with Mr. DuMont while he was here, or who might have followed him outside. He said there were at least three of them, perhaps four."

Mr. Roderick straightened, his expression serious. "Well that's shockin', that is." He put a meaty hand to his chin, then shook his head. "I can't recall seeing anything that would make me worry for him. It was a quiet evening. The only other person he was speaking to was Mr. Hugh Wakefield, and they seemed to be 'aving a pleasant conversation. No one was giving him any trouble, and he wasn't giving any. But Mr. DuMont left alone, and no one followed him."

"And you didn't hear anything?"

"No, Your Ladyship. But we had a full house last night. Hard to keep everyone in my sights."

After an exchange of pleasantries, Eleanore left the inn and walked along to the spot where, according to Mr. Schofield, he and Lord Ellsworth had discovered Mr. DuMont. During the light of day, it was open enough, but in the dark, there would have been long shadows to hide what was happening, and certainly, no one had intervened. They had dragged him to a spot where he might have simply frozen to death if he hadn't been found.

Was this attack just a random thing, fueled by alcohol and the petty squabbles of men's pride? Or was it more than that? Given what she'd just learned about Mr. DuMont, she could not help but wonder.

"Good afternoon, Lady Eleanore," called a familiar, congenial voice. "This is a fine, if unexpected pleasure. What brings you to town on this cold day?"

Eleanore gazed up from the step to see Mr. Wakefield walking down the street. He was, as always, elegantly dressed, with a pleasant smile on his face.

"I always enjoy a brisk walk, regardless of the weather." She tilted her head in the direction of the bakery across the square. "But I admit I am using the occasion to stop by Oliver's."

Mr. Wakefield nodded, signaling his interest, which Eleanore greatly appreciated. "I hope your driver is recovering."

"Slowly, thank you. It will be some time before he is capable of walking," she replied. "We will be eager to have him back in our employ. Mr. DuMont has been greatly attentive to his recovery."

"Yes, Mr. DuMont seems to be an excellent addition to the infirmary." He paused, then glanced around the square, as if collecting his thoughts. Then he turned back to her, his eyes, sharper than they were but a moment ago. "Interesting, don't you think, that such a small area would have a doctor and a surgeon handy. Most towns several times this size would not be so fortunate to have such a wealth of talent at their disposal."

Eleanore could not quite point to it, but there was something about his insinuation that put her on her guard, and she found herself eager to throw off any hint of suspicion. "Well, Mr. Wakefield, most villages are not fortunate enough to have an infirmary nor a physician they do not need to pay for," she said with a smile. "In truth, it was my brother's plan. He is interested in being able to provide fully for the people in the area. And, with Dr. Brayden away, it provides a measure of comfort."

Mr. Wakefield pursed his lips, as if considering the idea, then nodded mostly to himself, before turning his attention back to Eleanore. "Excellent thinking, indeed. Though, the poor doctor seems to have left his supplies behind." He gestured at Mr. DuMont's leather satchel in her hand.

"Yes. I am taking it to him."

"You should not have to trouble yourself," he replied. "Allow me to do you the favor. A lady should not have to do manual labor."

"I think this lady is quite capable of a little physical exercise, which is no doubt beneficial." She found herself clutching the bag a bit more tightly, holding it underneath the folds of her cape. "And it is no trouble, though I do appreciate your concern. I intend to consult with Mr. DuMont today about the state of my driver."

"Of course," Mr. Wakefield said, nodding smartly. "Allow me as well to congratulate you on a most engaging afternoon yesterday. I have been considering your initiative to create a foundling hospital. Allow me to make a contribution."

Eleanore put a hand to her chest, thrilled at the news. "That is most gracious of you, Mr. Wakefield! I had hoped, but certainly had no expectations, of your support." A weight lifted off her shoulders. Mr. Wakefield was a very successful entrepreneur, and a very influential one. That he might see the value in her idea gave her hope that others would follow.

"The well-being of my fellow man is always a concern, Lady Eleanore. And your impassioned plea has convinced me. Innocents should not be condemned because of the ill-conceived action of another."

Eleanore couldn't help but smile. This was the type of person England needed. Feeling. Caring. Understanding that there was reward in helping. "Thank you, Mr. Wakefield! That is most generous. The idea is still in its infancy, but I have already created some plans as to how the home will function. I am happy at any time to share those with you. Indeed, you might—"

Mr. Wakefield smiled, and held up his gloved hand. "I trust you implicitly, Lady Eleanore. A woman of your particular background has uncommon insight," he replied. "Please tell me how to do your bidding, and it will be done. I will instruct my solicitor to deliver a notice to you directly. And I hope you were able to secure a donation from Lord Ellsworth as well. He does us quite the honor to visit this area of the country."

"Indeed, he is visiting with my brother, who has also returned from London, and taking advantage of our clear skies to work on his scientific studies." she replied. "But I was very appreciative of his presence. His support, along with yours, I hope will encourage others."

"Scientific studies?" Mr. Wakefield shook his head, and smiled, though there was a touch of restraint in his manner. "Would it that we could all be so idle. I could not."

"Each of us has our passions, Mr. Wakefield."

"That we do." He paused, pursed his lips, then nodded. "The air is cold and I do not wish to keep you longer. I bid you good day. I look forward to hearing more about the progress with your little project." He tipped his hat and continued down the road.

Eleanore watched him go before continuing along toward Oliver's, torn between elation at Mr. Wakefield's decision to contribute to the foundling hospital and his probing questions about Mr. DuMont's presence in the community. Then again, perhaps she was being over-sensitive. Since Mr. DuMont's arrival, she'd fielded dozens of questions about him, many far more intrusive than Mr. Wakefield's had been.

It seemed the more she knew about Mr. DuMont, the more she wanted to know. Was it simple curiosity? She picked up her pace, suddenly eager to finish her tasks and hurry home. And, now that she had recovered his bag, she should return it.

Except Stephen had told her to stay away from him. Still, he couldn't deny the surgeon his tools, could he? What if he needed them?

Eleanore nodded, her body buoyed by a curious sort of lightness and excitement. Anticipation, perhaps. A sort of anticipation she had not ever felt, she realized, when she was with Lord Ramsay. And it was different than the kind when she was with Stephen and Rosalind, or even when she'd meet Edmund after his long absences from Barronsfield.

It must be fascination. That was all. Mr. DuMont was new, and he was different. And maybe he was a spy.

Or maybe it was something more. But it couldn't be. She was not meant for a fairy tale.

CHAPTER 17

*B*astien squared his shoulders, which, like all the other muscles in his body, were still tight and sore after his beating. He stood outside the door of Lord Barronsfield's study, where he'd been summoned. He wanted nothing more than to lie down somewhere and rest.

No. He didn't want to lie down just anywhere.

He wanted to be home. Wherever that was. Home, stretched out in front of a warm fire, a good glass of brandy in his hand. Watching Lady Eleanore as she sketched—the concentration in her eyes, her fingers as they gripped the edge of the pencil as she made little marks across the page.

This home was beautiful, but it engulfed her. Not that she didn't deserve a home fit for a princess, as the grand Barronsfield Manor clearly was. But she needed to shine.

He knocked, then opened the door and walked in. There, sitting around a small hearth was Lord Barronsfield and Lord Ellsworth.

"Come, DuMont," Lord Barronsfield said, standing and gesturing to a chair. "Can you stomach a cognac, or would you prefer something easier?"

"Non, merci," he said. He walked toward Lord Ellsworth, and bowed his head. "I owe you a considerable debt, monsieur."

"You look miserable enough at the moment to have repaid it, DuMont," the man replied. "But I'll keep it in my ledger, just in case."

DuMont nodded, acknowledging that Ellsworth no doubt felt a small matter of satisfaction at his current state of discomfort. Perhaps they were even.

Lord Barronsfield sat back in his chair. "We have some news."

"You heard from Hamilton?" Bastien stood fast, bracing himself for the news that things had turned for the worse for Tante Marie. "Tell me. What about the old woman?"

Lord Barronsfield exchanged a glance with Ellsworth. "Are you referring to Baroness D'Anville?"

Bastien nodded, impatient. "The old woman" had become a term of affection for her over the years. "Has her condition changed?"

"This came for me but an hour ago, though I suspect you should be the true recipient of it." The marquess held up a letter, clearly written in Hamilton's hand, which Bastien snatched out of his fingers and paced the room. Composed as nothing more than a friendly missive between acquaintances, Bastien scanned it to decode its meaning. "From what I can tell, she is improving. Hamilton is clear on that point."

Bastien scanned the lines and let go a breath he didn't realize he had been holding. Her wound was healing, and there had been no signs of fever. He kept reading, more intently. Apparently, Hamilton had another suspect he was watching, in London. Bastien turned the information over, uncertain what to think. He studied the note for some time before he realized the two peers were waiting for him to divulge more.

"There is a second person of interest being watched in London. Hamilton urges me to remain and continue my search until I hear otherwise." He looked up at Ellsworth. "The baroness also continues to insist that The Hunter is a lost prince of Weymouth."

He walked to the hearth, and dropped the note into the fire. Evidence was a liability.

"I wrote to my father after we spoke," Ellsworth began, "but I have not yet heard any word. I warn you that he might be reticent to speak of it, though I impressed upon him the serious nature of my request."

Bastien settled carefully into a nearby chair, and pointed to Ellsworth's shoulder. "I understand that birthmark on your neck is common in your family. Is it?"

"Common enough. My father does not bear it, but his sister does as do several of my cousins. It varies somewhat, but it is generally to be found in the same area."

"Unless you propose to conduct a search of all males over a certain age, I am not sure what we can do," Lord Barronsfield said. "That is not exactly common knowledge."

Bastien paused. If only Dr. Brayden was here. If anyone might have insight into such knowledge, it would be him. But then, maybe he did. Bastien just needed to find it.

"Perhaps not common, but your doctor may have known."

Bastien thought back to that conversation he'd had with the good doctor, not long after their meeting. They were in his study, at his home. *Every birth, even every death. There is always something to learn.*

The physician's words rang through Bastien's head. At the time, he had scoffed at the man's tedious attention to his note taking. Thought it foolish. If anyone had been the fool, it was Bastien.

"I don't understand," Lord Barronsfield said. "Why would the doctor know who the Red Hunter is?"

"He wouldn't. But his clinical notes are very detailed. If anyone bearing such a remarkable birth mark had been under his care, he might have noted it," he explained. "Or not. Stork bites are not uncommon. But it is the best possibility at the moment."

Bastien stood too fast, and let out an involuntary hiss of air as his muscles protested.

"I'm not certain you are in the best condition to be doing this," Lord Barronsfield said. "It can wait until morning."

"I have been in worse situations than this, thank you," Bastien replied. "If I have been unmasked, then I am working against time. He either suspects and will attack, or he will run. I will risk the first."

"Very well," Lord Barronsfield said, as he and Ellsworth rose. "I will send a carriage to take you back to Dr. Brayden's home. But be careful. Indeed, I might insist that you return here tonight. It might be safer, all things considered."

"Or it might give me away. No, my lord, I thank you for your hospitality, but this is mine to do. Mine to finish."

He nodded to Lord Barronsfield, then held out a hand to Lord Ellsworth. "I am in your debt, my lord."

Ellsworth paused, then reached out. "You're lucky you didn't vomit all over my good boots. The price would have gotten considerably higher." They shook hands. "If I receive any news, I will contact you immediately."

An hour later, Bastien arrived back at Dr. Brayden's abode. Happily there were no patients waiting for him. If he'd found he'd been needed while he was lying on his backside recovering from a drunken rout...

Why did this bother him?

The servant had already lit the lanterns and stoked the fire in the study. He began rooting through the shelf that held the physician's notebooks. Bastien grabbed the most recent one, a small, brown, leather-bound volume, and began flipping through the pages which were filled with Brayden's meticulous scribblings and some sketches the physician had clearly done himself. He scanned the pages, and it soon became apparent this was going to take much longer than he'd like.

He started to read a bit more quickly. He flipped a page, and a folded piece of paper fell out from between the binding. This drawing, one of a mother suckling her newborn babe, was clearly drawn by a different hand than Brayden's clinical drawings. This one had a certain tenderness to it. It was unsigned, but he knew instinctively this was Lady Eleanore's work.

Dr. Brayden's clinical notes were a treasure trove of information; more than a catalogue of the patients he had seen, they contained insights into the causes of the maladies, and the efficacy of his treatments. Some of his theories even seemed to confound and conflict with the current state of medical knowledge. In amongst those notes were a handful of mentions of patients who bore red marks similar to that of Lord Ellsworth—but in one case it was borne by an infant, and another was an older gentleman who'd died nearly three years prior.

Bastien lit a candle and continued poring over the notes, but he found his mind wandering. He'd been at it for an hour, and thus far, there was not even the hint of a birthmark mentioned on anyone over the age of three. Perhaps he was chasing nothing more than a ghost. There was no way to know if Tante Marie's lost prince of Weymouth did indeed bear a mark similar to Ellsworth.

The creak of the front door interrupted his thoughts, and truthfully, he was grateful for it. He was growing tired, as the fitful sleep he'd had last night, coupled with the pounding he'd been given, was taking its toll.

"Hello?"

The sound of her voice drove away his fatigue. He rose, pushing the book aside, and rushed out the door to meet her.

"Bonjour."

She stood in the doorway, wrapped up in her woolen cape, the dark red folds unable to obscure her beauty. Lightness crept into Bastien's heart at the sight of her.

"The servant let me in. I hope I am not disturbing you."

"What brings you here? Or are you determined to have your brother kill me?" He smiled, a miserable attempt at a joke.

She stepped forward, her steps tentative at first. "I hadn't expected you to be here, but when I was at the Darlings I noticed the carriage go by from their parlor." She frowned. "He didn't make a fuss, did he?"

"No." He shook his head. "I simply had work to be done." He left it at that.

"Well then, you should have this." She held out her hand, her gloved fingers wrapped around the handle of his black leather bag. He took it, his hand lingering a moment next to hers.

An unexpected relief flooded him at its return. "Where was it? I assumed it was lost." The weight of it felt good in his hand. He had bought it himself, while he was still in school. Over the years it had been tossed aside. Now it held tools of both his trades. That of surgeon. And that of the Wolf.

"Mr. Roderick gave it to me. He was quite concerned about you when he discovered what had happened."

"When were you at the inn?"

"I happen to be coming into town to do some errands, and to get some fresh air after our discussion." She smiled, blood flushing her cheeks. Was she thinking of their kiss? Her reaction brought a smile to his face, and a warring bout of sensations to his body. Delight. Desire. Desire not just for the touch of her skin, or the softness of her lips. But something more.

Did she care about him? Because something was there, in Bastien's awareness. Something new. Perhaps a bit protective.

"I asked him if he had noticed anyone follow you out," she continued. "He hadn't, by the way."

Much of the night had been a blur. "I am not your concern, my lady."

"Eleanore."

Her response came out in a breathless rush.

"Excuse me?" Bastien asked, uncertain he heard her correctly.

She bit her lip, then looked down a moment, as if she was in confession. "I was not born Lady Eleanore. I have never grown accustomed to it."

Bastien nodded, intrigued, but unwilling to prod her about it. "Very well. But you needn't check up on what happened to me. I am not your concern."

"Of course you are."

Bastien shook his head. "Of course I am," he muttered. Everyone was her concern. Why did this bother him so?

Her face darkened, and he regretted the way he'd dismissed her.

"I did not think you had recovered enough to return to work," she said. "You should return to Barronsfield."

"You sound like your brother," he replied. "But no, it is probably best for everyone if I remain here."

She looked disappointed. "There are no patients at present. But...

that is not your true purpose here, is it? You didn't come to assist Dr. Brayden. Not really."

"I cannot discuss it."

"Cannot?" She pulled her hood back off her head, her shyness disappearing and replaced with something else—exasperation. "Mr. DuMont, I find I am growing quite tired of the intrigues of the men in my life. I will go to my brother if you will not tell me. Perhaps you do not trust me to keep your secrets?"

"Trust has nothing to do with it."

"Trust has everything to do with it," she said. "Indeed, I happened to be speaking to Mr. Wakefield today. He was inquiring after you."

"Was he?"

"Yes, in fact," she replied. "And you may rest assured that I did not give him, nor any of the others who'd asked after you, any insights about what had happened. Despite what you might think of me, monsieur, I am not a busybody."

"I never thought anything of the sort."

"I told you, you are a horrible liar." She smiled.

"I will not involve you in my troubles."

"Aside from medical matters, you do not get to tell me what I should or should not do, Mr. DuMont," she said. "As you have said, I am not your patient. What should it matter to you what I do or not?"

What should it matter? Bastien put a hand to his chin, drawing his fingers along the side of his jaw, toiling over her question. He had no idea of the answer, but it was scaring the hell out of him.

"I do not want anyone putting themselves in danger on my behalf," he said. "Especially you."

Damn it. The words slipped out before he could take them back.

"I will ask again. Who is Le Veneur Rouge? Who are you that you would find yourself crossing such a man, Mr. DuMont?"

"I have been many things." A surgeon, a revolutionary, a mercenary, a spy. He shook his head, eager to rid himself of the sensation that she might care for him. He turned to a familiar one—bitterness—to turn her attentions away. "None of them make my troubles worthy of your attention. Go back to your charities. Your teas."

Instead of backing away, however, she stepped toward, him, crossing her arms.

"You keep trying to do that. To dismiss me. I will not be dismissed, Mr. DuMont."

"Why? Because you are the sister of the most powerful man in the county?" he countered.

"Because I thought I was your friend."

Her proclamation landed like a stone in his gut. Friend. With the exception of Edmund Pembroke, he had no friends. And yet, for her offer, he found friendship was not enough.

"Do you not understand it is dangerous to be my friend?" He strode past her, and locked the door.

"Who has the Red Hunter hurt?" she pressed, her voice measured.

Bastien paused. "You may have left London before news spread. Do you know the Baroness D'Anville?"

"Of course. I'm not sure there is anyone in society who doesn't know her. I had heard she had taken ill over the holidays."

"She was badly injured in a failed attempt on her life by Le Veneur Rouge—or by his associates."

She put a hand to her mouth, as if to contain her shock. "Is she going to recover?"

"She was very lucky. And she's a tough old bird, that one." He felt, for the first time, his voice tighten with emotion.

Eleanore paused, as if studying him for the first time. "She is someone close to you, isn't she?"

He nodded, waiting a moment for his voice to recover. He cleared his throat, and turned away, lest she witness any weakness before he could reel it back. "She is my great-aunt. And the only family I have in the world."

"I had no idea…"

"Until today, only one man knew the connection between us. It was to keep us safe."

"And you think this attack on the baroness was to get to you?"

"I don't know. But I cannot rule it out." He turned, taking her by the shoulders. "Do you not see why I have kept this from you?"

"Mr. DuMont…"

"Bastien. You have offered friendship. Please."

"Bastien," she began. "My brother was once a man alone, turning away all offers of help. It almost ruined him, and it certainly almost ended his chance at happiness. I would not be at Barronsfield today if he had not managed to overcome that. If your great-aunt has suffered at the hands of the Red Hunter, then you should be accepting every offer of assistance to find him and put an end to his handiwork. I am offering you that help."

He released her, then led her into Dr. Brayden's study and placed his bag on a nearby table. He pulled a second chair up to the desk where he'd been sitting, and picked up one of the physician's books of notes.

"Heaven knows this is against my better judgment, but having two sets of eyes looking for clues is better than one," he said. "Le Veneur Rouge has one, and possibly two, distinct marks on his body."

"Possibly?"

"The second one is a guess—a birthmark, perhaps three or four inches in length, in this area of the body." He pointed in a large circular area where her neck met her back. "Remember when you were angry with me for approaching Ellsworth?"

"Of course I do."

"I had good reason. Tante Marie gave me a note before she was hurt. In it, it said that Le Veneur Rouge was a lost prince of the house of Weymouth. But it wasn't your Lord Ellsworth."

"But he has a birthmark. I think his entire family does."

"Not all of them, but it does seem to carry through from one generation to the next."

"So Le Veneur Rouge is a long-lost cousin?"

"Perhaps. And it would, after a fashion, make sense. What better way to seek revenge on the peerage than to work toward their destruction? That's what he was doing when Edmund was kidnapped —building a network of revolutionaries here in England."

"I see. And you think Dr. Brayden might have made a note of it if he'd had the opportunity to treat him for any reason," she replied.

"Though I am not certain how remarkable such a mark would be, given how common birthmarks are."

"Correct. But he has a second mark, on his left shoulder. A scar that resembles a wolf's bite. It is quite distinctive."

"How on earth would he get a mark like that?"

"I gave it to him."

ELEANORE FURROWED HER BROW. "He was one of your patients?"

Bastien swallowed. Indeed he looked on the very edge of being miserable. He put his hand to his face, drawing it down to his chin, then smiled bitterly to himself. He retrieved the black satchel she'd brought to him, opened it, and methodically pulled out some of the tools of his trade, which were, she had to admit, equally fascinating and horrifying. An assortment of blades and saws, razor sharp and glistening.

At last he pulled out a small wooden box, which was a bit battered along the edges, and placed it in front of her.

She opened it. Inside was a piece of brass, shaped to fit the grip of a man's hand, like the pommel of a sword. On one end, was carved a wolf's head, the sole embellishment a glittering red stone set in the creature's eye. The other end, where a blade might have been, was capped with a flat, round piece of steel.

He reached over, his fingers gently wrapping around hers, then with his other hand, he removed the cap, revealing a maze of small, razor sharp blades.

"I don't understand."

"Turn it this way. Carefully. It is very sharp."

Following his lead, she turned the blades toward her, studying the pattern. It took a moment, but what she saw shocked her. A stylized profile of a wolf's head, it's jaws wide open.

This was no surgeon's tool.

Curiosity besting her, she put her finger to its edge.

"Don't!"

Bastien's sharp warning was too late. The metal had sliced into her finger, drawing a drop of blood. He quickly capped the device, laid it back in its box, then grabbed her hand to examine the wound. He drew her finger to his mouth.

"It's nothing." His touch, however, was not nothing. Heat rippled through her body.

They stood in comfortable silence for a moment, then he released her hand and gave her a clean handkerchief to press over the wound. "Hold it, like this. The bleeding will stop on its own in a moment or two."

"That is some sort of branding tool, isn't it?" she asked, motioning to the device lying in the box. "But instead of heat, it cuts into the flesh."

"The Wolf's bite." His voice was resigned, not boastful. "Le Veneur Rouge is believed to carry this mark. We have met before. I did not realize it until I arrived here. All these years I have been chasing that bastard. The irony of it is not lost on me."

"How? What is this for? You answer my questions with riddles."

"Let me tell you a fairy tale, mademoiselle. But I caution you, this is a dark tale, and there is no happily ever after."

He sat down and leaned back, as if trying to deduce where to start.

"Once upon a time, there was a young, idealistic fool."

"But a handsome fool, to be sure. With thick black hair, and sad, silver eyes."

He arched his eyebrows and smiled, devilish and teasing. "This is my story, but I will allow that embellishment. So this handsome fool wanted to change the world. To save the poor and the sick from a life of misery."

"A noble cause, to be certain." And not so different from her own, when she thought about it.

"A fool's errand. But he was determined, and he was gifted with the favor of a fairy godmother of sorts—or his great-aunt—who sent him to one of the best schools to learn to be a surgeon."

"And what magical kingdom was this?"

"Scotland."

"Magical indeed."

"He did very well there. And all was looking bright. But..." He paused and though the smile remained in place, there was something in his eyes that had faded. "But he returned to France, and to his good fortune, found a post in the army, where he put his skills to great use."

"You were a soldier? I can hardly imagine it."

"It did not last. Not so good at taking orders," he replied. He shook his head. "You're keeping me from burying myself in my *ennui*, chère."

"Apologies," she replied. The light returned to his face for a moment, and she basked in it.

"I—the fool, that is—returned to Paris, determined to make his mark. Still determined to save the world. He set bones made weak from the lack of proper food, hacked off limbs made black from putrefaction that came from living in filth. But the more he did so, the angrier he became. Because a surgeon could not fix those things."

"Bastien," she said under her breath, but he continued, unaware. He sat up, his eyes narrowed, as if he was caught up in the excitement of his own memory.

"By chance, the winds of malcontent grew thick in the streets of Paris and other cities. Voices crying, hungry for a new path. To this young fool, these forces offered another future. A future where the sick could be made well by curing the very thing that made them ill—poverty. It was more than even the greatest physician or surgeon could offer. So the fool became the disciple of this new path, and one of its most demanding leaders—John Paul Marat. The people love him. Even now, there are places that worship his image as though he were Christ himself.

"His words not only inspired, but they could whip people into a fury. And they did, the young fool along with them. Until that one day, in September." He closed his eyes and he paled, and for a moment Eleanore thought he was going to become ill. He took a moment to speak, and his voice thickened. "Those passions took a dark, deadly turn. The crowds had become hungry for passion—and that day, in September—it exploded in unchecked fury. The mob attacked the prison. Priests hacked to death, women..."

His voice trailed off, and his eyes were red-rimmed and bright.

"The September massacres," Eleanore cut in, eager to rescue him. She'd overheard Stephen speaking about them once. The stories of the savagery of that event had shocked everyone. And Bastien had been in the thick of it.

"The fool tried to intervene, but what could be done in the face of such savage devotion?" He looked at her at last, his eyes wavering under the weight of emotion. "Misguided devotion that would later see thousands of people led to the guillotine on a daily parade of blood and fear. The fool started to become a little less of a fool. He turned his back on Marat and those who were just as hungry for power as those they'd been trying to snatch it from. He turned away from the grand ideal and went back to doing what he knew how to do. Saving one life at a time. And he started with his own."

"What did you do?"

He shrugged, then reached out to check her finger where she'd cut it. The bleeding had lessened, but he kept his fingers wrapped around hers.

"I hid, at first. I couldn't return to Paris. I had no place there. I had to make my own way."

"What about your great-aunt?" she asked. "Could you not have come to England, and worked here, as you are now?"

"When I gave up the army, I went back to Paris and got caught up in the fervor of it. She and I—" He paused, his lips twisting into a bitter smile. "Well, we did not see eye to eye. She reminded me of my heritage. My mother was a minor noble. My father was...who knows. I am of noble stock—meaningless as it is. I told her I abandoned it in the manner my parents had abandoned me."

"And she was not happy about that," Eleanore said.

"You must understand, Eleanore, there is much about the Revolution I agreed with. That I still do, in fact. A man must be judged on what it is he does."

"And women too?" Eleanore could not help but think of her mother, and of men like Lord Ramsay. "Women suffer from a great inequality regardless of their social station, and they are judged with the same scorn for their actions. Actions men also commit, without the slightest worry of repercussion."

"The world is an unfair one. I have come to accept it is so. But at the time, I could not abandon France. It was my home. I had to make my own way, so I began looking for a new trade. I think that hurt Tante Marie the most." He paused again. "There was money to be made in secrets, and when you pretend to care, it is quite amazing what people will tell you. I learned I had a certain talent for it."

"Keeping secrets?"

"Pretending to care."

Eleanore was not certain of his talents in that regard, but did not press it.

"So you were surviving in a horrible situation. You sold secrets."

"I did more than that. You see, one day, I was approached by a man in Calais. The new government was looking for men willing to hunt down and capture, for a substantial reward, those noble families who were still escaping France. Escaping justice, at least in the eyes of the new regime. *Les veneur noblesse*. Rounding up families and sending them to justice."

"Dear heavens."

"I had inadvertently interrupted such a capture—a comte I knew to be a pig of a man. But his children—I got the children to safety in England. The baroness knew how to help them. She has been working for years to do so. And then I went back. And I hunted the hunters. Dispensing my own judgment."

"And this? You branded them with this?"

"The ones who got away, yes," he replied. His face hardened, but underneath it, there was something else. Fear, perhaps. "Not all of them walked away from our encounters."

Eleanore, for her part, was enthralled. Saddened by the weight of the events he still carried. "You saved people, Bastien. At great expense to yourself. Some would call that heroic."

He put a hand to his forehead, rubbing his temples. He took a moment before he faced her. "Are you even listening to me? I killed people, Eleanore."

"You were at war, Bastien," she replied, her voice soft.

"A war of my own making."

"If I may, you give yourself too much credit. You may want to take responsibility for the world, but in the end all we can do is choose how to respond to what is in front of us."

"I responded with violence. Against my own countrymen. And many of the people I saved...perhaps they did not deserve saving."

"You are determined to have me think ill of you." She reached up and stroked his cheek. "It is not for you to decide how I think of you. Nor Stephen for that matter. I have my own mind."

"I see how you look at me."

"Do you?" She lowered her hand to her side, exasperation finding release in a sigh. "Bastien DuMont, I am not the person from whom you need to seek forgiveness. The only person you need to make peace with is yourself. You do not have my pity, nor my disdain. But you do have my..." She stalled then. She wanted to say love. It was there, as surprising and as right as anything she'd ever felt. But she didn't trust the feeling. "My friendship."

"You are trying to redeem my sins in your mind. To make me a hero of sorts. But that is not how my tale ends, Eleanore."

"Your story is not yet over," she replied. "So what happens?"

Bastien gently lowered her hand, then began gesturing in that Gallic way of his she was quickly coming to adore. "Right. The fool found himself on the run from a maniac. All because he went against his better judgment and instead of selling Le Veneur Rouge's secrets back to him for a price, he gave the list to the bloody English king."

"I think you're telling this story wrong," she insisted. "You keep calling your main character a fool. But he is not."

"It's my story. I get to tell it as I see fit."

She sighed, shook her head, and looked down at her notebook in her hands. "You are stubborn, do you know that?"

"I am not the stubborn one. You would frame me as a hero."

Eleanore needed to change the subject, if only for her own sanity. "You said that you gave the Red Hunter a mark. Was he one of those men? Those hunters?"

"Oui."

"And he wouldn't recognize you?"

"Truthfully, I cannot say. I kept my face masked, but I don't know."

"So we must find him." She forced her attention back to one of Dr. Brayden's journals. "That mark would be unique. He would have hidden it."

"I think so. But he might not have thought about the birthmark as much."

Time ticked by, without success. At last, Bastien threw the notebook aside and closed his eyes. "This is pointless."

"I can continue." She looked at his lip, which was still swollen, and the nasty mark on his cheek. "Why don't you rest?"

"I cannot."

He closed his eyes, and Eleanore, unable to resist herself, reached over and gently put her lips to his temple.

"Rest," she whispered. "Doctor's orders."

CHAPTER 18

"Orders?" His mouth crept into a devilishly charming smile. "Are you a physician now?"

"Perhaps I am." A tingling heat prickled under her skin as her body responded to the hunger in his eyes. A hunger for her touch.

She put her forefinger and thumb to his chin, cupping it as she narrowed her eyes—mimicking a gesture she'd watched Dr. Brayden do many times before examining a patient. Apparently, the motion was not unfamiliar to Bastien as well.

"Would you like to examine me?" He hopped onto the edge of Dr. Brayden's desk, and held out his arms in invitation. "Ensure that I indeed have a heart beating in my chest?"

She crossed her arms, paused a moment, then stood opposite him. "I might not be a physician, but I believe I have enough grasp of anatomy to know that you have one. Indeed, I think your heart is healthier than you believe."

"Let's find out, shall we?" There was something there—a spark, perhaps even a dare, that emboldened her. Stirred her. Indeed, something had been stirring for quite some time. She could no longer deny it.

She stepped closer, reaching tentatively for the lock of hair that had fallen across his brow. The sensation as her fingers grazed his hairline rippled through her.

His eyes were fixed on her, and she couldn't help but notice that they did not bear the haunted look they had while he spoke about his time in France. There was something else there. Want. Need.

"What beautiful eyes you have," she said, her fingers tracing his brow line.

"All the better to look upon such a beautiful, remarkable woman."

Her heart jumped and she paused as the words settled like sunshine on a flower that had struggled in shadow. She ran her fingers along his jaw, along the little scar on his cheek, then down his neck to his collar. She savored every ounce of the sensation, until her exploration was foiled by the linen cinched at his neck. She frowned and bit her lip.

He breathed in sharply.

"Something wrong?" she asked, pulling her hand away. "Perhaps I should have been more careful." His bruises were still fresh.

He shook his head. "No. Let us say that you have a remarkable effect on me. Have you reached any conclusions?"

"That you need to remove your shirt if I am going to continue."

If the words hadn't come out of her own mouth, she could have scarce believed that she had uttered them. But the low growl and hungry smile that teased his lips as he loosened the cravat only emboldened her further.

She stepped back as he removed his jacket, waistcoat, and finally his shirt.

Dear heavens.

The sight of his firm chest and lean, muscled arms silenced her for a moment. Swallowing hard, she took a step forward and put a single finger on his skin. She was about to pull away when he reached out and took hold of her hand, placing it at the center of his chest. His skin was warm under her palm.

"Can you feel that?" He swallowed. "You do this to me. Every time I see you. Every time I think of you. There is no medicine or surgical technique that is as powerful as your touch."

The sensation created its own winding heat through her body.

"Touch me," he whispered. "Tell me what you feel."

"I am not certain what I feel." It was new. And intoxicating.

"Then you need to continue to examine me further."

She stepped closer, and put both of her hands on his chest, exploring the little ripples of skin across his abdomen. The gentle curve and hard muscle on his upper arms. The skin around one of his nipples. Her examination revealed some of the harshness that his life had become. Small scars here and there. They only added to his perfection.

The heat between her legs grew, winding its way through her body. Then she became aware of a new sensation—on the lower half of his body, pressing up against her.

"And your conclusion?"

"I..." She found herself falling forward, mere inches away from his lips. "You have a beautiful mouth."

"All the better to taste you with. If you wish it."

"I do."

The words had barely escaped her when she leaned forward, opened her mouth, and tasted him. It was a blind, urgent hunger. Perhaps she could not have a fairy tale love. But this moment was its own sort of magic, and she was taking it.

IF IT WAS POSSIBLE, Bastien would have swallowed her whole. That he sat in front of her now, half dressed, the agonizing sensation of her against him, was a moment of unparalleled exquisite torment.

Her skin, scented with vanilla and lavender, was flushed and warm from her desire. Her kiss was deep and probing, the softness of her mouth a contrast to the eagerness with which she kissed him. When she was done with his mouth, she moved to his jawline, and down his neck. All the while he kept himself holding on to the edge of the table as if his life depended on it.

She took one of his hands and brought it to her mouth, kissing his fingers. "What strong hands you have. Capable of such caring. Such healing."

"All the better to touch you with, chère."

"Touch me." Her breathless whisper, a subtle command, was all the invitation he needed to dig his hands into her hair. He ran his fingers over her exquisite breasts, still encased in her stays. But even through the fabric, he could feel the tautness of her nipples, and the sigh she let go damn near finished him.

He reached down, pulling up the layers of skirts and petticoats, drifting along the inside of her thighs. As he drew closer to her sex, she let out the most delicious little moans that shuttered through to his core. Holding onto the back of her neck with one hand, his other found purchase in her soft, damp folds.

She broke the kiss and her mouth fell open, her lips full and flush, calling his name in an urgent, hushed whisper. Driven by his own passion, he pulled her mouth to his, capturing her breath with his own.

He was rock hard, and the way she moved against the length of him, even through his breeches, was agony. It was all he could do not to lift up her skirts, thrust himself inside her, and exalt in her lush, tight heat.

"Will you touch me, chère?" he asked.

She nodded, still entranced by her own pleasure. He loosened the front flap of his breeches and guided her hand to his shaft. Her touch, moving in time with his strokes of her sex, the sensation of her tongue in his mouth, and finally, her climax, brought his own release almost immediately.

They rested their heads on each other's shoulders for a moment, allowing the wave of pleasure to ebb. The only sound was that of their breathing.

At last, he grabbed the linen from his cravat, and cleaned where his body had left the residue of his orgasm, and pulled his shirt back over his head. They were quiet, the two of them. As if words would dissipate the spell.

At last, she spoke. "That was..." her voice drifted off, and she was again almost afraid to look at him.

"That was beautiful."

"Beautiful?" Doubt dimmed her normally bright expression that Bastien had found so entrancing.

"Did you not enjoy it?"

"Immensely, yes." Her expression changed, but Bastien could tell her smile was forced. And whatever doubt she'd attempted to push away had returned. "It's just...I am the product of sin, Bastien." Her eyes were bright and sad, and the despair in her voice tore through Bastien in a way he didn't think was possible.

"Who told you this nonsense?" Bastien tensed, prepared, quite suddenly, to confront anyone who'd judge a soul as giving as hers. "You are an angel. Anyone who thinks differently is a fool."

She shook her head. "By the letter of the law, it is correct. My parents were not married. My father cared for her, but they were not in the same social sphere. My mother was a servant. My birth brought the end to their happiness."

Bastien went to her and wrapped his arms around her, desperate somehow to protect her from her own doubts. He held her a moment, reveling in the sensation of trust as she allowed him to bear her fears. After a moment, he loosened his embrace and rested his hands on her shoulders. "Their union produced a most beautiful, accomplished woman. I cannot imagine they would look upon you as anything but the culmination of their happiness. And certainly not a sin. That you would even think such a thing of yourself, when you work so hard to find the better nature in people who do not deserve it, I don't understand."

Her eyes were bright now, but with the sadness of tears. "Why do you think I came back here, to Elmsdale, in the middle of the night?" she said. "I ran. I was tired of not being good enough for them. Lords and ladies with pedigrees and lineages back to Elizabeth and further, looking down on me as if I am nothing."

Bastien bit back his anger. Lords and ladies indeed. "You are the daughter of a marquess."

"I am also the daughter of a baker. And they never let me forget it." She pushed the tears away with the back of her hand, and smiled sadly. "But here is the illogical part of all of it. I don't want to forget that I am the daughter of a baker. I don't want to forget my mother."

"Chère," he whispered under his breath. "There is no reason to. Without the bakers, the farmers, and the fishermen, the lords do not eat. The wise ones, like your brother, remember that."

She nodded. He opened his arms, and once again, she came to him. They sat in comfortable silence, until the sharp tinkling of icy rain started to hit the windows.

"I should leave," she said, a quiet resignation in her voice.

If only she could stay. But there was only one way for that to happen.

"Of course." Bastien went to his room to make himself presentable, then accompanied her to where the carriage was waiting for her. To spirit her away.

"Perhaps you could dine with us some evening?"

He nodded, his heart involuntarily leaping at the opportunity to see her again. But he was still seeking Le Veneur Rouge, and had at least another five journals to review, hoping against hope they might give up their secrets. Besides, her brother would certainly be not happy to see him at his table. Once his mission here was concluded, Bastien would take his leave.

"Perhaps," he said, deliberately noncommittal in his response. "But perhaps I should wait for an invitation from your brother." He shouldn't have cared, suddenly, what Eleanore's surly brother thought of him. But what Bastien DuMont was coming to care about was getting broader by the day.

He helped her into her carriage, then closed the door.

"Thank you again, Lady Eleanore, for returning my supplies to me," he said, if for no other reason than for the driver to take that excuse back to Barronsfield. He really wanted to thank her for the way she set his body on fire, and how she soothed his damaged soul.

How she made him feel wanted. And how, even though he stood in the icy rain watching her carriage disappear up the lane, the cold didn't seem to bother him when he thought of her.

He shoved his hands in his pockets and went inside, trying to force himself back to his task. But as he went to pick up the journal he'd been studying, another volume caught his eye. The one Eleanore had given him, stuffed full of notes and drawings. The one she'd pushed into his hands, begging him to look over. Challenging him to improve. Trying to learn how she could care better.

It had been a part of his life he thought served no purpose than to provide him with an ample source of guilt. A hardened sense of how the world actually worked.

But perhaps, he could help her to help others.

He wrapped his hands around it and settled into a chair. Could he be more than the Wolf?

Perhaps for the girl in the red cape, he would try.

CHAPTER 19

*B*astien walked through the clear, cold morning air from the Elm and Thistle, where he'd gone for breakfast on his way to the infirmary. He'd spent a long night poring over Eleanore's notes, and laid awake most of the night, his body burning for her. If he spent any more time alone, he was certain he would have gone mad. He made a few morning rounds to nearby patients he'd seen over the past week before indulging in a strong cup of coffee and breakfast.

Mr. Roderick, eager to atone for the beating Bastien had received outside his establishment, treated him to a large portion of eggs and would accept no coin for it. People nodded at him in salutation—Mr. Oliver, setting out the sign to his shop, and Mr. Battersby, walking along the cobblestones. The faces and names were becoming increasingly familiar and welcome.

And yet—among them lurked a killer.

He gripped his black bag, which held the tools of his trade and the weapon of his own personal war. When he'd showed it to Eleanore, he was certain she would be reviled by it and him. Judge him. Walk away.

But she had not. And he was uncertain how he felt about that.

He scanned the streets and lanes as he walked, unconsciously looking for a flash of red.

He should have made an offer for her, given what had happened between them. He had not ruined her, at least. They'd shared a magical moment of intimacy, and it was over. She'd offered her friendship, and that was all. If she expected more, she'd given him no sign.

The thought should have soothed his conscience. It did not. Neither did the notion that she deserved someone better. She deserved a hero. Someone to support her. Someone who could help her shine. Someone who saw her as he did.

Someone like him. And not like him at all.

While they were both of questionable noble blood, Lady Eleanore's standing in the community was by far more significant. Not that it mattered to him. But it no doubt mattered to Lord Barronsfield, and notwithstanding the marquess's rather pointed warning to stay away from her, there was the not so small matter that he would deny any offer Bastien made. He would make a guess as to the reasons behind Bastien's proposal, and he would be correct.

Besides, Lady Eleanore had already said she had hoped for love. For a fairy tale. He had no such happy ending to offer. Though her virtue was intact, she'd left him far more aware of the pleasures her body could provide.

Then there was the matter of her causes—her incessant need to save everyone, and her seemingly endless dogged determination to remind him that he was no less driven by the same desires. They would never agree on this point. He was done saving the world.

Though he tried not to, he could imagine a future with her, fluttering about, planning tea, seeing to matrons who'd help rear her foundlings. And when he wasn't thinking about the scent of her skin, or the flush in her chest, or the little sigh that escaped her after the rush of her climax was spent, he could imagine a morning where he could be having coffee with her over breakfast, or listening to her plans while they walked through the square in town.

It scared him to death.

But the most obvious reason not to offer his hand was because it was the honorable thing to do, and despite Eleanore's protest, Bastien

DuMont was not an honorable man. He was not here on a journey of redemption. He was not here to be saved. He was here to kill a man, and save the English king the trouble of creating a martyr.

There were a few more notebooks in Dr. Brayden's examination room that needed review. As he approached the stone edifice of the infirmary, he pulled out the key to unlock the heavy oak door. It pushed open effortlessly, even before he'd attempted the lock. He straightened, his body on alert as he cast a piercing glance around, then looked down at the ground, which was still frozen. It had not snowed during the night, so there were no footprints. His free hand tightened into a fist as he took a few cautious steps toward the door, then gently nudged it open.

The place appeared to be undisturbed. The fire had not been lit since he'd left last night, and a check on the storeroom saw no evidence it had been turned over.

But Dr. Brayden's examination room, where he kept his personal supplies and notes, had clearly been disturbed. It was not in complete disarray, but the notebooks were in the wrong order. A closer inspection of the shelf showed a space where one was missing.

He went to a few other cabinets which held some of Brayden's bleeding bowls and lancets. While nothing appeared to be taken, Bastien had become familiar enough with the physician's instruments to see they'd been picked over. On a hunch, he went to Dr. Brayden's traveling case. It was unlocked and rummaged through.

A sinking feeling gripped him. He stared at his own bag, which he placed on the examination table. At the bottom, secure in its case, was the Wolf's bite. Was this what they had been seeking? Proof he was their man?

"Mr. DuMont, sir?" Mr. Darling's voice called out from the entry.

At the sound, Bastien exhaled and walked out to greet the vicar.

"Bonjour, Monsieur. How can I be of service?"

He tipped his hat. "His Lordship wishes to see you at your earliest convenience."

Bastien swallowed. "Did he indicate the nature of the request?" While it could have been anything at all, he could not help but wonder if the marquess had discovered what had happened between him and Eleanore.

"He did not say. He received a special post last night, during dinner. Perhaps it is word about Dr. Brayden."

"Of course." Bastien breathed an unexpected sigh of relief. Bad news did not wait until after breakfast. "I shall leave immediately."

Within the hour, Bastien was being led by a footman through the halls of Barronsfield Manor. He couldn't help but wonder if Hanley was worse, or perhaps finally taking his advice to rest.

Bastien was led to the marquess' study, where the man himself was waiting, imposing as ever.

"Good morning, Mr. DuMont." Lord Barronsfield's greeting was congenial but no more than what was required. "You're looking a little less like the devil today. You're improving, I hope?"

"Indeed," he replied, impatient to get to the reasons he was standing here. "I understand you have news for me."

The marquess picked up a letter from his desk. "I received a missive last night from Hamilton. It contained some shocking, but I trust, excellent news."

Bastien's thoughts went to Tante Marie almost immediately, but he kept still.

"It seems Le Veneur Rouge was apprehended in London," Lord Barronsfield said.

The news dropped in Bastien's gut like a stone. London? How could that be? "Dead, or alive?"

"He was alive when they caught him," the marquess replied. "But he had been wounded, so it is impossible to say at present."

Bastien didn't know whether to sit or stand. Was there a mistake? Perhaps the true message had been written in code. "Let me see the note."

He snatched the parchment from Lord Barronsfield's outstretched hand, and studied its contents carefully. He recognized the hand—the quick upstrokes of the pen were undoubtedly from Hamilton's quill. He read the letter over once, then twice, but there was no mistaking the message.

The man they captured had what looked to be a scar that, while marred from perhaps a botched attempt at removal, appeared to be the mark of the Wolf. Not only that, he had been positively identified by several of Le Veneur Rouge's associates in Newgate.

The mechanism of a nearby clock marked the seconds. Bastien, out of a long protective habit, threw the paper into the fire, watching the flames lick the sides, curling the edges of the note until it had been completely consumed.

"So it is finished, then," Lord Barronsfield said, his voice interrupting Bastien's woolgathering.

"I suppose it is," Bastien answered, the words coming out of his mouth, but without conviction. Something about the entire thing that did not sit well with him. "I wish to confirm the facts of this myself."

"Excellent," the marquess replied. "I will see to the arrangements to get you to London."

A knock came at the door, drawing his attention. Eleanore swept in, a smile on her face.

"Mr. DuMont!" she said, walking to greet him with a polite smile on her face. "I had heard you were here. I hope you will be staying to take some tea with us."

Bastien cut a glance to Lord Barronsfield, whose mouth fell into a firm line.

"I thank you, Lady Eleanore, but I am afraid I am indisposed at the moment," Bastien replied, keeping his voice as clinical and polite as possible.

A wave of confusion crossed her face. "I am sorry to hear that."

"Mr. DuMont is being called to London," Lord Barronsfield said, the order in his voice clear.

"To London? When?"

"On the morrow," Bastien said. He needed to confirm the identity of the bastard Hamilton had caught.

"Has something happened?" Eleanore asked, worry stretching across her face as she took a step toward Bastien. "Nothing too terrible I trust. Will...you be returning, once your business is concluded?"

He did not miss the subtle catch in her voice as she'd asked the question he dreaded. The question for which he had no answer.

"I cannot say at present," he said. It was the truth at least.

Lord Barronsfield stepped forward, tugging at his waistcoat, his tone impervious. "Eleanore, please remember that Mr. DuMont has obligations beyond this household. For now, he is required in London. It is best we allow him to get on his way."

ELEANORE'S GAZE went from Stephen to Bastien and for an agonizing moment, it seemed that no one had taken even a breath. At last, Bastien bowed deeply to her.

"It has been a great pleasure, my lady."

She stood, her hands curled into fists at her sides to keep her from reaching out to him. And then he disappeared. His departure sent a wave of panic through her body. It must have been about the Red Hunter. Surely, he could return after he'd seen to his arrest. Why wouldn't Stephen encourage him to return?

"Stephen, what are we going to do with the infirmary?" she insisted, her gaze sliding over to the door. "It would be sensible to ask Mr. DuMont to return once his business is concluded, if only until Dr. Brayden returns."

"We have made do without him for short periods of time before," Stephen reminded her, his tone noticeably detached.

"'Tis true, but Daniel is not yet healed. Can Mr. DuMont not return until he is walking?"

"Eleanore..."

"If you are worried because of Le Veneur Rouge—"

"How in the blazes do you know about that?" Stephen's countenance hardened, his mouth a tight line.

Eleanore let out a low breath to settle her nerves. "Mr. DuMont had said the name in his sleep, the night you arrived." Stephen pursed his lips, and it occurred to Eleanore that reminding him of the evening he'd discovered her sleeping on the chair in Bastien's room was probably not the smartest thing to do, so she decided to drag someone else into it. "Lord Ellsworth gave it away, if you must know. He'd revealed that it was Bastien who saved Edmund. Bastien tried to tell me he'd just been in the area, by chance. But Edmund was a spy for a time, and that they were aware of each other seemed very coincidental, particularly if the Red Hunter is as dangerous as they say."

Stephen nodded his head and pursed his lips as he appeared to accept her explanation. Eleanore started to relax, until he crossed his arms and raised his eyebrow.

"I see. And did *Bastien* reveal anything else?"

Eleanore swallowed, a little knot tightening in her belly, heat rushing into her cheeks, but she stood her ground. "I do not understand your aversion to him."

"Perhaps you may wish to explain your lack of aversion to him."

"I—" How could she explain something that she could barely understand herself? Was it the little lines at the edges of his mouth when he smiled? The concern and care in his manner when he worked with his patients? The heat under his skin when she touched him, or the way he taught her to own her own pleasure? That he saw her as Eleanore, as if that was enough? "He is a good man, Stephen. And he's never been less than a gentleman to me. People here need him." *I need him.* "You weren't here when I first arrived. He was most attentive to Daniel, and very generous with his time when I asked it of him."

"Generous," he shook his head. "For his sake, I hope not too generous."

Anger bubbled inside her, sharpening her tone. "Stephen, do you not trust me or my judgment? I am not a girl any more."

Her brother blinked, as if stung by her question. "Of course I do," he said, his bluster disappearing. "You are a woman of much sense. But you cannot fault me for being protective."

"I do not." She went to Stephen, and took him by the hand. "You are all I have wished for in a brother. I love you very much. But I am asking you to trust me. I think Mr. DuMont should be encouraged to return. Not for me, but for the people in this community."

He stood in silence, regarding her carefully.

"If he has been as helpful as you say, I will consider it. But it is not my decision in the end, Eleanore. It is his. And while I do not know Mr. DuMont very well, what I know of him tells me he is not given to the role of a country doctor."

Eleanore nodded, knowing there was truth in what he said. But perhaps Bastien could be convinced. If he could see that people here appreciated his skills, that he belonged...perhaps he would stay. For them. And maybe, if she dared let herself think it, for her as well.

"Perhaps we could have him to dinner, tonight. And invite some of our neighbors. If he has serious business to attend to, then a dinner to wish him well would be in good form, I would think."

Stephen cocked his head, getting that familiar expression that Eleanore had come to love about her brother. The one that let her know that, despite the fact he might not be enthralled with the idea, he was willing to entertain it—for her.

"Very well. I will let you make the arrangements. But do not count on Mr. DuMont welcoming the idea, Eleanore."

She reached out and flung her arms around her brother's large frame, giving him a squeeze. "Thank you, Stephen."

"Go. Make your plans, before Mr. DuMont gets away."

CHAPTER 20

$\mathcal{A}$s if the heavens were smiling down on her, Eleanore learned that Bastien had gone to see Daniel, no doubt for one last visit before he left for London. She tore out of the house, taking only a moment to pull on her red cape, which caught in the air as she bolted to the steward's cottage. She arrived to find him just finishing his visit.

"Bastien," she said, putting a hand to her chest as she caught her breath. "I wanted to catch you before you left. Do you have a moment?"

He hesitated, then turned toward her, a flash of emotion that faded away into nothingness. It squeezed at her heart.

"Of course."

"How is Daniel?" she asked brightly.

Confusion crinkled his brow. "Improving."

He grabbed his hat, pulled up the collar on his coat, and grabbed his bag. He put his hand on the door, making ready to leave. "Good day to you."

"Wait!" She put her hand on his to stop him, and the heat of his skin, even through the layers of their gloves, jolted her. He paused, his eyes narrowing a bit.

She pulled her hand away. "Might we walk back together? It was not Daniel I came here to see."

The smallest hint of a smile on his troubled face buoyed her in a way that would have seemed difficult for her to imagine the day he'd arrived. It felt good...and still, even after all that had been between them...forbidden.

He opened the door, and they walked along one of the little lanes toward Barronsfield Manor.

"I spoke with my brother. He told me about the Red Hunter. It must be odd," she offered, breaking the strained silence between them, "having this come to a conclusion after so long a time. And in this manner."

Bastien nodded, silent.

"You said you wanted to see me?" he asked, a hint of impatience in his voice.

She nodded, her lips holding a smile while she wracked her brain for a reason other than the one her heart was afraid to own.

"My brother has extended an invitation for you to dine with us tonight."

The smile soured on his face. "Of course. One last meal before I depart."

"Not a celebration *because* you are leaving," she protested. "Rather, to celebrate that you have been here. But...is there no chance at all you might return?"

He slowed, and turned to her. "If the man in London is who he's believed to be, my work here is done. I have no reason to come back."

The words hit her in the chest. "I thought...I thought you might come back, at least until Dr. Brayden is able to resume his post." And maybe longer. She dared look up at him. His jaw tightened, as if he bore an unspoken weight on his shoulders.

"Edmund was not a spy forever. You could have employment here," she pressed. "I thought perhaps you might wish to stay, until Daniel is on his feet. And then decide."

"If I stayed in one place for every broken bone to heal, I would never have left Paris," he grumbled. His voice was light, but there was a dark edge in it that took her off guard. "I see you have been busy making plans for me."

"I was only trying to h—"

"Help." He sighed, the sharpness in his voice slowly dissipating. "I know. You always need to help. I must go to London. I am not certain how long I will stay."

"My apologies. I was not making plans for you. I am merely eager for you to know that you have a place, here. If you want it."

"Do you know what I want?" He stopped and took her by the arm, his grip gentle but firm, his glance both daring and dangerous. "I cannot have what I want."

"How do you know?" she persisted, ignoring the voice inside her. Forcing it down. "I am not certain you even know what you want, and that is natural. You've been chasing this man for years. He has done horrible things. And now it might be over. Perhaps you can search out a new life. And possibly…that could be here."

"I see—so you are writing this new fairy story for me?"

"I am not writing a tale, Bastien. Trust me when I say that I know fairy tales and their happy endings are not for me. All I am saying is that, for now, perhaps you might stay, and help Daniel until he can walk."

"I was never here to be your healer."

"But—I thought—you enjoyed your work."

"Now we both know you were mistaken."

Eleanore was stunned to silence. All the visits, the care, the times he tore away to help others. She shook her head. "But if you would come back, after your business in London is finished—you do not have to be the Wolf anymore."

A darkness crossed his face, his brow dipped, and he shook his head. "No."

"But Daniel—"

"Not, 'but Daniel,'" he said. "Tell me, Eleanore, why do you want me to stay?"

Her mouth opened. There were a thousand reasons. But the most important one was that she wanted him. Might even be falling in love with him. But love wasn't enough, was it? "I-I would miss you if you left."

His face softened at her confession, which enticed her to say more.

"I would miss the way you grumble when your patients don't listen to your advice. Or the smile on your face when they are improving. Or the way you smile that makes a person feel as though all will be right with the world."

"Eleanore…"

"And how you swear under your breath in French when you think no one can hear you. People here would miss those things." She paused and took a breath, daring herself to push past her fear. "I would miss them."

A chill wind stirred, sending a shutter of cold along her neck. He reached up and pulled her hood over her head.

"You don't want to catch cold," he said, his voice soft, causing a curious ache in her chest. "I am not certain I can be a country doctor. Not after the life I have lived."

"I am not asking you to return forever. Just until Daniel is better," she replied. "And if that is too much, just come to dinner this evening. For me."

They stood, face to face a moment, Eleanore afraid to breathe. Heaven help her, but she *was* falling in love with him, and not until this moment did she realize how much her heart ached for his smile. She stood still, fearful even to blink, looking for any sign that he could see what she was so afraid to admit to herself.

His mouth was pulled in a taut line, a weariness weighing on his shoulders. The only sound in that agonizing moment was the gravel scraping under his boots. He dropped his gaze and then, taking her hands in his, his silver gray eyes brightened before her.

"For you."

CHAPTER 21

The Red Hunter had one last man to hunt down. The Undeserving. The one who'd taken all that should have been his. Ironic that it was the Wolf himself who was unwittingly providing the opportunity. The Wolf and, of course, the lovely Lady Eleanore, who had sent such a pretty note to his home this morning with an invitation to dinner.

He poured himself a small cup of tea. He wanted brandy, but he needed his hands steady for the work in front of him. It was not every day one created a recipe for revenge. At least, not one as intensely personal as this.

He'd been obsessed with Middleton—he refused to call him by his title, the one that should have been his—an obsession that had only grown since the catastrophic events in Cumbria last summer. *No.* In truth, the man, who was little more than a boy in some ways —was so sheltered and naïve about the world he'd spent his time obsessed with the stars. He didn't even seem to want the title he would receive for no other bloody reason than he'd been the product of parents who were blessed with power that they didn't earn.

Wakefield had earned his power. His wealth. Every scrap. He did the dirty work—or built up a network of followers willing to do it for him.

He'd had terrific plans to strike out at Middleton at what should have been the great event of 1794—the marriage of the Marquess of Ellsworth to Lady whatever her name was. He'd been planning it for months, but dreaming of it for years. It would have drawn most of the peerage from Great Britain, and maybe even the mad king himself. A few well-timed explosives, brought in by some of his more devoted followers, would have made a spectacular show of defiance, and cleansed the land of much of the filth who claimed privilege over the rest.

And, most importantly, Middleton would have been dead. But the bastard couldn't even manage to get married. Fate, Wakefield decided, had brought the two of them together at last, away from the prying eyes of London society. And this time, he would not let the opportunity pass.

Did the Wolf know of his plans? For he was certain now, so certain, that the man currently favored by Barronsfield to look after his weaklings was, in fact, the Wolf de l'Ardoise. He involuntarily flexed his shoulder, the spot where the Wolf had bitten him all those years ago.

He could not help but wonder if Lord Barronsfield knew of DuMont's past—his treachery to his own people. Certainly Lady Eleanore could not. Lady Eleanore was a paragon of virtue, her common blood shielding her from the excesses of the landed class. She knew work. She understood sacrifice. In the end, she might die, but the deliciousness of killing both Ellsworth and Barronsfield—two of England's most powerful men, and two great symbols of English peerage—was an opportunity not to be missed.

His shoulder twitched again.

Was it too much that he wanted the Wolf as well? The man had been a thorn in his side since the winter of '92. He was the person most responsible for his current state of retreat—and for the hangman's ropes that had been wrapped around the necks of some of his most trusted associates. Leave it to the English to resist innovation and choose the crueler, slower method of hanging to rid themselves of their enemies.

Wakefield had to hand it to the Frenchman. DuMont had eluded every cutthroat that had been sent his way. Tracking down the Wolf had allowed Wakefield time to retreat and consider his next move. There were those within the French government who wanted to capitalize on English unrest and bring revolution to London. With allies in Ireland, who perhaps hated the English even more than the French, Wakefield had made connections. It was an astonishingly lucrative service. Discontent had always been profitable.

He turned back to his task, which demanded his full attention. After much experimentation, he'd managed to find an effective black powder recipe that would have made Guy Fawkes proud. The earlier attempt had cost him the hand of one of his best men. Tonight, Grimm himself would carry in the device, disguised as a barrel of brandy. Incendiary devices were perhaps cruder than pistols, but far more effective for making a grand statement.

If this was to be his last, it would be one for the ages.

꙳

ELEANORE SAT IN THE LIBRARY, trying to keep herself engaged in her guests' conversation. Though it had been a last minute affair, the Darlings, the Battersbys, and Mr. Wakefield had been able to join them. Only two gentlemen were left to arrive: Lord Ellsworth, who was expected very soon, and the guest of honor. All were present to wish Mr. DuMont well before he left for London. And, perhaps, to convince him to return.

She smoothed the skirt of her pink muslin, her mind wandering away from the pleasant, if mundane conversation in the room. She'd tried on four gowns. Four. Eleanore had never been so indecisive about dressing for dinner. Even the night that she'd first dined publicly with Lord Ramsay after their engagement, she might have fussed over two. Eleanore didn't fuss about clothes too much. At last, and no doubt to the relief of her maid, she'd settled on the pink muslin with a green ribbon at her waist, her hair braided and twisted into a knot at the back of her head. Around her neck she'd chosen a simple green ribbon—one of her mother's—which held a small cross her father had given her as a gift when she was just a babe.

Perhaps her consternation over gowns had nothing to do with Bastien. At least, not in the way she wanted to admit. Rather, her aim was to show him how much good he'd done, and how much he was appreciated, so he might be persuaded to return after his trip to London. For the good of everyone. *Especially me.*

A twinge of melancholy squeezed her chest. Every single thought she'd had about Bastien seemed to be forbidden—or at least destined for heartache. There was a small part of her that wondered if it wasn't best if he did leave. Though he was determined his story was not going to end happily, it was entirely possible it might. He was handsome, accomplished, and destined to do well in the world. If he did come back, he might find himself a wife—a wife that was not her. And that thought was somehow impossible to bear.

Eleanore gave herself a mental shake, determined not to wallow. She had to focus on the one thing that gave her purpose—bringing the foundling home into reality. But her thoughts were preoccupied with an embittered Frenchman with silver eyes and a veneer of clinical dispassion. A man who claimed not to care about anyone, but who was risking his own life to protect his family. Who complained about his patients but turned no one away. And who had the most passionate, tender kisses.

The memory sent a tendril of desire curling through her. She wanted to savor the moment he'd touched her in the most intimate way, but sitting in a room with her brother and the Darlings, it was neither the time nor place for such thoughts.

The clock on the mantle chimed seven, snapping Eleanore out of her reverie. She put her hands to her cheeks, as if trying to expel the unwanted emotion. Desire was dangerous. Desire was completely out of sorts with what she wanted. With what she was going to have. She would find love other ways—with her foundlings, and being a good aunt to her niece and nephew. Helping others find happiness. That would be enough.

At least, it had always felt like enough.

The doors to the parlor opened and the footman who'd stepped in for Mr. Hanley announced Bastien's arrival. Stifling a smile she rose, a thrill sliding down her spine. Ahead was Bastien DuMont, his black hair tamed with a brush and a dab of hair wax, freshly shaved, a dark burgundy coat stretching across his shoulders.

Eleanore froze, enthralled by the sight of him. He scanned the room, taking a cautious step inside, his face lighting up as his gaze rested on her. It took a moment for Eleanore to find her breath.

"DuMont," her brother said, extending a hand. "I am pleased you could join us at last."

He bowed graciously which seemed to take Stephen off guard, then entered. Eleanore waited but a moment, then went to greet him.

"Mr. DuMont," she said, desperate to keep her breath steady. She put a hand to her belly, which was full of butterflies, then pulled it away. "I am so glad you could come."

His gaze ran over her gently, and yet with such an unspoken urgency that it was as if she could feel his touch. "You are enchanting, my lady."

"Thank you," she said, almost breathless. She cleared her throat and squared her shoulders. "If I may, you are quite dashing tonight."

"My apologies for my tardiness," he said, turning his gaze to her brother. "I was seeing to a patient."

"How is Hanley?" Stephen asked, no doubt worried about their loyal butler. He'd been ordered to rest, as the cold and damp of the winter season was affecting him.

"Impervious as a lord," Bastien said, the hint of a teasing smile on his face. "But improving. There is only so much that can be done, but rest is not a bad thing."

"The guest of honor at last," said Mr. Darling as he approached, his hand out to taken Bastien's. "I am grieved to know you are leaving before you had the opportunity to dine with Mrs. Darling and me at the vicarage. I hope, when you return, that can be corrected."

Bastien nodded. "Indeed, I regret not taking the opportunity to know you better."

Eleanore could not help but notice his answer was completely noncommittal.

After greeting the guests, Eleanore sipped her warmed spiced wine, engaging in light conversation with the Battersbys and Mr. Wakefield. Occasionally she would be drawn to the sound of Bastien's voice, then she would catch Stephen's watchful gaze flick between them. Why he was so worried, she had no idea. Bastien had shunned all idea of love. As for Eleanore, her parent's coupling had reminded her that love could not last.

"Did Lord Ellsworth take his leave?" Mr. Wakefield asked Lord Barronsfield, concern in his brow. "I had been led to understand we would be graced with his company as well."

"Trust me when I tell you that there was no one more eager to send off Mr. DuMont than the marquess," Lord Barronsfield said, his tone light, though Eleanore could not miss the jab. "He had some business to attend to that took him away for a short duration. I expect him back any moment."

"Excellent," Mr. Wakefield said, taking a sip of wine. "In honor of this sad event, I brought a cask of my best brandy, just recently acquired. I would be most eager, after dinner, for the opinion of two of our kingdom's most esteemed lords."

Lord Barronsfield nodded politely. "That is most generous, and opportunistic."

"Opportunity is everywhere. I never fail to seize it when presented. If it pleases you, in addition to my donation for Lady Eleanore's foundling charity, perhaps I can auction off a few bottles and donate a portion of the proceeds."

Eleanore winced at Mr. Wakefield's announcement. She had not yet had the opportunity to discuss her plans with Stephen. Or, more truthfully, had not yet managed the courage to.

"Charity?" Stephen's brow dipped, turning his gaze to Eleanore. "What is this?"

"Something I've been musing over since London, when Rosalind and I went to visit Coram's," she said lightly. "Though a tragic event in Elsmdale last week only brought home the importance of it. I wish to have a foundling home in the area."

There. She said it.

"An admirable cause to be sure," her brother said, a flicker of hurt in his eyes. "I am merely surprised I am the last to know of it."

Eleanore smiled tightly, taking a sip of her wine to wash away the wave of unease. She should have told him. There was no good reason not to trust in his support.

She stood, desperate for a turn about the room, but the library, grand as it was, did not seem large enough. Between Bastien's impending departure and Stephen's thinly veiled disappointment in her, she wondered if the idea of a dinner had been a mistake. She rose, clasped her hands in front of her, forced her lips into a smile, then made the clumsy excuse that she needed to check on the arrangements for dinner. She practically bolted out of the room.

Letting out a long breath, she walked to one of the tall windows that looked out over the frozen gardens, peering out into the night, frost painting the edges in glorious little shapes.

"You are distressed, my lady."

Eleanore nearly melted at the sound of Bastien's voice behind her, his voice low, beguiling her. She wanted nothing more than to turn around and have him hold her. But it, like so many other things she wanted, felt impossible. She turned to him, her gaze slipping past him to the door to the library.

"What are you doing here?" she whispered.

"Wakefield is busy whipping up a tale that seems to have everyone enthralled. I merely excused myself."

"And followed me."

"I am still the Wolf de l'Ardoise," he said, a sly smile on his face. "Even without your red cape to mark you, I have become quite adept at hunting in the dark."

Her lips parted, excitement rushing through her body. "Aren't you afraid of being found out? Or perhaps," she paused, hating herself for asking the question, "this isn't the first time you've risked being caught with a lady."

Bastien's eyes narrowed, the slyness morphing to something more profound.

"Until now, there were none worth the trouble."

Eleanore willed her feet to be still, because her head was light and inexplicably happy.

"I have something for you," he continued. He dug into his coat pocket and pulled out the notebook she'd given him to review. The lightness in her chest lessened as her heart sank. He was no doubt returning it, unopened, before he left for London.

"Thank you," she said, attempting a smile as she reached out for it.

"I didn't have time to—"

"You don't have to apologize," she said, trying not to come across as very disappointed. "You had important work to do. I shouldn't have asked, but I…"

He put a finger to her lips, and Eleanore, for just a moment, forgot she had a voice. Cocking an eyebrow, he opened the notebook.

"I made a few notes, here and there," he said, pointing to comments, lists, and even little drawings he'd done in pencil.

Eleanore could scarce believe her eyes. Nearly every page had been annotated in some way, even if it was just a little checkmark, which indicated he'd seen it.

He turned to the last page. "I didn't have time to make as many suggestions as you might have liked. And there are still some issues I believe will take careful consideration before you proceed. But I do think your home needs a name. All the great houses in England have a name. This one should. So I proposed one. But it is just a suggestion. All of it is."

He pointed to the last page where he'd written two words. Martin Cottage.

Martin Cottage. Not Barronsfield, nor even Pembroke.

She swallowed deeply and took a moment to catch her breath, lest the well of emotion tightening her throat loosened, and she made a mess of her face before dinner.

"Bastien," she said at last. "Thank you."

"It is nothing."

She threw her arms around him, buried her face in his lapel, then, pulled away and stared deeply into his eyes.

"It is everything."

CHAPTER 22

*E*verything.

At this moment, Bastien was complete. Sated in such a way that made him understand, perhaps for the first time, that he'd been starved for so long. The years he'd feasted on bitterness only left him more empty. This wondrous sensation of Eleanore in his arms was new.

Glorious.

Enough.

And he wanted it forever. If she would have him.

Her faith in his goodness was unrelenting—and her unflinching acceptance of his past made him hope that a different future was possible. A future that included Eleanore.

In truth, he had only seen for himself a brutal, and perhaps futile, death. That he could even begin to imagine something else…he owed that entirely to her. After Le Veneur Rouge had been dealt with, he would speak with Tante Marie, and then return to ask Eleanore for her hand. He would give her whatever she'd asked of him, and in return, he would savor this glorious sensation—of being wanted, needed. If she would have him.

"Eleanore, I—"

The sound of heavy, quick footfalls approaching pulled them apart as the echo of her touch lingered. Bastien dropped his hands to his sides and let out a low, silent breath.

"DuMont."

Merde. Damn that man and his innate sense of timing. Lord Barronsfield was no doubt a kind and generous lord and a loving brother, but at the moment he was nothing more than an intruder. Reminding himself to behave, Bastien stiffened, turned to the marquess and acknowledged him with all the respect he could conjure. After all, he would have to find a way to earn Barronsfield's consent to marry his sister. But he was willing to do it. Willing to do anything for her.

"Eleanore." The marquess's gaze slid to his sister, a thin smile on his face. "I hope the arrangements with the kitchen are acceptable? Of course, I cannot imagine what oversight cook and the kitchen staff would require, since they have handled all our events with exceptional skill."

"Stephen," she interjected, tucking her book under her arm. "I merely needed some air, and did not want to appear rude. Mr. DuMont was merely taking the liberty of returning a notebook I had given him."

"I am quite certain he was taking liberties," Lord Barronsfield quipped, his gaze narrowing.

At that moment, Bastien wanted nothing more than to wipe that impervious look off his face. For Eleanore's benefit alone he bit his tongue, leaving a tense silence.

"Stephen," Eleanore said brightly. "Could I have a word, briefly? If Mr. DuMont would excuse us."

"Of course," Bastien nodded to both of them, and turned on his heel. He started walking away, watching over his shoulder as Eleanore led Stephen to his study.

As he re-entered the library, Bastien held his countenance steady despite the wave of emotions rolling inside him. In truth, he had been shaking since the moment Eleanore started turning the pages, studying his notes, disbelief and—dare he think it—affection in her eyes. It was the last bit of encouragement he'd needed. He would speak to her brother, and make an offer of marriage.

Refreshing his glass, unwilling to insert himself into the conversation of the other guests, he sauntered past the massive bookshelves on either side of the hearth. It was in the library, he'd learned from Mr. Roderick, that the steward's niece, now Lady Rosalind Barronsfield, fell in love with Lord Barronsfield. While he could entirely imagine falling in love with this room, dealing with Eleanore's brother seemed as farfetched as a fairy tale.

Part of him understood Lord Barronsfield's aversion to him. If their situations were reversed, he too would no doubt be casting a wary eye toward anyone intent on Eleanore. Her beauty and her fortune would be a draw to many. He would have to show Lord Barronsfield he was worthy. Bastien did have a little fortune, and the ability to make a living. And his devotion to Eleanore was unwavering.

He sipped his wine and scrutinized row upon row of books on subjects as varied as botany, classical philosophy, and even sensational novels. He pulled on one, which brought with it almost the entire shelf. Bastien took a step back and raised his arms, waiting for books to tumble down, when the movement stopped and a section of the bookshelf opened like a door. Recognition dawned that this was the hidden entrance to her brother's study that they'd used at the tea. Curiosity besting him, he took a step closer to examine the wonder. As he did so, he heard familiar voices from the other side.

"—my plans. For a foundling home. Like the hospital Rosalind and I visited last month in London. But smaller, of course."

Bastien positioned himself to get a partial view of the room. Lord Barronsfield stood over a desk, looking down at whatever had caught his attention. Across from him was Eleanore.

"They are ambitious," Lord Barronsfield said, flipping through the pages.

"Perhaps. But not unreasonable." Her voice was pitched a little higher than normal.

"Why am I learning this now? And from Wakefield? I didn't realize you had already begun fundraising." Irritation prickled his voice.

"Are you opposed to it?"

"Not in principle," he replied. "I only wish you'd come to see me. This is a significant undertaking."

DuMont could not help but agree. He also knew if anyone could make it a success, it was Eleanore.

"If you weren't so insistent on chasing him away, Mr. DuMont could help me," she replied. "His insights will be invaluable. Stephen, you must convince him to stay."

"Mr. DuMont?"

"Yes," she replied, her smile wide and a bit nervous. "We would be lost here without him."

"I see."

"Yes. We need him. He can't go until Daniel is on his feet. I don't want even the slightest chance of he and Allie not being able to wed, and knowing Daniel, he won't go through with the wedding if he can't work."

"And this is why you want DuMont here?"

Bastien's heart leapt into his throat, and he held his breath.

"Not the only reason." She paused. "He's endorsed my plans for the foundling home. And it took only a little persuasion to do so. You know he is not the type of man who would give an opinion he did not own."

A little persuasion. Bastien swallowed, bitterness at the back of his throat. The tea. Her smiles. Her kiss?

"Eleanore," her brother said. "Tell me the truth. I have seen the way you two regard each other. If you have feelings for him—"

"I don't. At least, not in that way," she replied, an edge of exasperation creeping into her voice. "I just ran away from a marriage in London. Do you really believe I wish to throw myself into the arms of a man just because he will support one of my charities? If that was the case, then I should marry Wakefield. At least he is giving me a donation."

Bastien gripped his glass as a sharp ache shot through his chest.

"I see," her brother replied.

And so did Bastien. He pursed his lips, nodding to himself. Things were becoming goddamned clearer by the moment.

"You cannot force Mr. DuMont away," she replied, each word cutting into Bastien's heart as surely as a scalpel blade. "This will fall apart without him. He has experience that can be harnessed to make this project flourish. Indeed, Mr. DuMont is a man who deserves a little kindness. His beginning in life was difficult. His work on the foundling home would not just help me, but himself as well."

A little kindness? A weight pummeled in his gut, as if he'd been punched. Used? Bastien frowned as he tasted bile at the back of his throat. She didn't just want help with her charity.

He *was* the damn charity.

"Mr. DuMont!" Mr. Battersby called. "Please come and join us. You can't spend your last evening alone."

A familiar hardness descended on him. He was alone. He'd been a fool to think it could be any other way.

A draft from a nearby window slid down his neck, underneath his collar. He swallowed the last of his wine, then set the glass down.

"If you will excuse me, ladies and gentleman," he nodded politely. He marched, with a new found purpose to the door. He was going to London. Where he would be the Wolf.

Devotion was for fools. It was a pity he had to learn the lesson again.

STEPHEN RETURNED TO THE LIBRARY, leaving Eleanore alone with her thoughts. She closed the notebook, leaving it on his desk. He hadn't dismissed the idea outright, and in truth, once she'd begun to talk about it with him, it was clear he was willing to see the merit in it.

Her fingers lingered a moment on the spaces in the margins where Bastien had scribbled his notes. Truly, it was a gift like none other she had ever been given. It was permission to pursue her ambition. Bastien had given her that.

Her smile faltered ever so slightly as she recalled her excuses to

Stephen about Bastien staying in Elmsdale. Whether she had feelings for him or not was quite beside the point. She could not act on them. Whether or not she loved him, he deserved long-lasting happiness. Her love might not be enough to give him that.

She left the study, eager to return to her guests. Pinching her cheeks before she entered the library, she caught the hurried countenance of Allie, one of the servants, rushing toward her.

"Allie, is there something amiss?" she asked.

"No, my lady," the girl replied, her normally cheery face now uneasy. "It's Mr. DuMont. He's asked for his coat and hat. He seemed quite cross."

His coat? Panic tightened at her throat. "Has he gone?"

"No, my lady," she replied. "I've been delaying him until you were aware."

Eleanore gave the girl a grateful squeeze, then dashed to the main entry, hoping there was some sort of error.

"Mr. DuMont!" she called out, racing to him. "I hope someone is not seriously ill."

His face was utterly devoid of emotion, which did nothing to calm her. "No."

"Then, I hope my brother did not say anything to chase you away," she replied with a tight smile. "He can be a bear at times."

"Lord Barronsfield's opinion of me is understood. At least with him, I know where I stand."

A clip of anger betrayed his calm demeanor. Eleanore swallowed, a slow-growing panic building inside.

"I don't understand." She blinked as tears pricked at the back of her eyes.

"Tell me the truth, if you dare. Why do you want me to stay?"

"You know why," she pressed, entirely confused. "Because I would miss you."

"Do not lie to me. You do not have the talent for it." His jaw flinched and he stepped back, as if eager to put distance between them. "Or perhaps you do. Because what I have learned is that you need me for your foundlings."

"Yes. No." Eleanore stepped toward him, reaching out, but he pulled back, away from her hands. "Your ideas are spectacular, I just thought—"

"—you could use me?" he seethed. "And I suppose, while I am here, I can soothe your overwrought conscience about Daniel Morehouse's injuries."

Eleanore blinked, realization settling heavily in her stomach. "You were eavesdropping on my conversation with my brother, weren't you? I thought I could trust you, Bastien."

Bastien recoiled, his reaction fleeting as he quickly replaced it with detachment.

"Old habits die hard, my lady. I came here as a spy, not a healer. That you chose to ignore that fact is not my problem. And neither is it my problem if Daniel Morehouse walks, or your orphanage gets built."

He brushed past her. Incensed, Eleanore caught up with him, blocking his path.

"I don't understand why you are so angry. I have offered friendship. A living. A purpose."

He raked a hand through his hair.

"I am not one of your little projects, *my lady*." He took her by the shoulders, the bitterness in his voice pricking at the back of her neck. "I do not even count as one of your friends."

"That is not true!" Eleanore replied, struggling to keep her voice low when all she wanted to do was cry out. "When I offered you friendship, I meant it."

"Using someone for your own ends, however virtuous in your eyes, is not friendship," he replied. "Trust me, I know. I am the Wolf de l'Ardoise. For one dangerous moment, you encouraged me to forget that."

"Not forget. Just move on. You are a healer too, and a good one. There is so much—"

"*Pas plus!*" he said through gritted teeth, his eyes gray and hard. "I am not one of your foundlings. I do not desire to be rescued. It's been attempted, and I'm sure if you asked the baroness she will tell you I am not worth your trouble. You want to fix me, make me believe that I can somehow be the better man so I can fit into this little world of yours, where you make everything right. But I don't belong here."

"But you do," she said, reaching out for him. He stepped away. She let out an involuntary gasp, before attempting to collect herself. "Bastien, you don't understand. Stephen was upset with me, and I do not like to disappoint him. I could not very well tell him about us. Not now."

His eyes narrowed. "About us? What is there between us, my lady?"

What was there between them? It could not be nothing. She could not feel this way about nothing. "I don't know."

He pursed his lips and nodded to himself.

"Well, I do. You didn't run away from London to fall into the arms of someone like me." He swallowed deeply, his eyes suddenly bright, as he recited back her ill-chosen words. "And you were right. Because men like me belong out there, in places like London, with the rest of the vipers you fled from."

"Bastien, please understand. I was just with Stephen, convincing him that you should stay."

"For whom should I stay?" He dropped his arms. "For your orphans? For Daniel Morehouse?"

"For me." *Because I think I love you.* Why couldn't she just say it?

"Liar."

The viciousness of the word took her breath. She stood, fixed to the floor, unable to find her voice.

"I am not one of your foundlings," he said. "I don't deserve saving, even if I desired it. And I do not."

"Bastien—"

"I know something about sin, Lady Eleanore. And trust me..." His voice grew thick a moment, and he paused to swallow. "The stain cannot be washed away with good deeds. And if there is one thing I have learned, good deeds always come with a price."

"Bastien," she whispered, her lower lip trembling.

"Do not give me tears." He turned away. "Save them for someone willing to be duped by them."

"Go then," she replied, swallowing her tears and letting the anger rise. "Turn your back on all of the people you supposedly care nothing about. Because I know the truth of it. I have seen it. You love this work. You were made to do it. So do not accuse me of cowardice when you are too afraid to care."

"You think you know so much about caring, about love." He paused, swallowed hard, and for a moment she thought she saw tears forming in his eyes. "But you cannot see it, can you? Not even when it is right in front of you."

Eleanore flinched as surely as if she'd been struck. The door opened, a rush of cold air hitting her, stinging her skin.

And then he was gone.

CHAPTER 23

*E*leanore returned to the library, where six faces greeted her expectantly. Her gaze flickered to Stephen, whose expression steeled as he knew, in that way he often knew, when someone he cared about was in pain.

"Mr. DuMont sends his regrets," she said, carefully keeping her voice calm, and steady. "He was called away by an urgent matter."

"Dear me," Mrs. Darling said. "I hope it is not too serious."

"I have no doubt whoever it is will be in good hands," Stephen said, his voice matter of fact. He nodded ever so slightly to Eleanore. "We shall continue with dinner. I am certain that he would not want us to stop on his account."

"Perhaps we should wait," Mr. Wakefield said, "until Lord Ellsworth returns."

"Ellsworth should be here within the hour," Stephen said. "I am eager to see this gift you have brought, Mr. Wakefield."

Mr. Wakefield nodded, obviously pleased his gift was so welcome. He walked behind Stephen and Eleanore as a footman led them to the dining room, where a glittering table waited. To one side was a large, intricately marked cask, flanked on either side by one of Mr. Wakefield's servants. The gesture, she supposed, added to the circumstance of the evening, even as the reason for it had become moot.

Eleanore's heart sank. She'd wanted everything to be perfect for Bastien. And now it didn't matter. She slid into her chair, a tight smile on her face. She'd had cook prepare some of Bastien's favorite dishes for this evening. The very idea of eating now turned her stomach.

He was wrong to think she had taken his good will for granted. She treasured it.

She'd watched him carefully since he'd arrived. She knew joy when she saw it. She'd studied it at length every time she was with Stephen and his family. The looks they exchanged when they thought no one watched. It burst from them.

Bastien had it too. She'd caught it. When he came from visiting Daniel, or the countless other times since he'd arrived when he'd helped people. Sometimes the medicine was brutal, and it wore on him nearly as much as it did his patients. But he was determined to deny the joy when he found it. As if he wasn't deserving of it. Like he was shutting off a piece of himself.

Just as she denied what she felt when she was with him.

You do not see what is right in front of you.

"Eleanore, my dear."

The sound of Mrs. Darling's voice snapped her out of her reverie. She swallowed, then pasted a smile on her face.

"Apologies, Mrs. Darling. I am distracted by my own thoughts."

"Not a worry, my dear. I was just concerned about Mr. DuMont."

Eleanore nodded and reached for her glass, putting it to her lips to allow her a moment to collect her wits. She was entirely scattered. In truth she would have swallowed the entire glass, and perhaps asked for more. Instead she took the smallest of sips.

"The trials of being a caregiver," Mr. Darling concurred. "The needs of others supersede your own."

No, she wanted to cry out. His need to walk away came before everyone else. Including her. And that was the unbearable part of it.

"I hope whatever business takes him to London will find him well," Mr. Wakefield said.

"I will be returning as well, now that my business here is concluded," Stephen replied. That business, Eleanore assumed, was Bastien.

"When do you plan to return?" Mr. Wakefield asked.

"In a few days," Stephen said. "I am always loathe to leave, but eager to be reunited with the marchioness and the children."

"And will you be returning as well, my lady?"

Eleanore looked up. She should. Face the crowds. Show them she was not afraid. That she had nothing to fear. She could return, be glittering, and trust Daniel to heal. And while she was there, she would raise funds and then come back to Barronsfield and begin work on Martin Cottage.

"I think I shall."

"Are you certain?" Stephen asked, concern in his brow. "I would not compel you to return."

"For the moment," she said, "I have no reason to stay."

"Perhaps you shall be able to see Mr. DuMont when you are there," Mrs. Battersby said.

"I think not," she said, cursing herself as she caught her voice wavering. Taking a breath and a drink of wine, she steeled herself to get through the rest of the evening. "I think not."

ta.

BASTIEN PULLED up the collar on his coat. Cold had settled in and while he could have waited for the offer of a carriage, he wanted Barronsfield and everyone attached to it behind him. His breath hung heavy in the air as he took the first steps down the stone staircase. The cold was bitter, and he wanted to savor it. It was, if nothing else, familiar.

He still burned from his encounter with Eleanore. Her tears had seared his heart like flame, which had surprised him. All the more reason to be walking away. It was the price he paid for opening up to her. Not that she had noticed. Perhaps she did care for him, in her own way, and maybe even more than she believed herself capable.

Or maybe he was simply a means to an end. Everyone had a

purpose for Bastien DuMont. Sir Richard Hamilton, Marat and his ilk that drew him into the cause, even Tante Marie. In the end, he wanted the sensation he'd experienced when Eleanore Pembroke had thrown her arms around him and told him he was everything. He was enough.

But he was not.

His foot hit the bottom step when the sound of an approaching carriage caught his attention. It slowed to a complete stop, and Lord Ellsworth hopped out onto the hard stone courtyard.

"DuMont," he said, coming toward him. "Just the man I need to see."

Bastien nodded, relieved to have something else to think about besides Eleanore. "Your news, I hope?" Though he did not expect anything that would deviate him from his plans to visit London, the more information he had about Le Veneur Rouge, the better.

"I am not certain it is, to be truthful. But perhaps you can make sense of it." Ellsworth pulled a note, emblazoned with the seal of Weymouth, from his pocket. Bastien squinted in the dim light from a nearby window to read the contents.

It confirmed Ellsworth's story about his great grandmother who, for reasons lost to history, had an earlier marriage to a man by the name of Howard Trimbel, which made her subsequent marriage, and the children she'd born the Duke of Weymouth, illegitimate. The title was moved to the line that made Ellsworth the heir.

"I should have never been destined for the title," Ellsworth said. "One might wonder what life I could have had."

Bastien glanced up at the man, catching the subtle tone of regret in his voice.

"Certainly not someone with the time or money to build telescopes," Bastien quipped, before turning his attention back to the letter.

The family left England in disgrace, the note continued, though they were hardly out of pocket. Ellsworth's own father had tried to search them out, without success. The only information they had was that they had gone to Bermuda and become involved in trade.

"I'm not certain there is anything of note there, I'm afraid,"

Ellsworth repeated, then started up the stairs. "Come. I am already late for dinner."

Bastien stood, re-reading the note, searching for any clue. Nothing. He folded it up and gave it back to Ellsworth. "You go on. I have an early morning ahead of me. I am in little mood for company at present."

Ellsworth's gaze narrowed behind his spectacles, but must have deduced that Bastien was in no mood to discuss it.

"Of course," he said. "I will be returning in the morning. If you can stand the company, you are welcome to join me."

Bastien nodded. "I will consider it."

He turned away, walking off into the night, the lights of Barronsfield and Eleanore Pembroke at his back. He wanted to be angry. Furious. In the end, with each step, there was a growing sadness. An emptiness.

He would leave his patients behind, but they would do without him. Daniel's leg needed time. Hanley's ankle needed a miracle, or at least, rest. The most seriously injured of his patients, the aptly named Jacob Grimm, was still alive.

At least Grimm didn't expect a damn thing from him except pain. He was a man who seemed to need little of anything. Just a bottle of rum and the meager belongings he'd brought with him to Wakefield's estate. The single wooden plank nailed into the wall that had robbed Grimm of his right leg below his knee, the name of the ship scratched into its surface.

Bastien pulled his collar around his neck more tightly, cursing the wind, the memory of that rough piece of wood slowing his gait.

Trimbel. That was the word scratched into the wood. Bastien stopped walking as his mind raced back to the day when Grimm complained about Bastien's stitching. Jacob Grimm had been on a vessel called the Trimbel. A merchant ship. A vessel owned by Hugh Wakefield.

A low, sick feeling rooted Bastien where he stood, then he wheeled around, looking back in the direction of Barronsfield Manor, where Wakefield and the others now dined. Wakefield, who warned Bastien about the whims and power of the aristocracy, and yet used that association to his advantage. Wakefield had been especially keen on knowing Ellsworth's whereabouts. He had boasted about a cask of brandy he brought, to be opened after dinner.

A dinner where Eleanore would be present.

Bastien closed his eyes, forcing himself to recall every detail of Grimm's injuries. Grimm had blown off his hand, claiming a rifle had misfired. Bastien had suspected even at the time the man was lying to him, but he'd written it off as the tale of a man eager to keep his job and cover up his own folly. He hadn't blown off his hand because he'd been sloppy with a rifle. He'd singed his hair and eyebrows, had powder burns on his clothes. His back had been significantly bruised, as if he'd been thrown backward. Bastien opened his eyes, clenching his hands. Grimm was probably involved in something else, far more deadly. More explosive. Something he was now bringing in to Barronsfield Manor, under Wakefield's orders. Concealed as a cask of brandy.

Bastien bolted inside the great house. It was eerily quiet. He bounded up the steps toward the dining room, and found a footman rushing by, a fresh bottle of wine in his hand.

"A cask of brandy was brought as a gift by Mr. Wakefield. Where is it?" Bastien asked.

"Mr. Wakefield had two of his servants bring it to the dining room. Mr. Wakefield insisted they guard it."

"Was one of them missing a leg by chance?"

The footman nodded, and Bastien's heart leapt in his throat.

"Take me. *Vite.*"

CHAPTER 24

*B*astien followed on the heels of the servant, who pulled on the door. It would not open.

"It's locked," he said, clearly confused.

Bastien grabbed the bottle of wine out of his hand. "I assume you have a key."

The boy fumbled with his key ring, but the door still wouldn't open. Bastien put an ear to the door, his gut clenching as he heard the sound of porcelain breaking and frantic cries.

A second servant, the girl he recognized as Daniel Morehouse's sweetheart, rushed to them.

"Mr. DuMont, sir. Thank goodness you've come. One of Mr. Wakefield's men drew a pistol and chased out all the servants."

Bastien pulled the two together, blood pounding in his ears. "That cask of Mr. Wakefield's is full of gunpowder. You need to get everyone out of the house—gather at the stables. You—" he pointed at the footman—"find Mr. Schofield at once and alert him to what is happening. Tell him not to approach the house until I give a signal."

"But what about His Lordship, and the others?" asked the girl, her voice shaking.

"Don't you worry about them." Truth be told, he was terrified at the moment, but he forced it aside. He needed to think. "How many of Wakefield's men are in there?"

"Just two—but they had pistols."

"*Bien*. Go on now. Get everyone out."

The two ran off, leaving Bastien standing at the door, fury warring with the need to be completely focused. He was going to kill Hugh Wakefield. If he so much as harmed a hair on Eleanore's head, he would do it slowly. And he wasn't going to let anger deny him the privilege.

He pulled the dagger out of his boot and stashed it in his sleeve, wanting it at the ready. He put his ear to the door, the stifled sobs of Mrs. Battersby mixing with the low, sharp tones of Lord Barronsfield trying to reason with Wakefield. Bastien knocked on the door. Silence was his response. He could not go blazing in—the man would panic, and panic would not do in a room with three pistols and a powder keg. He could not be seen as a threat, either.

Bastien, still gripping the bottle of wine he'd grabbed from the servant, found inspiration at last. Loosening his cravat and opening his collar, he took a healthy pull from the wine bottle, then drenching some in his hand, rubbed it into his neck, and through his hair. Feeling appropriately disheveled, he began pounding on the door.

"Lord Barronsfield," he yelled, letting his tongue loosen to mimic the sound of inebriation. "Let me in, you impervious English bastard."

A hushed sound came over the room, but there was still no response.

"Barronsfield!" he yelled again, pounding at the door. "Don't you want to tell everyone how you kicked me out of your house on a cold winter night because I dared to make eyes at your sister?"

The door flew open and Bastien tumbled forward, catching himself on one of Wakefield's men.

"Evenin'," he slurred, casting his eye about the room, trying to drink up every detail. Lord Barronsfield, closest to him, sat at the head of the table. To his left sat Eleanore and the other ladies. On his right, Ellsworth and the other two gentlemen, and the empty chair where Wakefield was supposed to sit. Everyone appeared unharmed, with the notable exception of Ellsworth, who appeared to have earned most of Wakefield's wrath, his nose bloodied. Eleanore, for the moment, was unharmed.

Wakefield had brought two goons with him, and both of them were armed. Off to one side, between the two lords, sat the large brandy cask perched on a caddy, a fuse trailing out the back. Even with the dagger in his hands, there was no way he could get to it without getting shot, especially since Grimm was standing next to it, his pistol drawn, looking more than eager to use it. No damn wonder Wakefield appreciated the man's loyalty. Grimm had blown half his hand off working on the ignition device that was inside that powder keg, and he was still ready to kill for Wakefield.

"M'lord," he said to Ellsworth, before falling forward on the table, scattering plates and forks, to a chorus of gasps. He scooped up a small knife into his hands, tucking it into his sleeve, making certain Lord Barronsfield saw what he'd done. He needed help if he was going to get people out of here alive.

Bastien felt himself being hauled off the table. He grasped his wine bottle, shrugging off Wakefield's lout, then walked behind Ellsworth, stumbling again, pressing the knife into his hands, before swinging wildly upright. He pointed a finger at Barronsfield. "You sir, are, as the French say, *un couillon*. I don't even want your sister. I need a woman with big..." He stuck out his bottom lip and flung his hands to his chest, pantomiming an oversized bosom.

Lord Barronsfield, apparently understanding his cue, roared at Bastien.

"So help me God, DuMont. If we get out of here alive, I am going to shoot you myself."

"The aristocracy." Bastien shook his head, took a swig from his wine bottle, then looked at Wakefield. "Too much inbreeding. You're lucky, Wakefield, you escaped the taint."

"Tie up the frog," Wakefield said, his voice cold and even.

Bastien found himself shoved onto a chair between Ellsworth and Barronsfield, the bottle pulled from his hands, his hands tied behind him.

Wakefield turned round, his face wild. "I knew it. The Wolf. I will enjoy knowing your guts will be strewn across the same carpets as the lot you helped escape justice. You're a traitor to your own people, DuMont. A disgrace."

Bastien let go a drunken laugh as he slid the blade out from his sleeve and started slicing through the ropes binding him. "Who's the disgrace? Tying up old women and commoners? Is this what you're reduced to? I suppose that man in London they've caught is just another one of your lackeys, ready to have his neck stretched on your behalf."

"Are you trying to be a man of honor, DuMont? The last time I saw you, you were drowning your sorrows in Mr. Roderick's cheap brandy and whimpering like the dog you are. Seems to be a habit. You smell like the floor of a public house." Wakefield sneered, leaning up against the edge of the table opposite Bastien, his eyes wide and manic. "Leave it to my cousin here to ruin my plans. I'm going to enjoy my breakfast tomorrow, knowing I've sent you to hell. And, yes, there is someone sitting in Newgate who is quite willing to take the glory for it. So I am quite safe."

His bindings were still not yet loose, or Bastien would have rushed him and gutted him where he stood. Instead, he cocked his head to one side, gesturing for Wakefield to come close.

"If you don't let them go," Bastien said, his voice now completely steady, letting go all notion that he was nothing but serious and quite sober. "I'm going to kill you. Actually, I might do it anyway. So if you are concerned about my honor, don't be. I merely wish to spare the lady the thrill I will have at spilling your blood on Barronsfield's expensive floors."

Wakefield squirmed but a moment, clearly uncertain about Bastien's threats. But he appeared unmoved.

"Lord Barronsfield, like every member of his abhorrent class, suffered from the lottery of being born to privilege. That privilege will end here. My tragedy, of course, is that I cannot have any witnesses of this momentous event—beyond the good people of Elmsdale, who will be the first to witness the strike of Le Veneur

Rouge, killing two of the most powerful men in the country." Wakefield gestured to Eleanore and the others, sitting across the table from Bastien, then shrugged. "They will be a necessary, if forgotten sacrifice. Just like all those priests in Paris, remember, DuMont? Except this will be quick. Painless. No messy trials. I am judge and executioner. Grimm!"

The one-handed man walked to the cask, located to one side near the head of the table, between Lord Barronsfield and Eleanore. He pulled a candle from one of the elaborate candlesticks on the table and lit the fuse. The hissing filled the room, followed by a series of gasps.

"You shouldn't have done that, Grimm," Bastien said, his voice light, desperate to keep his show of confidence. He was nearly through his bonds. "I'm going to have to take your other leg next, at the very least."

Wakefield bent over, a smug expression on his face. "Go to hell, Mr. DuMont."

Bastien, summoning up every ounce of his fury, smashed his forehead against Wakefield, sending the man stumbling back into the table before falling to the floor.

The crack of a pistol filled the room, the ball whizzing past Bastien's head, burying itself in the oak panel. Grimm came at him, but Lord Barronsfield, taking his lead from Bastien, threw himself, chair and all, at the one-handed man, knocking him over. Grimm landed on his still-healing stump, causing an ungodly howl to cut through the room.

To his left, Bastien watched Ellsworth working on his own bonds, and beyond him, a second pistol was aimed at his head. Bastien pulled at his fraying bindings, freeing himself at last, just in time to send his blade flying into the chest of Ellsworth's would-be killer. The pistol went off, shattering a decanter as the man slumped to the floor. The fuse continued to hiss, growing shorter with each passing second.

Bastien pulled his blade out of the goon's chest and rushed to cut the fuse, his hands sweating, the blood rushing in his ears. At last, the fuse fell to the floor and burned itself out.

The sound of a hammer being pulled on a third pistol cut through Bastien's relief. It was Wakefield, and it was aimed squarely at the powder keg. Bastien flipped the dagger, grasping it by the handle ready to strike, when Ellsworth, able to free himself, rushed the Red Hunter, the pistol discharging as it fell, the ball finding purchase in Grimm's body, silencing his moans. Both men scrambled on the floor, but before Bastien could assist, Wakefield was out the door, Ellsworth on his heels.

Bastien started after his long-sought prey, when the sound of Eleanore's voice brought him to heel.

"Bastien, please be careful."

He whipped around, his gaze focused on Eleanore. He was almost afraid to look into her eyes. Afraid she would see him for the killer he could be. Instead, he saw something else. Awe.

He went to her, crouching down to cut her bonds. As she brought her hands to her lap, he rubbed them quickly, trying to get blood into them. Then he wiped the dagger on his coat and placed it her hands.

"I have to help Ellsworth."

She took him by his collar, pulled him close, and kissed him. "Go. I will take care of the others."

Bastien paused, momentarily dazzled by the sensation of her lips, then smiled. "I know you will."

He sprinted as fast as his legs could carry him. Below, he caught Wakefield heading out the front door, Ellsworth hard on his heels. Ellsworth was unarmed. Bastien was not so confident Wakefield was as well.

At last, Bastien burst out the door, ready to strike, when he was nearly knocked to the ground by the force of Ellsworth and Wakefield wrestling atop the stone staircase. During their violent dance, Wakefield managed to get Ellsworth in a stranglehold, his arm curling around the younger man's neck.

"You're pathetic," he heard Wakefield snarl at his very distant cousin. "Hiding away, dabbling with your machines. You have power and you don't even know how to use it. No wonder your intended threw you off. No doubt she wanted a man, not a loiter sack."

Bastien watched as Ellsworth went deadly still, and for a moment, Bastien was certain he was finished. Instead, Ellsworth drove his elbow into Wakefield's gut, then grabbed hold of his arm and cast him aside. By the time Wakefield had righted himself, he teetered on the edge of the stairs, then lost his balance, tumbling violently down the hard stone steps to the bottom. Before Bastien could reach him, he knew by the unnatural way the man's head lay that Wakefield was dead.

Seconds passed, feeling like hours. Bastien flew down the stars, and stood above the man he'd hunted for so long, trying to understand that it was finished.

He crouched over Wakefield's lifeless body, the face wearing an expression of contorted surprise, as if at the very last he'd recognized he'd lost. Bastien wiped his hand over his brow, realizing only then that he was shaking. He let go a low, unsettled breath, then flipped the body on its belly. There was one more thing he needed to know.

"Bastien?"

The sound of her voice, still trembling, stopped him cold. Eleanore, wrapped in her red cape, ran down the steps toward him. Beyond her, Mr. Darling and Lord Barronsfield were assisting Ellsworth.

"You shouldn't be here." He went to her, deliberately standing between her and the body, trying to protect her from the grisly scene. "This is no place for a lady."

"I am more than a lady," she said. "I had to know that you were unharmed. I could not have borne it if...if—" Her voice grew thick, her lower lip quivering. He wanted nothing more but to end her tears with a kiss. Instead, he wiped away her tears with his thumbs, and smiled.

"I am well, as you can see," he replied.

"You were magnificent," she said, a smile on her face.

"The credit belongs to Ellsworth," he replied, gesturing to the top of the stairs where the marquess stood.

"None of us would be standing here, including Ellsworth, if it wasn't for the Wolf." She handed him back his dagger. "I don't know how we shall ever be able to repay you for what you have done."

A smile froze on his face. He knew the price his heart wanted. But he could not ask unless it was freely given.

"That smile is enough," he said. And perhaps it would have to be.

"Well done, DuMont," Lord Barronsfield said, as he came down to join them. He held out his hand. "That was the worst acting I have ever seen. Though you do smell like a cellar."

Bastien exchanged a look with Eleanore, who could not help but burst into laughter. Her brother, clearly unaware of the humor in his statements, merely shook his head.

"We have the powder keg being moved to a safe location. Eleanore, I've asked for a carriage to take both the Darlings and the Battersbys home," he said. "Why don't you wait inside while DuMont, Ellsworth, and I attend to this dastardly business. Perhaps you could send word to the servants that it is done."

She nodded, then looked to Bastien before sneaking a kiss on his cheek, then disappeared inside.

Ellsworth walked down the stairs, looking worse for wear.

Bastien stopped him. "You should sit, so I can look at your—"

"Don't you dare," Ellsworth countered, putting his spectacles back on his nose, a crack splitting one of the lenses. He looked down at the body of his long-lost cousin, his countenance one of grim resignation.

Bastien went back to the body, cutting a seam through the back of the man's clothes.

"What are you doing?" Lord Barronsfield asked.

"Making sure," Bastien answered. "I need a light."

Lord Barronsfield returned a moment later with a lantern, and held it up over the man's body. There, on the left shoulder, was the Wolf's bite. And, just above it, a large pink stork bite similar to the one borne by Ellsworth.

It was him. Le Veneur Rouge. The lost prince of Weymouth. And he was most certainly dead.

Bastien stood, silent, while the body was covered, then loaded on a cart along with the bodies of his accomplices. They would reside, ironically, in the morgue behind the infirmary until it could be decided what was to be done with them.

He'd wanted to kill this man for years. That he had been unable to do so, however, did not weigh on Bastien as he'd thought it might. Rather, as he looked up at the lit windows of Barronsfield Manor and saw Eleanore's silhouette in the window, he could not help but feel that his regrets ran in a different direction.

Ellsworth held out his hand, which Bastien took. "I suppose we are even now."

Lord Barronsfield similarly extended his hand. "I am in your debt, DuMont. Not just for my life, but Eleanore's as well."

Bastien nodded, his gaze drifting up to the window where Eleanore had been, his heart heavy.

"Is your plan still to return to London on the morrow?" Lord Barronsfield asked.

"Yes." He tore his gaze away from the window. "I have no reason to stay. I will have to give my report to Hamilton, and I wish to see Tante Marie to personally inform her she has been avenged."

Bastien prepared to hop onto the cart that was taking the bodies to the morgue. Before it pulled away, Bastien heard Eleanore's voice cry out.

"Wait!"

Bastien looked up to see Eleanore running down the steps, a heavy black cloak in her hand. She ran to the carriage and handed it to Bastien.

"I don't want you to be cold," she said, her voice breathless, a smile straining across her face while sadness ruled her eyes.

"Thank you," he replied, touched by her kindness. Of course, that was what she did. She was kind. He reminded himself not to read anymore into the gesture than intended.

As sorely as he wished it otherwise.

CHAPTER 25

*B*astien sat in what had become his regular spot at the Elm and Thistle, his hands wrapped around a cup filled with hot coffee, one of medical texts from Dr. Brayden's collection opened before him. It was over, Bastien kept reminding himself. It was over.

And yet, nothing felt resolved.

He'd sent a message through Hamilton's network of contacts that Le Veneur Rouge, also known as Hugh Wakefield, had been positively identified and neutralized. While it was entirely possible that someone else might try to claim the title, Bastien hoped whatever remaining elements of his network would wither.

There would always be other threats. Things were still unsettled in France. But Bastien found himself unwilling to return. He was done fighting the storm.

But a storm of ice and rain had kept Bastien from leaving for London. Still, he found Brayden's home to be too quiet, so he bundled himself up and ran the half mile to find Mr. Roderick's hospitality and warm fire. He was greeted with a cup of hot, if mediocre coffee, a hunk of cheese and bread, and Mr. Roderick's morning litany of local gossip before he was left alone.

He idly flipped through the pages of his book, wondering what the hell he was going to do now.

Most tempting was to stay here in Elsmdale, accept a living as a surgeon, and the torment of seeing Eleanore Pembroke, knowing she could not love him. Or he could take care of Tante Marie, if she would let him. He could be her personal surgeon, or establish a practice somewhere else. Either way, Eleanore Pembroke would haunt his dreams.

The heavy creak of the door was a welcome intrusion on his melancholy. Bastien peered up from his reading, then straightened when he saw Lord Barronsfield walking in the door.

"Your Lordship!" Mr. Roderick's voice boomed with a mix of surprise and pride, scurrying out from behind the counter, ready to take the man's cloak. "To what do we owe the honor of having you at the Thistle on this dreary morning?"

"Good day, Mr. Roderick," the marquess replied, removing his hat and shaking off his cloak, which he placed in the outstretched arms of the innkeeper. "I have business with our surgeon this morning. But first, I will have some of your hottest coffee, if you have any."

The innkeeper, moving faster than Bastien had ever seen, hung Lord Barronsfield's cloak by the fire and had a fresh cup of coffee in the marquess's hand before the man had settled himself opposite Bastien, who found himself perplexed by the company.

"It is positively miserable out there," the marquess began, pausing to test the coffee. His lips pulled back as he took a sip. "A perfect day for the sole quality of Roderick's brew—it is always steaming hot."

They sat in surprisingly comfortable silence, until Lord Barronsfield broke it.

"Tell me, DuMont, what are your plans now that this is over?"

Bastien shrugged, the answer no more forthcoming that it had been moments ago, when he was wrestling with this very question. "Return to London I suppose, and see to the baroness. She could use a caregiver, perhaps, though I doubt she'd admit to it. Maybe set up a practice somewhere. I think Tante Marie would like to see that her investment finally paid off."

"You are done with the world of intrigue?" Lord Barronsfield asked.

Bastien sat back in his chair and arched an eyebrow, annoyed by the question. "I am done with being at war with the world, if that is what you are asking." He paused, the image of Wakefield's body lying on the ground still fresh in his mind. "The Wolf de l'Ardoise died with Le Veneur Rouge. I have to learn to be simply Bastien DuMont once again."

Lord Barronsfield sat quietly, pursing his lips, as if considering Bastien's answer.

"Lady Eleanore—how is she?"

Lord Barronsfield paused, watching Bastien keenly, then shifted in his seat.

"We all had a fitful night, as you might expect. I saw her this morning, before I left." He smiled, though worry lingered in his brow. "She was in the kitchen, baking bread."

The image of her, her long fingers working dough, sprinkling flour on a board, sent an unwanted longing straight to Bastien's heart.

"She does that to be useful," Bastien said. "And to be close to her mother. She is not one to be idle, your sister."

"No. Definitely not. Heavens knows the man who deserves her will have to understand that. To nurture her need to be active."

I understand her. I would nurture her. But did he deserve her?

Barronsfield took a notebook out of his jacket and pushed it across the table at Bastien.

"Explain this."

Bastien's gaze fell upon Eleanore's notebook. The book that she'd showed her brother. The one that Bastien had pored over. It contained his advice, and perhaps a piece of his heart.

He shrugged, as if what he was looking at had no particular meaning. He reached out and opened a few pages, then, unwilling to torture himself any longer, closed it and pushed it back across the table.

"It's Lady Eleanore's notes to build her orphanage. A foundling home," he said at last, still staring at it. "She wants to save the world, your sister."

"I see."

Whether it was the tone of his voice, or the lingering pause before Lord Barronsfield spoke, but Bastien's gaze snapped up to the marquess's face, and he gave himself a mental shake. There was a knowing in the man's expression Bastien found uncomfortable. Perhaps it was because it reminded him too much of Eleanore, when she saw through his façade of nonchalance.

"What is the meaning of this visit?" Bastien pressed. "Le Veneur Rouge is dead. I am leaving, so you should be pleased. And if you are concerned, your sister sees me as a means to make her plans a reality. Nothing more."

"Let me tell you about Eleanore," Lord Barronsfield said. "And before I start, you should know that I would gut any man I thought would harm her."

"As is your right, of course," Bastien countered, determined to keep his tone neutral.

"But I wish nothing more than to see her happy. And, as much as it grieves me to say it, the last time I saw her truly happy was when she was speaking of you, last night, in my study, before whatever happened between you that drove you off."

"It was nothing."

"Do not lie to me, DuMont. I watched you two last night, when you put that book in her hands. I have never seen my sister filled with such gladness."

Bastien gripped his cup. "You were watching us? Goddammit, Barronsfield."

"Lord Barronsfield to you, DuMont," the marquess, continued, apparently nonplussed by Bastien's growing discomfort. "Whatever you had given her, it was more than just scribbles in a notebook. It was joy. It was—"

Just my heart.

"Nothing." Bastien glared at the marquess, angry. Perhaps he was treading too close to the wound that might scar him forever.

"You can tell yourself that, if it makes you feel better now," the marquess replied. "If anyone on this earth knows what it means to deny your own heart, and the havoc that it can wreak, it is I."

"Do you know what will make Lady Eleanore happy? Let her build her orphanage. Support her, but do not smother her. And leave my part of it in that book. It is all she wants from me...and she already has it."

The marquess straightened, took another sip of his coffee, then made a face, and pushed the cup aside.

"I see."

Bastien gathered his belongings, realizing perhaps too late that Lord Barronsfield damn well did see, and saw too much. "I have to go."

"We are not done."

Anger rankled in Bastien's shoulders at the sharp command in the marquess's voice, and he used it to propel him out of his chair.

"I am." This wasn't his goddamn country. Lord Barronsfield was nothing more to Bastien than another man with more money than he could spend.

"DuMont, we are not finished here."

Bastien kept walking, tossed a coin on Mr. Roderick's counter. Before he got much farther, a hand came down heavily on his shoulder. Bastien paused, his fingers curling into a fist.

He felt himself being spun around. Instinctively, he pushed the marquess back, sprawling onto a nearby table. Whatever satisfaction he gained was short lived, as the marquess got to his feet and sent his fist into Bastien's jaw. Bastien remained on his feet, but the sting of the blow went straight through him. He pulled back his hand when it was caught by Mr. Roderick, who then placed himself between them.

"Excuse me, Your Lordship, Mr. DuMont," he interjected, a fatherly tone that suggested, if it was possible, that he was disappointed with the two of them. "I don't allow brawlin' in here. Why don't you two sit, and I'll bring you each a warm cup of my best port."

Bastien looked over at the marquess, who, similarly chastened by the innkeeper's welcoming tone, nodded in understanding. They righted the bench and sat down opposite each other in silence until the innkeeper returned with two cups of warm, spiced port. Bastien examined the wine, the dark liquid glistening in the lamplight, the smells of cinnamon and cloves rising from the cup. Somehow, it reminded him of her. The scents of the kitchen. Warm. Welcoming. Intoxicating. He pulled together his scattered thoughts, and looked Lord Barronsfield in the eye.

"Lady Eleanore is a remarkable woman who lives every day of her life trying to please you. Trying to prove to you she is worthy of the love you have given her."

The marquess frowned. "She has nothing to prove, DuMont. She knows that."

"Are you certain?" he pressed, careful not to show any judgment. Indeed, he had not a hair of a doubt that Lord Barronsfield doted on Eleanore.

"I tell her so at every opportunity. I show her."

Bastien stretched out in his chair. "Barronsfield is a beautiful estate. The house is magnificent. Stately. Even welcoming. But it can cast a mighty shadow."

Lord Barronsfield paused, crossing his arms. "I understand what you are implying. Indeed, I know the weight of that legacy."

"But you were raised to it, my lord. It is different for you. For years, she lived another life. The life of a genteel parlor boarder."

A momentary flicker of sadness crossed the marquess's face. "That is my great shame."

"I am not here to be your judge, my lord. Indeed, she had many years with the Darlings, who are excellent people. She was not left to languish. Your father did well by her for a man in his time and place." He took another sip of his wine, eager to chase away the cold as he was momentarily caught by the memory of his own, very different experience. "I am simply reminding you that she is not just a Pembroke. She is a Martin. A child born to a working class woman. A woman she loved, but whose memory, whose legacy, she fears to celebrate, because she might appear ungrateful to the brother she loves dearly."

Lord Barronsfield straightened, his fingers gripping his cup, his gaze going past Bastien, somewhere into the depths of his own memory. He let out a low breath.

"Bloody hell," the marquess muttered.

"Do not blame yourself. Lady Eleanore seems to take a lot on herself."

"That, I fear, I can take that blame for. That is a Pembroke trait through and through. You know Edmund. He suffers the same affliction."

"Then you know how to address it with her."

Lord Barronsfield nodded. "I do. But I cannot protect her from everything, DuMont, as much as I may wish to. Society is a treacherous thing, and unlike my peers on the other side of the Channel, they continue to take their place in the world for granted."

"Perhaps another reason why she is fearful of publicly acknowledging her mother. All she has left of her is that red cape. She wraps herself up in it to hold on to that legacy."

The marquess shook his head. "I have tried for years to offer her a new one. A red one, even. But she politely refuses. No wonder."

"You are a concerned brother, and a powerful one, which is more than any other soul in her position is blessed with. And for that, perhaps especially because of that, she is torn. She knows how unique she is. A lady, and more than a lady."

"She is dear to me, and to my family," Lord Barronsfield said, the ferocity of his love edging his words. "Perhaps in protecting her, I have smothered her. It was not my intent. Is this why she hid her plans from me? For the foundling home?"

"I think Lady Eleanore was hiding her intent from herself more than anyone." Bastien sat back in his chair. "My understanding from Dr. Brayden is that the real name of the Elmsdale infirmary is the Jane Alexandra Memorial Infirmary. Why is that?"

"For my mother, and my young sister, who died of typhus, many years ago."

"I see. Do you?"

The marquess shook his head, impatient.

Bastien held out his hands, motioning to Eleanore's notebook sitting on the bench next to Lord Barronsfield. He flipped through the pages, and opened it to the drawing she'd made of the cottage. In pencil were the words *Martin Cottage*, which Bastien had scratched in himself. He turned the book around, pushed it toward Barronsfield, and tapped his finger on the name.

"Lady Eleanore's foundling hospital is not just wish fulfillment. It is a way to honor her mother. A way for her mother's memory to step out from underneath the shadow of the great man that Sally Martin fell in love with. Your sister has not been able to tell you, perhaps for fear of seeming ungrateful for the life and the kinship you have bestowed on her. She is proud of her Pembroke heritage. But perhaps that Pembroke pride has driven her to accomplish this as a Martin."

Bastien sat forward, an image of Eleanore's smile filling his chest. "Lady Eleanore is a magnificent woman. Yes, she is caring and thoughtful and the world would benefit from more like her. But she is more than that. She can organize people—work with them to accomplish great feats. If she were a man she might command an army. She reminds people of their better natures, and then, in a feat of something akin to magic, she harnesses that to further her work." Magic was the only word Bastien could conjure to describe the effect she'd had on him. "The only thing I have given her—which you saw last night— was this name."

The marquess peered down at the page, and stared at it for what felt like a long time.

"I think you underestimate yourself, DuMont," he said at last. He shook his head slowly, as if solving a puzzle Bastien could not see. "Tell me this, and do not lie to me, because despite Mr. Roderick's mother hen sensibilities, I will throw you out that window myself."

Bastien stopped breathing, put on his guard.

"Do you love my sister?"

Whether it was the warning in Lord Barronsfield's brow, or that he'd somehow become brave enough to own it, but Bastien nodded his head.

"My heart is not large enough to hold the love I have for her."

Lord Barronsfield settled back in his seat. "I see what you have given her, DuMont. Something that no one else has been able to. You have given her permission to celebrate all of who she is."

"She is worth celebrating, my lord."

"Stephen."

The two sat in amicable silence, a truce at last. When their cups were drained, the marquess rose. "Come. I have a horse and a driver in one of Mr. Roderick's stables, and I suspect both of them would rather be home. And so would I."

"I will remain here a while."

"You saved my life last night," Stephen said, his voice even, though the exasperation was unmistakable. "So I owe you a boon. And I will give you the most generous thing I have to offer, which is a chance to repair whatever happened between you. She deserves happiness, and maybe DuMont, you do as well. I know that love can save a man, if he's brave enough to let himself be saved."

Bastien had spent time on battlefields. On empty roads, being hunted by revolutionaries. Shot at by countless enemies. Facing down Le Veneur Rouge. In all that time, he'd never felt fear as he did at this moment. And then he thought of the light in Eleanore's eyes, and her horrible playacting, and the way she felt in his arms. How she looked at him as if he was the most remarkable being on earth. As if he was enough. The thought drove him to his feet.

Maybe he could be brave enough.

CHAPTER 26

*E*leanore sat in her bedchamber, feeling as empty as a London ballroom after the crush had gone. Stretching her arms to the ceiling, she yawned, tired from a sleepless night. She sat near the hearth in her room, under a thick wooden blanket, idly sketching by candlelight. The page was filled with a mix of squiggles and boxes and little flowers—disjointed images that reflected her own scattered thoughts.

So much had happened since yesterday. So much heartache. So much violence. So much death. As she'd watched Bastien use his deadly skills, she understood at last why he believed he was a man beyond redemption.

And yet, he was redeemable. She knew it.

He was a man who dedicated his life to saving others. As a surgeon. As the Wolf. As Bastien. He'd simply become blind to it.

It was in the notebook she'd given him. In the way he'd winked at her, across the table, letting her know, somehow, that they would be safe.

She just had to trust him. Trust him with her heart.

And she'd failed.

She pulled a wool coverlet onto her lap and watched the icy rain streak down the windows. The weather matched the weariness that lay heavy on her chest.

Despite all that happened, she should have been happier. After all, just as they'd sat down for dinner, the Battersbys and Stephen announced very generous donations for her foundling home, and Lord Ellsworth also provided her with a promissory note that provided enough that she could start searching out a property almost immediately. By spring she could begin improvements that would make it a suitable home. Of course, there was so much more to do, but she could finally start. Which was what she wanted.

Funny how that victory felt curiously empty.

A knock at the door interrupted her thoughts. She set down her sketch book and went to the door. It was Stephen, looking slightly worse for wear.

"You're bleeding!" she said, gesturing at the corner of his mouth. She took him by the arm and pulled him inside.

"'Tis nothing," he replied, putting a handkerchief to his cracked lip. He picked up a chair and sat it down next to where she'd been watching the rain, and invited her to sit next to him.

"It is not," she snapped. "What have you been up to?"

"Eleanore, tell me again about your foundling home. Or rather," he paused, and produced her notebook, "tell me how I can be a better brother to you."

She frowned, confused by the question. "I don't think you can be." Panic rose suddenly. "Do you object to the idea, or the promise of funds?"

He sat down, stretching out his legs, lacing his fingers together and resting his hands across his stomach. "Of course not. I'm extremely proud of you. But I know I can be a little bear-like, as Rosalind says, and you and I...we have never really discussed it. Why is that?"

She walked back to her seat and sat down.

"I don't know," she said, looking out over the gray-green, rain-streaked landscape. "You are a busy, important man. You have other things to occupy you than the fantastical plans of your little sister."

"Eleanore." He turned his head to her. "Far be it from me to point out the errors in others, as I am prone to my own. But you are speaking nonsense, and you know it."

She shifted, taken aback by his directness. "You are not important?" She smiled, attempting humor, but neither she nor Stephen were amused by it.

"There is much between us we have never spoken of. And that is my error."

"I don't—"

He swung himself around, sitting up straight. He held out a hand, which she took. "Eleanore. I am your only family that we know of. For the first crucial years of your life, I shut you out of mine, quite deliberately."

She shrugged. It stung, still, all these years later, but she knew it wasn't entirely his fault. "You had a good reason."

He shook his head. "It was a fantastical one. It felt real enough at the time, of course. But it was a fairy tale. And not all fairy tales are happy, as Rosalind would no doubt tell you. Mine threatened to be a dark one that nearly cost me a full life with a remarkable wife, a loving, accomplished sister, and a family." He paused, squeezed her hands gently, then released her. "And you were caught up in that tale, and we have never really addressed what that must have meant for you."

"Stephen—" She swallowed, unsure. "'Tis nothing. Being part of this family has been wonderful. Indeed, I have felt welcome—though perhaps overwhelmed, especially at the beginning. And yet, I was not born to this life. And the only reason I have it is because you have chosen to include me. There are plenty of 'unnatural children' living a much different life than I. I am a proud daughter of Charles Pembroke, our father. I am very proud to have the Pembroke name. But I am also the daughter of Sally Martin. And I don't want to forget her, either."

"This is why you have never worn any of the capes I have gifted you," he replied.

"It was a lovely gesture. But that cape is all I have left of her. That and a few recipes that Mrs. Darling saved for me. I cannot lose her." Her eyes stung as she fought back tears.

"Come here, you silly, wonderful girl." He stood, and pulled her gently to her feet, resting his hands on her shoulders. "I love you, Eleanore. And I am grateful to Sally for finding happiness with our father—you are the product of that happiness. So I will be forever grateful to Sally Martin for the gift of a sister."

Something opened up in Eleanore—a realization, a joy. She hugged her brother, and cried into his shoulder.

"And I think it would do her a great honor to name your foundling home after her."

Stephen's words cut through her tears. She straightened, wiping her nose with her handkerchief, and looked at him closely. "How did you know about that?"

"Mr. DuMont showed me, this morning."

"Bastien?" Eleanore's heart leapt into her throat. The moment his name escaped her lips, her gaze shot to Stephen. He stiffened slightly, put a few fingers to his split lip, and shook his head. And then, curiously enough, he smiled.

"Yes. Bastien DuMont."

"Oh dear. Did he do that to you?" Eleanore's heart sank. He was determined to leave—and obviously, determined to burn every bridge before he did so.

"We had a discussion. It became—animated. But it was nothing a glass of Mr. Roderick's good spiced port couldn't fix."

Eleanore furrowed her brow. And men always complained women were complicated. "You are confusing me."

"I went to see Mr. DuMont this morning. He was supposed to travel with Ellsworth to London this morning, but the weather has kept him in Elmsdale," he said. "Something had happened that had clearly upset you, and I wanted to speak with him about it."

Eleanore let out a low breath. He hadn't gone. Not yet. "What did you say? Please don't tell me you threatened him."

"If it is any consolation to you, my intent was to discuss his plans to return to London. The conversation happened to stray to other subjects."

"Like me."

Stephen leaned forward, his stare direct, but gentle. "Eleanore, what are your intentions toward Mr. DuMont? I have seen the way you two look at each other. It is not the way of friends. There is a yearning there I recognize."

Eleanore looked away, heat flushing her cheeks. "Am I so transparent?"

"Look at me, Eleanore. You are human. So I will ask you again—do you love him? Because if you don't, I will send him away. But if you do, you need to sort this out between you."

Eleanore tilted her head, her mind turning over what Stephen was suggesting.

"This is not fair," she began, shaking her head. "You told me to stay away from him. That he is not to be trusted." And yet, she was the one not to be trusted. Not with his heart, nor her own.

"I prejudged him. You see, Eleanore, I am human too," he replied.

"I have found Mr. DuMont to be a deeply honorable man. He has seen much of the world that is ugly, and tries to make it right. And though he convinces himself otherwise, he cares deeply."

"Eleanore, when a man cares deeply, it means he can be hurt deeply, too. It can cause fear—a fear so great he will bury that need— or run from it. It was that same fear that allowed us to be divided for so long," he said. "It is that fear Mr. DuMont is grappling with now. But he will do it, if he can dare to hope that you might be there to risk the journey with him."

"I am not brave, Stephen. I ran from London at the first sight of trouble. I want things to be good, and right, but I have risked nothing to earn them," she said. "I am afraid now...that perhaps I don't deserve the love of a man like Bastien DuMont. My parents had love, but it wasn't enough for them, Stephen. Why should I be any different?"

Stephen smiled.

"That was a different time. And very different circumstances. You and I are not privileged to everything that went on between them. If there is anyone I would wish happy, it is you. We are of our parents, Eleanore, but we are not them. We have our own destinies to follow. Our own stories to spin."

Eleanore swallowed. Yes. She tried to convince Bastien he deserved a happy ending. Did she not deserve the same?

"Bastien DuMont is a good man," Stephen said. "And I cannot believe I am saying this, but he deserves your honesty. If you love him, tell him. Be with him. And if you do not, put him out of his misery."

Eleanore grabbed her brother, moving up on her tip toes and gave him a peck on his cheek, determined not to cry. She flew to her closet, pulling her red cape from the hook. "How are the roads? Is he still at Dr. Brayden's?"

Stephen caught her by the shoulders and took the cape from her, tossing it on her bed. "You don't need that. He's in my study, looking for all the world like the most miserable Frenchman I've ever seen. And the day is gray enough without Bastien DuMont's glum face to make it worse."

BASTIEN PACED the floors in Stephen's study, wondering if he had made a colossal error in judgment. It wouldn't have been his first, but this might be his greatest.

The house was quiet, though calm, given the events of last night. He'd gone to visit Hanley, pleased to see that the swelling in his ankle had subsided and that, after a long conversation with Mr. Schofield and the marquess, he had decided to start planning for his successor. After a lifetime of service, Stephen had asked that he would stay on at the manor and receive a pension.

The door opened, the sound of the handle turning enough to make his heart stop beating in his chest. It was Ellsworth.

"Merde," Bastien swore, strangely relieved.

"Good morning to you too, DuMont," Ellsworth said. "Barronsfield told me you were here. I wanted to thank you for your service last evening."

Bastien took Ellsworth's outstretched hand, and shook it. "Hopefully that will be the last of that kind of service either of us have to render."

"I want to write my father and inform him of all that has happened, but I am not certain he will take it well," Ellsworth said. "He had tried many times to reach out to the family. I do not know if he knew of Hugh Wakefield's existence. The Red Hunter would have been as old as my eldest brother, had he lived."

"I see...you are the 'spare', as the English say."

Ellsworth nodded. "And then some. My parents were great producers of children, but alas, not spectacular with luck of seeing them to adulthood. I am their only surviving son."

"And you are not married."

"Don't you start on me, DuMont," Ellsworth said, his warning lighthearted. "I was supposed to be, as everyone well knows."

"I don't understand why you are in hiding, then. Is it because of this woman? The one with the letters?"

"Yes. And no. There was a remarkable event that occurred not far from here—a stone that fell out of the heavens, and I wished to see it for myself." Ellsworth said, then looked away, up toward the heavens though there was little to see except a blanket of heavy gray cloud. "That, and perhaps, trying in vain to convince Lady Amelia that we were supposed to be together. There are so few constants in life, DuMont, but she was supposed to be one of them."

Bastien shook his head. "Perhaps you need to open your self to the possibility that this part of your story has not yet been written. Would you not be excited by the possibility that you yet find a woman who can truly love you?"

Ellsworth turned away from the window, a shadow crossing his face. "I am not a romantic, DuMont. My sole purpose in life, at least as parents are concerned, is to procreate. I have been avoiding it, but perhaps it is time to give them what they want. Especially given all that has happened this past night. You and everyone in this house was nearly killed because of me. Because of a man who wanted everything I have, I admit, taken for granted."

The door opened, breaking the strained silence. Eleanore stood in the door, and Bastien's heart leapt into his throat. Her brother, interestingly enough, was nowhere to be found.

"Excuse me, Lord Ellsworth," Eleanore said clearly. "If you wouldn't mind, I would appreciate a word with Mr. DuMont. My brother is in the library, if you wish to join him."

Ellsworth shot Bastien a solemn look, bowed to Eleanore, and left.

Bastien stood, the thumping of his heart racing the ticking sounds of a nearby clock. He kept his hands at his sides, more nervous now than when he had performed his first procedure.

Her eyes were tired, like his, though there was nothing that could take away from their beauty. She had a shawl pulled around her shoulders, and she fiddled with the fringe along its edge.

"Bastien—"

"Eleanore—"

They stopped, each of them laughing to dispel the case of nerves that bound each of them.

"I want you to stay," she blurted out, shocking Bastien with her directness. She held up the notebook—the one he'd written in. "I want you to stay, for Daniel, and to help with the foundling home. I want you to stay because I think you will make the area a magnificent surgeon." Her lower lip started to tremble and her voice was low and thick with tears. "But mostly I want you to stay...for me."

"Eleanore, chère," he started, his voice low, but she kept speaking, her hands becoming charmingly animated as she continued.

"Because, this is selfish." She paused and looked him straight in the eye. "But I think I can be part of your happy ending. I know you are determined that you can't have one, Bastien, but you're wrong. I have been wrong about many things—accepting Lord Ramsay's proposal, not standing up for myself when Mrs. Waterstone was asking me about London, but not this."

"Eleanore, I—"

"You are a good man. Good, despite the many horrible things that have happened to you. You, of all people, deserve a happy ending," she said, pacing now, quite determined, quite endearing. She slowed and stopped in front of him. "And maybe, so do I."

Bastien held his breath.

"And I didn't believe that was possible until you. And maybe that is selfish. But I can't help it. I want a happy ending, Bastien. And I only know of one way to have it. I want you, Bastien DuMont. Just for me."

"You...want me?" Bastien asked, his voice shaking. He turned away, walked to the window, tears pricking the back of his eyes, fearful he would lose his composure completely. He let out a low breath.

"Yes, Bastien," she said, the response breathless. "Forever and ever do I want you. If you can bring yourself to forgive me for not trusting myself. Because I love you."

"Eleanore," Bastien went to her, stilling her with his touch. He took the book in her hands and pressed it up against her chest, then leaned his forehead against hers. "I did not know a happy ending was possible for me. I believed my heart was closed. Hard. Empty. You opened it. With your stubborn belief in me. My heart will not fail you."

Eleanore put her hand to his chest, tucking her fingers under his coat. "What a big heart you have, Bastien DuMont."

"All the better to love you with, chère."

He lowered his head to hers and captured her lips. A sweet torment filled him as her breathy little sighs escaped her throat, her body pressing up against him. There was nothing in the world he wanted more than to pleasure her, to give her all of the love—body and soul—she felt she could not have.

He broke the kiss, but held her, savoring the light touch of her fingers at the back of his neck.

"Eleanore Pembroke, will you be my happy ending?"

"As long as you will be mine."

EPILOGUE

Yorkshire, April 1796

Though Stephen had offered Eleanore and Bastien a special license, they had politely declined. There was much to be settled, between tidying up the last details of Wakefield's operations with Sir Richard Hamilton, and of course, seeing to Bastien's Tante Marie. Despite Bastien's insistence that the baroness would love Eleanore on first sight, and that they had met before at both Stephen and Edmund's weddings, meeting her as Bastien's fiancé was an entirely different matter. But she was incredibly gracious and welcoming, and they soon became confidants.

Spring had come at last, even in Yorkshire. Dr. Brayden had returned in February following the passing of his sister, and had insisted that until Eleanore and Bastien were wed, Bastien could continue to lodge with him.

The wedding was a joyous affair. It had, in fact, been a double wedding, as Daniel and Allie were married as well. Servants and gentry alike were treated to a lovely ceremony, and, in what was a Barronsfield tradition, each had a bouquet that featured roses from Stephen's spectacular rose bush.

After the breakfast had been eaten and the toasts made, Bastien scooped up Eleanore, and, to the cheers of all, took her away for their wedding night. The weather was pleasant—the perfect day for such an excursion, as they rolled through the now-lush green countryside, along a quiet country lane. Eleanore, the fingers of one hand laced with Bastien's, her head resting on his shoulder, was so utterly content and happy, she feared her heart would burst out of her chest. Her body ached for him, and if the carriage hadn't been open to the air, she might have been tempted to begin their honeymoon right where she sat.

They were still not far from Elmsdale when a pleasant house emerged beyond a copse of trees. Eleanore sat up, greeted by the fragrant scent of apple blossoms and pear trees.

"Bastien, look at this!"

He sat up, brushed his hair away from his eyes, and looked over to the house. "Do you wish to take a closer look?"

"Would it delay us too much, do you think?"

He pulled her close. "I have been waiting for months for this night. If it would make you happy, I would wait an eternity."

"I can't wait an eternity," she said, drawing her finger along the side of his jaw. "But I can manage ten minutes."

Bastien called ahead to the driver, and they turned down the country lane. They came to a stop near the small courtyard, which was skirted on all sides by flowers. The place was much, much smaller than Barronsfield—a tidy little country house, at best, sitting on a very pretty property with barns and a smaller cottage. Eleanore hopped out of the carriage and peered in the window of the front door. There was no evidence that the place was occupied.

"Do you like it?" Bastien asked.

"It is beautiful. Perfect in fact. The gardens, the trees...with the funds we've received, we could build Martin Cottage next door," she replied. "Perhaps when we return, we can make some inquiries."

"We could." He ran back to the carriage and pulled out a small box wrapped in a simple white ribbon.

"What is this?"

"Your wedding present. I wanted to wait, but since we have stopped, I thought you might like to open it now."

"Very well." Eleanore pulled on the ribbon and opened the box. Inside was a brass key. Eleanore looked up at Bastien in disbelief, then looked back into the box. He took her by the hand, and let her to the front door. He took they key out of the box and put it in the door.

"Turn it."

Her hand shook but turned the key, the lock making a satisfying click as the door gave way. Overwhelmed, she put her hands to her mouth and turned to Bastien, whom she hadn't seen so nervous since that moment they'd met in her brother's study, back in January. That seemed so very long ago now.

"Do you like it?" he asked.

"Oh Bastien, it's perfect." She wiped the tears running down her cheeks. "Can we go in?"

He scooped her up into his arms, and walked across the threshold.

"Of course, Madame DuMont," he replied, a devilish smile teasing his lips. "May I suggest we begin with a tour of our bed chamber?"

THE END

HISTORICAL NOTES

Readers will notice that Bastien uses the term of address "Mister", rather than "Doctor" to refer to himself in his role as a surgeon. This is a tradition dating back to the earliest days of the profession, where physicians were primarily Medical Doctors (MD's) with university education. Though some surgeons, like Bastien, were formally trained, at this time in history, most were not. Thus, the term "Doctor" was not commonly applied to surgeons at the time. Though the practice of surgery became more professional in subsequent decades, the term "Mister" because a badge of honor amongst surgeons in Great Britain (where Bastien would have been trained) and the Republic of Ireland. This practice continued well into the twentieth century.

For those of you interested in further reading, there is an excellent little article by the medical historian Irvine Loudon from the British Medical Journal (2000 Dec 23; 321(7276): 1589–1591) entitled *Why are (male) surgeons still addressed as Mr?.*

ર.

For those readers who might be interested in a real life cliffhanger, I highly recommend *The journal of a spy in Paris during the reign of terror, January-July, 1794,* which is a fragment of an account left by an English spy working in Paris during the height of the terror. This gripping account provided much of the insights into the world Bastien DuMont inhabited, and the treacherous conditions for those living in Paris at the time. In it, the author speaks of the men I had named *Les veneur noblesse*—those who were hired to hunt down noble families fleeing France. It also inspired a line Bastien utters about the impact of starvation on the French people.

Unfortunately, the account ends abruptly, just before the death of Robespierre. The fate of the author is unknown.

CONNECT WITH MICHELLE

I hope you enjoyed *Never Trust a Rogue in Wolf's Clothing*! This is the third installment in my *Enchanted Tales* Series.

If you're new to the series, re-introduce yourself to Stephen Pembroke in **Not Your Average Beauty**, and follow with **No Prince Charming**, where Bastien first makes his appearance. I'm currently hard at work on Colin's story, **Nothing Magical about Midnight** (*Book 4*).

Reviews are welcome - and super important to indie authors, so if can leave a review, I'd be super grateful! Feel free to post one where you purchased the book, or on Goodreads.

My website is www.michellehelliwell.com. You can sign up for my newsletter and get a heads up on new releases.

You can also find me on:

Facebook

Twitter

Pinterest

Instagram

ENCHANTED TALES

NOT YOUR AVERAGE BEAUTY

When beauty is a curse, only love can break the spell

Stephen Pembroke, the Marquess of Barronsfield, believes that where his love of beauty goes, death follows. Cursed to a loveless existence, and with his legacy at stake, Stephen makes a desperate proposal of marriage to Rosalind Schofield, his steward's new ward - and the plainest girl he has ever met. Rosalind has spent a lifetime being overlooked for prettier faces. When she is singled out for her lack of beauty by the Marquess, she begins to doubt if she is deserving of the love she inwardly craves.

When unusual things start happening around her, Rosalind can't help but wonder if Lord Barronsfield or his curse are who and what they appear to be. When she openly challenges Stephen about the curse, he begins to doubt everything – and comes to realize that this apparently plain, ordinary woman is not as unremarkable as he believed. Strange things *are* happening in Barronsfield. As they move closer to the truth, Rosalind unwittingly finds herself in the sights of the real beast in Barronsfield, and Stephen must decide if his growing love for Rosalind will be his salvation or her doom.

❧

NO PRINCE CHARMING

Love is the fairest of them all

Dashing off in a daring elopement with a prince handpicked by her mother, Lady Gwyneth Snowdon anticipates a lavish future. But when a mysterious stranger kidnaps her, Gwyneth fears her happy ending is doomed.

Used by his maniacal father, Edmund Pembroke turned his back on society.

Seizing the opportunity to say good-bye to his past forever, he makes a deal to separate the pampered countess from a gold-digging imposter. But when Edmund discovers her life is in danger, he is forced to protect the beautiful, well-born Gwyneth Snowdon and to confront his ghosts.

Separated from her plush surroundings, Gwyneth learns she's capable of so much—including love for a man with neither title nor fortune. But she begins to suspects there is more to her rugged, handsome guardian than he's chosen to reveal. After finding herself at the center of a sinister deception, can she dare to trust her heart to a man who's spent years deceiving himself?

ABOUT THE AUTHOR

Michelle Helliwell started writing her first novel, a time travel fantasy, when she was 15. She moved on to half-hearted attempts at something more literary, then nearly gave up on the writing all together until one fine day in 2005 a co-worker put a romance novel in her hands and told her to "get over yourself".

She did, and the rest, as they say, is history.

Michelle lives with her husband and two sons in Nova Scotia, Canada where moody weather and bagpipes are plentiful, but alas, guys in puffy shirts are too few.

Connect with me online!
www.michellehelliwell.com

www.ingramcontent.com/pod-product-compliance
Lightning Source LLC
Chambersburg PA
CBHW021218250626
47155CB00008B/2855